Lana Ferguson is a sex-positive nerd whose works never shy from spice or sass. A faded Fabio cover found its way into her hands at fifteen, and she's never been the same since. When she isn't writing, you can find her randomly singing show tunes, arguing over which Batman is superior, and subjecting her friends to the extended editions of *The Lord of the Rings*. Lana lives mostly in her own head but can sometimes be found chasing her corgi through the coppice of the great American outdoors.

CONNECT ONLINE

LanaFerguson.com

 Lana-Ferguson-104378392171803

  lanafergusonwrites

The Nanny

LANA FERGUSON

PIATKUS

PIATKUS

First published in the US in 2023 by Berkley Romance
An imprint of Penguin Random House LLC
First published in Great Britain in 2023 by Piatkus

3 5 7 9 10 8 6 4

Copyright © 2023 by Lana Ferguson
Excerpt from *The Fake Mate* copyright © 2023 by Lana Ferguson

A CIP catalogue record for this book
is available from the British Library.

ISBN 978-0-349-43963-1

Printed and bound in Great Britain by Clays Ltd, Elcograf S.p.A.

Papers used by Piatkus are from well-managed forests
and other responsible sources.

MIX
Supporting
responsible forestry
FSC® C104740

Piatkus
An imprint of
Little, Brown Book Group
Carmelite House
50 Victoria Embankment
London EC4Y 0DZ

An Hachette UK Company
www.hachette.co.uk

www.littlebrown.co.uk

To my sweet mother, who once asked me:
"Wouldn't you rather write children's books instead?"

The
Nanny

I told myself I wouldn't be nervous.

They can't actually see me, so why is my heart pounding so hard?

I adjust my camera for the fourth time, checking the angle before I assess my outfit again. It's a cute bra, and the underwear match—what comes next is nothing that I haven't done a thousand times before.

It's just that now, I'll be doing it for unseen viewers for pay.

I take a deep breath, reminding myself that I need the money. That it's my body, and I'm taking ownership of it. Everything that I do from this point onward is my choice, and I'm in complete control.

That thought makes me feel brave.

I take a deep breath. I check my wig. I adjust my mask.

I can do this.

I start the camera.

CHAPTER 1

Cassie

"I'm going to be homeless."

I hear Wanda clucking her tongue all the way from her kitchen (which, incidentally, isn't that far away in a seven-hundred-square-foot apartment), and when I raise my face from the aged velvet of her couch, I can see her shaking a spatula at me. "No pity parties," she tells me. "You aren't gonna be homeless. You can take the couch if need be."

I make a face at the aforementioned velvet couch, glancing from it to the pile of newspapers at the end of it to the television that defies time by refusing to die inside its wooden shell. "I couldn't . . . impose," I say tentatively, not wanting to hurt her feelings. "I'll figure something out."

In my third year of grad school for occupational therapy—losing my job as a therapy assistant at the children's hospital was not part of the plan. I've barely been making rent *with* the salary they were giving me, and now that they've had to downsize, my even tinier apartment across the hall from Wanda's place is looking more and more like it will be a thing of the past very soon.

"Nonsense," Wanda argues. "You know you're welcome here."

I blow one auburn curl away from my face, pushing up from the couch cushions to a sitting position. I've known Wanda Simmons for about six years now; I met her when she invited me in for tea after I locked myself out of the apartment my first week here. A seventy-two-year-old woman as my best friend wasn't exactly on my list of things to accomplish here, but she might be more interesting than I am, so I guess there's that.

"Wanda," I sigh. "I love you. You know that, but . . . you have one bathroom and no Wi-Fi. It would never work out between us."

"It's the age difference, isn't it," she pouts.

"Absolutely not. You will always be the only woman for me."

"I'm just saying. The option is there."

"And what are you going to do when you bring home your bingo men, and I'm sitting here on your couch?"

"Oh, we won't bother you. We'll go to the bedroom."

I grimace. "I am all for you getting yours, but I absolutely don't want to be on the other side of these very thin walls for it."

Wanda chuckles as she stirs the sauce for her meatballs. "You could always go back to doing those booby cams."

I groan. "Please don't call them booby cams."

"What? It's a camera. You show your boobies. You get paid."

I let my face fall back against her couch. I sort of regret telling Wanda about my . . . *history* with OnlyFans, but I hadn't quite anticipated that she would be able to handle her tequila better than I did the night I bared it all. Not that I'm ashamed of it, by any means. It was good money. Taking cash from people looking to get their rocks off was an easy decision when faced with a looming tuition bill that I couldn't begin to pay for otherwise. I mean, good tits should really earn their keep. I think Margaret Thatcher said that once.

"You know I can't," I sigh. "I deleted my whole account. All my subs are gone. It would take me another two years to build them back up."

Besides, I learned my lesson the first time around. At least I kept *that* part to myself.

"Then what are you going to do? Have you been looking for another job?"

"Trying to," I grumble, scrolling through the same help wanted ads on my phone that have mostly not panned out. "Why put out help wanted ads if they aren't going to get back with you?"

"Too many people in this city," Wanda tuts. "You know, when I moved here, you could actually walk down the street and recognize folks. Now it's like a beehive out there. Always buzzing. Did you know they have a damned grocery store you don't even use your card in? Just walk in and walk out. Thought I was stealing the whole time. 'Bout gave me heart palpitations."

"Yes, we talked about the new Fresh store, remember? I helped you set up your account."

"Oh, yeah. Next thing you know, they'll be flying groceries right to your door."

"Wanda, I hate to break it to you, but they already are."

"No kidding? Hmm. You should set that up too. Save me a damned walk."

"I guess you're not so opposed to the future after all."

"Yeah, yeah. What about the diner on Fifth?"

"They won't let me off for my on-campus labs."

"You know, Sal was saying he could use some help with—"

"I am not working at the deli," I tell her firmly. "Sal is too handsy."

"I always sort of liked that about him," Wanda laughs.

"Aren't you too old to be this horny?"

"I'm old, Cassie," she snorts. "Not dead."

"Seriously, I don't know what I am going to *do*," I groan.

"Check the ads again. Maybe you missed something."

"I've checked them a dozen times," I huff.

Wanda is still grousing at me from the kitchen as I pore over the help wanted section again regardless, thinking that if I scan it enough times, some miracle ad will jump out at me that I didn't notice before. How can it be so hard to find a job that will let me do my schoolwork at night and be off every other weekend for my on-campus courses? I mean, this is San Diego, not Santa Barbara. There's got to be *something* that I can—

"Oh, shit," I say suddenly.

Wanda steps out of the kitchen, spatula in hand. "What?"

"*Wanted: full-time live-in nanny position. Experience with children is a must. Free room and board. Serious inquiries only.*"

Wanda humphs. "You don't want to be stuck taking care of someone else's—"

"*Entry salary . . .* Holy shit."

"Is it good?"

I look up at Wanda with an open mouth, and when I tell her what they're offering, Wanda says a word she usually only reserves for when the Lakers lose. She blows out a breath afterward, patting at her neat white curls in that flustered way of hers. "I guess you'd best be calling them then."

hadn't expected Aiden Reid to get back to me as quickly as he did after I emailed him, and I certainly hadn't expected him to seem so eager, in setting a date for an interview. And speaking of date, I *definitely* hadn't expected him to ask me to meet him at one of the poshest restaurants in the city—one I cannot afford to eat at and one that I am pretty sure I am too underdressed to even *be* in. Is this how rich people hold interviews? I doubt Sal at the diner would be treating me to a five-star restaurant to get me to slice turkey for him while he *accidentally* brushes his hand across my ass.

Still, I've put on my favorite black sheath dress, the one that I wore to my college graduation, and I hope it makes me seem a lot more put together than I feel right now. Since I am now under the suspicion that the family I am trying to nanny for is more well-off than I first thought, I'm thinking a little false confidence will do me a world of good.

I mean, I love kids. And I learned working at the children's hospital that they're the target demographic of my terrible jokes, so that's a plus. Besides, the entire reason that I am pursuing a career in occupational therapy is to try to be that person who is there for children when no one else seems to be—so with that in mind, this job should be a piece of cake, right?

That's what I keep telling myself.

I swear the hostess can smell my vanilla body spray from Target, and she somehow *knows* this means I can't afford the appetizers here, but she pastes on a smile, much to her credit, and leads me to a table after I give her my would-be employer's name. Is this what it feels like to have pull? I take a seat in the silk-covered chair, feeling like a fish out of water amid the lit candles and the elegant music. Hell, I'm afraid to put my elbows on the table.

A waiter comes by to ask if I want to start with any appetizers, and since the hostess with the judgy eyes was absolutely right—I ask for water instead while I wait. I sip it as I wait for this Aiden guy to show up (seems kind of rude to be late to your own interview), trying to look like I totally eat at places like this all the time.

The restaurant itself is the nicest I've ever been in. I've never seen so many crystal centerpieces in my entire life, and Wanda would lose her shit if she saw the prices on the menu. I can't wait to tell her later and watch her eyes bug out of her head.

"Excuse me," someone says.

The deep voice murmured so closely to my ear nearly makes me choke on my water, a bit dribbling over my bottom lip and down my chin as I cough through it. I press the back of my hand there to try to wipe it away, noticing big hands in my now-blurred vision as a face comes into view.

Holy. Hell.

My brain short-circuits for a few seconds, trying to make sense of the sudden appearance of a large man with thick chestnut hair that's pushed away from his forehead and strong jaw and stronger cheekbones, and is his mouth softer looking than mine? He's tall too. Not the sort of tall that makes you think he plays basketball or something (although he totally could, if he wanted to), but the kind of tall that makes you want to ask him to grab something off the top shelf for you just so you can watch the way his shoulders move under his shirt. I realize this thought process makes little sense, but all I know is I am five seven with tits worth paying for, an ass built on squats and an emotional connection with bread, and this man makes me feel *tiny*.

And if these things aren't enough to leave me dumbfounded (which I am, I mean, I'm literally drooling sparkling water)—his eyes would do the trick. I've heard of heterochromia; at the very least I'm pretty sure my biology professor mentioned it in passing when I was an undergrad, but I have never actually seen it in person. His eyes are a clash of one brown and one green, the colors not bright but subtle, like warm tea and seawater that are hard to look away from.

I realize that this is exactly what I'm doing. Staring at the poor guy.

"I'm sorry," I sputter. "Sort of caught me off guard."

I grab the napkin to start patting at my chin, noticing now that the man is wearing a white chef coat with a matching apron tied around his waist.

"Oh," I start again. "I wasn't going to order anything yet, I was waiting for someone."

"Right." He flashes a row of perfect teeth that my orthodontist would be ecstatic over, looking almost like he regrets having walked up to the table. Or maybe I'm projecting. "I think you're waiting for me. Are you Cassie?"

"I—" Oh no. No, no, no. I did not spit water all over myself in front of the guy I'm trying to get to hire me. "Are you Mr. Reid?"

He makes a face. "Aiden, please. Mr. Reid makes me feel old."

Which he isn't. I don't think. I mean, he's older than me but not *old*. He can't be any older than thirty, I'd wager. I'm still sort of gawking at him. "Right," I say, trying to collect myself as I push away from the table and extend my hand awkwardly. "I'm Cassie. Cassie Evans."

His mouth quirks at my extended hand, making me immediately regret holding it out like I'm doing an off-Broadway rendition of the Tin Man in *The Wizard of Oz*, but there's no taking it back now. He shakes it in what I can only assume is an attempt to be nice, gesturing back to my seat and waiting for me to sit before he takes the one across from me.

I clear my throat, trying to forget that a minute ago I almost spit water on the hottest man alive who I very much want to pay me a ridiculous amount of money to watch his kid. *His kid,* I remind myself. This is a *job* interview. Which makes it totally inappropriate that I'm still thinking about his massive hands. Hands that my hindbrain actually notices aren't sporting a ring of any kind.

Cut it out, brain.

I should stop staring at his hands, in any case. Even if they are large enough to make a girl mentally calculate when her last date was.

"So," I try awkwardly. "You're a cook." I groan, instantly regretting my choice of words. "Sorry. I mean a chef. You're a chef. Right?"

Miraculously, he doesn't call to have me removed but smiles instead. "Yeah. I cook here."

Oh, bless him for humoring me.

"That's . . . awesome. Really awesome." I nod appreciatively as I glance around us at the glittering chandeliers and the piano player somewhere behind us. "It's a snazzy place."

"It is," he agrees. "I've been the executive chef here for a few years now."

"No kidding? Fancy."

"Fancy," he echoes, looking amused. "Right. Sorry to ask you to meet me at work. I've been, ah . . . well. It's been crazy lately."

"It's no big deal. I thought it was weird to do one of these things over dinner, especially at a place like this, but I figured . . ." It might have been nice if it had dawned on me *before* I had started sputtering my nonsense, but nevertheless, it does hit me. The implications of what he's said. My mouth snaps shut as heat floods my face, and I duck with embarrassment as I cover my eyes. "Oh my God. This isn't a dinner interview. You wanted to talk to me on your break."

"I should have . . . been more clear in my email."

Oh God. He's trying to defend me. Someone bury me.

"I'm unbelievable."

"No, no," he tries. "It's fine."

"God, I'm an idiot. I wore this dumb dress, and—"

"It's a very nice dress."

"You probably think I'm bonkers—"

"Really, I don't."

"I can be so dense sometimes, I'm sorry."

He still looks amused. Like he's finding my mental breakdown funny. I don't know if that makes things better or worse.

"You can order something," he offers. "If you want. I don't mind."

"Um, thank you, but I might need to go throw up now. I should see myself out, right? This is already a disaster."

"Wait, no." He holds out a hand as I move to stand. "Don't do that."

I stop trying to slink away. Surely he can't still be considering me, can he? Maybe he's bonkers too. "You still want to interview me?"

"To be honest," he sighs, "no one has applied with anything near your credentials. CPR training, a bachelor's in occupational therapy with a minor in psychology? I mean, your last job was at a *children's* hospital. And they had nothing but good things to say about you there when I checked your references. It almost sounded like they hated to let you go."

"Yeah, I was pretty bummed when they did," I admit. "There was a funding issue, unfortunately. I loved the work."

"Well," he laughs, "I'm hoping their loss is my gain. I couldn't believe it when you sent me your résumé."

"But now that you've met me, you're beginning to think I forged it, right?"

He sort of laughs, his mouth barely opening as he casts his eyes down at the table, like he's afraid of making me think he's laughing *at* me, which would be well within his rights, considering this awful first meeting.

"No," he says. "I don't think you forged it. Though, I am curious why you're looking at a nanny position with your background?"

I sink back down into my chair, heaving a sigh as I lean over the table. "Can I be totally honest with you?"

"I'd prefer it," he says, leaning in and looking intrigued.

"I'm in my last year of the graduate program for OT, and like I said in my email, I got let go from my job due to downsizing. Rent in this city is ridiculous, and honestly, I need the money. And even *more* honestly, the free room and board isn't anything to turn my nose up at either. It would be great to not have to worry about that on top of everything else."

"Right. About that." He frowns then, and I assume this is the part where he tells me that he actually can't allow a spitting lunatic like me anywhere near his kid. "It *is* a live-in position, but full disclosure . . . it's just me and my daughter. You would have your own room, of course, practically your own floor, even—full privacy, and all that, but . . . I want to be completely transparent with you in case that makes you uncomfortable."

Twenty-five years old, and the first time I live with a good-looking guy is in a full-on *Uptown Girls* scenario. I'm dying to ask about the other parent in this situation, if only to squash my mental drooling, but my brain is screaming that this is the wrong move. Still, he's got a good job and a nice smile and doesn't give me total murderer vibes.

I paste on my most professional smile. "I don't think that will be a problem. However, in the spirit of being transparent . . . I'm in a hybrid program at St. Augustine's over in San Marcos."

"What does that mean?"

"It means that most of my coursework is online, which I have been taking care of at night after work, but two weekends a month I have to attend on-campus classes. It takes longer than the usual program, but since I've been paying my own way, it makes working easier. Most of the jobs I have been applying to haven't been able to work with me on my schedule, though, which is sort of a deal breaker." I chuff a laugh. "It seems that you're the only one who thinks my credentials are impressive. Diners, dives, and department stores? Not so much."

Aiden frowns, thinking. "I won't pretend that I get home at a reasonable hour every night. My job is stressful—that's actually an understatement. My job is a *nightmare* sometimes. I have most mornings off, and sometimes I don't have to go in until the afternoons . . . but my nights can get late. Do you think it would be a problem? Sophie normally gets into bed by nine. I'm sure that as long as she's fed and ready for bed, you could work on your schoolwork."

"Sophie? Your daughter?"

Aiden smiles a new kind of smile, one that feels warm and proud, but it clashes with the flash of sadness that sparks in his eyes. "Yes. She's . . . really great. She's nine, but she seems so much older than that. She's too damned smart for her own good."

"Little girls usually are," I laugh, thinking of myself. "And the weekends that I have school? I could be home by late afternoon. So I can still cover dinner, surely."

Aiden considers this. "I can make it work. I mean, I have so far, anyway. If worse comes to worst, maybe you could pick her up here on those days? She could play her little game system in the office while she waits. She's, ah, used to that by now, unfortunately."

"And your daughter? Is she okay with all of this? The nanny situation?"

Aiden nods thoughtfully. "She's had them before. None have really . . . fit though. I . . . Can I be honest with you again?"

"I prefer it," I tell him, echoing his earlier sentiment.

Aiden laughs again, and I determine that I am going to have to make it a point not to make him laugh very often for my own sanity's sake, if I'm going to be living with him. It's a very nice laugh, okay? "I just . . . I need some help, Cassie, if I'm being blunt. I'm doing this all alone, and it's much harder than I thought it would be. Or maybe it's exactly as hard as I thought it would be. I don't know. Sophie can be very . . . strong willed, and that's made it difficult to find someone who is willing to stick around. I've been looking for a replacement for the last nanny for weeks, because I wanted to find the best fit for Sophie, and absolutely no one has applied for the job that has been half as qualified as you. It's been weeks of juggling schedules, and at this point, I'm desperate."

"That's . . . very honest."

"You can run away screaming at any time."

Strangely, I have no desire to do that. Something about this tired-sounding man with his pretty eyes and his stomach-fluttering laugh makes it kind of hard to say no to him. Not to mention, there is still the ridiculous amount of money he's offering.

"So, how would this go? If I say yes."

"Well, I'd love for you to start as soon as you can," he tells me. "Maybe you could come by this Saturday? I could introduce you to Sophie and show you the house. Where you'd be staying and all that . . . If you take the job, that is."

I'd be silly not to, right? I mean, when is anything else this good going to come along? Sure, it's daunting, the idea of being directly responsible for someone's kid, not to mention living in their house . . . especially *this* guy's house . . . Still. I don't think it's an offer I can actually afford to refuse in my position.

"Okay."

I nod down at the table as I come to a decision, meeting Aiden's eyes and once again sticking out my hand across the space in a thoughtless way that I immediately regret.

Seriously, why do I keep doing that?

Thankfully, Aiden sighs with relief, taking my hand again and enveloping it in his much larger one. "So you want the job?"

"As long as you want me," I say with what I hope is confidence.

I try not to think about the way his eyes widen with my weird phrasing; it won't do to regret my nervous word vomit now. Thank God he's so desperate.

And I'm definitely not thinking about how his hand swallows mine.

⋮

@alacarte
Ⓢ **sent you a $20 tip** Ⓢ

♥

I love the way you come.

▶

CHAPTER 2

Cassie

By the time Saturday rolls around, Aiden and I have already hammered out my schedule and the specifics of my salary. In that time, I've been able to convince myself that this is going to be a great gig, even if only to ease the nerves of living under a hot guy's roof and hoping his kid doesn't hate me. As sure as I am about my new career path, however, Wanda is not so convinced. The entire time I have spent finishing up bagging my clothes on the morning I'm supposed to head to Aiden's (an easy task, given that there is so little I've collected over the years that I've deemed worth saving outside of the essentials), Wanda has taken it upon herself to interview me about *my* interview, grilling me for every detail about the mysterious man I'll be living with all *willy-nilly.* (Her words, not mine.)

"What if he doesn't even have a daughter?"

I roll my eyes. "He has a daughter."

"It could all be some elaborate scheme to lure you to his house so he can lock you in his basement."

"He lives in a town house," I tell her. "I don't even think they have basements."

I'm not *entirely* sure about that, seeing as I've never been in one, but Wanda doesn't have to know that.

"We need to think of some sort of code word."

I pause from shoving socks into my overnight bag. "Code word?"

"Right." Wanda nods thoughtfully from my couch/bed (all hail the futon). "In case he won't let you speak freely."

"How many Lifetime movies have you been watching?"

"You won't think it's very funny when he's feeding you baby food and making you play dress-up."

I laugh at that. "You know that's actually a kink, right?"

"You're kidding."

Her shocked expression makes me laugh harder. "People pay good money to feed cute girls baby food and play dress-up."

"Hot damn." Wanda shakes her head. "Where was that when I was younger? Could have saved me a lot of shifts at the library."

"You loved working at the library," I remind her.

"I'd have loved it a hell of a lot more if someone had paid me to get naked in it."

"In another life," I chuckle, "you would have ruled the entire camgirl scene."

"And don't you forget it," she tuts.

Even as I throw the last of the clothes from my closet into a bag, I feel her eyes watching me from across the room. I wait until the sack is full and tied off before I give her my attention. "What?"

"I just want you to be careful," she says a little more gently. "There are a lot of weirdos out there."

"I'm going to be fine," I assure her, pretending that her concern doesn't make me want to smile. She may be cantankerous ninety percent of the time, but Wanda cares about me more than my own mother ever bothered to. "I promise. It's good money, and he was incredibly nice. I scoped his Facebook, too, and he has a daughter." A pretty one too. Seriously, the *genes* in this family. "Besides, if the vibe is bad, I can leave, okay?"

"You kids and your vibes," she grumbles. "When I was your age, we didn't have vibes, we had instinct."

"You realize it's practically the same thing, right? Also, you could stop griping and help me pack something."

Wanda crosses her arms. "Gotta rest my back. Got a bingo match tonight."

I don't ask for elaboration, not wanting to know if she needs to rest for bingo or for whoever she will inevitably bring home after. She and Fred Wythers got into a fight last week, so I imagine he's on the outs.

"Aren't you the one always saying that you're old, not dead?" She gives me the finger, and I laugh. "Hey, did you know the middle finger is the fastest growing nail?"

"Oh, to hell with your damn Snapple facts."

I bite back my smile as I give my attention back to packing. When the tiny space is packed away in various boxes and bags, I nod appreciatively at a job well done, thinking that the place looks bigger somehow when it's mostly empty like this. The furniture stays, seeing as it was here when I got here. Plus, I won't need it since I get my own furnished room at Aiden's place.

There's only a *tiny* flap of butterfly wings in my stomach when I am reminded that I will be under the same roof as Aiden Reid.

"I think that just about does it," I tell Wanda.

"I guess so." Wanda eyes the scattered bags on the floor. "I just know they're going to let a weirdo come in here after you."

"Maybe it will be your soulmate."

Wanda snorts. "Don't need one of those."

You have to admire her independence, that's for sure.

Wanda has never settled down in her long life, as far as I know, always bouncing from one man to the next. She makes it seem fun, don't get me wrong, but surely it has to be lonely sometimes. I like to think that the two of us needed each other equally as much when we stumbled into each other's lives. She became an unlikely surrogate mom and best friend all rolled into one, adopting me into her life and treating me like the kid she never had. I'm not entirely sure that I knew what real affection looked like before I met her.

"And you're *sure* this is a good idea? You could still do the booby cams."

I consider that, knowing that Wanda likes to live vicariously through my OnlyFans endeavors (seriously, this woman missed her true calling), and it *would* be easy money if I could build a following again, but I can't bring myself to. Not after what happened.

"I'm sure." I nod, mostly for myself. "You can tell me you're going to miss me, you know."

"Miss you?" She snorts as she pats me on the shoulder. "You don't come visit, I'll come looking for your ass."

I pull her into a hug, breathing in the familiar scent of her White Diamonds perfume and a bit of talcum powder underneath that I've always found strangely comforting. "It's going to be great. You'll see."

Wanda still looks unconvinced when she pulls away, and as I start to pile up what's left of my things in preparation for the moving service that will bring the rest of my things tomorrow, I do my best to seem as confident about the whole thing as I'm pretending to be.

———

A iden's town house is located in a gated community, a quiet residential area of three-story homes lining the street. Aiden's in particular has a cute little yard, lined with a block wall and closed off with an iron gate. My old Toyota parked in front looks out of place amid the rows and rows of shiny-looking town houses but to be fair, so do I. I check the house number one more time in my emails as I unlatch the gate, feeling only a little nervous as I approach the front door.

I pull the strap of my overnight bag tighter against my shoulder when I finally summon the courage to ring the doorbell, having packed only the essentials to get me through the night until everything else gets here tomorrow. Suddenly it's hitting me that I will be *living* with virtual strangers, and what if Aiden *is* some kind of weirdo?

God.

I try to fish my phone out of my pocket to let Wanda know I've made it, managing to pull it halfway out before my bag slips from my shoulder and onto the ground, the only half-zipped opening allowing for some of my stuff to spill out onto the porch. I drop to my knees to start scooping the scattered items back in, thinking that this is the last thing I need, for my new boss to find me picking up my underwear outside his front door.

"Fuck, fuck, *fuck*."

And because the universe is a fickle bitch, this is exactly how Aiden Reid finds me. In the middle of a personal fiasco, cursing on his porch and holding my underwear. But then again, judging by the splotches of flour covering his black (fitted, it's very fitted) T-shirt and matching black apron and even higher on his cheeks, not to mention the sticky . . . something that is dripping down the front of his pants (less fitted, but no less distracting), I think maybe this time we're even.

"Are you"—my eyes take in his disheveled appearance—"okay?"

His eyes flick from my still-crouched form to the heart-patterned, neon-green underwear in my hand to my face. "Are *you* okay?"

"Oh." The back of my neck heats as I hastily shove my underwear back into my bag, pulling the strap over my shoulder as I stand back up. "I'm fine. Just had an accident." I'm actively choosing not to think about how Aiden just saw my underwear, pointing at the goop on his pants. "It looks like you had one too."

Aiden makes a helpless face, and the quiet sigh that escapes him makes my stomach do something funny.

"Yeah." He looks down at the mess on his shirt before giving me a sheepish grin. "Do you . . ." He bites his lip. I mustn't dwell on this. "Do you happen to know anything about pancakes?"

"Pancakes?"

Aiden jerks his head in a nod, gesturing to the staircase behind him. "Come on up."

I follow him out of the entryway and up the stairs to the second level, the top of the stairs spilling out into what seems to be the main living area and kitchen. I recognize a little girl at the counter in the kitchen as we approach, her hair the same shade as Aiden's and her mouth pressed into a full pout. She looks terser than she did on Aiden's Facebook. I also notice that the mess on Aiden's shirt and pants extends to the kitchen floor and half of the countertop.

"We, ah . . . wanted to do something nice for you," Aiden tells me. "For your first day here."

"*Dad* wanted to," the little girl grouses from her place at the counter, just loud enough for me to catch it.

Aiden shoots her a stern look. It looks good on him. I mustn't dwell on this either. "*We* thought you might like pancakes, but, ah . . . This is embarrassing."

"You seem to be having some trouble," I point out with amusement. "I've never seen such a mess over pancakes."

Aiden looks at his feet like a child who's broken his mother's vase and is reluctant to tell her. "I dropped the bowl of batter. It's a disaster in here."

"I can"—I let my eyes sweep down the front of him again, for purely investigative purposes, of course—"see that."

"I'm . . . not very good at making pancakes," he admits, almost like it pains him.

I cock my head. "Aren't you a chef?"

"There are no pancakes on my menu." His mouth does something that is dangerously close to a pout, and it shouldn't work for a man his size, but it weirdly does. "Sophie says she doesn't like them, but I'm pretty sure she just doesn't like *mine*, so it's personal now. I was trying a new recipe, but . . ." He gestures to the mess. "Obviously, it didn't turn out the way I hoped."

I flash him a grin, realizing he really *does* need some help. "Whew, boy."

I drop my bag by the stairs as I take in the space. The kitchen is sleek and modern with black cabinets and a gray marble countertop—everything you might expect from an upscale house in this part of town. The tiles are a similar shade of gray, maybe lighter, going all the way to the edge of the open living room just beyond where it blends into soft-looking gray carpet that rests under black leather furniture.

I'm gathering Aiden isn't very big on color here.

"This is a nice place," I tell him. "I like what you've done with the, ah . . . color scheme."

I peek back to find Aiden frowning. "I . . . like black."

"I would have absolutely never guessed," I tease. It dawns on me that he's still covered in goo. "Right. Pancakes." I scan the kitchen, searching. "Do you have another apron?"

Aiden rushes to a tall, slim cabinet just beside the black stainless steel fridge to pull out a (surprise) black apron. I throw it over my head, reaching behind me to tie the strings as I flash a smile toward the girl, who is still silently sizing me up at the counter.

"You must be Sophie," I try. "I'm Cassie."

"You're my new nanny," she says with only a hint of bitterness.

"I am. I heard you've had a few."

"Only four," she mutters.

"How old are you, Sophie?"

"Nine."

"Wow. You're practically grown up. I doubt you even need a nanny."

"That's what *I* said," she huffs. "I can take care of myself."

"Of course." I nod seriously before leaning in closer to lower my voice. "Between you and me . . . I just needed some company. I don't have many friends. Practically had to beg your dad to give me the job, you know?"

Sophie looks suspicious, her lips pressed together for a good number of moments before she finally casts her eyes down to the countertop. "I don't have a lot of friends either."

"Well . . . we could be friends. Maybe? What do you think?"

Sophie looks me up and down, seeming to consider. "You're pretty," she says finally.

"Not as pretty as you," I gush. "Look at those freckles!"

Sophie narrows her eyes. "Freckles aren't pretty."

"You're right," I sigh as I prop my fists on my hips. "They're *gorgeous.*"

Sophie rolls her eyes, but there's a bit of a smile at her mouth as she does it. I notice she doesn't have the same condition as her dad, but her eyes are the same soft green of his right eye, complementing the pretty shade of her hair. She's adorable now, but I can already tell she's going to be a real knockout when she gets older. Seriously, the *genes.*

"Right," I say again. "So let's clean up your first attempt, shall we?"

Aiden still looks utterly dumbfounded, like he still can't believe he could have messed up such a universally known thing at his level of culinary prowess, but silently trudges to that same slim cabinet to pull out a broom and a wet mop.

"Sorry," he tells me. "We really did want to try and do something nice."

I shrug, pulling the elastic from my wrist and reaching to tie up my hair. "It's fine. Sophie and I have got this, right?"

"Why do I have to help?"

"I need a capable assistant if I'm going to make pancakes," I say seriously. "You look like the perfect girl for the job."

She still doesn't look like she trusts me very much, but her desire for pancakes must exceed her wariness of me, and she tentatively hops from the barstool to cautiously cross the kitchen to stand beside me. "I guess so."

She absolutely doesn't smile.

I like her already.

The second attempt at pancakes goes much smoother than the first, the mess cleared away and one very large chef (but not pancake maker) and his little mini me humming around syrup and cake.

"These are so good," Sophie gushes. "Dad never gets them right. They're always too mushy."

"Oh, so you *do* like them," Aiden snorts. He looks down at the pancakes like they've offended him. "I should buy an actual mixer."

I smile around my fork. "How do you not own a mixer?"

"I don't bake a lot."

"Clearly," I say with a grin. "You know they have a box mix."

"A box mix goes against every fiber of my being," Aiden scoffs.

I keep my expression serious, pointing to the soaking dishes in his sink with my fork. "Yes. Clearly this is better."

"Cassie has to make all the pancakes from now on," Sophie says matter-of-factly.

Aiden shares a grateful look with me, and it takes a lot of effort on my part not to let my gaze linger on the clashing brightness of his eyes.

"I think for the safety of your dad's kitchen, that's best," I deadpan.

Aiden stifles a laugh. "Everyone's a critic."

When the plates are empty and the forks are clattering against them, Sophie pats her belly with a satisfied sound, a content little smile on her face. "You're all right, I guess," she tells me, quickly masking her smile into a more stern expression. "But you can't come into my room."

"I wouldn't dream of it," I assure her. "You can come into mine, though, if you want. I have board games coming with my stuff tomorrow." I look back over at Aiden. "Where is my room, by the way?"

"Oh. Yeah. Of course." He slides from the barstool, pulling his apron over his head as the muscles in his biceps roll and flex against the fitted cotton of his sleeves. It's not something I've ever found myself noticing on a man, biceps against sleeves. "It's back downstairs. I can show you . . . ?"

"Awesome." I hop down from my own stool, grabbing the bag I left by the stairs and slinging it over my shoulder. "Lead the way."

"So the whole first floor will be yours," Aiden tells me when we're near the bottom landing. "The bedroom has an attached bath, and there's a TV in there, so you should have everything you need, but you can just ask if there's something else I need to get you."

Aiden gestures to the door right off the entryway so that I can open it, and beyond is a room nearly bigger than my entire apartment. The queen-sized four-poster is covered with thick, gray (shocker) bedding; the chest of drawers and end tables are a sleek black that matches the rest of the house decor. I gape around the room in awe, trying to think back to a time when I've slept in a bed this nice. If ever.

"If you want to change something," Aiden says quietly behind me, "we can—"

"It's perfect. Seriously, this is nicer than my whole apartment."

I hear Aiden sigh in relief. "Good. I want you to be comfortable here."

"Really struck out in the nanny department, huh?"

"You have no idea." Aiden leans against the doorframe. "She's been through a lot. I think that's why she acts out sometimes. I'm always trying my best to get her to open up and talk about it, but she's . . ." He breathes in through his nose just to blow it out his mouth, shaking his head. "It's like we speak a different language, sometimes."

"Did something . . ." I drop my bag to the carpet, reaching to scratch at my neck awkwardly. "I hope I'm not overstepping, but I thought I should . . . Just so I don't say something insensitive by accident, you know. Sophie's mother . . . is she . . . ?"

He doesn't answer for a moment, chewing at his lip as if trying to decide how to broach the subject. I know there has to be a story, and I hate asking on my very first day, but I hate the thought of accidentally putting my foot in my mouth at some point because I *don't* know even more.

"She passed away," Aiden says finally, half whispering. "Almost a year ago. Stroke."

"Oh God." I had expected a bad divorce or something. Not *that*. "That's terrible. I'm really sorry for your loss."

"It was . . . sudden. None of us expected it. She was so young, after all." Aiden sighs, running his fingers through his hair. "She was great," he tells me. "An amazing mom. She was a lot better at this than I ever was. I'm still figuring out how to do this without her."

I suddenly feel *so* much worse about all my lingering thoughts of his catcher's mitt hands, voluntary or not. "I really am sorry," I say lamely. "How long were you married?"

Aiden's eyebrows scrunch together. "What? Oh. No. We weren't. We weren't even together." I must look confused. That must be why Aiden chooses to clarify. "Sophie was . . . ah, unexpected. Rebecca and I met at a party during our senior year in college and were seeing each other casually for a little while. When Rebecca found out she was pregnant, we attempted an actual relationship, but it was pretty clear early on that it was never going to work out between us. We did our best to co-parent as smoothly as we could though. For Sophie's sake."

"Oh." I look down at my shoes, still feeling awkward. "I'm sure it's been rough for Sophie."

"It has," Aiden agrees. "Sorry for dumping this on you. I thought it might help you understand her better. If you knew."

"No, I'm glad you told me," I say honestly. "Thank you."

"Truth be told, I could have been there more these last few years. When I was promoted to executive chef everything got so hectic, and I . . . I didn't make the time I should have for her. I'm paying for it now."

I feel a twinge of sympathy for Sophie then, knowing *exactly* what it's like to come second to a parent's career. Still. Aiden seems to be trying now, at least.

"I mean . . . it's never too late, though, right?" I try for an encouraging smile. "She's still so young. You'll figure it out."

Aiden gives me a similarly soft smile. "I hope you're right."

The big room seems smaller now that I'm just standing there like an idiot, smiling at the pretty man in my doorway, and I finally have to pull the old distracted look around the room, pretending to admire the painting of . . . oh. Is that smoke? Abstract smoke? I really have to sneak some color into this house.

"Okay." Aiden must sense my awkward energy, since he chooses right now to push away from the doorframe. "Well. I'll . . . let you unpack then."

"I don't have much," I admit. "The rest is coming tomorrow."

"Right. Well. I can finish showing you around when you're done. The living area is all on the second floor. Mine and Sophie's rooms are on the third."

"Cool," I say.

Why is that cool? Why did I say that it was? Do people even say cool anymore?

"I'll leave you to it then," Aiden says.

I don't breathe until he's out of sight, cursing under my breath at my very *un*cool behavior, acting like I've never seen a hot guy before. But then again, I actually haven't ever *lived* with a hot guy before. Especially not one who attempts (and fails, but it's sort of cute) at pancakes and worries about how to connect with his kid.

It's a job, I remind myself. *It's just a job.*

I bet Aiden's bedding is black too.

Not that I'm thinking about it.

It's the first gift anyone's ever sent me.

The packaging is sleek, but it's what's inside that really grabs my attention.

The toy is bigger than anything I've used before, and I gulp just pulling it out of the box. Can I even take something this big? I pick up the note that came with it, a strange thrill coursing through me as I consider the fact that one man out there wants to watch me use this. That he's out there imagining it right now.

I can't wait to watch you use this. —A

CHAPTER 3

Cassie

I finish putting my stuff away and head back upstairs after the pancake debacle, finding Aiden sitting in the living room and reading a newspaper, with Sophie nowhere to be found. I assume she's up in the room I'm not allowed in. He's changed his shirt to a clean one (still black, but a different shade of black, if that's possible, so I guess points to him), but I am not complaining about the monochromatic tone of his gray sweats with the way they fit him. His hair is less styled than it was the night I met him, mussed and curling at his temples like he simply toweled it dry after showering off all the batter from earlier. It makes him look even younger than he normally does.

He looks up from the paper when he notices me awkwardly lingering at the top of the stairs, folding the pages and giving me a little smile. "All settled?"

"Yeah." I cross my arms, feeling strange. The idea that I actually live here now is sort of crashing down on me all at once. "The room is great."

"I'm glad. Make sure to tell me if you need anything. I can take care of whatever you need."

Oh boy.

In lieu of answering, I move to the armchair across from the couch he's sitting on, pulling my legs up to tuck them beneath me. I'm actually grateful for his casual attire, making me feel better about my leggings and long tee. I mean, I know he didn't mention a uniform or anything, but still.

But damn if those sweatpants aren't distracting.

I nod toward the paper he's still perusing. "Anything interesting in there?"

"Not really," he says with a shrug. "I mainly get them for the crosswords."

Why is that cute?

"Did you know that someone good at crosswords is called a cruciverbalist?"

He lowers the paper to cock an eyebrow at me. "How on earth do you know that?"

"I read it on a Snapple lid," I say. "It's where I get eighty percent of my knowledge from."

"You must drink a lot of Snapple."

"Oh, tons. I bet I bleed peach tea at this point."

Aiden smiles, shaking his head. "Any other interesting facts I should know?"

"Humans are slightly taller in the morning than at night."

His brow wrinkles. "That can't be true."

"It totally is."

"I don't know about that," he laughs.

"I bet you'll measure yourself now to check though."

"Hmm." He considers this with a guilty expression. "I plead the Fifth."

He's still smiling as he turns another page, and I tap my fingers against my thigh. "So . . . no cooking tonight?"

"I'll have to go in later. Before the dinner service." He cuts his eyes at me. "I wanted to make sure to be here when you arrived though."

"I appreciate it."

There's a bit of an awkward silence then. The product of two near strangers now cohabitating, I'm sure.

"So . . ." I shift a bit in the chair so I can look somewhere other than Aiden's face, which is also pretty distracting. "Do we think Sophie will put dirt in my bed tonight, or will she let me get a false sense of security before she goes full *Home Alone* on me?"

Aiden laughs again, and I'm reminded of how nice of a sound it is. "Maybe you check the tops of the doors before you open them, just to be safe."

"At least I get my own bathroom," I point out. "Maybe I can keep a better eye on my shampoo so she doesn't put Nair in it."

"The worst she might do is leave her towels on the floor," Aiden grouses, all dad-like. "You buy the girl a towel rack, and she drops it right next to it. Don't even get me started on her shoes on the bedroom floor."

"No towels on my bathroom floor," I say seriously. "Got it."

"Oh." He actually looks mildly embarrassed. "No. It's your room. Don't listen to me, I'm just . . ."

"Neat freak?"

"I wouldn't say that," he mumbles. "I like things in their place."

It's weirdly cute that he's trying to pretend he isn't a total control freak when it's written all over his face.

"Gotcha." I keep my expression even. "So this is probably a bad time to tell you about my collective network of ant farms then?" Aiden looks horrified, and I can't help but burst into laughter. "Kidding."

"Hilarious."

More silence. I hate silence. It always makes me feel anxious. I decide to change the subject. "It must be a huge adjustment for Sophie. This year."

"It's been tough for sure." He lays the paper down beside him on the couch. "They were close. I mean, I'm sure you know what it's like, the whole mother-daughter bonding thing."

I try to smile, but it's forced. "Not really."

"Oh. Shit. I'm sorry. Did she . . . ?"

"She's alive, don't worry." I laugh bitterly. "My parents weren't ever the nurturing type. I haven't spoken to them in . . . a long time."

"I'm sorry," he says again. "That's terrible."

"It is what it is. I guess you can't fault them for being terrible parents when they never wanted to be parents in the first place."

"I mean, you can," he argues. "As a mostly subpar parent myself, I'm the expert on the subject."

I grin. "I don't think you're a subpar parent. I mean. You're here. You're looking out for her. That's already half the battle."

"Right." Aiden's eyes suddenly gain a faraway look. "I'm trying."

"That's all a kid wants, to be honest. They just want you to try your best."

Aiden's mouth does this thing, not quite a smile but sort of, and his eyes flick to meet mine, the soft green and brown hard to look away from. "I appreciate that."

"So, we should go over what you need from me a little more," I say, changing the subject again.

Aiden's eyebrows raise. "What I need from you?"

Oh shit. Did that sound weird? It didn't sound weird in my head.

"I know the basics here, and you gave me your schedule and Sophie's allergies, but does she have any after-school clubs? Any soccer practices I need to know about? What about an approved list of emergency numbers of relatives or something like that? I don't want to let in a weirdo pretending to be her uncle or something."

"Oh." Aiden watches as I untuck my legs, following the way I let my feet fall to the floor, his gaze thoughtful. "She hasn't joined any clubs yet. It's a new school year, after all, and she's still settling. No weird uncles that I know of. My parents live across country, so we only really see them around holidays. Rebecca has a sister, Iris, so she might be around from time to time to see Sophie. I can leave you the number to the restaurant, and of course we should exchange numbers."

"Numbers?"

"It's not really practical to keep emailing each other forever," he points out. "Since we're living together and all."

He just had to remind me.

I'm *living* with this gorgeous man. Not that there is any reason to be so flustered by the reminder, since it's all contractual. It's not like it matters, anyway. It's completely irrelevant how nice Aiden is to look at, since I'm the nanny, and he is absolutely, positively off-limits. I might almost laugh at this entire line of thought; Aiden is successful and good-looking and way out of my league. He's probably bringing home dates on the regular.

Oh God. I hadn't thought of that. I sincerely hope it's not something I have to find out anytime soon.

"Right," I manage. "Numbers. Give me your phone, and I'll send myself a text."

Aiden lifts his hips from the couch to dig in his pocket for his cell phone, and I don't think that I need to elaborate on why this move on a hot guy in gray sweats has me averting my eyes. He hands me his phone, and I immediately notice his wallpaper of him and a smiling Sophie at what looks to be a park. The wind is ruffling their hair, and Sophie's smile is wide and bright and slightly snaggletoothed here, one of her incisors still growing in.

"This is a nice picture," I note as I pull up his texts.

"It was a good day." Aiden smiles fondly. "It wasn't very long after, um . . . after Rebecca."

"Sorry," I say, afraid I've touched on a sore spot. "I didn't mean to—"

"No, no. Seriously. It's fine. It was the first time I can remember Sophie smiling like that. After it happened. I like to remember it."

"I get it," I answer quietly. "It's a great photo."

"Thank you."

I shoot myself a text, feeling my phone vibrate in my pocket, then I hand Aiden's back to him. "All done. I'll be sure to text you if I burn the house down."

"I appreciate that," Aiden laughs.

I shrug. "I figure it's common courtesy."

"Of course."

He opens his mouth to say more as footsteps come thudding down the stairs, a flash of chestnut hair in my peripheral as Sophie lands at the bottom.

"Dad, the batteries in my remote are low," she huffs. "Do we have any more?"

Aiden closes his mouth, whatever he'd been about to say dying on his tongue as he stands from the couch to walk toward the kitchen. "They're in the drawer by the sink," he tells her. "Let me get them for you."

I turn my head to notice Sophie eyeing me. "Are you going to make lunch?"

"That depends," I say smoothly. "Are you going to help me?"

"Isn't it your job to feed me?"

I press my lips together, nodding as if I'm considering. "It might be. But you know I hold all the power when it comes to deciding if you're getting borscht or pizza, right?"

"What is *borscht*?"

"It's beet soup, essentially," Aiden tosses over his shoulder, still searching for batteries. "It's very good. Kind of sour though. It's good with smetana."

"*Ew.* She can't feed me that, can she?"

Aiden turns to lean against the counter, holding the batteries he's found and shrugging as he gives Sophie an aloof look. "She's the boss when I'm not here."

Sophie turns to narrow her eyes, frowning at me as I give her my sweetest grin. "Fine," she relents. "I'll help. But no beets."

She takes the batteries her dad is offering as she trudges back up the stairs, and Aiden smiles at me from the kitchen, looking amused. "You're going to give her a run for her money, aren't you?"

"That's the plan," I assure him. "Until you guys get rid of me."

Aiden's smile hitches wider. "You might be the only person in this city who has a real shot at handling my daughter," he says. "I don't think I can let you leave, sorry."

I know he's joking, but it still does something funny to my insides.

"So," I say, pushing out of the armchair and clapping my hands together as I raise my voice for dramatic effect. "Where do you keep the beets in this place?"

"No beets!" Sophie's voice calls from up the stairs.

Aiden covers his mouth with his hand to hide his laugh.

The rest of my stuff comes Sunday afternoon after Aiden has already left for work, and I spend some time putting it away, giving the enigmatic little girl who is determined not to get too close to me a moment to breathe before I go upstairs and start trying to make her like me. My attempts so far have been met with a lukewarm reception at best.

"I think she might hate me," I tell Wanda, using my shoulder to hold the phone to my ear as I hang up my jeans. "But I'm pretty sure it's more about principle than me as a person, so I'm not taking it personally."

"It's all those preteen hormones," Wanda muses.

I wrinkle my nose. "She's only nine."

"Well, maybe it's a personal choice to be difficult then, I don't know."

"I'm still a stranger," I laugh. "I think we can cut her some slack. Besides, I'm totally going to win her over. Just wait."

"I'll bet," Wanda chuckles. "How is the house? Is there a basement? Has he asked you to wear a diaper yet?"

"The house is amazing. My room might be bigger than my entire apartment. No evidence of a basement though. Also, it's more of a padded underwear situation, and he asked nicely, so . . ."

"One of these days you're going to give me a heart attack with your nonsense, and who'll be laughing then?"

"Well, not you, presumably."

"Oh, ha ha. So what do you think of the family?"

"Sophie is cute as a button. Stubborn as hell though. I can tell she's going to be a tough nut to crack."

"And the dad?"

"Aiden is . . ." I still with my hand on a hanger, considering how best to describe him. "He's really nice. You can tell he loves Sophie, and he seems determined to make sure I'm comfortable here. Sounds like they've had some bad luck in the nanny department lately."

"They're probably all in the basement."

"Well, at least I'll have company when he throws me down there."

"You laugh now, but don't come crying to me when he brings out the zip ties."

Wow that shouldn't sound halfway appealing. I tell myself it's a natural reaction to someone who looks like he does, and that it will get better the more I get used to him. Surely.

I definitely can't tell Wanda that Aiden is hot. She'll be completely insufferable about it, I'm sure.

"They're perfectly nice people, and this is a perfectly nice house, and I am perfectly safe. I promise."

"Yeah, well. You make sure you keep that tracker thing going on your phone."

"We're sharing locations. I don't have to turn it on."

"Well, as long as I can find you when he throws you in the basement."

"Yes, I love you too."

"Yeah, yeah."

"How was bingo?"

"I won a succulent."

"But you have a black thumb."

She scoffs. "It's a cactus! You don't even have to do anything with it."

"No, you definitely have to water it."

"No, you don't. They make their own water."

I shake my head, thinking about that poor plant that is absolutely going to die.

"Just throw some water on it every once in a while," I insist. "Humor me."

"Oh, whatever."

"I'd better let you go," I tell her. "I'm done unpacking, so it's time to go and try to tame the cute little beast."

"The trick is to not show any fear."

I smile into the receiver. "Noted."

"Call me tomorrow."

"I will, I will."

We say our goodbyes before I stow my phone in my pocket, taking one last glance around the room and nodding in satisfaction. I still can't get over how big it is. I could practically open a dance studio on either side of the bed. I figure I've afforded Sophie about as much space as I can manage at this point, and I give myself a pep talk before I leave my bedroom in an attempt to coax her out of her room.

It's my first time going upstairs, since last night she claimed she had homework and sequestered herself in her room. I knock on her bedroom door, careful not to step inside even after she answers, peeking my head around the door instead.

"Hey. More homework?"

She pauses her Switch to frown up at me. "I finished it."

"Oh, that's good."

"Did you need something?"

I know she's trying to be a brat, but she's so cute it still sort of makes me want to smile. "Oh, nothing much. I have this huge bowl of popcorn downstairs and all three Shrek movies on Blu-ray."

Her nose wrinkles. "What's Shrek?"

"You've never seen *Shrek*?"

"No."

"Sophie. It's a cultural phenomenon. An epic love story. A comic masterpiece. I can't in good conscience allow you to continue through life without having seen it."

"It sounds weird."

I push her door open a tad wider, leaning against the frame. "There are princesses in it."

"I'm too old for princesses," she says stoically.

"Well, when we're done we can visit the retirement home."

Her lips purse. "You're not gonna leave me alone, are you."

"Not a chance, doll." I beam.

She looks annoyed the entire walk down the stairs, and then begrudging, when she settles onto the couch in the living room, but I notice that she doesn't hesitate to grab a fistful of popcorn, even if she munches on it with a little more aggression than needed.

"Why is it called *Shrek*?"

I push play as the DreamWorks logo glides across the screen. "Because that's his name."

"That's a weird name."

"Well, he's an ogre. So."

"Ew. I thought you said this was about princesses?"

"No, I said it *had* princesses."

She makes a face as the opening scene starts. "What is this weird song?"

"Oh my God, Sophie. I will not let you sit there and slander Smash Mouth."

"Is that old people's music?"

I pull my popcorn bowl away from her extended hand. "Ma'am, do you want to lose your popcorn privileges?"

"Fine," she huffs. "I guess it's okay."

Her barrage of questions continues up until Donkey's proclamations about staying up late and swapping stories, finally laughing when Shrek kicks him out of the house and makes him pout. I give her a look, and she immediately tries to mask her glee. "I guess it's kind of funny."

"Just wait until you meet Lord Farquaad," I say.

She looks like she'd rather pull out her hair than admit she's enjoying the movie, and I notice her eyeing our dwindling popcorn.

I grab the bowl. "Want me to make some more? We've got all night. We can totally have a marathon."

I can see the wheels turning in her head as her eyes dart from the popcorn bowl to the TV screen, her obvious desire to keep watching warring with her determination to remain disinterested in the "enemy" that is her new nanny.

"I guess that sounds cool," she finally concedes.

I do a silent victory dance behind her back as I go to the kitchen for more popcorn.

don't know when I fell asleep; Sophie passed out sometime after dinner near the end of the second movie, and I distinctly remember starting the third, but when I'm awoken to the feel of a warm hand on my shoulder and a warmer mass at my side, my eyes blink open to mostly darkness. Sophie has wormed her way against me as she sighs softly with sleep, and when my eyes adjust to the darkness of the room lit only by the soft glow of the menu screen of the third Shrek movie, I see a familiar face looming over me as Aiden's hand gently rouses me awake.

"Sorry," he says quietly. "Didn't think you'd wanna spend all night out here."

I sit up straighter, careful not to disturb Sophie. "What time is it?"

"Just after nine," he tells me. "I guess you guys didn't finish your movie?"

I stifle a yawn. "I have been giving your daughter an important education on film classics."

"Clearly," Aiden laughs as he eyes the menu screen still playing on the TV.

"How was work?"

"A surprisingly slow night," he says, coming around the other side of Sophie's sleeping form to sit beside her. "It's not often I get home this early." He reaches to brush Sophie's hair away from her forehead, smiling. "Seems like she's warmed up to you a little bit."

"Don't be fooled," I tell him quietly. "It's like taming a feral cat. When she wakes up again, she'll be her cute little hissing self."

"I appreciate your valiant effort." Aiden's eyes me curiously. "Are you thinking of disappearing in the middle of the night yet?"

"Oh, my go-bag is currently hidden under the stairs," I say seriously. "I'm waiting for an opening."

Even when he looks exhausted, his smile makes my heart stutter. "I guess I should get better locks."

"Have I told you yet about my friend's basement theory?"

He grimaces. "Do I want to know?"

"That depends. Where do you stand on kidnapping jokes?"

"I think this is a good time to make it clear that I don't actually have a basement."

"My friend would say that's what you *want* me to think," I answer grimly.

His answering laugh quickly morphs into a yawn, and he reaches to rub his eyes. "I'm going to pass out mid-conversation if I'm not careful."

"Oh, right. Let me—"

I throw the blanket I'd grabbed from the back of the armchair from my shoulders with the intention of untangling myself from Sophie, so Aiden can put her to bed, only noticing after it's gone that the neckline of my oversized T-shirt has slipped over my shoulder to bare a good bit of skin and bra strap and—judging by the cool air—even a bit of cleavage. Great. Aiden coughs as he averts his eyes while I adjust it, and I'm grateful for the darkness of the room as I pull everything back into place.

"Sorry," I mutter.

Aiden sneaks a peek to see if it's safe, shaking his head. "It's fine. I should get her to bed. School tomorrow and all."

"Right. Sorry. I didn't mean to fall asleep. She was getting into the movies."

"It's fine," he assures me. "I'm happy you got her out of her room."

"Thanks for waking me up," I tell him, rubbing my neck. "I'd have been sore in the morning if I slept out here all night."

"Yeah," he shoots back, gently scooping up his sleeping daughter. "I figured it would be better to put you to bed."

He stills when he's standing again with Sophie in his arms, looking surprised at himself. "I mean . . . I meant *send* you to bed."

"Right," I answer dryly, my face flushing slightly. "Yeah. I know what you meant."

"Sorry, I'm tired."

"Of course." I rub my arm awkwardly. "I'm sure."

He lingers there for a moment, Sophie still tucked away in his arms, looking at me like he isn't sure what to say now. I decide to save us both.

"Anyway . . ." I put on a smile. "See you in the morning?"

"Sure. Good night, Cassie."

Now, Aiden has said my name before, during the interview, if nothing else, but something about hearing it in a dark room, with only the soft light of the television touching his black slacks and his black T-shirt that he must wear under his chef coat, feels different somehow. It gives me a weird sense of déjà vu that I can't explain. Like I've heard it before. I must be really tired.

"Good night, Aiden," I say back softly, not sure where my voice went.

Thankfully, as dark as it is, I know he won't see the blush creeping up my neck as I move quickly from the den toward the stairs, hearing his quiet footsteps shuffling in the other direction as he carries Sophie to the next floor. I peek behind me to catch Aiden's back as he goes before I head down to my room, catching sight of him leaning to press a kiss to Sophie's sleeping forehead and feeling something tug at my heart for reasons I can't explain.

He really is trying, I think.

I smile all the way down the stairs.

Chat with @lovecici

⋮

I was wondering if you
did private shows.

 Sometimes. I'm still
kind of new at it.

How much?

 It's $100 for a twenty-
minute show.

You sent @lovecici
 a $100 tip
♥

I want one, please.

CHAPTER 4

Aiden

"Sophie!" I call up the stairs for the second time. "We're going to be late!" I pull my cell phone back to my ear and continue my pacing on the first floor. "Sorry. Tell me what happened."

I hear Marco, my sous-chef, sigh on the other end of the line. "Alex forgot to put the scallops in the fridge last night after prep."

"What?"

"Yeah. They're ruined."

"You've got to be fucking kidding me."

"Nope." I can hear him rummaging around in the kitchen back at the restaurant. "And as far as I can tell, that was our entire supply from this week's delivery."

"What the *fuck*."

"I know. We're out until they deliver again on Friday."

"So we have to tell a hundred people that we fucked up, and now we're out of our most popular appetizer."

"If it makes you feel any better," Marco says, "I made Alex call Joe and tell him himself."

I roll my eyes. Joseph Cohen is many things, but a hard-ass is not one of them. He'll be comforting Alex before that conversation is over. All of the hard-assing at Cohen's is left to me.

I pull the phone away from my ear, still looking for my daughter. "Sophie!"

"Do you want me to take Sophie to school?"

I startle as I notice Cassie standing near her bedroom door. "Did I wake you up?"

"Oh, no," she assures me. "I've been up." She eyes my phone in my hand, where Marco is still chattering about something. "But I can totally take her, if something came up."

"Oh. No, I—" I bring the phone to my ear and murmur to Marco to give me a sec. "I want to take her. We're having a mild scallop disaster at work that I have to deal with."

"Oh, okay. If you're sure." She grins at me then. "Did you know that a scallop can produce up to two million eggs?"

I make a face. "Snapple?"

"Snapple," she answers with a nod.

I catch myself smiling despite what's happening on the other end of my phone. "Good to know."

"I'll go see if I can rustle up your daughter," Cassie says, frowning up at the stairs. "I bet she can't find her shoes again."

I can distantly hear Marco calling my name, but I'm ignoring it. "Thanks," I tell Cassie. "That would be great."

"Don't sweat it," she says, waving me off.

She starts to climb the stairs in search of Sophie, and I catch myself watching her go for a second longer than I mean to. I tear my eyes away when I realize what I'm doing, turning my back to the stairs and giving Marco my full attention again.

"Listen. Call the servers and have them come in early for a staff meeting. We can make them aware, and they'll have to let the tables know as they seat them. I can go tomorrow morning to the seafood market across town and get enough to last until the truck comes back."

"Okay. Sure." Marco scoffs. "I'm going to let Alex call them. Let him get bitched out by the servers."

This makes me laugh despite my growing headache. "Sounds like a plan. I'll be in later."

"We'll be here."

"Right. Bye."

I hang up the phone, stowing it in my pocket as I hear footsteps coming down the stairs. I turn to see Sophie taking the stairs two at a time, Cassie close behind. I throw my hands up in question. "What's the holdup?"

Sophie frowns. "I couldn't find my shoe!"

I glance at Cassie, who gives me an "I told you so" look.

"Well, come on," I urge my daughter. "That teacher with the whistle is going to yell at me again if we're late."

Sophie adjusts her backpack. "Okay, okay."

"Thanks for getting her," I tell Cassie.

"No problem," she says. She waves her hands in a shooing motion at us both. "Go on, both of you. Can confirm the whistle lady is scary."

I take Sophie's hand to pull her out the front door toward the car, and despite what's waiting for me at work tonight, I catch myself smiling.

W hy isn't Cassie taking me to school?"

"I had time this morning." I meet Sophie's gaze in the rearview mirror. "I thought we didn't like Cassie?"

Sophie purses her lips, face turning toward the window as she shrugs. "She's okay."

"Just okay?"

"She's kind of weird."

"Oh, really? How so?"

"She's always trying to hang out with me," Sophie huffs. "Doesn't she have any grown-up friends?"

"Maybe she likes you," I suggest.

Sophie tries to look casual, but I don't miss the way her eyes dart to the side to meet mine again in the mirror. "Do you think she does?"

"I doubt she'd keep trying to hang out with you if she didn't," I assure her. "Maybe you should be nicer to her."

"I'm nice to her," Sophie mutters.

"Uh-huh."

"She's not as lame as the last nanny," Sophie says after we pass another block.

"I'm glad you think so," I tell her.

I mean it too. After going through four nannies in the last year, I was damn near desperate by the time Cassie's résumé had reached my inbox.

Bringing Sophie to the restaurant is fine as an intermediary solution, but doing it too regularly had started to wear on us both. So it had felt like an actual miracle when Cassie applied. I had been prepared to offer whatever it took for her to take the job, convinced by her résumé alone that she was the answer we'd been looking for.

But then I met her.

I don't even know what I expected; I only gave a thought to her credentials in the short period between answering her email and seeing her for the first time, but I can definitively say that Cassie took me by surprise. Even with the slight disaster of our first meeting, it had been hard to pretend that I wasn't distracted by her.

It's not appropriate in the slightest for me to have noticed how silky her auburn hair looks, or how pouty her mouth appears. It's *definitely* not acceptable that my eyes had drunk in the way her black dress hugged dangerous curves before I forcefully packed those thoughts away—and that's what I've been doing ever since.

I have to remind myself once a day of all the things I shouldn't be noticing about Cassie. Like how pretty her smile is, or how bright her blue eyes seem to appear when she laughs, for example. Ultimately, I'm one hundred percent sure now that she *is* the best person for the job, and finding her attractive in any capacity only serves to potentially fuck up the good thing we've started to find. Sophie is more important than a few wayward thoughts I can never give voice to.

Even if they are sometimes louder than I'd like them to be.

"What happened at work?"

Sophie's voice pulls me out of my own head, reminding me of the scallop fiasco. "Someone not paying attention," I grumble. "We're going to be out of a popular dish tonight. People are going to complain."

"What are you out of?"

"Scallops."

Her nose wrinkles. "Ew. What is that?"

"Kind of like little clams."

"Gross."

"Well, I'm glad that you aren't put out by this," I laugh.

"Cassie said she's gonna show me how to make mini pizzas from tortillas for dinner," Sophie says. She tries to look like she isn't excited, but I can tell it's a front. "I bet they're gross too."

"Sounds pretty cool to me. I'm sad I'll miss it."

Sophie pouts. "I wish you could stay home tonight."

"I'm sorry." I frown, feeling like a dick. "I have to deal with the gross scallops." I eye her in the mirror. "It's going to get even busier in the next few weeks. We're adding some things to the menu."

"Okay," she answers quietly, trying not to let her disappointment show as guilt pangs in my chest.

Our last year hasn't been easy. At times it's been a downright nightmare, and I've thought more than once that if I'd known Sophie and I would end up here, I might have chosen a different profession. I love what I do, but I hate not being able to spend more time with her. She pretends that it doesn't bother her, my frequent late nights, but I know better. There's just nothing I can do about it right now.

"You'll have to tell me all about the mini pizzas tomorrow though," I offer.

Sophie nods. "Okay."

I notice her school coming into view, signaling with my blinker as I prepare to turn in to the drop-off line. I know in the coming weeks I'll have far fewer opportunities to drive her like this, and that only increases my guilt. I think that's why I'm so desperate for Cassie and Sophie to hit it off. If I could imagine Sophie having fun and not holing up in her room, I might be able to not *completely* hate myself for being absent.

"Tell Cassie it's my turn to pick a movie tonight," Sophie tells me before she hops out of the car. "She picked yesterday."

She's still trying to look as if she isn't very interested. It almost makes me laugh. My daughter is a lot of things, but hard to read is not one of them.

I grin at her. "I'll do that."

———

don't go home immediately; I take advantage of the extra time this morning to stop by the gym on my way back, if only to cut down on the amount of time I will be alone in the house with Cassie without Sophie as a buffer. I've found during this last week that a long run on the treadmill usually helps ensure I am too tired to even think about whatever Cassie is wearing or how she's fixed her hair. She has a habit of throwing it into a messy bun on top of her head, and while there's nothing particularly special about the way she does it, it makes her neck look longer, makes it easier to notice. It's one more thing I shouldn't be thinking about.

By the time I *do* get back to the town house, I'm worn out and sweaty and in good need of a shower. Thankfully, it's nearly lunchtime, which means when I finish up everything else I need to do before work, I can escape to the restaurant and avoid any dangerous moments alone with Sophie's nanny.

The house is quiet when I step through the front door. I hang my keys on the hook beside it as I notice Cassie's closed bedroom door off the stairs. I consider stopping to check on her, but deep down I know there's no real reason to, so I walk past instead to climb the staircase. I mentally go over my list of things to do before I go into work in a little while. I'm still working through my checklist in my head as I step off the landing to head toward the kitchen. Maybe that's why I don't notice her at first.

I cross the kitchen, opening the refrigerator door to look inside and noting several things we are getting low on. I guess I need to add a trip to the grocery store to my list. If I can find the time today, that is.

"I can go later, if you want," I hear Cassie call from the living room, startling me. "I just have a few more assignments to work through."

I stand there with the fridge door open, distracted momentarily by messy auburn tresses piled high on her head. It's an actual chore to keep my eyes there and not let them dip lower, focusing on her face instead. Where it's safe.

"I didn't see you," I tell her. "Sorry."

She shakes her head, shifting in the armchair to move the laptop sitting between her crossed legs. "You're fine. I had a few lessons I thought I'd get ahead on since you took Sophie. I totally would have taken her, by the way."

"No, no, it's fine," I assure her. "I wanted to."

"Any news on the scallop situation?"

I scoff as I shake my head. "Tonight is pretty much shot. I'm hoping to be able to find some more for tomorrow night, at least. If we have to make it to the end of the week without any, people will lose their minds."

"Oh, no," she says with a hint of amusement in her voice. "A clam-tastrophe."

I groan at her terrible joke, but I can't help but grin as I cover my eyes. "That was awful."

"That's sort of where I live, humor-wise. Somewhere between awful and lame." Cassie's lips curl in a smile, and that, too, is distracting. At this point in our living arrangement, I just hope I'm not unconsciously making a weird face when I look at her. "I don't have a lot left to do here though," she tells me. "I can run to the grocery store if you want. Save you a trip."

I glance back in the fridge, remembering my earlier train of thought before I grab a water bottle from the inside. "That would be great, actually. I can leave you with my credit card. Just get whatever you guys need."

"It makes sense anyway since I've been doing most of the cooking," she points out.

I grimace. "I'm sorry about that."

"What?" She looks genuinely confused. "Don't be. It's my job, right?"

"Yeah," I answer, unscrewing the cap on the water while I round the counter, leaning against it as I keep a safe distance from the living room. "Right. Sorry."

Cassie laughs quietly. "You have a habit of apologizing when you don't have to."

"Sorr—" I frown. "I don't even realize I'm doing it half the time." I notice her gaze flick down to my T-shirt that is still pretty drenched with sweat, and I give her an apologetic look. "I need a shower."

"Kind of," she chuckles. "I don't know where you find the energy to work out with the late nights you've been pulling."

I shrug. "You get used to it. Just have to steal time where you can."

"Couldn't be me."

I nod toward her laptop. "What are you working on?"

"Nothing fun," she sighs. "But I have to get it done before my on-campus labs this weekend, and I promised Sophie we'd make mini pizzas tonight and watch a movie."

"She told me." I smile. "She also told me to tell you that it's her turn to pick."

Cassie snorts. "She would say that. She totally tricked me into picking the one she wanted last time. This will have to be our third time watching *Encanto* at this point."

"*Encanto?*"

She looks at me like the question is an offensive one. "Really? 'We Don't Talk About Bruno'?"

"Why don't we talk about Bruno?"

"How have you missed this? I feel like Sophie has sung this song at least eight dozen times in the last week."

"Wait. Is this the one about a wedding?"

"It's catchy as hell is what it is. I haven't been able to shower without that damned soundtrack making an appearance."

Don't think about her in the shower. Just don't.

"I guess I need to watch the movie."

"Oh, don't worry. She'll corner you eventually and force you."

I laugh at her expression, disgruntled and yet somehow affectionate. "I think she likes you."

Cassie perks up. "You think so?"

"I do. She likes to act tough, but I can tell she's already warmed up to you."

"She could throw me a bone and let it show."

I can't help but laugh. "That would be too easy. She's got to make you think you earned it."

"She's so stubborn," Cassie says, grinning. "I sort of love her."

"I am . . . very glad to hear you say that."

"She's an awesome kid," Cassie says seriously. "It's kind of hard not to."

There's still a touch of a smile at my mouth as I look down at my feet. "She is."

I think I dread one-on-one conversations with Cassie because they are so *easy.* Sure, there are sometimes lulls or awkward silences where I am trying not to notice her in all the ways I shouldn't be—but every time I talk to her, it's almost as if we've been talking forever.

"I meant to tell you," I start, changing the subject. "Outside of the . . . clam-tastrophe"—Cassie gives me an *aha* that I roll my eyes at—"work will be busier for a while."

Her brow knits. "Oh?"

"Yeah. We're testing a few new dishes for their potential as additions to the permanent menu, and that always means more time to assess any feedback and refine any details. I'll have to meet with the new suppliers, and go over the recipes with my sous-chefs . . . It's usually a nightmare."

"Oh." She nods idly. "I get it. Gotta work, right?"

"Stay in school as long as you can," I huff. "It's shit out here."

Cassie laughs. "I bet the whole steady paycheck thing makes it worth it though."

"One might argue that, yes."

Her smile really is . . . very pretty. It usually tilts on one side first, like she's thinking about it, but then the other lifts to join it as she grins in earnest. It makes it hard not to look when she smiles like that. I should let her get back to her schoolwork, I know that; I should turn around and head to my room to shower and leave her be.

I walk to the couch instead, settling into it as I take another swig from my water bottle. I reason that I am just resting for a second.

Don't make things weird.

"Did you always want to go into occupational therapy?"

"Mostly," she says. "Since my sophomore year of undergrad. Maybe earlier. The money is good, and the work feels like something I would enjoy."

"I mean, you're amazing with kids . . . Is that who you want to work with?"

"I think so. I told you my parents were sort of shitty, right?"

It hits me harder than it should, being reminded of it; maybe it's because of my own situation. "You did."

"Yeah, well. I kind of like the idea of being there for kids like that. You know? Kids that don't think they have anyone else."

Every new thing I learn about Cassie makes talking to her that much more dangerous.

"I get it," I say, crinkling the plastic of the water bottle as I nod down at my knees. "It's good motivation. Plus, it seems like you've had a lot of practice, with the children's hospital. You worked there for almost a year right? What did you do before that?"

She looks surprised by the question, a strange blush at her cheeks as she averts her eyes, looking suddenly very interested in her laptop screen. "Oh," she says. "Random odd jobs. Nothing nearly as cool as the hospital. I tried the whole full-time student thing for a bit, I guess."

"Ah." There's something sort of nervous about her behavior, and I can tell that whatever she did, she must not want to talk about it. Which is odd, but also none of my business, I guess. I take her dodgy reaction as my cue not to pry. "Well. I'm sure it was very rewarding. It will be good experience, too, I imagine. It's all very admirable. What you're doing."

"Makes for a lame personal life though," she laughs. "My best friend is in her seventies."

My brow furrows. "Really?"

"Oh, you'd love Wanda, if you can get around the fact that she's still not entirely convinced you don't have a secret basement, that is."

"Oh, *that* friend."

She beams back at me. "She's kind of a worrywart."

"I hope you brought her up to speed on the basement situation."

"I did, but she hasn't entirely ruled out the possibility that there's a hidden door around here."

"The more I hear about Wanda, the more terrified I am to meet her," I snort.

"Oh yes. You should be very afraid. She's one hundred and thirty pounds of pure terror." She looks pensive then. "I would actually love to take Sophie to meet her eventually, if that's okay? I think they'd really hit it off."

"I don't see why not," I say after thinking for a moment. "Sophie would like that, I'm sure."

"I definitely think Wanda would get a kick out of it. That is, if you're sure you're okay with it. I mean, you're welcome to come, if you're free . . . ?"

"Oh, no, that's okay. I'm sure I'll still be busy. Let me know the address and when you'll be there. Maybe text me when you get back home so I know where you guys are. Actually, maybe we should turn on location sharing, that way if anything happens—"

I notice she's smiling again, and I shut my mouth quickly.

"I sound silly, don't I."

"You sound like your run-of-the-mill control freak dad. It's not a bad thing. I can do whatever makes you feel best."

There's no reason for me to think twice about this statement; I know it's perfectly innocent, but that doesn't stop the strange sensation from coiling in my chest. "Right. Sorry."

"Apologizing again," she chuckles.

"I'm sure Sophie would love to get out of the house for a bit," I reason. "I'm sure she's over being cooped up here with me every day that she wasn't hanging out at the restaurant."

"Sophie loves hanging out with you," Cassie asserts. "She talks about you all the time."

My mouth parts in surprise. "Really?"

"Literally. All the time. Give yourself more credit."

I nod slowly, considering. "I . . . Thanks."

"Just calling it like I see it."

"Shit." I frown. "That reminds me—Iris is supposed to be coming by later."

"Iris?"

"Sophie's aunt. I mentioned her, right?"

"Oh." She nods in recognition. "Right. I remember."

"She asked to see Sophie."

Cassie laughs. "Why do you look so uncertain about that?"

"Iris is . . ." I sigh. "I suppose I should just tell you. Things can be tense between us sometimes."

"Uh-oh."

"Yeah. She means well, she really does, but she's always been so involved in Sophie's life . . . I think suddenly not being able to see her whenever she wants really eats at her. She's tried to talk me into a joint custody situation several times."

"But you're her dad," Cassie answers.

I nod. "Right. And I'm happy to let her see Sophie when I can, but I want Sophie to have a stable environment."

"That makes perfect sense," Cassie says, and hearing it feels nice, like I hadn't even realized how much I needed to hear another person validate it.

"She can have a habit of being . . . terse. With the nannies. In the past."

"Is she going to go all WWE on me?"

This makes me laugh. "No, no. Nothing like that. I think it just bothers her that I feel the need to hire someone in the first place. Iris thinks I should just leave Sophie with her. But again . . . that feels like a slippery slope. I want her to know that this is *home*. I think she needs that in her life right now."

"I might be biased," Cassie starts, "because, you know, you're paying me"—we both laugh—"but I really think you're doing the right thing. Kids need to feel like they have a place that's theirs, you know? Even if you're not here all of every day, I imagine it's a comfort to Sophie to know that you'll always come home to her. If that makes sense."

I'm nodding dazedly, wondering how someone who barely knows us could encapsulate everything I've been striving to do after such a short time with us. "It does," I say. "Perfect sense."

Cassie tucks a strand of hair behind her ear. "Don't worry," she says with a grin. "I can handle Iris."

"Good," I chuckle.

There's awkward silence that settles once again because I don't know what to say, the soft sound of crinkling plastic crackling in the air as I anxiously squeeze the water bottle. Again I tell myself to go, to leave her here and go on about my business, but I'm still finding it difficult to do so, not quite ready to be done talking to her.

"So, you said you had labs this weekend, right?"

"Yeah. Is that okay? I'll be back in time to make Sophie dinner."

"Oh, of course. Sure. I was just getting it in my head so I wouldn't forget." I nod aimlessly. "How did you meet Wanda, anyway?"

At this point, I'm grasping at straws to talk to her a little longer.

"She was my neighbor at my old place. I got locked out of my apartment back when I first moved into the building, and she made me tea while I waited for the locksmith. She's ornery as shit, but I love her." Cassie grins as she shakes her head. "Even if she was pretty convinced you might have been some sort of criminal luring me here with a fake kid."

I snort. "Why does that sound like something I might worry about if Sophie was in your position?"

"Don't worry, I promise you can't be as paranoid as Wanda."

"What a relief," I deadpan.

"Seriously, it's sort of hysterical that she would even worry about me like that. She's the one picking up random bingo dates every other weeknight and bringing them back home."

"You're kidding."

"I wish I was. The woman gets more action than I ever will."

Don't think about that statement. Just don't.

"She sounds . . . like a character."

"She's kind of wild. Honestly, her dating life is sort of impressive. She's always trying to give me tips, and I swear to you, they are just as ridiculous as you might imagine. Thank God I'm not worried about it right now."

Don't ask. Don't you dare ask, Aiden.

"So, you don't date?"

You ass. You utterly dense ass.

She looks surprised by the question, and why wouldn't she? It's an inappropriate question. I quickly try to correct.

"I just meant—" Surely, she can tell I'm floundering. I hope it isn't showing on my face. "I realized that we never discussed, ah, how we'd handle it. I mean, of course your dating life is a private matter, but it might confuse Sophie if you were to bring anyone here." I want to crawl into a hole and never come out. "I mean, maybe if she was asleep, and you stayed downstairs—"

"Oh." It takes her a moment before her eyes widen with realization. "*Oh.*" She laughs, which makes me feel slightly less ridiculous, but only slightly. "No, no. Don't worry. It's not going to be an issue. I don't exactly have a lot of time for it either. School keeps me busy. Doesn't leave a lot of time to meet Mr. Right, you know?"

There's no reason for this news to please me. Absolutely none. I shouldn't feel *better* hearing that she won't be bringing some random man into my house, because it shouldn't matter to me in the first place.

"Sure," I say finally, unable to look her in the eye. "That's . . . understandable."

She laughs again. "The only boyfriend I'd have time for at this point would have to be a live-in willing to get down at the weirdest hours." I think I stop breathing, but only for a second. I watch her eyes go wide and her cheeks flush ever so slightly as she seems to realize what she's said. "Wow, I did *not* think before I spoke. Sorry. I sort of lose the whole filter thing when I get nervous."

I know the longer I don't respond the more awkward it will be, but my tongue feels glued to my mouth at the moment. I can't stop wondering why she would be nervous. Is it because of me?

Doesn't matter. End this fucking conversation.

"No worries," I say tightly. "It's fine."

And I'm going to leave now, because it's clear I can't have a conversation with Cassie today without making a total ass of myself, and I'm about to make an excuse and leave when she says, "What about you?"

This throws me, forgetting what I'd been about to do. "Me?"

"I mean, surely someone like you isn't hurting for dates."

I can feel myself blinking dazedly at her. "Someone like . . . me."

"Well, yeah, you know."

I absolutely do not know, so I tell her so. "I don't."

She rolls her eyes, making a slightly frustrated sound. "Oh my God. Obviously, you're good-looking. And you're this big fancy chef." I feel my brows raise, still stuck on *obviously you're good-looking*. "I mean . . . do I need a place to take Sophie when you bring someone home, or is there some sort of sock-on-the-door policy?"

Something about knowing that at this very second Cassie is thinking about me being intimate with someone, even in this strange offhanded capacity . . . it's not good. What it does to me. There's absolutely nothing about it that should be expanded or considered.

"Sock on the door," I echo dumbly before a dry chuckle escapes me. "No," I tell her. "You don't have to worry about that. Between work and Sophie, it hasn't been an issue for . . . a while."

Especially since my last attempt was such a disaster.

But that's an entirely different story.

I tell myself I am imagining it, the expression on her face that almost looks like relief but is gone as quickly as it comes, knowing that my nonfunctioning brain is just supplying what it wants to see. She's probably just happy she doesn't have to be subjected to something awkward, and I'm over here thinking things I shouldn't. Again.

I check my watch, not actually looking at the time. "I'd better go shower. I still have some stuff to do before work."

"Okay." I catch her nodding from the corner of my eye, but I still can't bring myself to look at her fully. "I didn't mean to chat your ear off," she continues.

I do look at her then, because I can't help it. "No, no. You didn't. Just . . . lots to do."

"Sure."

I push off the couch, giving her a nod before I retreat upstairs to leave her to her schoolwork. I don't look back at her as I go, mainly because I'm afraid she'll see how much I want to kick my own ass, but I note that I don't hear her start to type again until I am nearly out of sight.

Don't make things weird.

So much for that.

"Can you tease your nipples for me, Cici?"

God, his voice. It's low and gravelly, but it makes
me feel tingly all over. Especially since he seems
to know exactly what he wants me to do.

My fingers tweak my nipples, and I can hear his
breath huff against his speaker.

"Just like that. They're so pretty. I bet they taste fantastic."

I wonder idly if it's supposed to feel this intimate. I can't see
him, and he doesn't know my real name.

None of this stops me from coming exactly
how he tells me to.

CHAPTER 5

Cassie

"I'm just saying, it could be a long con," Wanda tuts on the other end of the phone that's pressed against my ear.

I laugh, shaking my head as I flip Sophie's grilled cheese. "I've been here for over a week. I think it's safe to say they aren't plotting to kidnap me."

"You never know." I hear the clanging of pots on the other end of the line. "I can't find my damned saucepan."

"It should be in the cabinet to the right of the oven."

"I already looked th—oh."

"Told you."

"How in the hell do you know where my stuff is better than I do?"

"Because you have the organizational skills of a pack rat with amnesia."

Wanda scoffs indignantly. "Such a bully."

"Yeah, yeah."

"What about the kid? Is she a terror?"

I glance past the kitchen into the living room, where Sophie is lounging on the couch playing her video games, her little brow furrowed in concentration and her tongue poking past her teeth. It makes me smile.

"She's great," I tell Wanda quietly. "I mean, she *is* sort of a terror, but I kind of like it."

"Sounds like someone else I know," Wanda snorts. "I'm glad she's real. You know, I half worried this Aiden fellow might have been one of your booby-cam stalkers."

"Yeah," I chuckle. "Right. I don't think someone like him needs to visit sites like that."

"Oh? Someone like him?"

"I mean . . . I'm sure he could see the real thing for free anytime he wants." I lower my voice. "He doesn't look like the type who would have any trouble bringing women home."

"Cassie Evans. Are you telling me your new boss is handsome?"

I pause, cursing myself. She wasn't supposed to know that part. I try to keep my voice casual, like I haven't given it much thought. "I wouldn't say that he's unattractive."

"Oh, Lord. He is, isn't he? How hot are we talking?"

"I don't know. I haven't paid much attention."

"You know I know when you're lying, right?"

"Fine," I huff with defeat. I glance at Sophie as I half whisper, "He's insanely hot, okay?"

"Whew, boy. You should send me a picture."

"I am absolutely not going to do that. Also, would you even be able to figure out how to open it if I'm not there?"

"Such a bully," she mutters again. "You be careful, you hear? Handsome guys are trouble."

"I'll be sure to guard my virtue carefully," I say seriously. "But trust me, there's no chance it will be an issue. He's way out of my league on my best day."

"Oh, shut up. You know you're a looker."

"Yeah, yeah. What about you? Met anyone new yet?"

I can hear the sound of running water as Wanda works on her own dinner. "No one worth mentioning," she snorts. "Damned Fred's been calling though. Can't seem to get the hint, that one."

"Maybe he just finds you irresistible."

"Well, no one is arguing that," she says matter-of-factly. "But I'm not that lonely yet. Even if you did leave me high and dry over here."

"Aw, is this your way of telling me you miss me?"

She clucks her tongue. "Maybe. Maybe not."

"I actually want to come visit soon, if that's okay. I'd love for you to meet Sophie. Aiden already cleared it, if you're up for it."

"Well of course I want to meet the little hellion. I have to make sure she's making you earn that big fat salary they lured you away from me with."

I flip the grilled cheese, laughing again. "Of course."

"Bring her over for dinner, and I'll make my meatballs."

"You know the way to my heart."

"I tried to talk you out of leaving me, but you *had* to go . . ."

"I know, I know. I'll pick a day soon and let you know. Sophie's dinner is almost done. I better get her fed before she starts biting my ankles."

"I heard that," Sophie's voice calls across the room.

"Well, all right," Wanda says. "I'll let you go. Just make sure you come by. I sort of miss your face."

"I love you too," I chuckle.

"See you soon."

"Right."

Sophie has wandered into the kitchen by the time I hang up the phone, peeking at the grilled cheese I'm sliding onto a plate. "Can you cut mine into triangles?"

"Well, obviously," I snort. "The triangles make it taste better."

I'm rewarded with a toothy grin. "Yeah."

"Do you want milk or juice?"

"Um." Sophie considers, weighing her options. "Milk. No, juice. Yeah. I want juice."

"I think we have some apple juice left," I tell her. "Go check."

"Okay."

I finish up the second grilled cheese I've made for myself as she paces over to the fridge, pulling open the doors to peek inside as I turn off the stove. It's not the fanciest meal anyone has ever made, but thankfully, it doesn't take much to impress a nine-year-old. I can hear her half climbing up onto the countertop to grab her own glass, which is pretty par for the course for my independent little charge, and I am just getting ready to scold her when I am distracted by the sound of the doorbell. I look back at Sophie with a curious expression; I don't know who could be coming by this late since Aiden has already left for work.

Then it dawns on me. "Oh. That's probably your aunt. Your dad said she was coming by."

Sophie's eyes light up. "Aunt Iris!"

She bounds off even as I'm calling after her, wiping my hands on a kitchen towel before I start down the stairs to follow her. Sophie already has the door open, hugging a tall, thin woman with soft blond hair falling around her shoulders. Her face is lit up in a bright smile as she clings to Sophie, and it's only when she peeks up at me that her expression changes, her delicate brow that is the same shade as her hair turning down and her smile faltering.

I decide not to let it bother me. "Hi," I greet cheerily. "You must be Iris. Aiden said you were coming by."

"Right," she answers flatly, and I don't miss the way her eyes dip down and back up again, like she's sizing me up. "You must be the new nanny."

Oh boy.

"That's me," I say, keeping my cheery tone. "We were just making dinner . . . Do you want to come up and join us?"

Iris looks around. "Aiden isn't here?"

"He's at work," I answer, noticing the tense nature of her tone.

"Hmm."

It's all she says, but she does close the door behind her to step inside, so I guess she's taking me up on the meal offer. "I was just making us some grilled cheese sandwiches," I tell her, turning to start toward the stairs. "But I can make something else if you'd rather—"

"I already ate, thank you," Iris says stiffly.

She's going to be a tough nut to crack, I think.

I let the silence linger as I step off the landing and move back to the kitchen to get Sophie some juice.

"So how long have you been working here?"

I look up from the counter to find Iris has settled on the couch, watching Sophie climb onto one of the stools at the counter as she readies for dinner.

"Not long," I say. "Just over a week now."

"You just seem so at home," Iris notes.

"Oh, well . . . Aiden and Sophie have been great."

"Sorry if I sound rude," Iris says. "I've just always hated the idea of Sophie being left with strangers."

"Of course," I answer with a smile that doesn't quite reach my eyes. She watches me for a minute as I pour Sophie's juice, not speaking again until I slide the cup across the counter to Sophie's waiting hand.

"How old are you, anyway? You seem kind of young to be a nanny."

"Twenty-five," I tell her tightly.

Be nice, I mentally chant.

"Wow." Iris laughs. "You really are young. You must be barely out of school."

"Still in, actually," I correct. "I've been working my way through."

"Oh? And what are you going for?"

"Occupational therapy."

"Oh, wow." She nods, looking almost impressed, albeit begrudgingly. "That's admirable."

"Let's hope so," I respond before taking a bite of my sandwich. "And you? What do you do?"

"I own a flower shop," she tells me.

I laugh excitedly. "Oh my God! That's so cute!"

Iris looks at me strangely.

"Because of your name," I clarify.

"Right . . ." She's looking at me like I've lost it. "Well. I used to run it with Rebecca. It's been harder doing it alone."

My smile dissipates. "Oh. Of course. I was so sorry to have heard about that."

"Were you," she says flatly.

I take another bite, and then another, wanting to escape this awful tension. I chew roughly as Sophie gives me a thumbs-up about her own sandwich. "Mom used to give me flowers for my birthday every year."

I smile. "Oh, yeah?"

"They were really pretty," she tells me.

"That sounds very sweet."

I notice that Iris is watching this interaction, like she's studying me, trying to find some fault.

I pop the last bite of my sandwich into my mouth, deciding that I'm obviously in the way here. "Soph, how about I go work on the laundry while you and your aunt visit?"

"Okay," Sophie says flippantly.

"Great." I smile as I drop my plate into the sink; I'll wash dishes later. "I'll be around if you guys need me. Just let me know." I try to flash a smile in Iris's direction, one she doesn't return. "It was nice to meet you, Iris."

Iris nods stiffly. "You too."

I make my escape quickly, climbing the stairs to the third floor to gather up Sophie's laundry that's probably scattered on her bedroom and bathroom floor. Sophie seemed to be unaffected by the strange first meeting between her aunt and me, but I can't pretend I'm not a little uncomfortable. It's very clear that Iris thinks I'm not needed here, and I can only wonder how that might make things weird going forward. Still . . . based on everything Aiden has told me, I can't help but be a little sympathetic. It must be hard to have lost a sister and a niece all at once. I would probably be bitter too. I tell myself that there will be plenty of time to get on Iris's good side, and who knows? Maybe we can even be friends. Eventually.

I think back to Iris's cold expression, my optimism wavering.

On second thought.

The encounter with Iris stays on my mind for the rest of the night—through a round of board games and even while getting Sophie ready for bed before tucking her in—and maybe that's why it feels impossible to get to sleep. I toss and turn for maybe an hour trying to drift off, and eventually I doze at some point, but it's restless. Like one of those instances where you're awake enough to know you're asleep but asleep enough not to be awake. If that even makes sense.

At some point, I give up on the idea of it altogether, swinging my legs over the side of the bed in a huff and deciding to head up to the kitchen for a drink. If I can't get sleep, I can at least get hydrated, I guess. I rub my eyes as I leave my bedroom, closing the door behind me and trudging up the stairs.

I don't notice him at first, my eyes still heavy and my yawn meaning I'm not really looking where I'm going as I shuffle across the living room, but just before I round the counter I hear him startle, making me do the same thing.

"Aiden?"

He looks surprised to see me there, almost like maybe he'd forgotten I was even here—his eyes exhausted with dark circles underneath them and his button-down half-undone to reveal a stark white T-shirt underneath. "Cassie? What are you still doing up?"

"Sorry," I offer, stifling another yawn. "I couldn't sleep."

"Oh." He nods, standing in the light of the open fridge with an amber bottle in his hand. "I hope I wasn't being too loud."

I wave him off. "No, no. It wasn't you. Just a long day."

"You're telling me," he huffs, finally closing the fridge door, making it so that the only thing casting any light is the soft glow of the bulb from the vent hood over the stove.

"Brutal?"

He pops off the cap of his beer. "Very."

"Sorry about that."

He takes a swig, making a satisfied sound when he pulls the bottle away. Even haggard looking, it's hard to miss how good he looks, which is a sharp reminder that we're alone here in the near dark just staring at each other. Probably not the best idea.

I scratch my scalp sleepily. God, I'm exhausted. "I met Iris today. She's . . . a character."

Aiden's mouth presses together in a tight line. "She wasn't awful to you, was she?"

"Well, I'd be lying if I said she was going to be inviting me to her birthday party anytime soon," I tell him. "But it could have been worse, I guess."

Aiden leans against the counter near the fridge. "I'm glad she wasn't rude, at least."

"I didn't know Sophie's mom ran a flower shop," I point out, making conversation for reasons that escape me, given that it's so late.

"Oh, yeah." Aiden nods before taking another sip. "It's a pretty popular shop. Iris runs it by herself now."

"She really seems to love Sophie," I note.

"Yeah. She's great with her. Half raised her, really."

"She wasn't entirely happy that Sophie came straight to me after Rebecca died. She seems to think she was the better choice, since, in her words, I was never there for Sophie like she was. It made for a lot of arguments in the beginning."

"But you're her dad," I argue. "Of course she should be with you."

"The courts agreed, but Iris . . ." He shakes his head. "Part of me thinks she's just waiting for me to fuck all this up somehow."

Oh. I know I'm sleepy, but something about Aiden's deep voice uttering such a dirty word makes my stomach flutter. Definitely not the time, I think.

"It doesn't help that I'm in the busiest time of my life, careerwise," he goes on, sighing. "It keeps me away from home more than I'd like."

I won't pretend this doesn't plunge my thoughts into my own childhood, thoughts rushing back of my parents and their jobs and the financial burden that I was constantly being reminded that I was. I am almost one hundred percent certain that Aiden is nothing like my parents, since he actually seems to enjoy spending time with Sophie and tries to do so every chance he's able; I pack away my own bias to try to see his side.

"I get it. You have to work. Plus, it's not like you're just leaving her here by herself. And you spend all your extra time with her when you aren't working, right?"

"As much as I can," he says with a nod. "I just . . ." He makes a frustrated sound. "I'm doing my best, but sometimes it feels like it's not enough."

"I'm sorry," I say again. "I'm sure this isn't what you wanted to come home to. I didn't mean to hit a nerve."

"No, no. I'm sorry for dumping this on you. It just weighs on me."

"Don't be," I assure him, finally moving to the fridge to grab a water bottle. I pull it open. "We'll just say that mild therapy is part of my duties. I'll send my bill in the mail."

His mouth quirks. "Obviously."

"Anyway . . . I'm sure you're tired. I'd better get back to not sleeping."

"Yeah, I wouldn't want to keep you," he chuckles.

"It's thankless work, but someone has to do it."

I close the fridge door with the intention of leaving him to himself, but he surprises me when he reaches out to grab my wrist loosely. I stare down at his thick fingers that are warm against my skin, looking back up to meet his concerned expression.

"Sorry," he says quietly. "It's just . . . You're okay, right?"

I blink with confusion. "What?"

"I mean . . . she didn't say anything to upset you, did she?"

"Me?"

Aiden nods. "It's just . . . I hope she didn't scare you off."

"Oh."

The thought hadn't even crossed my mind. I mean, yeah, she was icy toward me, but I'm a big girl, and it'll take more than Iris to rattle me.

"I'm fine," I assure him. "Don't worry. I'm not going anywhere."

He visibly relaxes. "Good." I think he realizes it then, that he's still holding my wrist, his face turning down to take it in before he quickly drops it. "Sorry. I'm tired. I wasn't thinking."

"It's fine," I answer quietly, that fluttering in my stomach now a rampant flapping of wings. "We should go to bed."

His eyes widen a fraction, and then it dawns on me what I've said.

"I mean—" I feel my face heat. "I meant separately. Like, you go to bed, and I go to bed, and—"

"Right," he says, saving me. Is it just me or is his voice lower than it was a second ago? "I know what you meant."

"Okay."

The air-conditioning feels chillier than it did before, goose bumps breaking out across my skin and my nipples tightening under my thin T-shirt, reminding me for the first time since I left my room (and much too late, I might add) that I'm not wearing a bra. It only fully hits me when I notice Aiden's gaze dip down in a way that feels almost like a reflex, like he can't help it. I hear his sharp inhale as heat rushes down my neck, and I quickly cross my arms over my chest as embarrassment floods through me.

I decide that not acknowledging it is the least mortifying option, looking down at my toes instead of his face. "Okay. Well. I'm going to bed. I'll see you in the morning."

"Sure," he answers slowly. "See you in the morning."

I pad away as fast as I can without actually running, only pausing at the landing turn back slightly. "Night, Aiden."

"Good night," he calls back, and I notice he hasn't moved from where he's standing.

I don't think I take a full breath until I'm safely back in my room with the door closed behind me, leaning against it to cover my eyes with my hands. I can only hope the entryway was dark enough that I didn't give Aiden a *complete* eyeful; the embarrassment of knowing my very-hot-but-off-limits boss might have seen most of my nipples was enough to make me want to stick my head in a toilet.

I huff out a sigh as I shake my head at my own carelessness, staring out into the dark of my room and telling myself it's not a big deal. That we're bound to run into a few faux pas in a situation like ours. That surely Aiden will have forgotten all about it by morning.

Right, I think as I tuck myself back into bed. *It's absolutely not a big deal.*

Even if I'm still thinking about the way he looked at me.

Chat with @alacarte

@alacarte
⑤ **sent you a $50 tip** ⑤

♥

I haven't stopped thinking about your pretty pink nipples all week.

CHAPTER 6

Cassie

Worrying about my late-night encounter with Aiden proves to be all for naught, given that after that night, I hardly see him for a week. He takes Sophie to school every morning in the days that follow, spending all his remaining free time at the gym when Sophie isn't home and sneaking in and out of the shower before he disappears off to work. If I didn't know any better, I'd say he was avoiding me, which makes me even more anxious about the whole thing. I worry about the possibility of having made things awkward between us, fearing that I may have ruined the easy rhythm we'd begun to fall into. By the following Saturday, I can count on one hand the glimpses I've had of Aiden Reid, even living in the same house.

I mosey into the kitchen that morning earlier than usual, hoping to spend some alone time with the coffeepot before Sophie wakes up. I think I've got some time before Aiden wakes up and busies himself with something or another that will allow him to avoid talking to me. I've decided at this point that I will not be letting this bother me, that if things *are* weird between Aiden and me, it will be his fault, not mine.

I mean for God's sake. The guy has seen nipples before. And it isn't like I didn't use to show mine to half the internet on a regular basis. I don't even know why I'm so unsettled by it. It's not the end of the world.

I stretch while the coffee brews, my robe slipping from my shoulders a bit to drape around them loosely when I settle back against the counter. I roll them as a well-known tightness prickles at my back, reaching to rub at the raised skin there and sighing like I always do when I'm reminded of my scar.

When the coffee is done, I add more sugar to my cup than is socially acceptable—but whatever. I close my eyes when the first sip of hot heaven hits my tongue, humming contentedly as I let it finish the job of waking me up. I'm still standing there in the misguided sense of safety that comes from thinking I've got a decent amount of alone time ahead of me, still leaning casually against the countertop with my robe askew and my hands preoccupied with my cup when I finally pick up on a large body stepping off the stairs that lead to the third floor.

Aiden yawns, his hair in sleep-mussed disarray and his arms high in a stretch that makes his gray T-shirt creep up enough to flash the toned lines of his abdomen above his low-slung flannel pajama bottoms. My eyes are drawn to the well-honed muscle that must be his reward from all the escapist workouts, struck dumbfounded at the counter. I shouldn't be ogling him, I know that, but looking the way he does . . . I can't exactly help it.

And that's when he notices me.

"Cassie?"

I realize I'm just standing there gawking. "Oh, hey. You're up early."

"Yeah." He runs his fingers through his hair absently, still blinking sleepily. "I have a staff meeting this morning."

He still hasn't moved away from the foot of the stairs, almost like he's afraid to approach me. It only feeds my suspicions that things are weird between us.

"I made coffee," I offer. "If you want some."

"That would be great," he says.

His eyes flick from my face to my pink baby doll T-shirt, reminding me it's the same one I'd been wearing during our last disastrous encounter. Is it my fault that I'm so partial to it? At least I'm wearing a bra this time; I definitely learned my lesson about going sans bra outside of the safety of my bedroom.

But I can still tell that he recognizes it.

I hastily readjust my robe after I set my coffee cup on the counter—righting it and belting it across my front to hide my shirt. The last thing I need is for Aiden to be thinking about my nipples while he's trying to talk to me.

I clear my throat, trying not to think about how obvious I'm being. "So, coffee? How do you take it?"

"Black is fine."

I purse my lips. "Really?"

"I don't like all of that extra stuff," he admits.

I can't help it. It makes me smile. "You know, I've always said that people who drink black coffee don't love themselves."

"I don't know if that logic is sound," Aiden counters, his mouth quirking.

I don't answer, turning to make him a cup instead. I can hear him finally crossing the living room to join me in the kitchen, the scrape of a barstool behind me alerting me to his nearness. It's the closest he's been to me since last weekend, and I have to admit it puts me on edge. I can almost feel his eyes on me as I work, and I can't help but wonder if he's remembering the last time we were this close. Is he still thinking about what he saw, or am I the only one fretting over it?

I turn to hand him his cup when I'm done pouring his coffee, and when he reaches to take it from me, his fingers brush against mine. I feel little sparks where they touch, and he doesn't immediately withdraw his hand. A second passes, maybe more, before he takes the cup from me, and I raise mine in a mock toast, keeping my place against the counter on the other side and trying not to hyperfixate on how broad his shoulders look in his T-shirt or how warm his touch was.

"So," he starts, taking a careful sip from his mug. "Damn, that's hot." He frowns as he continues. "Did I miss anything interesting this week?"

"Well, I've been introducing Sophie to my underground gambling ring, but she hasn't impressed me yet."

His mouth twitches. "Have you?"

"Yep." I sigh dramatically. "The kid has no poker face. I don't think she's cut out for it."

"I'm not sure if I should be grateful or disappointed."

"Definitely disappointed. If she can't handle blackjack, how are we ever going to get to Texas Hold'em?"

He nods seriously. "Well, this does sound much more educational than multiplication tables."

"Oh, she's definitely not ready for that. She blows past twenty-one nearly every hand."

Aiden is laughing now, and I'm grateful to see something other than furtive glances and his retreating figure as he ducks out of a room to avoid me. I could easily just keep up this "let's pretend it didn't happen" game and hope that carried us back to normal, but unfortunately, I am a glutton for punishment at heart.

I avert my eyes as I bring my cup to my mouth. "So, you weren't kidding when you said things were going to get busy, huh?"

Aiden sighs, blowing softly on his coffee. "It's been a nightmare. One of our suppliers had problems delivering this week. That's why I have a meeting today; I have to meet with another supplier to try and get things back on track."

I can tell by the sound of his voice that his frequent absences are more likely to get worse before they get better. It makes me think of all the times this week Sophie has mentioned her dad, knowing that Aiden can't help that his job is hectic but still feeling sympathy for the little girl who had to have hoped she'd at least get to see him on the weekends.

I know I should mind my own business, but it's hard. "Sophie will miss hanging out with you this weekend."

"She'll have a better time with you than she ever would with me," he says with an airy sort of laugh.

I wish I knew why Aiden insists on putting himself down all the time when it comes to his parenting. I wonder if he actually thinks his daughter wouldn't prefer to spend her time with her *dad* rather than some random lady he hired.

"She misses you when you're not here," I counter, trying to keep my tone casual. "I can tell."

Aiden's brow furrows as he stares down into his cup, thinking. "I miss her too. I'm hoping things will slow down soon."

I wrestle with telling him that Sophie isn't the only one who's noticed his absence, wondering if it will only make things weirder. I mean, there's no doubt in my mind that he's been purposefully avoiding me lately, and I can't decide if addressing it would be worse than pretending it isn't happening.

"I know how busy you've been," I point out carefully before taking a sip from my own cup. "Feels like I haven't seen you this week."

There. I said it. I'm probably going to regret it, but I said it.

"Oh." I notice the way his jaw tenses, just as much as I notice he doesn't look up at me. "Yeah. We've had a lot of early prep work to do."

"Oh." Maybe it's the truth. Maybe I'm reading too much into it. Still. "I thought . . . well." I shift nervously from one foot to the other. "I guess I was worried you might be . . ."

He does look at me then, those pretty eyes of his meeting mine and throwing my train of thought off course. "Worried that I might be what?"

"I . . ." I swallow thickly, unsure how to bring up what I've been referring to in my head as *the nipple incident* in a way that won't be incredibly embarrassing for us both. "I guess I thought maybe you were avoiding me. After . . . you know . . ."

I can't read his expression at all, his stony countenance only made worse by the tight line of his plush mouth and the hard set of his eyes. I'd give anything to know what he was thinking right now, to have some way to prepare myself for a scolding or an incredibly awkward conversation, and by the time he opens his mouth to speak, I might actually be sweating.

"Cassie, actually I—"

"G'morning," a sleepy voice mumbles from behind him, startling us both.

Sophie shuffles into the kitchen to join us with barely opened eyes and wild hair, having gone unnoticed by us both until this very second. Aiden looks back at me for only a moment, like whatever he was about to say is still hanging on his tongue, but he quickly pastes on a smile and ruffles his daughter's hair when she sidles up beside him.

"Morning. Someone slept wild last night."

Sophie frowns. "What do you mean?"

"Look at that hair," he laughs.

Sophie reaches to pat at wayward tufts that stick up this way and that. "Yours looks weird too."

"Does it?" Aiden reaches to do something similar, frowning when he notices he's in no better shape. "I guess you get it from me."

Sophie places a hand over her stomach. "What's for breakfast?"

"I have pancake mix," I chime in. "We could have another go at those that won't end in a disaster this time, hopefully."

Sophie grins. "As long as dad doesn't help."

"You're both hilarious," Aiden remarks dryly. He checks the time on the oven display. "Unfortunately, I can't stay for breakfast, but at least you know I won't be able to muck up the pancakes."

Sophie looks disappointed. "You're going back to work?"

"I'm sorry," Aiden tells her, sounding like he actually is. "I have to."

"Oh." Sophie looks down at her feet, shrugging. "I thought you were gonna go to the beach with us today."

Her demeanor and tone touches something inside me, sparking memories of eating alone and wishing for anyone's company other than my own. I know Aiden is a far cry from my parents, but seeing Sophie make the face that she is in this moment, triggers emotions I thought I'd long packed away.

"I wish I could," he says, sounding sincere. "You two are going to have a much more fun day than I will."

Suddenly I'm struck with the image of Aiden in nothing but swim trunks, and that imagining might actually be bad for my health.

He glances over at me. "Which beach are you going to?"

"Coronado. I figure we can get lunch at the Del."

"ENO's has great pizza," he says. "I'll leave you some cash."

I try to wave him off. "Oh, no, it's okay, I can—"

"You're going to be wrestling a nine-year-old at the beach all day," he says bluntly. "I'm buying your lunch."

"Fine," I concede, rolling my eyes.

It feels weird accepting money from him for something that's most likely going to end up being fun for me, too, but I reason with myself that it *is* still technically an on-the-clock activity, and that makes me feel better about it.

I'm distracted by this line of thought when Aiden's eyes find mine again, something in them making me feel as if he had more to say from before Sophie interrupted, like he still *wants* to say it. It makes me even more curious about what it might have been.

"I should get a shower," he tells us, giving us a smile that doesn't quite meet his eyes. "Don't want to be late."

"Okay," Sophie mumbles, still looking dejected.

"Thanks for the coffee," Aiden tells me, his expression still hinting at what remains unspoken.

"It's black coffee," I answer, making a face. "I don't know if you should be thanking me."

"Right." His smile is warm, and it makes me feel similarly. "You girls have fun today," he says, bending to kiss the top of Sophie's head. "Stay out of trouble."

I don't say anything more as I watch him leave the kitchen, and I might be embarrassed by the way I'm watching him, if not for the fact that I catch him peeking back at me one last time before starting to climb the stairs.

I down the rest of my coffee in one go, letting it linger in my mouth as thoughts bounce around my skull. One question stands out more than anything else, though, one I suspect I'll be wondering about for the rest of the day, if not longer.

Just what had Aiden been about to say?

———

t was a great idea to bring Sophie here. She looks happier than I've ever seen her, and I think that maybe Aiden was right when he said she would like to get out of the house. She's cheered a little since we left, but not entirely, currently busying herself with an elaborate sand castle she's making with the variety pack of beach toys she had stashed away at the house.

I'm distracted while I watch her, the memory of Aiden's expression and the soft way he'd said my name weighing on my mind. I might be making what happened earlier seem like more than it is, but the way Aiden has been keeping his distance from me has left me in a constant state of unease, and I'm not even sure why. I'd like to say it's because I'm worrying about my job . . . but I'm not sure that's the whole truth. Deep down, I think I just miss talking to him. It's probably silly of me to be so preoccupied by it; it's more likely that he was just going to tell me that we should pretend it never happened, which would most likely be the best course of action.

Even if it is easier said than done.

Sophie's earlier zeal has died down a bit since we had lunch, but not enough that she's made any indication that she's ready to head back yet. She'd probably stay out here all day if I let her.

"Hey, kid," I call finally, brushing the thoughts of Aiden far away. "I need to put some more sunscreen on you."

She makes a face. "I'm not burning."

"You think that, until I get you home later and you look like a lobster."

"*Fine*," she huffs, pushing up from the sand and dusting off her hands before she comes to sit with me on the blanket.

She gives me her back, wrapping her arms around her knees and tucking her chin against them. I grab the bottle of sunscreen from my bag nearby, squirting some into my hands before starting on her shoulders that have already started to turn a shade pinker than they should be.

She winces, and I cluck my tongue. "See? We caught it just in time."

"Yeah, yeah," she grumbles.

"Are you having fun?"

She shrugs. "Yeah."

"Wow, way to rain on my parade," I tease. "You sound like I have you out here pulling weeds."

"I don't know . . ." She sighs. "I wish Dad could have come."

I pause in what I'm doing, sympathy panging in my chest. There is part of me that still thinks it isn't my place to pry into their relationship. That I should do my job and earn my paycheck and not worry about anything else—but it's hard. Especially with the way I've grown to care for this spunky kid who might be smarter than I am.

Not to mention the way I'm still thinking about how her feelings might align with mine from another time; a time when I, too, had wanted nothing more than to spend more time with the people whose attention should be a given. I finish applying the sunscreen thoroughly before I wipe the remainder on my towel, alerting her that she's good to go. She doesn't immediately move, still staring out at the slow roll of the waves against the shore like she's lost in thought.

"You can talk to me you know," I offer tentatively.

She shrugs again. "It's nothing."

"Secrets don't make friends," I say seriously. "And we're friends now, right?"

She nods, and I resist the urge to do a victory fist pump. "I guess so."

"So, tell me what you're thinking about so seriously."

"I just thought Dad might not be so busy today."

Something constricts in my chest. "I'm sure he'd rather be here with you."

"I guess so," she mumbles. "I hate it when he's busy."

"Does it happen a lot?"

She shrugs again pitifully. "Sometimes. His job is stupid."

"Ah, come on, it's not stupid. He's gotta work so he can buy you more video games, right?"

"I guess."

I scoot up to sit beside her, and she glances at me from the side.

"It just . . ." she starts. I can tell she's wrestling with her words, her voice softer now, like she's embarrassed. "It makes me miss my mom when he's gone a lot."

"Oh, honey." I extend my arm to press my hand on her back, rubbing a slow circle. "Of course it would."

Her soft sniffle breaks my heart, the first sign of vulnerability she's shown since I met her. "She was awesome."

"I bet. I mean, she'd have to be, since she made a cool kid like you."

"She was so funny," Sophie tells me. "She told the best jokes. And she used to read me stories every night." A single tear rolls over her lower lashes, trickling down her cheek. "Dad works late a lot, so."

"You know, I'm a pretty good reader."

Sophie reaches to wipe her nose, still trying her best to look stoic. "I'm too old for bedtime stories."

"Says who?"

"I don't know."

"Well, I'm super old, and I still like bedtime stories."

She perks up minutely. "You do?"

"Yep. I was just thinking the other day how much I wish I could read a good story. Maybe you could help me out with that?"

Sophie bites her bottom lip to keep from grinning, averting

her eyes as she tucks her chin against her knees again. "I guess I could. Since you want to."

"You'd definitely be doing me a favor."

I've only known this little girl for two weeks, but I'm starting to think there isn't much I wouldn't do to make her smile. Especially since I get the feeling she could use as many smiles as she can get with everything she's been through.

"Okay." She nods into her knees. "Sure."

"Hey, did you know that you can't hum while holding your nose?"

Sophie's lips press together. "What?"

I pinch my nose, making a ridiculous face as I give it a go. I feel my eyes bugging out and my cheeks puffing, and Sophie giggles. "See? Impossible."

"Nuh-uh," she argues. "I can do it."

Her face screws up with concentration as she copies me, pinching her nose and tensing her whole body as she tries to force her throat to produce a sound. She does it until her face starts to turn red, and I finally have to tug her hands away so she doesn't bust a blood vessel. I can't help but laugh at her irritated expression, looking like she's angry to have been bested by my Snapple fact.

But I notice she doesn't look sad anymore, so it's worth it. "I told you it was impossible."

"I could figure it out," she grumbles.

"I'm sure you could," I chuckle. I nudge her with my elbow again. "Hey. Why don't we get out of the house again tomorrow? There's a park nearby. This girls' day thing has been nice, right?"

Her eyes widen, her interest piqued. "A park?"

"And maybe we can find a bookstore that sells good bedtime stories. You know. To help me out." Her toothy grin is my reward, and I reach out with my other hand to wipe a stray tear still clinging to her cheek. "No more tears, okay?"

"Okay."

"Now, let's get this sandcastle finished before we both end up looking like lobs—"

I make a surprised *oomph* sound when her little arms wind around me suddenly; her small body pressing to mine as she clings to me in a warm hug. I'm only thrown for a second or two before I smile at the top of her head, circling my arms around her shoulders and pressing my cheek to her hair.

"You're not so lame," she mumbles into my shirt. "For a nanny."

I close my eyes as I breathe in the soft scent of her watermelon shampoo mixed with ocean water. "I will take that as the highest compliment."

I crawl across the sand to help her with her castle, grabbing a bucket as she starts to boss me around about what should go where. Her earlier melancholy seems to dissipate after our talk, and even though my own anxious thoughts still race through my head, knowing that she's relatively okay does make me feel better, for the most part.

I tell myself that it's because of Sophie that I am so worried over what Aiden had tried to say earlier, that it is simply because I'm afraid he will decide against me being the right fit for them, and I will miss out on more time with this little girl I'm growing so attached to. Anything else would be ridiculous. Especially any latent interest in said little girl's father who is so off-limits he might as well be my own personal Area 51. Even if he continues to avoid me, that is perfectly okay, as long as I can continue working here.

I try to focus more on the sandcastle and less on Aiden and all that comes with him, deciding it would be better that I stop thinking about his unsaid words and his unreadable glances. This isn't something I should be trying to figure out. I should be spending this energy on Sophie.

Cassie, actually I—

Yeah. Don't think about it.

———

We get home that night a little later than expected; Sophie talked me into ice cream and then a visit to the arcade that bled into getting dinner. By the time I'm carrying all seventy-five pounds of her through the front door because she's worn herself out, it's nearly nine. She's out like a light as I struggle to get her through the front door, holding her tight with one arm as I fumble with my keys. I'm just about to resign myself to waking her up so that I can get us inside, but then the door opens on its own, taking me by surprise.

"Aiden? What are you doing home?"

"Just got here," he says. "Slow night." He notices me struggling, reaching to take Sophie. "Looks like she had a big day."

"Oh yeah." I let him juggle Sophie from my arms to his. "She talked me into a lot of side trips after the beach."

"Yeah," he chuckles. "She's good at that."

I'm still standing on the porch. It takes Aiden a second to realize this.

"Shit. Let me—" He moves out of the way so I can step in. "I'm sure you're . . . cold."

And it's only then that I realize that I'm wearing nothing but a sheer cover-up over my bikini top and shorts that feel completely too short all of the sudden. Aiden clears his throats as he averts his eyes, and I squeeze past him, conscious of the fact that the see-through black material leaves little to the imagination. It hadn't felt like a big deal when we'd been out and about today, this is California, after all—but four feet from Aiden Reid with half my tits on display so soon after *the nipple incident* feels like too much.

Just this morning I had been trying to halfway apologize for it, to try to clear the air between us, and now I'm standing in the foyer in a bikini while he does his best not to look. Which I have to give him credit for. He is currently *very* interested in the color of paint on the entry wall.

"I'm glad you guys had a good day," he says tightly.

I cross my arms over my chest. "We really did. She missed you though."

"She did?" He does glance my way then, an unconscious movement that I don't think he catches until he's already looking right at me. He seems to remember shortly after why he wasn't in the first place, averting his eyes to the floor. "I wish I could have been there."

"Maybe next time."

He nods. "Maybe."

God, do things really have to be so awkward? We have got to figure out a way to handle things like this if we're going to live together. I have tits. His face is tailor-made to induce butterflies. We'll deal with it.

"Well, anyway," he says. "I guess I'd better get Sophie up to—"

"Can I ask you something?"

I shouldn't, probably. I know that. But it's been on my mind all day, and watching him try so hard not to look at me doesn't make it feel any better.

He doesn't hesitate. "Yes."

"What—" I have to take a deep breath for courage. "What were you going to say this morning? Before Sophie came in."

His mouth opens only to close, lips pressing together for a brief moment before he answers quietly, "I was going to tell you that I was. Avoiding you. I'm sorry."

"Oh." Definitely not what I expected, I think. "I mean, I get it. It was sort of awkward."

"No, I mean—" He makes a frustrated sound. "I was afraid you felt uncomfortable. I didn't want to make it worse."

"I . . . oh. I mean . . . I didn't. Stuff happens, right? It wasn't that big of a deal."

"Right," he says. "Okay. Good. I'm glad you don't . . . feel uncomfortable."

"I don't," I assure him. "I just don't want things to be weird between us. We're bound to have some mishaps here and there, in a situation like ours."

His eyes meet mine, less hesitant than before. "You're right. I'm sorry if I made things worse."

"Don't." I wave him off. "I'll, ah, try to be more careful too. There will be no more nipple-related incidents in this house."

Shit.

I really had meant it as a joke, but the minute it's out of my mouth, I'm cursing my complete lack of filter when I'm nervous. Aiden's eyes widen a fraction, and his throat moves subtly with a swallow, and the nod he gives me is wooden, like it's forced.

"Right," he answers, his voice lower than a moment ago. "That would be . . . Yeah."

Cassie, you really are a class A dipshit sometimes.

"Anyway . . . I guess I'd better get to bed."

"Sure." Aiden nods again, just as rigid as before. "I'll get Sophie upstairs too."

"She's heavier than she looks," I tease.

"Mm-hmm."

Despite what he says, he doesn't move as I squeeze past him, and I give him an awkward wave before slipping inside my bedroom and closing the door behind me. I don't know why the universe is intent on making things weird between Aiden and me, but it's doing a great job of it. Then again . . . it's just a bathing suit. This *is* California. It's something Aiden has surely seen a thousand times. Right. It's no big deal.

Apparently brushing off awkward incidents with my hot boss is just my nightly routine now.

Great.

It's a complete accident. I've done well so far to keep it out of view, and now that one of my top subscribers has seen it—I feel too exposed, embarrassed, even.

"I know it looks awful."

My hand reaches over my shoulder, my fingers grazing the rough skin of the scar that is seared there. I realize I'm sitting here, post orgasm, waiting for him to log off and stop coming back for these private shows.

"I don't think it looks awful at all," he says finally, and his tone leaves no room for a lie. I feel my anxiety lessening, even more so when he speaks again. "I have a scar, too, you know."

CHAPTER 7

Cassie

"Be careful! I'm not coming up there if you get stuck."

Sophie laughs from the top of the jungle gym. "Scaredy-cat."

"You'll change your tune when you want me to come help you down," I call back from the bench beside the playground.

She's been playing for nearly an hour now while I work on an assignment on my laptop, making sure to check on her every few seconds to ensure she's still okay.

She's going to hate hearing that we'll need to go find lunch in a bit; I can already hear her groaning about not wanting to leave. I make a mental note to bring her back here soon. I think it's good that she's been able to play with some kids her age as well, knowing by her own admission that she is still struggling to find friends at her school.

When I'm done with my assignment, I take a second to check my emails, grimacing when I notice I have a new one from Only-Fans nudging me about some special they have going on. I still get them regularly, and I know I should unsubscribe from their mailing list, but I haven't yet. It's not like I have any plans to return, and I don't even have any need to, with what Aiden is paying me now, but even a year after deactivating everything, I can't bring myself to put it fully behind me. It's silly, I know that; it isn't like there's even a possibility anymore for anyone to contact me through the site, but even knowing that, here I am still wistfully deleting emails that serve no purpose.

I pack my laptop away in my carrying case after I delete the message, because I do, as always—disregarding my brief dip into bad memories and walking over to the swing set where Sophie has migrated. She is a better object of my attention, anyway. I set my case nearby on the ground where I can see it, taking the empty swing beside Sophie and settling into it.

"Bet you can't go as high as me," she challenges.

"Oh, I have no doubts," I tell her. "You seem way more advanced at swinging than me."

She grins. "Yep."

"Are you having fun?"

"Yes! Can we come back after school tomorrow?"

"I'd be willing to bet we could," I tell her with a grin. "Maybe we can invite your dad?"

Her expression immediately falters. "He'll be too busy."

"Maybe not," I try. "He can't be this busy forever."

"I guess," she grumbles.

I straighten the swing, starting to sway backward and forward slightly. "Have you tried talking to your dad about this? I'm sure he'd want to know how you feel."

"I don't want to make him mad," she admits quietly.

"I don't think he'd get mad. Your dad doesn't seem like the type to be mad about something like that. He loves you, you know?"

She gives me another slow nod. "I know. He's just busy."

Again there's that pang in my chest as I'm thrust back into buried memories of putting myself to bed, and it takes everything I have not to let my feelings sway my conversation with Sophie, knowing my bias isn't fair to her or Aiden. I know Aiden is different from my parents, that his absence is an oversight, not a conscious choice.

"Why don't we go find some lunch," I say, wanting to pull her out of her darkening mood. "You've gotta be hungry after all that climbing."

"I am kinda hungry," she admits.

"All right then." I push up from the swing to retrieve my laptop case. "We still need to stop by the bookstore, too, but after that, we'd better get you some food. Have to protect my ankles and all."

"I *don't* bite," she giggles.

I cluck my tongue. "Says you."

"Can we have pizza?"

"We had pizza yesterday."

"But I want it," she pouts.

"Oh, well, when you put it *that* way," I laugh.

Can I carry the pizza?"

"It's too hot," I tell her. "You're in charge of the books."

She's picked out three books about talking pumpkins, friendly monsters, and a lost unicorn, respectively, guarding them like her life depends on it.

"I can do both."

"I've got it. We're almost home, anyway."

"I can do it," she argues.

"Yes, but then you might burn your hands, and you'll use that as an excuse not to help with the dishes."

"I will not!"

I feign suspicion. "I don't know . . . sounds like a trap to me."

"You're so weird," she huffs.

"Tell me something I don't know, kid."

"Okay, but when we get home I wanna—"

"Sophie?"

We both pause on the sidewalk, noticing a familiar figure lingering outside of the gate in front of the town house holding a paper sack. Aiden hadn't said anything about Iris visiting today, so it throws me to see her here, and I momentarily falter before I paste on a smile. "Hey! What brings you by?"

"I don't need a reason to check on my niece," Iris says bluntly.

Yikes.

"Well, no," I offer with an awkward laugh. "I guess not. I just thought if you let me know ahead of time next time, I'll make sure to have her back here sooner."

"Mm-hmm." Iris gives Sophie a smile then. "Can't you give your aunt a hug?"

Sophie grins back, bridging the gap between us to hug Iris.

"How was school this week, honey bear?"

Sophie shrugs. "It was okay."

"Made any friends yet?"

"Not really," Sophie sighs.

"You will," Iris urges sweetly. She really is a different person with Sophie. "Don't worry."

"I brought you some books," Iris says. She eyes the pile in Sophie's arms. "I see someone beat me to it though."

I am seriously not winning any brownie points with this woman.

"That's okay," Sophie says. "Cassie can read yours too."

"I'll just bet she can," Iris answers.

Sophie takes the sack Iris is holding and grins at me, and I do my best to return it. I have no idea how to handle this strange situation I've gotten mixed up in, but I try to look unbothered for Sophie's sake as I move toward her.

"Hey, Soph, do you mind taking the pizza inside? I'll be right behind you." I hesitate before handing her the box. "But be careful," I warn. "It's still hot."

"Okay," Sophie says brightly, taking the box from me and balancing her books on top before looking back at her aunt. "Bye, Aunt Iris."

"Bye, sweetheart. I'll see you soon."

Neither of us says a word as Sophie moves through the gate, Iris waiting until she's safely inside the house before she speaks again, her earlier sweet tone nowhere to be found.

"I notice her dad isn't around again."

"He's working."

Iris laughs, but it's off. "He's always working."

"I'm sorry, but I don't think it's a bad thing that he's providing for his kid."

Iris's eyebrows shoot up. "Why do you care? You're just the nanny." I watch as her expression turns curious. "Unless you're more . . . invested somehow. What exactly is your role here?"

"I'm here to take care of Sophie," I tell her. "Look, it feels like we got off on the wrong foot. I would never think of getting in the way of your relationship with Sophie. She needs all the love she can get, I imagine. I don't want her to be confused."

"I'm sure she's already confused, given that her dad can't be bothered to spend any real time with her."

I cross my arms. "That's not fair."

"There are a lot of things about this situation that aren't fair," Iris answers bitterly.

"Listen, I think I get where you're coming from, but you can't—"

"You have no idea where I'm coming from," she says, cutting me off. "You don't know me. You barely know Sophie. I don't know what Aiden has told you, but he isn't—"

"*Hey.*"

She blinks in surprise, looking as shocked by my outburst as I am.

"Sorry," I say more quietly. "But I can't sit here and listen to you bad-mouth her dad to me. You're right. I *don't* know Sophie and Aiden that well yet, but I can tell he's trying. I mean, he's her dad. Don't you think being with him is what's best for her?"

Iris looks at me for a long moment, almost like she's trying to figure me out. "I don't need a lecture from you," she says finally. "You don't know anything. About any of this. Frankly, it's none of your business."

"Whether you like it or not, *Sophie* is my business," I counter. "It's my job to look after her, and you randomly dropping by makes it my business."

"It's funny," Iris notes after a short time. "You're much younger than any of the other nannies Sophie has had. Prettier too. I wonder why that is?"

What she's saying makes my ears feel hot, but I decide I don't have to validate her insinuations with a retort.

"I think you should leave," I say as politely as I can manage. "Clearly, you're upset."

"Upset," Iris chuckles dryly, still looking at me in a way that makes me feel icky. "Sure. Tell Aiden I'll be in touch."

I watch her stalk off toward what seems to be her car down the street, waiting until she's tucked into the driver's seat and pulling away before I head inside, cursing under my breath the entire way. I can't fathom what I could have done in the *two* instances of meeting Iris to make her loathe me, but it's clear that polite talk and pasted-on smiles aren't going to put a dent in the chip she's carrying on her shoulder. God, even when I make it inside, I'm still rattled, recognizing that Iris was on the money about one thing at least. I *am* more invested in this than I should be.

And I thought it was going to be weird talking to Aiden about *Sophie's* feelings.

made sure that I was fully dressed this time, bra and all. I had this whole speech planned out, when I decided to wait up for Aiden on the second floor after Sophie went to bed, thinking that I would have a quick chat about everything Sophie and I talked about and then tack on a careful mention at the end of my most recent encounter with Iris. Easy peasy.

I didn't, however, intend to pass out on the couch long before he showed up.

I don't know what time it is when I come to, woken by the sound of hissed cursing and something hitting the counter in the kitchen. I blink in the darkness as I lift my head sleepily, noticing a glow from the vent hood of the oven offering only a little light. The sight there immediately rouses me from my half-asleep state, going completely still when I notice that, for some reason—Aiden is standing shirtless in the kitchen.

It takes me a moment to piece together what I'm seeing: Aiden holding what I assume is his shirt in his hand as he uses it to mop up something from the counter. There's a beer can sitting nearby that I can just make out, and I reason that he must have spilled some and decided his shirt was the best bet in cleaning it up. Not the most sensible course of action, I think, but who am I to judge? I know I should say something, that I should do something to make him aware of the fact that I'm frozen on his couch in the dark living room, but I'm finding it a lot more difficult than it should be.

Especially since I can't seem to tear my eyes away from his shirtless state.

I can only see him from the chest up from this side of the counter, but what I can see suggests that all those trips to the gym have . . . really paid off. Aiden looks firm in all the right places, eliciting an urge to touch the hard lines and cut ridges in a way that is *absolutely* not appropriate for someone looking at their employer. Not that anyone would blame me, I think, if they were seeing what I'm seeing. Aiden says another filthy word in that same quiet voice that had woken me up, and everything about it makes me feel things that are also wholly inappropriate.

It isn't fair that he is so good-looking. Paired with the fact that he's sweet and funny and doing his best as a single dad . . . my ovaries are forming their own fan club at this point.

I know the longer I sit here the more awkward it will be when he finally notices me, and despite the urge to quietly watch him until he escapes upstairs, I know I waited up for him for a reason.

"Aiden?"

He startles, face whipping up to peer into the living room, shirt still clutched tightly in his hand. "Cassie?"

"Sorry," I offer, pushing up from the couch to a sitting position. "I fell asleep on the couch."

"Oh. That's . . ." He looks down at himself as if remembering that he's half-naked, standing up straighter and bringing what I assume is a wet shirt to his chest to offer some coverage. Not that it helps. "I spilled my drink."

"Yeah. I can see that."

"I should . . . get another shirt. Sorry if I woke you up."

"Aiden, wait."

He stops midstep, still behind the counter as he watches me slide off the couch. I pull my robe tighter as I approach the kitchen, thinking that at least *one* of us won't be exposing ourselves to the other tonight.

"I actually wanted to talk to you," I start. "That's why I was waiting on the couch."

I have no idea how I will be able to have this conversation when I can see Aiden's nipples.

How the tables have turned, I think idly.

"What did you want to talk about?"

"It's about Sophie."

He immediately looks concerned. "Is she okay? Did something happen?"

"She's fine, don't worry," I assure him. "It's just . . . she's been talking. About how much she misses you when you aren't here."

I see his expression fall immediately, almost making me regret my decision to talk to him. "Oh."

"I don't even know if it's my place to say any of this, but it hurts my heart hearing how much she misses you."

"No, I'm glad you told me, but I don't know how I can change it right now. I told you that we had a lot of things going on at the restaurant."

"I know," I press. "But it really seems to be taking a toll on her."

"Well. I did tell you that my job was a nightmare sometimes."

"And I totally get that," I say carefully. "But . . . lately, even on the weekend when she's here all day, you've been shipping off to the restaurant practically right after breakfast. If not earlier."

"It's not something I can exactly control," he says wearily. "It's my job. I can't just say, 'Piss off,' to it."

"I'm not trying to lecture you," I assure him. "I'm just worried about her. I can tell she doesn't like to talk about her mother, but . . . when you're not here, it makes Sophie miss her more."

Aiden's mouth parts, his expression softening. "She told you that?"

"She did," I tell him gently.

Aiden scrubs his hand down his face. "She never talks about Rebecca. Never. I'm always trying to get her to open up, but she—" He closes his eyes, taking a deep breath. "She always acts like she's fine."

"I think she worries about you," I venture. "I think she's afraid of how her feelings might make *you* feel."

He laughs bitterly. "Even my own daughter thinks I'm not fit to take care of her."

"Hey. No." I take a step, having to stop myself from going to him. I know that's not my place. "I don't think that's the case at all, Aiden. I just think that she is thinking of your feelings just as much as you're thinking of hers."

"I really am trying," he says. "I know that Iris probably thinks I'm the shittiest dad in the world, and maybe I was there for a while, but . . . I'm *trying.*"

"I believe you," I say, because I do. "I'm sure it's harder to know what to do with someone like Sophie. She seems so tough."

"She does," he agrees. "Tougher than me." He shakes his head. "This probably isn't what you signed up for," he says with a dry laugh. "I'm sure you didn't take the job expecting to have to be a family therapist."

"No, it's okay. Really. I can just send you another bill," I say, trying for some levity.

I'm rewarded with a choked laugh. "Right."

"Listen, I feel terrible to be dumping all of this on you on top of everything else you're dealing with, but I just . . ." I can see the exhaustion on Aiden's face, and not only from a hard day. I can see an exhaustion that seems to weigh on him from the inside out. "I really care about you guys." His eyes widen a fraction, and

I avert my gaze. "I just know a little bit about how Sophie feels, and I don't want her to ever grow up with regrets like I did. You, either, for that matter."

"I don't want that either," he stresses. "And I'm sorry for bringing up bad feelings for you."

"Oh, no, it's—" My mouth drifts closed as memories crop up unbidden, and I feel something heavy in my chest. "You're nothing like my parents, Aiden. I promise you."

"Was it that bad?"

"Worse." I huff out a bitter laugh. "My parents were shit. The entire time I was growing up, I had to hear about how the only reason they had to work so hard was because of *me*. Like I was some sort of burden. I mean, they didn't want me from the start."

Aiden's brow knits in sympathy. "They didn't?"

"I guess I should count myself lucky that they were so religious," I snort. "Might not be here otherwise."

"Cassie . . ." I can tell he's struggling with what to say, and I can't believe I'm actually blurting all of this out. Normally, I do my best to avoid talking about it at all. "I'm so sorry."

"It's fine," I answer flippantly, ignoring the slight ache in my chest. "I'm only telling you this because my parents . . . they were *never* there. I put myself to bed, I made my own dinner, I spent weekends talking to a ridiculous number of imaginary friends just to simulate some sort of human contact. That kind of loneliness can really fuck a kid up." I give him a pointed look then. "But you aren't them. And I know that because I know what shitty parents who don't care look like. I *know* you care, Aiden."

Aiden is looking at me strangely, like he's seeing more than I'd like him to. I feel mildly embarrassed for oversharing now, wishing that he'd say something to clear the air.

"I'm sorry," Aiden says again after a beat. "I didn't . . . I really appreciate you telling me this."

I take a deep breath. "I'm sorry if I overstepped."

"No, I . . . you're right," Aiden goes on. "Of course you're right. I'm doing a shit job at this."

"No, you're not," I argue. "You're human, Aiden. It's okay not to get it perfect. I just . . . thought you would want to know. How much Sophie misses you when you aren't here."

Aiden hangs his head, reaching to run his fingers through his hair in exasperation as he heaves out a sigh. "I know. I need to do better."

"I'm not trying to make you feel bad," I assure him. I chew at the inside of my lip, afraid of overstepping again. "I just want to see you guys happy, that's all."

The way Aiden is looking at me makes my skin warm, his expression softening into something that is far too heavy for what we are. It makes me feel dizzy.

"I'm sorry you had to pick at old wounds," he says softly, breaking the spell slightly. "But I appreciate you sharing with me."

"It's fine," I answer softly. "It's all in the past now."

"Still," he says. I meet his eyes, and that same warmth threatens to do me in. "Thank you."

I remember then that I had another reason for waiting for him, and it feels almost cruel to tack on another heavy load, one after the other. Best to rip it off like a bandage, I guess.

"Right. Also, I should tell you . . ." I make a face. "Iris came back today."

"Of course she did." He breathes in deep just to blow it out. "I've tried to convince her to check in with me first before she visits, but sometimes she likes to be difficult. I think she'd love to prove what a shit dad I am."

"You're not a shit dad," I stress. "I told you, remember? All kids want is for you to try."

He nods solemnly. "I can do better. I can. I'll make sure to be here more. When I'm supposed to be off. I promise."

"Sophie would love that."

So would I, I don't say.

I fidget, knowing I should say more but unsure of how to broach it. I rub at my arm idly as I frown down at my feet, clearing my throat.

"Anyway, I thought I should tell you that Iris made some . . . insinuations," I go on. "About me."

"What?" Aiden's expression turns hard. "What did she say to you?"

"Well, she was bad-mouthing you, and I just wanted to defend you, and she might have . . . made the implication that I was . . . more involved than I should be."

Aiden doesn't immediately catch my drift. "What do you mean?"

"She . . ." God, he's going to make me say it. "I think she might have been implying that there was something . . . inappropriate going on between us."

"What?"

"I know, ridiculous, but . . . I didn't want to somehow be something she uses against you, so I thought you should know."

"Right." I notice his throat bob with a swallow. "Ridiculous."

Ouch. I mean, I know I just said it, but hearing him repeat it stings.

"I just thought you should know. I don't know . . . maybe we could work out some sort of schedule for Iris to come by more. I'm sure Sophie would love to do more things with her aunt."

"Maybe that's a good idea," Aiden muses. "I should talk to her."

"It couldn't hurt," I offer.

He still looks a little out of sorts. "You defended me?"

I stop midturn in my attempt to quickly retreat. "I . . . Yes?"

"You didn't have to do that."

"I didn't say anything I didn't think was true."

"Oh. I . . . appreciate that."

"I told you," I urge. "You *are* a good dad, Aiden. I promise."

He nods slowly, looking at me with an expression I can't read. I decide I should retreat like I planned, not wanting to make this encounter any more awkward than it already is.

"I'm starting to think we shouldn't have discussions after eleven o'clock," I say with a laugh.

His lips twitch. "They do seem to always go south, somehow."

"Yeah. Well. I'd better get to bed."

"Sure." He starts to move from his side of the counter, and I have to try to not let my eyes drift south when I am reminded that he still isn't wearing a shirt. "I'll make some calls in the morning so I can be here for breakfast. And I'll talk to Iris. I promise."

"I definitely think Sophie will be—"

I forget everything I was about to say when Aiden rounds the corner, and it has absolutely nothing to do with the fact that he isn't wearing a shirt. I can barely make it out in this light, but even having never seen it before, it makes my heart start to pound in my chest and my blood start to rush in my ears. I don't know how long it takes Aiden to realize I'm staring at the place to the left of his navel, his skin darker there, more raised.

"Oh," he laughs. "I know it looks weird. I've had it forever."

"It's . . . a heart."

"Yeah, it looks like one, doesn't it? I got it in culinary school." He touches the scar absently. "I dropped hot oil on myself. Damned pan slipped right out of my hand. Not my best moment as a chef."

I don't think I'm actually breathing; everything he's saying only makes my panic worse. It seems impossible, what I'm seeing, what I'm *hearing*—the coincidence of it all too much to comprehend. My eyes remain glued to the heart-shaped burn on his abdomen for longer than is appropriate, and I finally tear them away to meet Aiden's increasingly confused-looking face.

"I'm tired," I blurt out, my knees feeling oddly weak. "I'd better get to bed."

"Oh . . . kay," he says slowly, probably wondering why I'm acting weird all of a sudden.

I can't help it. I need to get *away*.

"Good night, Aiden," I say quickly as I turn away from him, his scar still fresh in my mind along with all the memories attached to it.

No, no, no, this can't be happening.

If he thinks me half sprinting down the stairs is strange, he doesn't come after me to ask about it. I don't slow down until I'm safe in my room, my heart beating out of my chest as I cross to sit at the edge of my bed in a daze.

"I have a scar, too, you know."

"Really? I bet it's not as bad as mine."

"It's pretty big. And it looks like a heart, which means it doesn't even look cool."

"How did you get it?"

"I dropped hot oil on myself a few years ago while I was cooking. Not my best moment."

It's a story I've heard before. A story I've heard murmured through a computer mic from a man whose face I've never seen. A man who—until he suddenly disappeared from our message threads and subsequently my entire life—had almost made me believe he might have cared about me.

I'd known him as *A*. Isn't it ridiculous that I could have misplaced his voice in only a year? That I didn't make the connection until right now? I thought when he disappeared it was just a bad experience I was going to have to chalk up to naïveté, the consequences of allowing myself to grow too close to someone who was ultimately paying to watch me come. And here I am, a year later, still unable to unsubscribe from OnlyFans emails because of some silly fantasy that he will somehow try to find me after all this time, even though it would be nearly impossible even *if* he wanted to, given that I nuked my account in some pitiful post-breakup-like depressive episode. Which makes no sense, since we were never actually together. He was just some guy I deluded myself into thinking I knew better than I did. Just someone I had never seen and thought I never *would* see. Which I'm realizing now isn't the case at all.

The truth is obvious, I think, as terrifying as that is. That my time online that I thought was well behind me has brought itself front and center in the form of the very reason that made me leave it in the first place. The man who had made me feel something and then made me feel utterly stupid for doing so when he logged off and never came back.

Because Aiden Reid, very-hot-but-very-off-limits boss, used to watch my channel.

He used to watch it *a lot.*

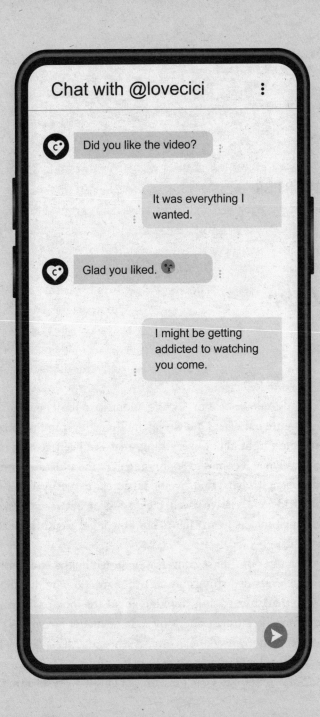

CHAPTER 8

Aiden

Twenty minutes after Cassie went to bed, I'm still trying to figure out what I did wrong, mulling it over in the shower. I know she's right about everything, that I've been getting in my own way when it comes to Sophie and even the situation with Iris, and I meant it when I said I would take steps to rectify it. I thought that it had gone relatively well, the discussion between Cassie and me, which means I can't figure out how it got weird there at the very end.

Even after our tense conversation, it felt by the end that we'd somehow mended things, or so I thought. So why did she run off like that? I can't stop thinking about the look on her face—something like surprise and panic, and no matter how many times I go over it in my head, I can't make sense of it. It's a far cry from the way she'd looked at me before that, at least.

That's something I can't exactly get out of my head either.

There had been a lingering way about how she'd looked at me, and sure, I hadn't expected to be surprised by her so late at night while being shirtless in my kitchen after a quick but dumb decision, but I know I'm not imagining the way Cassie *looked* at me. I'm well aware that I shouldn't be acknowledging it, that I should be actively ignoring it, but I would be lying if I were to pretend that I was doing any of the things that I should be.

Maybe it makes me a creep, the things I can't help but think about her. It probably does, I know that, but surely it counts for something that I have been actively trying incredibly fucking hard to bury those things. Especially given our . . . incident. That night when she'd told me about her first run-in with Iris.

I press my head against the inner wall of the shower, closing my eyes as the water drips down my hair. It's not something I do on purpose, recalling her too-tight T-shirt in soft pink, shaping against parts of her I'm not supposed to have seen. In fact, I've done everything I can in the last week to *avoid* remembering, including keeping my distance from Cassie as much as possible. Because I shouldn't think about her soft mouth telling me she isn't going anywhere, or about her blush when she'd misspoken that we should *go to bed*, and I definitely shouldn't be recalling the shape of her tight little nipples pressing against her shirt every time I close my fucking eyes.

It's absolute torture, trying to actively not be a creep.

I blast the cold water on myself to try to combat my traitorous thoughts, shivering a bit in the spray before shutting it off altogether. It helps, but only a little. I'm still wondering what it is that made Cassie's mood shift so quickly, and what it was that had her practically sprinting away from me only seconds after we were laughing together. I glance down at the darkened skin of my scar at my abdomen, frowning. It was almost like she'd been spooked by it, but by any account, that doesn't make sense.

It's incredibly late by the time I'm toweled off and dressed, my eyes burning with a need to sleep as I shuffle down the hallway from my bedroom to Sophie's so I can peek inside. She's sprawled on her bed like a starfish, one leg poking out from underneath her comforter as she snores softly. I smile as I cross the carpet quietly to lean over and kiss her forehead, recalling all of the things Cassie said and feeling that familiar pang of guilt in my chest.

That kind of loneliness can really fuck a kid up.

I make another silent affirmation to be here more. I know Sophie deserves that.

I back out of Sophie's room just as quietly, sighing softly to myself as I pull her door shut behind me. I'm on the third floor, but my thoughts are two floors lower, where I know they shouldn't be. It's ridiculous to even entertain the thought of going downstairs to check on Cassie, even to me that sounds like a terrible idea, and I stow the thought away as I trod off to my own bedroom. It's well after midnight, and I know I should get some sleep after the day I've had, especially given that tomorrow night will be a shit show since I promised I wouldn't go in early, but even when I'm tucked into my bed, I can't seem to shut my brain off.

You are a good dad, Aiden. I promise.

Why does it feel so important to me that she thinks so?

I close my eyes, letting my head thunk against the headboard. I might be in real trouble. I told Cassie that I'd been avoiding her for her sake, and sure, that's partially true, but the whole truth of it is that I've been avoiding Cassie because after that night, I *haven't* been thinking about her in the way a boss should. Especially given our situation. The way I've been thinking about Cassie would have her quitting in an instant, and given that she seems to be the first nanny Sophie has ever actually *liked* having around, that's not something I can risk. I laugh bitterly to myself, thinking that I have a real way of picking the worst women to be interested in.

It's always the ones that I shouldn't be involving myself with that seem to catch my eye.

My fingertips ruck up the edge of my shirt before they begin to trace the puckered edges of my scar as I think back to another time when I'd told a woman I'd begun to care for about it. It's no wonder that Cassie's reaction would bring up memories of the woman I try so hard not to think about on any given day; she'd been as surprised to hear about it as Cassie was to see it. Come to think of it, I think the woman in question might be the last person I've talked about it to. Some desperate attempt to connect with a person who had been vulnerable about her own scars. Now *that was* the dumbest thing I've ever done.

I had been no stranger to the phenomenon that was OnlyFans when it blew up. It seemed like everyone had heard of it, at the very least, and I was no exception. It's just that before I went looking, I thought it was something I wasn't interested in.

I think maybe it had gotten to me, the loneliness that comes from my packed work schedule that made it so hard to meet people. Maybe that's how I ended up surfing OnlyFans late one night at the suggestion of a coworker. I'd found her profile by complete accident, something about her drawing me in even though she kept her face half-covered by a mask.

It started with innocent scrolling, checking out her non-subscriber feed, which had been designed to make you want to become an actual subscriber. Which I did, obviously. It hadn't taken anything at all to get me to do that. At first, I would just buy her videos when they came out. They were always solo sessions, always her, front and center and set to some soft music, but something about this woman whose face I couldn't see and whose hair always sat covered under some bright wig . . . something about her *hooked* me.

So I started paying for private shows. Actually, that's laughable. I started paying for *a lot* of private shows. It was so easy to hop over to Skype with my camera off. So easy to indulge in the fantasy of a show put on just for me. Like I was the only person in the world, as far as she was concerned. I think it was the idea of sharing her with other viewers like me that made me feel . . . jealous. Somehow. And isn't that outrageous? Isn't it ridiculous that I would start to romanticize my encounters with a woman I was paying to watch touch herself?

Except . . . she seemed lonely too. She even told me so. More than once. Maybe that's what made everything seem like more than it was in my head. It was easy to let myself believe that I was special to her, but it was never real. She never had plans to meet me in person. Even *if* she pretended to. Her disappearing completely was evidence enough of that.

I can still remember the soft curves of her body even now, hips that begged for my hands, and breasts that begged for my mouth, and when she touched herself, when her slim little fingers slipped between wet folds to tease me night after night . . . well. It's no wonder I became a little obsessed. Especially when there were *so many* nights when it felt like it was all for me.

The memory alone is enough to make me stiffen in my pajama pants, an ache building there as the thought of a woman whose name I never knew is, as always, enough to make me hard. Even after all this time, she still affects me. She'd gone by Cici, but I'm not dense enough to think she'd given me her real name. It's another reminder that it had all been a fantasy.

I hiss between my teeth as I press my palm against the straining cotton, feeling pathetic for resorting to this but knowing that there aren't many other options of release for me at this stage of my life. Between the demands of my job and Sophie . . . there hasn't exactly been time for dating. My eyes flutter and my teeth press against my lower lip when I reach inside my pants to wrap my fingers around the heat of my cock, a shaky breath escaping me when I start to pump my fist up and down to relieve some of the pressure. I can feel slick liquid beading at the tip that coats the inside of my fist to glide back down the length. In my head I am safe in the memory of that masked woman with a fake name, her fingers teasing between her legs and pinching at her nipples all for me, just for me.

Even then I had thought about what she would feel like if I were ever able to touch her. If it were *my* hands teasing her, instead of hers. It was something that I had almost thought was a possibility at the end. She had made me feel like she wanted me as much as I had wanted her. So where did she go? I hadn't been gone very long, had I? While I was dealing with Rebecca's death? Why had she completely disappeared when I came back to apologize?

Because it had never been real.

I grit my teeth as I work faster, a tightness in my chest as my pulse races and my blood rushes faster with the increasing pleasure that pools with every stroke of my fist. I can feel it, like a hot pressure that builds and builds and *builds*, my head falling back as my lips part with short bursts of air escaping me.

I'm trying to focus on the memory, the one that is safe in my head—clinging to that faceless woman with her soft curves and her perfect body and pretty tits that I still dream about sometimes, but my thoughts are drifting elsewhere beyond my control. Drifting to thoughts of soft cotton stretched tight over the shape of tighter nipples. I don't mean to think of her, I really don't, but without my consent my brain starts imagining a very *not*-faceless woman with a sweet smile and bright eyes and a body that is just as tempting, if not more, even fully clothed.

Without my consent, my traitorous thoughts are turning to *Cassie*.

My breath is trapped in my lungs, my back bending as I work my cock faster while that same pressure builds to the point of bursting and my thoughts flit between old memories and new ones until I can't seem to differentiate where the faceless woman ends and Cassie begins. And why is it that it is so much harder to breathe now that Cassie's face is cropping up in my thoughts? Why do I feel so much *closer* now that I'm thinking about her?

And when the hot release spills over to coat my hand as I pulse into my own fist, the memory is gone completely, leaving only Cassie's face behind as I come against my palm. I'm trying to catch my breath after, my eyes open and fixed on the ceiling but not really seeing it, trying to come down from the high as the guilt of what I've done slowly creeps in.

You'd think that I might have learned my lesson the first time.

Hadn't my last experience with caring about a woman out of my reach taught me anything? How much of a disappointment had it been when I let my loneliness drive me to make terrible judgment calls only to be delivered a rude awakening when I had learned none of it had been real? I close my eyes even as my chest still heaves, cursing under my breath.

Here I am, an entire year later, becoming enamored with another woman that is completely out of my grasp and probably out of my league. What in the world would Cassie want with a workaholic single dad barely even able to keep his shit together on an average day?

It's ridiculous to even consider, for all sorts of reasons.

I really care about you guys.

I have to remind myself that she couldn't have meant that the way I'd like to believe. That's just who Cassie is. I'm sure that she only cares about me as a single father struggling to connect more with his daughter, like a pet project. Nothing more.

I walk to my bathroom in a state of shame to wash my hands,

frowning down at the sink as the cold water brings me back to slight clarity. When it's done, and I'm drying my hands on the towel hanging beside the sink, I catch sight of my still-flushed face in the mirror and shake my head at my own reflection.

"You dumb prick," I mutter.

I fall back into my bed face-first, still cursing myself for being a delusional asshole but feeling less tense, at the very least. Even now, after slipping further into villainy without meaning to—I'm still thinking about her. Just as much as I have been since the moment she moved in, if I'm being honest. It's ill-advised, and it's *definitely* inappropriate, but there it is.

I sigh, pushing my arms under my pillow and burrowing into it as I try to push Cassie's face from my mind. I tell myself that tomorrow I will work on burying this asinine crush deep, deep down where it belongs. That when I wake up tomorrow I will have breakfast with Cassie and Sophie and act like I didn't just abuse myself to the thought of the nanny, because even *thinking* about it makes me feel like a creep.

Hell. Maybe I am.

I absolutely get no sleep that night, but that's pretty much what I expected.

*I'm about to tell him goodbye, because by all accounts
we're done here; he's watched me come, he's
paid his money—so why am I hesitating?*

*I can still hear him breathing on the other end of the Skype
call, and it isn't the first time I've found myself curious
about what he looks like. His voice does unspeakable things
to me, that much is clear, and surely someone with a voice
like that must have a face to match?*

*I'm going to end the session. It's ridiculous
that I'm hesitating.*

*I clear my throat, about to tell him thanks for buying
another private show, but he surprises me by speaking first.*

*"I'm curious . . . how much would it be to
keep talking to you?"*

I know that my heart shouldn't skip a beat.

CHAPTER 9

Cassie

I wish I could see what he looked like.

His voice is low, like a constant murmur, always offering quiet instructions as I jump to fulfill his every whim. Something about the way he asks for what he wants from me with complete confidence, without the slightest bit of embarrassment or uncertainty— it makes my skin tingle all over, almost like he's actually touching me.

"Spread your legs, Cici," he urges through the microphone. "Let me see you."

I don't hesitate, parting my thighs wider in front of the camera so he can see exactly how wet I am. Exactly how turned on he's made me.

"Touch yourself," he commands. "Touch your clit."

I circle my fingers around the little bundle of nerves, feeling sparks in my belly with every swipe. "Like this?"

"Just like that," he groans. "You're so pretty. So fucking wet."

"I wish I had your fingers instead," I coo, a practiced act that is hardly an act with him. I actually wish that I did.

"I'd give you more than fingers," he promises huskily. "I'd have you full of my cock for the rest of the weekend."

"Yeah?"

"Would you like that, Cici? Would you like to come on my cock?"

"Mm-hmm." I move my fingers a little faster. "I wish I could see it."

"Maybe you will," he murmurs. "If you want."

I nod, my lashes fluttering. "I want it. I want you."

"You have no idea how much I'd like to fuck you, Cassie."

Cassie?

That's not right.

He only knows me as Cici.

My eyes fly open, surprised to find my camera has disappeared, Aiden sitting in its place and watching me intently. His eyes burn as they drink in the way I'm touching myself, and even though I'm shocked that he's here, my only thought is to beg him to come do this for me. To touch me with his hands and his mouth and his cock until I can't even remember my own name.

"Cassie."

His voice is clearer now. Stronger. Touching my skin like the brush of fingertips. He says it again and again as I work myself faster and faster, feeling my orgasm so close that it makes my legs shake. I know if I do what he's asked of me, he'll close the distance and do all the things I want him to.

I'm so close. So impossibly close. And he's still watching me, and I just need a little more, and I'll—

I shoot out of bed, still sweating and flushed and out of breath—

all from a damned dream. I can still see Aiden's eyes on me even now, and the memory is enough to ensure there is a very real tingling between my legs.

Get it together, Cassie.

Obviously, I still haven't completely come to grips with my discovery this morning, my conversation with Aiden last night still fresh on my mind. I'm still on edge with the knowledge that the man whose house I'm living in, and who for all intents and purposes is my *boss*—has seen me naked. Has seen me naked *a lot*. It makes me equal parts flustered and "I would like to crawl into a hole and die, please," and thinking about all of the things Aiden has paid to watch me do sends me into a tizzy.

God, the things he has *paid* to watch me do.

Not to mention all the other questions that pop up whenever I think about it, which admittedly has been most of the night, since I've barely slept. Questions like: Where the fuck did he go? Why did he suddenly disappear after mentioning that he wanted to meet me? Meet me for *real?* Not only do I have to relive the embarrassment of what had turned out to be nothing more than cyber–pillow talk, but I have to relive it in person, face-to-face with the person who even now, even a year later, still holds a dominant corner of my thoughts whenever I am careless enough to let them stray.

I reach blindly for my phone and check the time. It's still early, but I know that anytime now Sophie will be doing her morning zombie walk down the stairs and expecting breakfast. Breakfast that we will now be sharing with Aiden, who I now know is *A*. What a horrible time to push him to spend more time at home. I think this might be my punishment for ogling my shirtless boss.

God, how in the hell did I manage to form a crush on the *same* man twice? One who is as out of my reach now as he'd been then?

It's not like Aiden will ever be interested in me outside of the job he hired me to do. *Especially* if he finds out I'm the same woman he left behind like a box of old rocks.

It's so ridiculous it doesn't even feel possible.

Still . . . I'd always wondered what *A* looked like. Given the nature of our relationship, it hadn't even struck me as odd that he interacted with me via voice chat only. It was a common practice that I had more than become accustomed to, but I won't pretend that I hadn't (and haven't since) spent countless hours wondering what sort of face might have gone with the low, hushed voice that would quietly direct me to touch myself in a myriad of ways. The reality of it is . . . decidedly more than I could have ever expected, given that sometimes it seems like Aiden was specifically designed with the sole purpose of driving me to distraction.

This is going to be the most awkward breakfast in the history of breakfasts.

I manage to pull myself out of bed, knowing that if I don't, Sophie will come looking for me, or worse, Aiden will—and Aiden in my bedroom is not something I'm equipped to deal with yet. So I force myself into my robe like that fickle bitch universe didn't drop the mother of all surprises on me only hours earlier, tying it tight as I shuffle to the bathroom to tame my hair into something slightly presentable. There are dark circles under my eyes, which I guess makes sense, given how little sleep I got last night, and I splash some cold water on my face in an attempt to wake myself up more.

Not the best I've ever looked, but I guess it will have to do.

I can hear Aiden and Sophie's voices upstairs in the kitchen when I leave my bedroom, closing the door behind me and taking a deep breath to steady myself before I join them. Because of course they're both already awake. I tell myself that I can do this, that I can pretend like nothing is wrong and keep doing my job—

because I *need* this job—reasoning that Aiden has long forgotten about our past at this point, and that I can do the same thing.

They're both sitting at the counter when I reach the top of the stairs, both laughing about something I didn't hear as Aiden reaches to ruffle Sophie's sleep-mussed hair. I notice that Aiden looks as tired as I feel, sporting the same dark circles and a bit of a five-o'clock shadow to boot. It's completely unfair how much better tired looks on Aiden than it does on me. Although, I highly doubt we are tired for the same reasons. I find a bit of comfort in that, at least. *Aiden* wasn't up half the night thinking about the person at the opposite level of the house.

He notices me then, the bright green and soft brown of his eyes turning my way before his lips curl in a careful smile—almost like he's worried he might spook me. I guess that's fair, given that I practically ran away from him last night.

"Good morning," I offer, trying my best to look like the sight of him doesn't make my heart race.

Sophie turns to notice me. "Cassie! Tell my dad that chocolate chips are better than blueberries."

"Well, that depends," I tell her, stepping closer to the kitchen. "In what context?"

"For pancakes!" She shoots her dad a disgruntled look. "Dad says blueberries are better because they're *healthier.*"

"Well, he has a point," I say, taking the open barstool on the opposite side of her. I hear Aiden make a triumphant sound before I lean in closer to Sophie to lower my voice. "But chocolate chips are *way* better."

Sophie beams, shooting her dad a smug grin. "See? Told you."

"Fine, fine," Aiden laughs. "I guess I'm outnumbered."

He catches my eye then, looking at me in a way that feels like a question, and that same fluttering sort of panic sparks in my chest, my heart pounding a bit harder as a flood of memory washes over me. I bury it deep as I give him a smile that hopefully says anything but "you used to watch me touch myself." All I can hope for now is that he doesn't ask about my strange behavior last night, because I am not confident that I will have any explanation to give him that will make any sense. I know that telling him the truth is not an option, because the most likely outcome of that will be him kicking me out of his house and out of his life, for the *second* time, I might add, and there is more at stake now. Not just the money, which I desperately need, but also the connection I've formed with Sophie. I can't abandon her now, not when I've just gotten her to trust me. She doesn't deserve any more disappointment.

And if there is a small part of me not ready to see Aiden disappear from my life again . . . Well, I tell myself that it is normal, and not completely pathetic, to feel that way.

"So . . . will you make pancakes?"

Sophie's expectant question draws me out of my fervent thoughts, tearing my gaze from Aiden's and meeting Sophie's instead as I pretend to consider. "Hmm. I don't know. Your dad told me he was staying for breakfast today, and since he seems to be anti–chocolate chips, it might be a problem."

"What?" Sophie turns toward Aiden excitedly. "You're staying for breakfast?"

His eyes crinkle with a smile. "Yep." He reaches to tap her nose. "Gonna try to make sure I'm here for breakfast more often."

Sophie's entire face lights up, but I find myself watching Aiden. I can see it, the way he notices that such a simple thing makes all the difference in his little girl, can see the way it pleases him, and it sets off an entirely new sensation in my chest—one that is warm and fuzzy and strange. It makes me happy, I realize, to see the two of them happy, and I also realize it has nothing to do with the strange history between Aiden and me, and everything to do with this tiny little family that is slowly worming its way into my heart.

It's something that could be dangerous, and that, unfortunately, *does* have everything to do with Aiden and our strange history.

I watch them continue to chat happily as I slide off the barstool to start busying myself with pancakes, a strange influx of emotions keeping me quiet with my own thoughts as I consider all that's happened in the last twenty-four hours. I am well aware that there is some part of me that will always wonder what happened with *A*, or rather, Aiden, I guess, but I know that my best course of action is to bury every emotion I have that is connected to anything we shared a year ago, bury it deep so that it can't ruin what I've found with this little family that I so desperately want to find happiness. Because the one thing I'm sure of, more than anything else . . . is that Aiden can never know what I know.

No matter how badly I want to ask.

t's still bothering me later when I'm stepping into the campus building of St. Augustine's, trudging to the lab room to find my seat before class starts. I'd been excited about today, since we're working with the Anatomage table—but now I'm preoccupied with thoughts of the past and the present all colliding to make for one very confusing living arrangement. I miss the instructor's introduction entirely, huddling over my desk as I chew the end of my thumbnail.

It isn't until we break for group study that my lab partner, Camila, finally comments on my strange behavior. "What's up with you? You were barely paying attention when she was explaining how to use the table settings."

"I know," I sigh, flipping through the instruction guide. "Just some weirdness at home."

"Oh. Are you still nannying?"

"Mm-hmm."

"Is it the kid? You said she was nine, right? I have a niece that age. They can be mean as hell."

"No, no, she's great," I assure her. "Just some weird adjustments on my part."

"Uh-huh."

Camila looks at me with a cocked eyebrow before leaning over the large, lit-up table to take the veins away from the digital cadaver so that she can get a closer look at the bones of the wrist. "You said it was just the kid and her dad, right? That's got to be weird. Living with a strange guy."

"He's not strange," I insist. "They're both really great."

It's just that the dad has told me exactly how to make myself come on numerous occasions.

But I can't say that.

"My abuela says that a young lady living with an unmarried man is a recipe for disaster."

"Thanks," I mutter. "That makes me feel better."

Camila laughs. "She's also, like, eighty. So I tend to tune her out sometimes."

I can't help but think of Wanda, the timeless bachelorette, wondering what she would have to say on the matter. I roll my eyes. She'd probably just tell me to bone him and get it over with.

"Camila," I start carefully, thinking an impartial third party might be just the thing I need. "What would you do if you met someone you used to know . . . really well, but they don't remember you?"

She wrinkles her nose. "Does that actually happen? Do you mean from childhood?"

"No, not childhood . . . It's complicated."

Camila stops playing with the settings on the table, glancing over at the instructor, who is deep in conversation with another group having difficulties. "How well did you know them?"

I mean . . . he's watched me play with my nipples.

"Pretty well," I say instead. "But it was more of an . . . online friendship."

"Hm." Camila taps her chin. "If it was mostly online . . . it does make more sense that they might not place you. Maybe you should just tell them? They'd probably be happy to realize it was you. Unless it ended on bad terms or something."

I frown down at my feet. There's no good way to explain the way that Aiden, or rather *A*, and I parted ways. Which is to say we didn't part ways at all. He just . . . disappeared.

"Things ended kind of weird."

"Well," Camila says, "maybe it's a good thing they don't remember then, yeah? Could be hella awkward otherwise."

She goes back to the table to start separating the metacarpals; her words bouncing around in my head to make me both relieved and strangely . . . more depressed.

Maybe it's a good thing they don't remember.

Then why does it make me feel so shitty?

Aiden keeps his promise that week to make himself more present in the mornings and early afternoons, making sure that he spends as much possible time at home before he has to leave for work. A week ago, this would have elated me, but now that I know what I know, it means I am constantly on edge. I tell myself that if he hasn't recognized me by now, there is no chance that he will. I mean, the mask and the wig I wore during my time on OnlyFans seem to have done the exact job I meant for them to, and I know that I should be relieved that Aiden seems to have no inkling of the fact that he is living with a woman he's paid to touch herself many times over.

So why *does* it sort of bum me out? I don't *want* Aiden to recognize me. He *can't.*

After a few days of awkward breakfasts and tiptoeing around him, I am grateful to be out of the house, taking Wanda up on her offer of dinner and using it as a chance to clear my head. She and Sophie instantly hit it off, which I expected, the little girl's spunk matching Wanda's in a way that didn't allow for any other outcome. Like calls to like, after all.

"Now, be careful with those," Wanda chides as Sophie picks through an assortment of souvenir shot glasses. "Some of them are older than you are."

Sophie shows her one in particular. "Did you really get this from Alaska?"

"You're damn right I did," Wanda says. "I used to travel a lot when I was younger. Wanted to collect one from every state." Wanda points down the hall. "Got some photo albums in my bedroom," she tells Sophie. "Go get that red leather one on my bookshelf, and I'll show you some pictures."

Sophie's face lights up with a nod, and she bounds off down the hall in search of her prize, leaving Wanda and me alone.

"You wanna tell me what's up with you?"

From the couch, I frown at my friend, watching her study me from where she sits at her padded rocking chair on the other side of the living room. "What do you mean?"

"Don't give me that," she huffs. "You've been distracted since dinner. I know when something is wrong with you, girl."

"There's nothing wrong with me," I argue. "It's been a long day." *Long week is more like it.*

"Now, you know I'm not ignorant, so why act like it? I can tell when you're worked up about something. So why don't you spill it before that girl finds my album."

I laugh dryly, leaning to let my face fall in my hands. "Is it that obvious?"

"It is to me."

"I don't even know how to begin to tell you what is up with me."

"Just open your mouth and tell me what's bothering you," she grouses. "It's not that difficult."

I glance toward the hall to make sure Sophie is still out of earshot, taking a deep breath just to let it out slowly. "It's about my OnlyFans."

"Did you boot it back up? Because I told you that you could—"

"No, no," I say, shaking my head vigorously. "I'm not doing it again, but . . . I never told you why I deleted my account."

"Gave me some bullshit about getting tired of it," Wanda says. "How anyone gets tired of easy money is beyond me."

"Well, I mean, that was true, but not . . . *entirely* true."

"Oh boy."

"It's embarrassing, okay?"

"Honey, I wear a Poise pad every day. What the hell do you think you have to be embarrassed about with me?"

I smile despite everything, shaking my head as I fall back against the couch cushions in a slump. "There was a guy."

"There always is," Wanda sighs.

"He was . . . I mean, I know he was a subscriber, I'm not completely delusional, but he . . ." I blow out a frustrated breath. "God, it sounds so stupid."

Her expression turns sympathetic, and it only makes me feel that much sillier. "Got too close, huh."

"He seemed different. We . . . I mean, he watched me like everyone else, but we . . . talked too."

"Well? What happened?"

"He disappeared one day. We even set a date to meet up, but then he just . . . didn't show. He disappeared after that. I thought . . . I thought he liked me. Isn't that dumb?"

The old sting settles in my chest as I remember sitting in a coffee shop for over an hour before realizing that he wasn't coming.

"First of all, you assume any fault to be had is with the man. You have good tits and a better brain, and that means you are automatically hands above the rest."

I can't help it, I laugh. "Should we put that on a T-shirt?"

"Just don't be calling yourself dumb over some man. I don't wanna hear that again. Got it?"

I smile wistfully. "Got it."

"So I gather this mystery dummy isn't as gone as you thought, right?"

"How did you know?"

"I'm old, Cassie. I know everything."

"I . . . yeah. He isn't."

"Did he contact you?"

I make a choked sound that I think is supposed to be a laugh, covering my face with my hands. "It's Aiden."

"Pardon?"

I pull my hands away. "It's *Aiden.*"

"Your boss?" It might be the first time I've ever seen Wanda look speechless, and it only lasts a good ten seconds before it turns to anger. "Did he hire you because of that?" Wanda pushes out of her chair, pointing a finger at me. "I swear on all that's holy, I will put this hip implant to good use and put my foot right up his—"

"*Shh.* He didn't know," I tell her, looking back at the hallway to make sure Sophie is still back in the bedroom. "He still doesn't know."

"Then how the hell did you figure it out?"

"He has a scar," I answer quietly. I point to my belly. "Right here. He told me about it once. It's not . . . It's too big of a coincidence not to be him."

"Does he know about yours?"

I reach unconsciously to rub my shoulder. "He's seen it."

"Recently?"

"No, of course not. There's no way he wouldn't put two and two together if he saw it again. It was back when I still had my channel. He was . . ." My eyes turn toward the floor, and I feel a squeezing sensation in my chest. "He was the only one I ever let see it."

"So he definitely doesn't know who you are."

I shake my head. "He can't know."

"But aren't you curious why he—?"

"Of course I am, but . . . he disappeared for a reason. He obviously wasn't as invested as I was, and don't you think it would make him feel awkward to know who I was? Awkward enough to fire me, I'd wager."

"Shit." Wanda crosses her arms, frowning at the carpet. "You think so?"

"I mean, would *you* want some woman you saw naked and then cyber-dumped living in your house? I can't exactly think of a more awkward situation than that one."

Wanda taps her foot aimlessly, thinking. "Well, I'll be damned."

"Right. Like I said, awkward."

"So what are you going to do?"

I throw up my hands. "What can I do? I just have to make sure he doesn't find out. If he hasn't put it together by now, I think it's safe to say he won't. As long as he doesn't see"—I frown as the marred skin on my back prickles in reminder—"I think it will be okay."

"But will *you* be okay?"

"I . . ." I press my lips together, a tightness in my chest that hasn't gone away in the last week. "I'll be fine. It's old news. I mean . . . I'm over it, and I need this job."

Wanda looks unconvinced. "Mm-hmm."

"I'm *fine*," I stress. "Seriously."

"Cassie, only liars say they're fine. You know that right?"

"I don't think that's right."

"Sure it is. I know more than you."

"You can't *always* play the old card whenever it suits you."

"It's worked okay so far," she says with a shrug. She looks at me with concern then, peering over her glasses. "I don't want to see you get hurt, girl. Just . . . be careful."

"I found it!" Little footsteps patter down the hall, drawing our attention. Sophie comes back into the living room with her leather-bound prize, looking entirely too excited for a bunch of old pictures. She plops the book down on the coffee table before sinking to her knees beside it. "Do you have any pictures of polar bears?"

Wanda chuckles, settling back into her rocker. "Never did see a polar bear, sugar. I think you'll find a great picture of a moose in there somewhere though."

Her eyebrows shoot up. "A *moose?*"

"Antlers and all," Wanda says with a grin.

"Cassie, have you ever seen a moose?"

I shake my head. "Never."

Sophie pats the spot beside her on the carpet. "Come look with me."

"All right, all right," I laugh, pushing up from the couch to join her on the floor.

Sophie points out every snowy photo from the album that catches her eye, actually squealing with excitement when she finds the aforementioned moose photo. Wanda tells her all about how they came across the massive creature, and while they talk, I think about what Wanda said.

Only liars say they're fine.

It's laughable, given how accurate it is, because the truth of it is that I'm not fine, not really. In fact, I'm living in a nightmare of my own making. A purgatory built on my own choices. Because I can pretend I don't care why Aiden disappeared from my life a year ago, I can pretend that it doesn't matter to me anymore, or at least, I could have, maybe . . . before I met him.

I've been lying to myself in all sorts of ways lately. I've been lying to myself and saying that I only want to make this work for Sophie's sake. I've been lying and telling myself that it doesn't matter that Aiden is *A*, because at the end of the day, this is just a job, he is just a guy, I am just the nanny, and there's no reason to let any of this bother me.

But he has a face now. He tells jokes. He asks about my day. He kisses his daughter's hair. He ruins pancakes. He listens to me when I tell him my concerns. He worries about how I'm feeling. And sure, he's so good-looking it kind of hurts to look at him sometimes—but that's not nearly as important.

Because as much as I would like to pretend otherwise . . . I *like* Aiden. As much as I thought I'd liked *A*. And as much as I tell myself again and again that I don't want him to find out who I am and cut ties with me again because it would hurt Sophie, I know deep down it would hurt *me* too. It would hurt for him to disappear again, and knowing that is the most dangerous thing of all.

Especially since, if he finds out . . . that's exactly what he'll do.

Chat with @alacarte

@alacarte
 sent you a $50 tip

♥

Thanks for the
conversation.

CHAPTER 10

Cassie

"Did you have fun at Cassie's friend's house last night?"

Sophie nods around a bite of her Frosted Flakes. "She's so weird."

"Weird?" Aiden looks at me curiously. "Is weird good?"

I nod. "In Sophie-speak . . . I think it is."

"Ah," Aiden chuckles. "Of course."

It's a normal Sunday morning. We woke up as usual, we're eating breakfast as usual, and everything seems easy and sweet and worry-free. And it is, mostly. Except for me.

I keep wondering if he'll notice that I have a hard time looking at him, if at any given moment he'll notice the way heat rushes into my cheeks and my ears when I do it for too long. Every time it happens, every time my gaze settles on him and remains there for longer than a handful of seconds, I remember everything that Aiden has seen, how much he doesn't even *realize* he's seen . . . all of me. I remember hushed conversations and sweet, filthy words all murmured in a dark room that he probably doesn't remember.

All that time I wondered what he looked like, and now that I have a mouth to match the words, hands to match all the things he said he wanted to do with them . . . it's hard to think about much else when I look at him.

"What do you think, Cassie?"

I blink back at Aiden, spoon halfway to my mouth, having not heard any of the last few seconds of their conversation. "Sorry, what?"

"I asked Sophie what she wanted to do for her birthday," he tells me. "It's on Thursday."

Sophie pushes up from her barstool. "I want to go to Disneyland!"

"Oh wow," I say with surprise. "Disneyland?"

"Pretty lofty goals with my schedule," Aiden chimes in bemusedly.

I laugh. "Yeah, how would you swing that?"

"Come *on*," Sophie whines. "Please?"

"It might be hard to do with how busy the restaurant has been," Aiden says woefully. "Maybe in a month or so?"

Sophie's face falls, her face turning to her cereal bowl as she pushes her spoon through the milk dejectedly. "Oh."

"Sophie," Aiden sighs. "You know I would love to—"

"Mom was supposed to take me," she interrupts quietly. "For my birthday last year."

I meet Aiden's eyes, seeing the guilt there as he gives me a helpless look. I shrug, not knowing what to say, nodding toward Sophie in what I hope is an encouraging gesture. Aiden heaves out a sigh before running his fingers through his hair, reaching to pat Sophie's head.

"I guess we can . . . make it work."

Sophie brightens immediately. "Really?"

"I think I can manage a day off," he tells her. "Anaheim is an hour's drive . . . We could spend a day at the park and then come back the next day before work . . . I'll figure it out." He shoots her a stern look. "But you'll have to ask your teacher if they can send home your schoolwork for the days you'll miss."

"I can run in and talk to them when I take her to school tomorrow," I offer.

Aiden flashes me a grateful smile that makes my stomach flip. *Curses.* "That would be great."

"And Cassie can come, too, right?" Sophie asks expectantly.

Aiden and I both look at each other, Aiden looking unsure. "I don't know if Cassie wants to do that . . . ?"

"She wants to come," Sophie asserts, looking at me. "Don't you?"

"I . . . I would hate to intrude on your family time."

Sophie pouts. "It won't be as fun without you."

"I . . ." I glance at Aiden, looking for help. "I don't know if—"

"You're welcome to come," Aiden assures me. "If you want to." He gives me a shy sort of smile. "It wouldn't be as fun without you."

"Oh." I can tell by the look on Sophie's face there is no way to turn this down. "Well . . . if you're sure that you want me to."

"Maybe we could sneak away Wednesday morning?" Aiden pulls out his phone to check something. "It's a day early, but midweek is usually our slowest time. Probably be better. Would that work? Do you have any plans?"

"Sounds perfect," I say tightly, calculating cost in my head. "If you'll tell me how much the tickets are—"

"Oh, no," Aiden says with a shake of his head. "Don't worry about anything. I'll take care of it. I can make reservations tonight on my break."

"I couldn't let you—"

"I want to," he says firmly. "Don't worry about it."

"Okay."

Sophie shakes her dad's arm. "Can Aunt Iris come too?"

"Oh, I—" Aiden looks unsure. "I don't know if she'd want to." He shares a look with me, and again, I nod encouragingly. Aiden gives Sophie a thin smile. "I'll call and ask if she would like to."

Sophie is already chirping with excitement, her cereal forgotten as she asks me if she can go call Wanda and tell her about the trip. Aiden looks confused after I give her my cell phone and she runs off with it.

"I cannot stress enough how much she and Wanda hit it off."

Aiden smiles. "Clearly."

"They're practically best friends now," I joke. "I am being edged out as we speak."

"I'm glad you took her," he says. "That's all she's talked about this morning. It seems like she had a great time."

"Wait till you meet Wanda," I laugh. "You'll get it."

"Something to look forward to," he notes. He looks worried then. "Is inviting Iris a terrible idea?"

I shrug. "Uncomfortable, maybe, but not terrible. It could be a good opportunity for you two to bury the hatchet."

"Right," he says absently, nodding. "You're right."

I take another bite of my cereal if only so I don't have to look at him anymore, every second looking at his face meaning another few beats that my heart rate picks up. Was it this awkward before? Stupid question. Of course it was. It's definitely more so now that I know he's seen me naked though.

"I haven't properly thanked you," he goes on.

I peek up at him. "For what?"

"Just . . . for sticking it out with us. I mean, with Sophie, that is. She loves you."

This part is easy, no anxiety attached to my feelings for the little girl. "I love her too. She's such a great kid."

Aiden nods, looking relieved. "I'm glad it was you that answered the ad."

"Oh, well . . ." I swallow, feeling that familiar heat at the tips of my ears. "So am I. It's been great."

"We're both lucky to have you, Cassie," he goes on, making me flush further. "I hope you know that."

He's just happy you're so good with his kid. Don't get beside yourself.

"I . . . thank you," I manage, hoping that my hair is at least covering my neck, which is growing warmer with every passing second. "Really."

"I hope you're still . . . happy here? You've seemed sort of quiet lately."

Well, shit.

"Have I?"

"Maybe I'm reading too much into it," he says, shrugging. "It feels like you've been . . . I don't know. I thought maybe you were upset with me."

"What?" This takes me by surprise. "I'm not upset with you."

"Oh. It's just that . . . it feels like you've been avoiding me since we talked."

"I'm not upset," I assure him. "I've just had a lot on my mind lately."

Aiden frowns, something in his expression seeming like he wants to ask something more but can't quite figure out how. There's a wrinkle at his brow and a set to his mouth that doesn't give me the slightest insight into what he's thinking, and I worry in this moment that he somehow knows what *I'm* thinking, that he can see right through my flimsy lies to the truth.

There's no way he could know. You're fine.

"I really am sorry," he says. "For dumping all of that on you."

"Seriously, it's okay." I try for a smile, but as nervous as I feel right now, I can only imagine how forced it looks. "I think it's a side effect of caring about Sophie."

"Right." He nods. "I hope you know how much I . . . appreciate you."

I hold my breath.

It's just because of the job you're doing. Stop reading into it.

"I'm glad," I manage. "I'm happy here. With you guys."

There's a moment where neither of us says anything, and I know I should avert my eyes, that it's weird to sit here and keep staring into his, but the problem is . . . he doesn't look away either. Once again I find myself wishing I could know what he's thinking.

"Good," he says finally, his expression still hard to read. "I'm glad."

I'm opening my mouth to say something, exactly what, I'm not sure, but Sophie chooses that moment to rejoin us, and it ends up not being an issue.

"Wanda says to take pictures," Sophie tells me. "And to bring her back a shot glass."

Aiden's brow quirks. "A shot glass?"

"Yep." Sophie nods. "It's this tiny cup thing. I don't know what you drink out of them though. They wouldn't tell me. She has one from Alaska!"

"She has one from almost everywhere," I chuckle.

"*And* she's seen a moose," Sophie says.

"I know," Aiden says amusedly. "You've told me about the moose. Several times."

Sophie hands me my phone back, looking at me expectantly. "So what are we going to do today?"

"Well," I start. "I thought maybe we could go back to that park you liked. That was fun, right? It's supposed to be a nice day to-day."

"Yes! That sounds awesome." She looks at her dad excitedly. "Can you come? Please? Just for a little while? I can swing *super* high. You've gotta see."

"Oh, I . . ." Aiden looks at me helplessly, and I can only shrug. "Yeah," he sighs, and I can tell by his expression that this is going to put him behind, but strangely that makes it that much sweeter. "I'd love to see the park. Why don't you run upstairs and get dressed while I shower?"

Sophie squeals with glee before she makes a beeline for the stairs, Aiden hanging his head wearily before he tilts his face back up to meet mine. "I have to say . . . that smile does make the shitty night I'm going to have worth it."

"Super dad," I praise.

The corner of his mouth turns up, and I think it's moments like these that make me the most unsure. Seeing him so carefree, with his easy smile and his pretty eyes and his hair still sticking up in places in the same way that Sophie's does when she wakes up . . . it makes it that much harder to pretend I'm not more invested than I should be. That I'm not wondering what his hair might feel like under my fingers or what his smile might feel like against my skin.

"I guess I'd better go hop in the shower," he says, sliding off his barstool.

I give him a tight nod as he heads off to the stairs, not relaxing until he's out of sight and I'm alone. I blow out a breath, letting my face drop to the granite countertop and letting it cool the flush at my cheeks.

I'm not thinking about Aiden in the shower. Absolutely not.

———

don't know who is having more fun on the playground—Aiden or Sophie. The last hour has been filled with her squeals and his laughter, Aiden satisfying her every whim, be it pushing her on the swing or following her up the jungle gym ladder that is considerably too small for him, his above-average frame trying to maneuver through each section very entertaining to watch.

I keep my distance on the bench at the edge, content to watch them spend time together. Every so often, Aiden smiles at me like we're sharing a secret, something that feels ironic considering we *are* sharing a secret, he just doesn't realize. I don't know how long it is before he plops down on the bench beside me while Sophie busies herself on the merry-go-round with a few other kids out this morning, his cheeks flushed and his breath labored.

"I think I'm getting old," he laughs.

"Spare me." I roll my eyes. "You're barely over thirty."

"Thirty-two in four months," he points out. "Practically over the hill."

"I'll be sure to start picking out your room at the nursing home."

Aiden gives me an expression of mock relief. "Well, that's one less thing to worry about, I guess."

"It's my master plan," I say seriously. "Edge you right out of the house and raise Sophie as my supervillain sidekick."

"Good luck with that one," Aiden snorts. "Sophie fights me to brush her teeth some mornings. Something tells me she won't have the patience for organized crime."

"Well, shit." I shake my head. "There goes my five-year plan."

The sun is climbing higher in the sky, and Aiden turns up his face, covering his eyes as he frowns. "Maybe I should have brought Sophie some sunscreen."

"She'll be getting hungry soon, anyway. She'll be fine."

"You're right. I'll let her play a little longer, and then we can go. I don't want her to burn."

"Did you know that pigs can get sunburns?"

Aiden somehow looks incredulous and amused all at once. "Where do you keep these, exactly?"

"You got me." I raise my fist to knock at my own skull. "They're probably taking up all the extra space I should be saving for something more important. Like tax law, maybe."

I notice his mouth quirk from the corner of my eye, and I have to bite back my own smile to keep from looking too giddy. We both sit quietly for a time, watching Sophie enjoy herself, and I don't even realize I'm still grinning to myself until I catch Aiden watching me out of the corner of my eye.

"Sorry," I say sheepishly. "She just looks so happy."

He's still watching me, that same unreadable *something* in his expression that has me wishing I could read his thoughts. "No, it's . . . there's nothing to apologize for."

"I know I overstepped when we last talked, but . . . it really has made a difference, I think. Her being able to spend more time with you."

"You didn't," he counters, finally averting his gaze to watch Sophie. "Overstep. You didn't say anything that wasn't true."

"Still. I'm sure it's annoying for someone who's barely been around a month acting like she knows everything."

Aiden laughs quietly. "It's so weird. It feels like it's been longer than that."

"Really?"

"Maybe it's because you and Sophie hit it off so well."

"She never did put dirt in my bed, at least."

He smiles softly, still watching Sophie. "I'm just glad you're not angry with me."

"I swear, I never was."

I am trying to pretend that I'm not sneaking glances at him, not noticing the way the wind ruffles his hair or the way his jeans fit or how his dark gray Henley hugs his chest—but it's hard to do that when Aiden keeps catching me, stealing glances himself.

"Good," he says finally. "It just felt weird. Like you were avoiding me."

"Yeah, well . . . you avoided me first."

Aiden's face splits into a grin. "We aren't very good at handling our emotions, are we?"

"I don't know what you're talking about. Avoiding awkward situations is the absolute best way of handling them, in my experience."

"So you admit it was an awkward experience," he teases.

More than you can ever know, I think bitterly.

"I mean, I've never had a meaningful conversation with my boss while he was half-naked, so I think I handled it okay, all things considered."

"Yeah . . . I'm not sure what led me to believe my shirt was the best option for cleaning up my beer."

"There *were* perfectly good hand towels in the drawer."

"I was very tired, okay?"

It's a moment that feels too easy, one that makes me almost forget all the other shit going on in my head that makes me anxious if I dwell on it too long. Does he have to be so fucking nice? It makes it a hell of a lot harder to do the smart thing and pack all my feelings away.

I decide it's best to change the subject. "So . . . Disneyland?"

"Yeah," Aiden sighs. "I can already hear my boss bitching."

"But just think of how happy she'll be," I point out.

"You're right," he says. "She's going to lose her mind."

"Have you ever been?"

He makes a face. "Absolutely not."

"Oh boy. This is going to be extra fun."

"How badly am I going to regret this?"

"Don't worry, I'll be there to handle all the hard stuff."

"The hard stuff?"

"Oh, you know . . . taking pictures with the princesses, Sleeping Beauty Castle—you realize she's going to want to be dressed up, right? How do you feel about roller coasters?"

Aiden looks like he might be feeling queasy. "What are the chances she'll want to spend a good chunk of the day at the *Star Wars* attraction?"

"I wouldn't hold my breath," I laugh. "I think you're in for a lot of princess-adjacent fun. Maybe we can catch a parade!" The look on Aiden's face only makes me laugh harder. "This is going to be so much fun."

"I'm glad you're looking forward to it," he mumbles.

I reach over to pat his hand. "I'll make sure you don't get lost, don't worry."

It had been an innocent gesture, placing my hand over his, but when my laughter dies down, I notice it's still resting there, and Aiden's staring at where my hand is touching his in a way that makes me lose my train of thought. I don't know how long we stay like that before I remember myself, clearing my throat before pulling it away as quickly as I can without seeming weird.

"Sorry."

"It's fine," he says too quickly. "I'm glad you're coming."

"Yeah?"

He nods, not looking at me. "For Sophie, I mean. I'm sure she'll enjoy herself a lot more with you there."

"Oh. Well . . ." *For Sophie.* Why does that sting? It's the only reason I'm here, after all. "I think it'll be a lot of fun."

Aiden clears his throat. "I called Iris."

"You did?"

"She can't get anyone to cover the store for two days," he tells me. "Since we're getting an Airbnb after."

Please don't remind me, I think woefully. Although, why sharing a rental with Aiden makes me squirm when we *live* together is beyond me.

"That's too bad," I say, meaning it, weirdly. "I know Sophie will be bummed."

Aiden nods. "She's going to come by before work on Friday."

"Well, that's good at least. Was it weird? The phone call?"

"I . . ." He purses his lips for a moment before shaking his head. "She sounded . . . grateful. That I asked. It might be one of the easier conversations we've had in the last year."

"Maybe she sees that you're trying to meet her halfway."

"Maybe." He glances over at me. "Thank you for suggesting it."

"Ah, well . . ." I try to look nonchalant. "Just looking out for Sophie."

And you, I don't say.

I think maybe we both sort of run out of things to say then; a quiet settling over us both as we watch Sophie, who has moved on to the monkey bars. We stay like that until a woman pushing a stroller passes us to take the bench next to us, huffing as she drops a diaper bag on the ground beside her. "Do you guys mind if I sit here?"

"No, of course not," Aiden tells her. "Please."

The woman looks like she's a few days short of a good night's sleep, her hair tossed into a messy bun and her eyes lined with dark circles. "Thank God for the park, right?" She laughs as she fusses over the baby girl's bow in the stroller. "I'd lose my mind if I couldn't bring her brother here to burn off some of his energy."

I lean over to get a better glimpse of her baby. "She's adorable. How old?"

"Six months," she tells us. "She's a handful, but at least she's stationary." She nods her head toward a dark-haired little boy currently climbing up the ladder to the jungle gym. "*That* one never seems to get tired." She gives us a kind smile then. "Which one is yours?"

"My daughter," Aiden offers, pointing toward the monkey bars. "She's over there."

"She's a cutie."

Aiden smiles with gratitude. "Thank you."

"You guys make such a cute little family," she gushes, my cheeks instantly feeling warmer.

"Oh, we aren't—"

"Daniel! What did I say?" She gives us an apologetic look. "Sorry. I need to go make sure he doesn't break something."

She leaves us there, pushing her stroller in a hurry to check on her son, who is now hanging upside down on the ladder, and when I finally find the courage to look over at Aiden, he looks as embarrassed as I do.

"I guess it was bound to happen," he says with a shy sort of laugh. "No big deal."

"Right." I reach to tuck a stray tendril of hair behind my ear, looking down at the concrete. "It's ridiculous though."

Aiden cocks his head at me from the side. "How do you mean?"

"I mean . . ." I think, in my attempt to make things less awkward, I am digging a deeper hole into that very thing. "Well, obviously you're out of my league. On a whole other planet, really. So I doubt many people would make the same mistake."

"You think I'm out of your league?"

Jesus Christ, what have I done? Is it still too late to run away?

"I mean . . . objectively speaking, it's obvious that you're—"

"I don't think it's that obvious," he says flatly. "Objectively speaking."

The breath I'd been about to take gets trapped in my lungs, and when I find the courage to peek up at Aiden, his expression seems wholly serious.

"What?"

"If anything," Aiden says, "you'd be out of mine."

My mouth parts in surprise. "What? There's no way that—"

"Cassie, you have to know . . ." He blinks then, seeming to realize the content of the conversation we're having. "Okay. I think maybe I'm the one overstepping now."

"No, it's okay, I didn't mean to—"

"I just don't think you should ever imply that you aren't good enough for someone," he says matter-of-factly. "Least of all me."

I have no idea what to say to that, left sitting on the bench with my mouth open and scrambling for some sort of response. Is he saying that he *is* in my league? Like he's considered it? Or is he just being nice? I'm too afraid to ask; everything about this conversation is screaming *dangerous*.

We both stare at each other for what feels like much longer than the ten seconds it more than likely is. I notice the way Aiden's eyes dip to my mouth, the way his throat bobs with a swallow and his chest rises and falls heavier than it did a moment ago.

"Hey, Dad! Come push me!"

Aiden snaps his head away, still breathing harder than he should be as he finds Sophie waving at him from the other side of the playground. He looks from her to me to her again, finally shaking his head before he stands up from the bench.

"Sorry. That was . . . I shouldn't have—" He takes a deep breath through his nostrils, only to expel it from his mouth. "Just forget I said anything."

I say nothing, because I have no idea what to begin to even say, watching his back as he walks away from me. Over and over, my mind is picking apart and piecing together every single thing that he just said, to try to find the meaning of it, coming to all sorts of conclusions, each one making less sense than the last. Did Aiden really just tell me in some strange roundabout way that I am well within his league? That he is in mine?

And what the hell does it mean if he is?

It takes a long time for me to move from the bench as my thoughts race, knowing that I will be doing the absolute opposite of what he'd urged me to do.

Just forget I said anything.

Right. Fat chance of that.

Chat with @alacarte

 Fucking hell, Cicí. That was incredible.

You asked me to be loud. 😊

 I'm not going to be able to sleep tonight thinking about you begging for me.

 You have no idea how badly I want to fuck you.

I think I'm starting to get an idea. 😏

CHAPTER 11

Cassie

A iden at Disneyland turns out to be one of the most hysterical things that I've ever experienced. He looks out of place
in his black shirt and his black shades and his dark jeans—a good
head taller than most of the other guests and a permanent expression that is equal parts nervous and stoically resolved. Even
so, he takes everything Sophie throws at him in stride. He wears
the ears that match mine and hers that she begged for. He waits
patiently in the costume shop (it turns out she wasn't too old for
princesses, after all) as she garbs herself in the whole nine yards:
dress, tiara, wand, and shoes. He even rides every ride that she
asks him to, even though I'm pretty sure he might be scared of
heights. His knuckles were the color of chalk when Sophie made
him go on the Incredicoaster.

It would be the perfect day . . . if it weren't for the awkward air
between us.

After Aiden left us at the park to go to work on Sunday, the extent of conversation between us from then until now has been nothing more than awkward hellos and goodbyes and a clipped text about tickets and reservations to some Airbnb nearby. He hasn't said anything more about the strange exchange we had at the park—in fact, Aiden hasn't said anything more than he's had to since then. Even on the hour-long ride into Anaheim this morning, it seems like he only spoke to me when absolutely necessary, starting our back-and-forth cycle of avoiding all things awkward all over again.

Our communication skills do seem to devolve into elementary-like levels when either of us thinks we've overstepped. It would be annoying if I wasn't being just as idiotic about it; I can't seem to make myself bring it up, either, so I don't think I can actually be upset with him.

By midday, I can tell Aiden is already exhausted, hiding under a shady tree on a bench as Sophie and I come out of the Matter-horn. Supposedly he needed a bathroom break that just couldn't wait, but I'm not entirely convinced he isn't scared of the Yeti. The birthday girl is chattering about the ride, adjusting the tiara she got from the Bibbidi Bobbidi Boutique (blue, because pink was just too girlie for her princess gown, apparently) and skipping alongside me just as she spots her dad.

"Dad, *Dad*," Sophie squeals excitedly as she rushes toward him. "It was awesome!"

"I'll bet." He reaches beside him to grab for two drinks, handing one to each of us. "I figured you guys might be thirsty."

I shouldn't be this happy over a bottle of Snapple, but I can't help it. I only mentioned my favorite flavor once in passing, and apparently Aiden deemed it important enough to remember. I shake it back and forth, giving him a grateful smile. "Peach tea."

"I'm told you bleed it at this point."

I give my attention to the bottle just so he doesn't see my goofy grin, reaching to unscrew the cap. I turn it over to read the fact, laughing.

Aiden cocks his head curiously. "What?"

"I can't make this up," I snort, holding the lid so I can read it to them. "'The hundred folds in a chef's hat represent the hundred ways to cook an egg.'"

Aiden laughs, holding out his hand. "No way."

I drop the lid in his hand. "*Can* you cook an egg a hundred ways?"

"I . . ." He frowns. "I don't actually know. Am I supposed to know?"

"All the professional cooks I know are egg aficionados," I tsk.

Aiden's lips tilt up, and it might be the first normal moment we've had since Sunday.

Sophie is apparently not interested in this exchange, gulping down a swig of her Gatorade and *aah*ing loudly after. "I want to go on the Matterhorn again," she whines. "Can we do it again?" She gives Aiden a pleading look. "*Dad*. You would *totally* love it. Can we?"

"Oh, I . . ." He smiles at her but looks nervous. "You know, there's a lot of stuff we still need to get to. How about I go on the next one?"

"Okay," Sophie pouts.

I elbow Sophie gently. "I think your dad is scared of the Yeti."

"What?" Sophie looks at her dad with concern. "Are you scared?"

Aiden raises one eyebrow. "I am not scared of the Yeti."

"That sounds exactly like what someone who is scared of the Yeti would say," I tease.

"Sure it is."

"I'm just saying." I shrug. "The minute you heard Yeti, you suddenly needed a bathroom break."

"Hilarious," he deadpans. "Are you guys hungry yet?"

Sophie covers her stomach with her hand. "I'm starving."

"I saw a couple of food carts back that way." He points back toward Fantasyland. "We could go and see what they have."

"We still have to go on Peter Pan!"

"We'll get there," Aiden assures her. "We still have the rest of the day."

"*Okay,*" she huffs. "As long as we—"

It takes Aiden and me a second to realize that Sophie has stopped following us, and when we both turn, it's clear that something else has completely captured her attention. I follow her line of sight up toward Fantasyland, squinting my eyes to try to see what she's seeing.

"Is that . . . ?"

Sophie squeals. "It's Mirabel!"

She grabs my hand and begins to pull me along, leaving a very confused-looking Aiden in our wake as she tugs me toward the Disney princess in question. A very pretty actor with dark curls and golden skin is skipping nearby in an embroidered teal skirt and flowing white blouse. It's the glasses that give it away, though, round and bright green. They stop to wave at the little kids she passes, and Sophie is close to hyperventilating the closer we get.

"Cassie! Cassie! It's Mirabel!"

"I see her," I laugh. "Do you want to go meet her?"

"Can I?"

"Go on," I urge, pushing her toward the actor, who is only a good ten feet away now. "We'll be right here."

Sophie practically sprints in Mirabel's direction, only slowing when she's a foot or so away as she hangs back patiently, waiting for the actor dressed as Mirabel to finish speaking with a boy who looks to be a tad bit younger than Sophie.

"Am I supposed to know what just happened?"

I glance over at Aiden, who has finally caught up. "You have got to get up to speed with the *Encanto* craze," I chuckle.

"Apparently." He stands next to me, shoving his hands in his pockets. "I'm not sure I've ever seen her this excited."

"She's obsessed with Mirabel," I inform him. "It's a cute movie. You should watch it."

"I'll try to make a point to ask her next week," he promises.

We both watch as Sophie finally gets her turn to approach Mirabel, her face lighting up when the actor squats down to her level, giving her a bright smile. I can't hear what they're talking about, but given that Sophie looks like she's met the child's equivalent of the president, it must be good.

"You're surviving Disney pretty well," I point out, unscrewing my drink to take another swig. "I thought the ears were going to do you in."

He reaches to touch the Mickey Mouse ears that Sophie insisted on getting only to chuck hers for a tiara the second she saw the boutique. "I'm guessing this is what dad rock bottom looks like."

"They're cute, don't worry," I laugh.

He clears his throat subtly. "Are they?"

"Yeah, they're—" It's a mistake, looking up at him, because how in the world does someone wearing all black at Disney and sporting Mickey Mouse ears manage to look so tempting? I can't see his eyes behind his sunglasses, but it doesn't matter, I think, because it's obvious that he's looking right at me. "You pull them off," I say a little more quietly.

I watch his jaw work subtly for only a moment before he looks back toward Sophie, who is having Mirabel sign her autograph book. "So do you."

You could just ask him, something whispers in my head. *You could just ask what he meant at the park. What's the worst that could happen?*

He could tell me he was just being nice. That's what.

"Hey, Aiden, about—"

"Dad! Cassie!"

I whip my head around to catch Sophie frantically pointing at a bush just behind her, just able to make out a curly head of hair and an emerald-green poncho. The actor looks as nervous as their namesake, peeking up from behind a branch and giving Sophie a shy wave as she rushes over to them.

"So, we're gonna talk about Bruno," I half sing.

Aiden frowns. "What?"

"Nothing," I laugh. "We better go get her before she hyperventilates."

It's probably for the best, I think. *Curiosity killed the cat.*

Forget the cat, it's my damned feelings I'm more worried about.

I don't attempt to bring it up for the rest of the day.

We spend every second of the entire day exploring Disneyland—Sophie dragging us from one attraction to the next until well after the sun goes down. Aiden physically has to carry her out when it is all said and done, the little girl being more than happy to stay until closing. It's hard to explain to a newly ten-year-old that it's not a great idea to keep her out past midnight.

She falls asleep in the car on our way to the Airbnb, but even with nothing but the sound of passing cars outside, Aiden and I still can't seem to find a way to break the tense silence. He hasn't looked at me once since we left the park, and even though the sun has set, I can just make out his features in the streetlights outside if I steal a glance in his direction. It's going to be awkward trapped in the small space of the Airbnb if this keeps up, not having the safety net of an entire floor between us like we do at home.

I don't know how long we stay like that before it gets to me, but by the time I've listened to the tapping of his fingers against the steering wheel for the fourth time, I can't take it anymore. "I think it's safe to say that today was a hit," I point out. "She's probably going to try to wear that princess dress to school when we get back."

Aiden laughs softly. "It was worth the shit show I'm going to come back to at work."

"Super dad," I say, echoing my statement from the other day.

I can just make out his barely there smile. "Yeah."

"I bet she doesn't even budge when you carry her to bed."

"You're probably right," he agrees, and when I look again, I see him glance in the rearview mirror. "She's had a full day."

"Did you have fun?"

"It was definitely something."

"Maybe you can wear the ears to work when you get back."

"Oh, sure. I'll do that," he snorts.

I grin in the near dark, turning my face toward the window. It's funny how things can seem so easy between us only to turn uneasy moments later. Aiden clears his throat then, drawing my attention, apparently not done.

"You did say they looked good on me," he mentions, his voice lower than it was a moment ago. "So."

I turn my head slightly, feeling my heart beat faster. "Yeah. I did."

"You were going to ask me something earlier," he goes on. "What was it?"

"Oh." I swallow, my mouth suddenly dry. "I was just . . ." It's not a good idea, and I know that. I should drop this, but I don't do that. "I was going to ask what you meant the other day."

"The other day," he echoes quietly.

"Yes, you—" I shift in the car seat, straightening my back as my hands grip my knees. "At the park. When that woman said— when I said you were—" *God.* "You said it wasn't obvious."

I can only hope he is picking up this scattered mess that I am laying down, because I can hardly even hear myself think over the way my pulse is thumping away inside my ears. My chest is alight with flutters and sparks that make it harder to breathe.

"Oh."

I wait for him to expand on his *oh,* but he doesn't say anything else for at least a minute. At least sixty seconds of me growing increasingly more panicked for having touched on this subject again.

"You said it was obvious that I was out of your league," he half whispers.

I might not be breathing. It's hard to tell. "You said it wasn't."

"Because it isn't."

My lips part, and I'm not stealing glances anymore; in fact, I am almost fully turned in my seat to look at him. "I don't know what that means."

"I'm not sure I do either."

"You have to know," I manage. "That's what you said. *You have to know.* What do I have to know, Aiden?"

I notice his fingers are gripping the steering wheel now, and he still isn't looking at me. "I don't know if we should be talking about this."

"Oh." Every spark in my chest goes out all at once. "Right. Of course."

"It's just, I don't think it's a good idea to—"

"I get it," I say, cutting him off. "Sorry. You're right. Totally inappropriate."

"Cassie, it's just—"

"I get it, Aiden." I turn my face toward the window. "Seriously. I was just curious. No big deal."

He goes quiet again, and I find myself regretting bringing it up, just like I knew I would. The streetlights still pass by outside, and my heart's still beating too fast, but it holds none of the strange anticipation from a moment ago, just embarrassment and mild disappointment.

You should have just kept your mouth shut.

keep waiting for Aiden to say something more as we drive to the Airbnb, but he never does. I'm starting to think I've messed things up—that I've created a situation that we will have trouble getting over. It's clear that I should have just let things lie, that it's becoming increasingly more likely that Aiden was just being nice and now he has to worry about his nanny reading too much into things. I guess if I were him, I'd feel awkward too.

I lock myself in the bathroom while Aiden tucks Sophie into their room, brushing my teeth aggressively as I recount the day's events in my head. I try to find where I might have gone wrong in thinking that Aiden might have meant something with everything he said and even everything he didn't say.

Cassie, you have to know—

God. That one is going to keep me awake.

I spit my toothpaste in the sink before turning off the water, dropping my toothbrush on the counter and gripping the edge to peer back into the mirror. It's probably ridiculous in the first place, the fact that I had actually *hoped* he might have meant more; there's nothing about it that screams good idea, and in the long run—there's no way it would end well. Even *if* Aiden were interested. Which he isn't. Or maybe he is, he just knows that it's a bad idea. Maybe I'm just tossing that idea into the hat to make myself feel better. I don't know.

I run my fingers through my hair and blow out a breath, shaking away these no-good thoughts that ultimately won't get me anywhere. I have to remind myself again and again that it doesn't matter if Aiden is the person who used to watch me. It doesn't matter if he's the person I thought felt something for me, because in the end, he disappeared. And if I keep imagining things that aren't there, that's exactly what he's going to do again.

I quietly shut the door to the bathroom behind me when I'm done, stepping out into the hallway. It's dark here, only a thin sliver of light coming from the lamp still on in the living area at the end of the hall—and maybe that's why I don't see him at first. I run straight into a big, solid mass when I move to head toward my bedroom, the very object of my concern colliding with me in the darkened hallway and throwing me off guard.

Aiden's hands grab for my shoulders as if by instinct, steadying me. "Cassie?"

It takes my brain a second to catch up to the fact that the person I've been obsessively stressing about is now a foot away from me and also touching me.

"Sorry," I sputter. "I didn't see you."

"No, it's okay. I was just . . ." He seems to notice then that he's still holding my shoulders, jerking his hands away quickly. "I was getting a drink."

I glance down to the other end of the hall, where the bedroom Aiden and Sophie are sharing lies a good ten feet from mine. "Is Sophie asleep?"

"Out like a light."

"Well, it was a big day."

He nods. "It was."

We both just stand there uncomfortably, Aiden rubbing at the back of his neck as I stare down at my feet.

"You had fun today," he tries. "Right?"

"Of course," I assure him. "It was a great day."

"Good, good."

Cassie, you have to know—

I should just go to sleep. I should go to sleep and forget this day happened, forget everything I know about who Aiden is and what he's seen—that I should wake up tomorrow and commit to doing my job without any distractions. I can do that, right? I can pretend that Aiden means nothing more to me than being Sophie's dad. I *can.*

But apparently I can't stop opening my mouth.

"Listen, about earlier—"

"Yeah?"

His eager tone catches me off guard, and when I look up, I notice his expression matches his voice. My brain is grasping at it like a straw. I have to forcibly tell it to shut up and sit down.

"I just . . . I'm sorry. If I made you uncomfortable. I don't want things to be weird between us."

"Oh." He nods slowly, that eager look fizzling out. "Right. No. You didn't."

"I think I just made a lot of assumptions that were silly," I say, trying to make it into a joke.

"Silly," he parrots, not sounding amused at all.

He doesn't make anything easy.

"Of course you were just being nice, and I read it wrong. I just don't want you to think I can't do my job or something because I thought you might be serious."

He doesn't say anything, and when I peek up at him, I notice his expression now almost looks pained. I must be making this worse. He looks like he wants to die right now.

I clear my throat, making a move to step away so I can escape to my bedroom and think up different ways to pass away. "Anyway, I guess I'd better—"

Suddenly, Aiden has his hand around my upper arm, not

squeezing exactly, but applying enough pressure to let me know he would like me to stay put. I glance down at his hand in confusion, then back up at him to find him still staring at the spot I'd just stepped away from, looking just as confused that he reached for me as I am.

"Aiden?"

"It's not," he says tightly, still not looking at me.

My brow knits. "What?"

"Silly," he says. "It's not silly."

My heart starts to race. I tell myself not to hope, not to read too much into this, every instance of doing so thus far has left me disappointed.

"I don't know what that means."

Aiden shakes his head. "I'm not sure I do either."

"You have to give me more than that," I say, frustrated. "You're being confusing."

Aiden laughs, but it's strange. "I *feel* confused around you."

"What? What does that even—"

"Because I shouldn't be thinking about you as much as I do."

All the air leaves my lungs in a rush. "What?"

Aiden looks right at me then, and even in the dark I can make out the hunger in his eyes. It's enough to take my breath away. "And I shouldn't be thinking about you the *way* that I do."

I know in this small space there's no way he misses the way I swallow. "Aiden, I—"

"You don't have to say anything," he sighs. "You probably shouldn't. I know that I'm overstepping. It's just . . . I feel like I'm going crazy. I'm starting to think this entire arrangement was a bad idea, but Sophie just loves you so much, and I can't be the reason to fuck all of that up with the way I can't seem to stop—"

I'm not sure if it's the darkness or the way he's slipping into this word-vomit-like speech that is a stark contrast to his usually collected self, but he doesn't notice when I pull away from his grip, when I step just close enough to bridge the short distance between us. His words die on his tongue as he looks down at me, and I can just make out his eyes, one bright and one dark and both fixed on me. I can still feel my heart beating a tattoo against my ribs, still hear the blood pulsing in my ears as I question myself, even now, but something about the way Aiden is looking at me gives me courage.

"And what if"—I swallow thickly, my gaze dipping from his mouth back up to his eyes—"I don't want you to stop?"

I hear his quiet gasp. "What?"

"Who says that you're the only one? What if I've been thinking about you too?"

I don't think it's a conscious thing, the way his hands raise and his fingertips graze the bit of skin between the hem of my T-shirt and my cotton shorts that I'm just now remembering have little hearts all over them.

His voice is impossibly soft now, almost hoarse sounding. "Have you?"

"For weeks," I admit, feeling bold.

He grips my hips. "This is crazy, isn't it?"

You don't know the half of it.

"I don't mind a little crazy," I breathe, my mouth inches from his.

I feel the hot warmth of his palm slide under my shirt, shaping itself against my waist as he glances down to my chest. "You're wearing the shirt again."

"It's my favorite."

He makes a sound I've never heard him make before, something like a groan and a whine that I feel all the way down to my toes. "It's mine too."

He goes impossibly still when I press my hands to his chest, when I let them push higher to grip his shoulders—finally allowing myself to feel the shape of his body against mine, like I've been daydreaming about. If the hard *something* pressing against my belly is any indication, I think it's safe to say Aiden is telling the truth when he says he's been thinking about me.

"This is crazy," he whispers again.

I let my hands slide back down to the firmness of his chest. "It would be crazier if you kissed me."

"Can I?"

"Aiden."

He doesn't need any more hints.

His mouth is as soft as it looks, exploring but gentle as his lips curve against mine. I can feel the searching press of his tongue as it licks along my lower lip like a question, and I don't need any more prompting to open and let him inside. When his tongue touches mine, it's like a switch has been flipped, and suddenly his hands are at my jaw and in my hair and everywhere else—tugging and touching everything he can reach. I swallow down his needy sounds as he presses me against the wall, tucking each one away in my memory so that I can take them out later like little treasures.

He's still hard against my stomach, and his hips rut upward in an almost thoughtless way, like he doesn't realize he's doing it. I feel his teeth nibble at my lip and then his breath hot against my jaw, the sensations all blending together as his touch sets me on fire.

"We can't." His voice sounds pained against my skin. "We shouldn't—"

I feel a flush of panic. "What? We can't?"

"Not here," he groans softly. "Sophie. She could . . ."

Like hell am I letting him stop after riling me up this much. I push him backward toward the bathroom door, grasping behind him to turn the handle as we rush inside. He reaches to turn on the light, and now that I can see him all lit up—hair a mess, mouth red from kissing—everything feels extremely real.

Are we really doing this?

Apparently so, if the way Aiden is kissing my neck is any indication.

"This shirt is very distracting." I tilt my head back when his mouth wanders, kissing at the bit of my exposed collarbone as his hand slides up the front of my T-shirt to cup just below my breast. "I haven't stopped thinking about it. About what's underneath."

"I didn't mean to—"

I make a sound when his mouth suddenly covers my nipple through the thin material, a soft cry that sounds louder echoing against the tiles in the bathroom. Aiden pulls away immediately, looking up at me with hooded eyes. "You have to be quiet," he murmurs. "Can you do that?"

"I can—" My gasp is softer when his lips cover me again to suck, but no less heavy. "I can be quiet."

He hums against my nipple as the increasingly wet cotton starts to rub me in a way that tingles, and my fingers find his hair to push through it, holding him close. It's everything I imagined it would be, him touching me, both now and a year ago—and part of me is struggling to make sense of all of it.

Not that Aiden gives me much time to overthink.

I feel his hand sliding from my waist to press against my stomach now, his thumb stroking the material between my legs in a featherlight way. "Tell me to stop," Aiden says roughly. "Tell me to stop, if that's what you want."

"It isn't," I reassure him, tugging at his hair to force him to look up at me. Both eyes seem dark now, his pupils dilated and his breath ragged as I grab his face to bring his lips up to mine. My voice is barely there when I whisper against them, "I want you."

His kiss is fiercer now, his hands more insistent, and when my fingers curl at the waistband of his pants, hooking at his underwear to tug it all away, his answering hiss elicits a heartbeat somewhere other than my chest.

"Fuck," he grinds out against my mouth.

It still does things to me, his mouth uttering filthy words, but wrapping my fingers around the hard, thick length of his cock does more. It twitches against my hand, throbs in my grip when I slide my fist down to pump him, and when I come back up to the tip, I can feel a slick wetness there that coats my palm.

Aiden leans back to watch me touch him, his hands finding my hips as his eyes remain fixed on me stroking him. His mouth parts as he lets out a shaky breath, and the way he seems to be hanging on to his control by a thread makes me feel oddly powerful.

"You're going to make me come," he groans.

I smile. "I think that's the point."

"I don't want to come in your hand."

My hand stills. I press my thumb against the wet slit at the head, purposefully coating it before I bring it to my mouth to lick it away before returning it to stroke him again, never tearing my eyes from his. "Where do you want to come, Aiden?"

He leans into me, his lips brushing against my jaw and his tongue hot against my skin. "Inside you."

"We can—" We're pressed so closely together that I can feel the heat of him against my belly, even through the cotton of my shirt. I reach for my shorts hastily with my free hand to try to shove them away. "I can get these off, if you'll just—"

"We can't," he huffs, like it pains him.

Something inside me deflates. "Oh. I'm sorry, I didn't mean to—"

"I *want* to," he clarifies, "but I don't have anything. Not here."

"Oh. *Oh.*" I swallow nervously. I'm hyperaware that I'm still touching his cock. "I have an IUD," I tell him. "And I'm not—I have regular checkups, so, if you wanted . . ."

He looks at me with wild eyes, and I watch them travel from my face all the way down to my hand that is still touching him.

"I do," he says. "You have no fucking idea how much I do."

"And do you . . . you know. Are you—"

"I'm clean," he tells me.

"Oh. Well. If you want to—"

Placing his hands at my hips, lifting me in one motion as he turns to set me on the bathroom counter, seems like his answer. It takes him only seconds to roll everything down my thighs to leave me naked from the waist down. His fingers tease through my wet folds as my breath catches, and then I feel his other hand cupping my ass to pull me closer until the heat of his cock slots against me to actually take my breath away. His lips are at my throat again, kissing that spot I hadn't even known could affect me like this, and his voice against my skin makes me shiver.

"Do you know how much I've thought about this?"

I shake my head, or at least I think I do. My brain feels fuzzy.

"Fuck, Cassie, you are"—he lets a finger slip inside me as my head falls back—"perfect." The way he pumps his finger in and out of me feels like a tease, each push and withdrawal leaving me wanting more. "The things I want to do to this pretty pussy of yours."

Jesus.

I haven't heard him use that word since before I knew his name. I haven't heard it since he whispered it to me through a computer speaker, in a time that feels so long ago right now.

I whine when he pulls his hand away, but it's short-lived when I feel him settling between my legs, guiding his cock to nudge at my entrance. His mouth covers mine to swallow my whimper when he notches there, slowly easing inside to fill me, and he shushes me gently as I take all of him.

"Quiet," he reminds me. "You said you could be quiet, Cassie. Remember?"

I feel myself clench around him, and if I weren't already sitting, my knees might give out. It feels so reminiscent of another time, one where he'd whispered filthy things to me without even knowing it was *me*, and it makes me all the more turned on. All the times I'd imagined this, what he'd feel like—none of it can compare to the real thing.

I nod breathlessly, feeling his shuddered breath wash against my lips.

"You feel so good," he rasps. "So fucking good."

His hips are flush with mine now, every hard inch of him rooted deep inside. He fills me until there's no room left, and I tremble against him, struggling to keep still on the counter. "Can you—*ah*. Can you just—"

"Do you want me to move?" He kisses me slowly, rolling his hips just enough to stir me up. "Do you want me to fuck this perfect pussy?" I can feel him slide against my inner walls, and I have to grip his shoulder with my free hand just to steady myself. "Tell me you want that."

I nod shakily. "Yes."

"Thank fuck," he groans.

He grips my hips tighter then, pulling out just to push back inside. He grunts when he fills me, the sound harsh and sending a shiver down my spine, but I don't have time to dwell on it with the way he does it again.

Aiden thrusts harder, and I cry out, "*Ah.*"

"Shh," he soothes, his hand reaching to cup my jaw as his thumb presses against my lips. "Be good, Cassie. You have to be good so I can fuck you."

I think I nod, maybe, but I can't tell. Not with the way he's begun a steady rhythm, each thrust bottoming out as the soft sound of our bodies coming together rings out against the tiles. I really am trying to keep quiet, but it's getting increasingly difficult to be sure.

"Aiden . . . Aiden, can you—"

"Tell me what you need," he grits out. "Tell me how to make you come."

"Touch me," I whine. I grab his hand, bringing it between my legs. "Can you touch me?"

He presses against my clit immediately, rolling the swollen bud beneath his fingertips as my head lolls and my stomach clenches. I'm already so close, the delicious friction of his cock inside me making me lose my mind—and the added pressure of his fingers against the most sensitive part of me only makes the hot pressure building between my legs that much more imminent, like it might burst at any moment.

His breath huffs against my jaw. "This okay?"

"Just like that," I breathe.

"Fuck, I'm gonna come," he moans softly against my mouth. "Are you close?"

I'm trying to move with him now. His fingers slip against my clit as I brace my hands against the counter to try to meet his thrusts, each one bringing me *right there.*

"Just keep—*right there*—oh. *Oh.*"

"*Cassie,*" he groans.

Maybe it's the way he says my name that does it. Maybe it's the searing heat of his mouth against mine just as his tongue slips inside. Maybe it's his hands or his cock or the warmth of his body—regardless, I feel myself begin to shake as every muscle in my thighs goes taut and my insides tremble around him with my orgasm. I can feel it when he lets go only moments after, like he'd been waiting for me. I can feel his cock twitching deep inside and hear his low grunt in my ear that sets off butterflies deep, deep in my stomach—and then his face is buried against my throat and his chest is heaving against mine.

We stay like that for a moment, neither of us speaking and both trying to catch our breath, and I wait for the regret to sink in, for the worry about what this will mean, but it doesn't come. There is nothing but the sated quality of my limbs and the comforting warmth of his body as his hands continue to stroke at my skin.

When he finally pulls away to look at me, the expression on his face is equal parts dazed and awed, like he can't quite believe that what just happened was real. My hands cup his face to pull him in for another slow kiss, catching his groan in my mouth when he carefully slips out of me.

I kiss him again, softer now, and I feel his lips curve against mine in a smile as a breathless chuckle escapes him. "This feels like a dream," he murmurs.

I'm still kissing him. I can't seem to stop. "Not a dream."

He buries his face against my chest, nuzzling back and forth against my breasts and making me giggle quietly. "This damn shirt," he grumbles. "Been driving me crazy."

"Maybe I should ask for a pajama stipend from my boss," I tease.

"I think he'd tell you it wasn't in the budget." He looks at me seriously then. "Was it . . . weird?"

I rear back. "Weird?"

"It's just . . ." He looks unsure now. "It's been a long time, and you're so . . ." His eyes travel down my body, making me shiver. "I got carried away."

Oh.

Do you want me to fuck this perfect pussy?

"It's okay." I kiss him gently. "I liked it."

I don't know how to tell him that I know all about his filthy mouth—intimately so.

"Good," he rumbles. "Because I don't see myself magically gaining any restraint when it comes to you in the foreseeable future."

I can't help my smile, the anxiety that's been building this last week dissipating and morphing into this strange calm. But still, I can't help but wonder:

"What—" I clear my throat. "What does this mean for my job?"

"What?" He looks genuinely confused. "You don't want to leave, do you?"

"No, no, of course not! But . . . is this . . . is this going to make things weird?"

"Not if we don't let it," he assures me. "We just have to make sure we keep things separate."

"Separate?"

"From Sophie," he says. "Until . . . until we know what this is."

It shouldn't make me feel the way it does, hearing it—it's a perfectly reasonable thing he's saying, after all. It wouldn't be fair to Sophie to expose her to this without knowing what it is.

So why do I feel so anxious all of the sudden?

My mind travels back to sleepless nights and red eyes after Aiden disappeared from me once, and I think now it would be so much worse, now that I know him.

Maybe that's why I say nothing, even when I know I should.

I could tell him now. I could tell him everything I know about us, about what we've shared—but there is a tiny voice in my head that warns me against it. He walked out of my life once, and I survived that, but could I do it again? Now? These questions have me shoving down all the things I know I should probably be saying, but instead I lean in for another lingering kiss.

"I'm okay with keeping things separate," I tell him. "For Sophie."

He pulls me close, forcing me to meet his gaze. "But that doesn't mean this ends tonight," he tells me pointedly. "Right?"

My lips curve in a shy smile. "I don't want it to."

"Good," he sighs. He kisses me again. "Because I'm not done with you, Cassie. Not by a long shot."

I hadn't realized how much I needed to hear him say this until he did. It makes me feel giddy.

He carefully helps me dress before tucking himself back in his pants, pulling me down from the counter before tilting up my chin to kiss my cheek. I feel his smile there, feeling his other hand sliding against my hip as if to memorize the shape of it.

He flicks off the lights in the bathroom as he pulls me out in the hall, holding against me for longer than necessary, like he's not ready to let me go. I can definitively say that I know the feeling.

"Good night, Cassie."

"Night," I whisper back, his low voice making my knees weak.

His hand slides down my arm when I peel myself away from him, his fingers grazing my skin until they find my fingertips, clinging to them for a few seconds before he finally lets me go. I turn from him to head back to my room, and it takes everything I have not to selfishly beg him to come back with me, just like it takes an incredible amount of effort not to turn back to get one last look at him.

Especially since I feel his eyes on me the entire way.

---◆---

I've been waiting for Cici to log on for half an hour.

I think it's officially safe to say that I'm a little obsessed.

Doesn't stop me from continuing to wait.

---◆---

CHAPTER 12

Aiden

I spend the entire night thinking about her.

Sleep has been impossible, and I'm left staring at the flat white ceiling of the Airbnb with a snoring Sophie sprawled out next to me, wishing I'd booked us a place with a double bed room, or maybe even another bedroom for her altogether. I go over all the reasons why it would be a bad idea to sneak off to see Cassie again. Every time I close my eyes, I'm met with the memory of her soft sounds and softer body—the sensation of how it felt to be inside her practically overriding every corner of my brain and making a home there.

I eventually give up on sleep altogether sometime in the early morning, leaving my room while Sophie is still sleeping and closing the door quietly behind me with the intent of making coffee. I lose my train of thought when I spot Cassie in the kitchen, who apparently had the same idea. I haven't actually considered the morning after yet, how we might act together after last night; maybe I thought it would be awkward with the things we said and the things we did, but seeing her now—wide-eyed with her auburn hair slightly mussed and her lips still red and a bit swollen from my kisses—all I can think about is how much I want to touch her again.

She's no longer wearing that fucking shirt that drives me crazy, but even in her cotton T-shirt and jean shorts, it's hard not to think about what her skin feels like against my hands underneath her clothes.

"Good morning," she says shyly, hiding her smile behind a mug. "I made coffee."

I return her grin, trying not to think about how I know what her nipples feel like against my tongue or how much I regret the fact that she's wearing a bra this morning. "Morning."

"Do you want me to make you a cup?"

"After."

"After?"

I cross the space between us quickly, taking her by surprise when my hands rest at her jaw, tipping up her face to press my mouth to hers. She sighs softly into it, parting her lips to chase after my tongue, and I can taste the sweetness of the sugar and cream from her coffee there. Before I pull away, I take just enough to get me through the day, unsure of when I will be able to properly touch her again.

"After," I clarify.

"Well, I'd say this is a better wake-up call than coffee," she teases.

"Did you sleep last night?"

"Not really."

"Neither did I."

I reach to tuck one stray tendril of hair behind her ear, letting my thumb linger at her cheek to swipe back and forth. It might be the first time I've allowed myself to really drink her in, too afraid before this to let my gaze linger for too long. Everything about her—from the delicate shape of her nose to the fullness of her mouth and the brightness of her eyes—seems meant to draw me in. It's making me want to kiss her again very badly.

I shake my head. "How am I going to keep from touching you all the time?"

"You're just going to have to learn some self-control, Mr. Reid."

My cock doesn't seem to have gotten the memo that we have to keep things discreet. "I probably shouldn't like that."

"I thought it made you feel old?"

"Not when you say it like that, it doesn't."

"Hmm." She transfers her mug to one hand, reaching out with the other to tease her finger back and forth against the bit of skin just under the hem of my T-shirt. "I'll keep that in mind." She pushes up on her toes to press another quick kiss to my mouth before giving my stomach a gentle push to put distance between us. "Now go sit down so I can make you a cup."

"Yes, ma'am," I murmur.

I settle on a barstool at the counter, letting my chin rest against my fist. It's easy to watch her work; all I've wanted to do for weeks is watch her more openly, and now that I'm allowed to, I think I'll have a hard time doing anything else. She sets my coffee in front of me from the other side of the counter, leaning over it to take a slow sip from her own mug as she holds my gaze. There's a tension there that speaks of everything we've done and everything I still hope to do—already calculating how I might get her into my bed or insert myself into hers.

She cocks her head at me. "So how does this work?"

"How do you want it to work? You hold all the power here, Cassie."

Her mouth quirks. "Oh, do I?"

"Absolutely."

"Well . . . I'm hoping you'll stop making yourself scarce while Sophie is at school."

"I think you can guess why I was doing that in the first place."

Her smile turns coy. "I don't know what you mean."

"Don't you?"

"Maybe you should explain it to me in more detail."

"Are you teasing me, Cassie?"

"I would *never*," she assures me, looking innocent for all of two seconds before she winks at me. "Unless you asked me to."

I have to stifle a groan as I hear the bedroom door open down the hall, tensing when I hear Sophie's little footsteps and quiet good morning as she shuffles into the kitchen. "I'm hungry," she complains.

Cassie has none of the trepidation that I do. "There's princess Sophie," she gushes. "Do you feel ten today?"

Sophie makes a face. "Not really."

"You look ten," Cassie says seriously. "Did you get taller since yesterday?"

"What?" Sophie reaches to press her hand to the top of her head. "No, I didn't."

"I don't know . . ." Cassie casts me a sly look. "We might have to let you drive us home."

"I can't drive!"

I laugh at the pair of them. "I'll be doing the driving, thank you."

"Oh, hold on," Cassie says.

She turns from us both and heads toward her room, disappearing for a moment before she returns with something behind her back. She bends down to Sophie's level, flashing a brilliant smile as she pulls out a small bouquet that consists of bright sunflowers and daisies and some light blue flower I don't recognize. Sophie stares at it for a moment with an open mouth, taking several seconds to meet Cassie's eyes and gingerly take the flowers.

"Happy birthday, Sophie," Cassie says softly.

Sophie's little lip quivers slightly, gently laying the bouquet on the counter before she collides with Cassie's waist, wrapping her arms there for a hug. "Thank you," she mumbles into Cassie's shirt.

Cassie squeezes her tight before kissing her hair. "You're welcome."

I'm still not entirely sure what's happening, but seeing the exchange between Cassie and Sophie is making my chest feel tight. Watching them, it almost feels like they've been in each other's lives forever. How does Cassie make everything seem so *easy*?

"Don't cry," Cassie fusses, her voice thick as she reaches to wipe under Sophie's eyes. "You'll make me cry. And I'm a super-ugly crier."

This elicits a watery laugh from my daughter, and Cassie urges her to turn before pushing her toward the bedroom she came out of. "Go wipe your face. We'll talk about breakfast when you get back."

Sophie nods heavily before heading back down the hall. I wait until she's out of sight before I open my mouth, still a little confused. "What was that about?"

"Oh." Cassie looks sheepish now. "She told me the other day that her mom used to give her flowers on her birthday. I just thought . . ." She rubs her arm. "I had time this morning since I couldn't sleep, so I googled and found a shop nearby."

For a moment, I'm too stunned to say anything. Not just because I am reeling over the fact that I didn't know this about Sophie and Rebecca's relationship—Sophie has certainly never mentioned it—but also because Cassie *does* know this about Sophie and Rebecca's relationship. And not only that, but apparently her first instinct upon learning it was to go out of her way to replicate it just for no other reason than to Sophie happy. I'm having a hard time even pinning down what the emotion is that I'm experiencing over this.

"Thank you," I say thickly. "That was . . ." My heart is beating so loud. Can she hear it? "That was amazing of you."

"It's no big deal," she mumbles, looking at her shoes.

I want to kiss her so badly, it actually hurts. "It really is," I assure her. "Trust me."

Cassie's lips turn up in a shy smile, and I can do little more than sit at the counter, wrestling with the swirling emotions raging in my chest.

"I'm still hungry," Sophie announces, choosing that moment to burst back into the kitchen. Apparently she's gotten over her bout of emotion from earlier. "Can we eat?"

"Okay, okay," Cassie chuckles. "What are we hungry for?"

"I want pancakes."

"You *always* want pancakes."

"Funny how she used to not like them," I murmur.

"So I don't have anything here to make them," Cassie tells Sophie, "but I bet we could find a place to get you some pancakes."

Sophie looks skeptical. "With chocolate chips?"

"*Of course* with chocolate chips," Cassie tells her. She opens her arms then to beckon Sophie closer, pulling her in to smooth her hair as she gives Sophie a playful smile. "Your hair is as wild as your dad's when you wake up."

I watch Cassie fuss over Sophie's hair as they both laugh, that same constricting sensation in my chest when Cassie pulls her in for a hug and presses another kiss to her hair, just like I often do. Watching them together makes me feel odd, something about the natural way they have come to care about each other throwing me off guard. It makes me feel—for lack of a better phrase—warm and fuzzy inside.

"We have to get on the road soon anyway," I tell them both. "I do have to go in early tonight since I missed last night. We can find some non-dad pancakes on the way."

Sophie flashes me that toothy grin that makes my heart hurt, and Cassie pulls her along with a promise to fix her hair. She looks back at me from over her shoulder as she leads Sophie toward the bathroom, sending a wink my way that makes me feel warm in a different kind of way.

I finish my coffee alone, my mind far away and on the two ladies in the other room.

I might be in real trouble.

The trip home takes longer than expected since the pancake place that Sophie picked was thirty minutes out of the way, but the way she hasn't stopped talking about the chocolate-chip-birthday-cake pancake monstrosity she had there makes it worth it. And she hasn't. Stopped talking about it. Not even when we're walking into the house.

"But how did they get the little colors in there? They tasted so *good*. Like sprinkles! But on the inside!"

Cassie laughs as she sets her bag at the foot of the stairs. "It's like a Funfetti cake."

"What's that?"

"You don't know what a Funfetti cake is?"

Sophie shakes her head, and Cassie gasps theatrically. "Okay. We will be going to the store and buying a box mix of Funfetti cake as soon as your dad goes to work."

Sophie fist pumps. "*Yes.*"

"Box mix?" I raise my eyebrow in Cassie's direction. "Really?"

She shrugs. "Don't worry, I'll be sure to get rid of all the evidence before you come home so it doesn't offend your delicate chef sensibilities."

"Can I call Wanda?" Sophie tugs on Cassie's hand expectantly. "I told her I'd call her and tell her about the trip!"

"Yeah, okay," Cassie says, digging her phone from her pocket. "Tell her we'll bring her some cake in a little while."

Sophie's eyes light up as she snatches the phone away, already bounding up the stairs toward her room. I wait until she disappears beyond the landing, listening to her footsteps on the stairs for a few moments.

"You know," Cassie teases while I watch the stairs distractedly. "If you ask nicely, I *might* save you some cake. But you're going to have to say something nice about box mi—*oh*."

She makes a surprised sound when I suddenly crowd her to the other side of the stairs, backing her into the little alcove beyond the settee and cupping her face to tilt her mouth to mine. It only takes her a second to melt into it, her arms winding around my neck and her fingers teasing through my hair as she kisses me back. I don't know what it is about Cassie that causes me to devolve into a rutting teenager, but it's taken every bit of my patience to wait as long as I have to touch her again.

She's smiling when she finally pulls away, her lips a little redder than they were a moment ago. "Hi."

"I'm sorry," I murmur. "I've been wanting to do that for hours now."

"Wow, you must have been suffering. I couldn't even tell."

"Just assume going forward that I always want to do that."

She bites her lip to keep from grinning wider. "Good to know."

"I'm going to have to figure out a better method of restraining myself," I sigh.

"Or not," she says innocently. "I kind of like you unrestrained."

"You make it very, very hard to be good."

She presses up on her toes to kiss my cheek. "Maybe you should be bad then."

I have to close my eyes and think about something else just to keep from getting hard. This is absolutely not the time. "You're going to kill me."

"Never." She untangles herself from me, patting my shoulder playfully. It's amazing to me that one night could somehow eradicate all the tension between us. If I'd known this was the solution, I might have proposed it sooner. "Pretty sure you're supposed to be getting ready for work."

"Yeah," I sigh. "Gonna be a great night."

"Maybe I should give you something to look forward to?"

It's probably pathetic, the way I visibly perk up. "Oh?"

She comes closer, reaching to let her fingers trace the shape of my bottom lip. "Something to come home to."

"It's going to be late . . ."

She smiles sweetly then, reaching again, and I can feel my eyes closing in anticipation of her kiss. "It's fine." She presses her lips softly against mine, pulling away after and bringing her hand up to tap my nose. "I'll just leave your piece of cake on the counter."

She's laughing as she skips away, and I'm left dumbfounded for a few seconds before it clicks what she's said. I shake my head, pinching the bridge of my nose as I hear her start up the stairs after Sophie.

"She really is going to kill me," I mutter to no one.

Work is hell, just as expected.

Two of my line cooks were out with a bug that's apparently going around, and I had to send my sous-chef to the fucking hospital after an incident with a knife that required stitches. It's like the universe decided to punish me for taking a night off.

I was so ready to leave by the end of the night that I hadn't even bothered taking off my chef coat, only unbuttoning the top button as I step through the front door of the house and sighing with relief to be home. I hang my keys on the hook as always, stretching as I'm finally able to shake away the stress from tonight's dinner service.

My eyes find Cassie's closed bedroom door, a flicker of temptation sparking inside as I check my watch, but it's nearly midnight.

"Damn," I mutter.

Not that it would have been acceptable to wake her up just to touch her an hour ago, but still I can't pretend I'm not thinking about it. I undo another button of my coat as I run my fingers through my hair, pushing the desire away and starting up the stairs as I resign myself to a shower and bed. I tell myself I can restrain myself for one night. I've been doing it for weeks, after all.

My decision means that it's a complete surprise when I feel a tug at the back of my coat that pulls me backward into a now open door. It closes behind me as a smaller, softer body presses me against it, and then I'm met with a tempting smile lit by the nearby lamp.

"Cassie?"

"I told you I wanted to give you something to look forward to."

Everything I've been trying to pack away starts trying to claw itself back to the surface. "What happened to the cake?"

"Oh, it was a huge success," she assures me. "If that's what you'd rather have, there's still some upstairs . . ."

"Hardly."

"Mm." Her finger teases at the third button of my coat that's still done. "Long night?"

"Fucking terrible."

She pops open the button easily, not looking at me. "Boo. What can I do to help?"

"Are you sure you're not tired? It's practically mid—"

She pops open another button, shushing me. "Are you really worried about my sleep right now?"

"I—" Another button, enough fabric gapping so that she can slip her hand inside and press her palm to my chest. "No. Not really."

I'm rewarded with her smile as she reaches with her other hand to undo the second to last button. "This chef jacket thing is actually kind of hot."

That's one I haven't heard before.

I notice what she's wearing now, frowning. "I see I'm not the only one wearing buttons."

"Someone complained about my pajamas last night."

I press my hand to her hip, letting my thumb flick at one of the large white buttons on her purple pajama shirt. There are cats all over it. "Are you a cat person?"

"Who isn't a cat person?"

"They're kind of pretentious."

"Oh, wow." Cassie laughs. "Did you know cats have more than a hundred vocal cords?"

"Are you really giving me Snapple facts right now?"

"I'm sorry." She pulls at the pieces of my coat before she teases her fingers under the hem of the T-shirt I'm wearing underneath. "Are you not turned on by useless trivia?"

I close my eyes as her fingers slide over my abdomen. "This seems one sided."

"You don't like my pajamas?"

"I'd like them better on the floor."

She bites her lip. "You never told me how I could help you feel better."

"I could think of a few ways," I murmur, toying with her buttons now. "If you'd take this off."

There's a flash of something in her expression then, just a tiny flicker of hesitance before she starts pulling me back toward her bed. She tugs at my coat until I'm forced to crawl over her, her back falling against the comforter as she tugs my mouth down to hers.

I'm still fumbling with her top even as she helps rid me of my coat, and by the time she's yanking up my shirt to urge it over my head, I've managed to undo all of her buttons as her shirt parts so that I can see more.

"Fuck, Cassie," I breathe, mouth suddenly dry.

Feeling her is one thing, seeing is another. She's all soft swells and pretty pink nipples—her breasts spilling out of my hand when I cup them as the stiffening peaks beg for my mouth.

"*Ah.*"

Her soft cry when I wrap my lips around her nipple to let my tongue tease there only worsens the growing situation in my pants, but I tell my cock to back the fuck off and let me enjoy this. I've been fantasizing about doing this for as long as I've been mentally kicking my own ass for fantasizing about doing this. Her fingers tangle in my hair as I pull at the taut bud with my lips, swirling my tongue there just to elicit more of her sounds.

Because they are *addicting*.

Cassie doesn't hide them, doesn't try to quiet herself, and I am very grateful for the floor between us and Sophie's room as her quiet mewls blend into sharp gasps that have her back bowing.

"I thought I was supposed to make you feel better," she says breathily above me.

I flick my tongue across one nipple as I reach to roll the other between my fingers, speaking directly against her skin. "This is making me feel better."

"*Oh*." She squirms when my teeth graze just below her breast, kissing a path over her ribs. "Don't you want to—"

I reach to pin her hip against the bed. "Be still. This is what I want."

"O-okay," she manages airily, and I can feel her relaxing. "I'd hate to get in the way."

I chuckle against her belly. "I appreciate it."

I'm holding my breath when I start to roll her soft shorts down her thighs, leaving her in yellow underwear that are covered in Popsicles. "Is everything you own in some sort of print?"

"All of my underwear, at least."

"Something to look forward to," I mutter. I peek up at her when I hook my fingers into the elastic band at her hips. "Is this okay?"

"I mean." Her lips tilt up dreamily in a shy smile. "If that's what makes you feel better."

It's all the invitation I need. I'm not sure where her underwear ends up since I practically toss them over my shoulder, and right now I don't care. Her thighs are soft and inviting, pressing together prettily as if she's embarrassed by the way I'm looking at her. I urge them apart with my hands as I brush my palm up the inside of one, swallowing when I can see all of her.

Her neat curls are the same deep red of her hair, a perfect contrast to the slick pink between her legs that makes me feel feral. I slide a knuckle through the wet crease of her, her hips shifting impatiently and her breath catching.

"Aiden . . ."

"You're so pretty here," I manage, my voice tight. "Can I use my mouth?"

"What?" She looks concerned. "Oh. I don't—"

I can't stop touching her, still teasing her with my fingers. "You don't like it?"

"It's not that, I just . . ." She bites her lip. "I've never been able to come that way."

"What?"

"I don't know. I probably have a busted vagina."

I snort, and I think she might have been about to laugh, until it breaks off into a choked sound when I tease her entrance. "No. You don't."

"I'd just hate for you to waste your time. We could just have sex."

I frown, watching her look up at me with worried eyes as I think about all the assholes who apparently didn't take the time with her that they should have. Which only makes me feel strangely furious, knowing some other asshole has touched her. I didn't even know I was the jealous type until this exact moment.

"I can promise you"—I'm already urging her thighs to part wider as I settle between them—"that this is not a waste of time for me."

"O-oh, well, if you're sure you—*oh.*"

I close my eyes when my tongue first glides through her wet folds to taste her, her flavor on my tongue erotic and heady and almost too much. Her thighs tremble under my hands when I do it again, and I shift against the mattress to seek some release for how hard she's made me, just from this.

I tease my tongue up her center until I find that hot little bundle that is just a little firmer, circling it slowly as her breath catches. I'm taking my time to work her up to it, wanting to make up for all the times she's never come this way. Fuck, I think I could spend *hours* between her legs if she'd let me.

Because Cassie is fucking *intoxicating.*

It's the way her breath hitches when I touch the right place, the way she presses against my face when she needs more, the way her thighs cinch against my ears when she thinks she can't take it. By the time I've wrapped my lips around her now-swollen clit, sucking at it to draw out every drop of her pleasure that I can—I'm having to hold her down to keep her from writhing away from me.

"Be *still*," I murmur against her. "You're going to come on my tongue, Cassie."

"I'm—I think—"

I don't want to give her time to think, flicking her clit with my tongue before resuming my mission of trying to suck it into my mouth. Her fingers find purchase in my hair, and even with the slight sting, my cock throbs, her hips rolling against my face evidence that she's lost in it. That she wants me to make her come just as badly as I want to give it to her.

I can tell when she's close—her hips lift from the bed and her fingers tangle in my hair—every little movement and sound making me that much harder, that much more desperate to fuck her. But I'm determined to hold out until I've reduced her to a shaking mess against my tongue. Her stuttered breath has turned to whimpered pleas of *more* and *right there*, and I hold her steady as I work her clit with my lips and tongue to push her over the edge.

"Aiden. *Aiden.* Keep—right there—oh. *Don't stop.*"

She doesn't fully let go until I slide two fingers to dip inside her, keeping her full while I devote all my attention to the taut bud between my lips. I'm still thinking about filling her with something else when we're done here, and that's enough to have me dizzy when her fingers grasp at my hair. She makes a pretty sound when she comes, a quiet gasp that seems to come from deep inside her, and her entire body trembles and shakes as she falls apart.

It's fucking beautiful.

I don't stop until she's actively pulling me away, whimpering my name over and over as she says she can't take any more. I lift my head to see her flushed face, feeling out of breath and too warm as she smiles at me with glazed eyes.

"That was . . . something."

I turn my face to slide against her thigh, wiping my mouth on her skin. "I feel much better."

"I'm happy to be of service," she murmurs. "Come back anytime."

I'm laughing when I crawl over her, running a finger down one side of her open pajama top before dragging it over her chest that still heaves slightly. "I've got something else in mind now."

"Well." Her arms wind around my neck as she pulls me down closer. "Whatever makes you feel better, Mr. Reid."

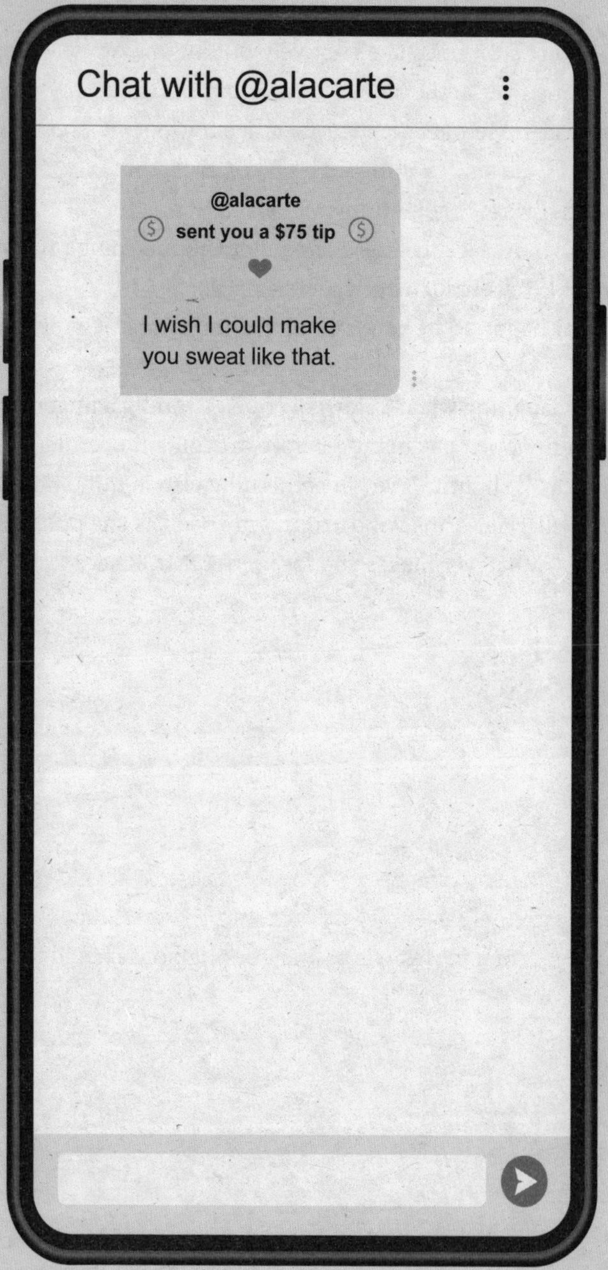
Chat with @alacarte
@alacarte
sent you a $75 tip
I wish I could make
you sweat like that.

CHAPTER 13

Cassie

Even after a blissful night of orgasms, it's hard not to be a little tense the following morning. I keep checking the clock on the kitchen stove as I count down until the time that Iris is supposed to arrive this morning, left to my own devices since Aiden ran out to the gym. (I suspect his convenient absence during Iris's visit might even be on purpose, although he avidly denies it.) I am placating myself with remembering how excited Sophie is to see her aunt.

By the time the doorbell rings, I'm downright jumpy, and I shoot up from the couch even as I hear Sophie bounding down the stairs and rushing past me down to the first level as I toddle after her. Iris always looks different with Sophie—her terse demeanor fading in the embrace of this lovable little girl, and I can't help but wish I could find some bridge to *that* Iris. I know it would do this entire household a world of good if I could somehow draw that side of her out more. As expected, her expression changes when she notices me lingering at the bottom of the stairs, giving me a curt nod as she breaks away from Sophie's grasp.

"Hey," I offer, giving an awkward wave.

Our last encounter is still fresh on my mind, and I imagine the same can be said for Iris. It makes for a tense greeting, that's for sure. Especially since all the things she had insinuated about me have turned out to be decidedly true.

Another nod for my trouble. "Morning," Iris answers.

Sophie notices the gift bag in Iris's hand then, squealing excitedly. "Is that my present?"

"Yep," Iris says with a grin. "Do you want to open it?"

"Yes!"

Sophie snatches the bag greedily, flouncing away from the both of us as she skips up the stairs back to the living room, leaving Iris and me lingering in the entryway. I clear my throat as I rub my arm, trying for a polite smile.

"Have you eaten? I was going to make breakfast soon."

Iris shakes her head. "That's okay," she tells me. "I had a bagel on the way over."

"Oh, okay."

There is another long span of seconds where we both just stand there, until I decide I can't take it anymore. "Hey, about the other day—"

"I should apologize," Iris cuts in.

I blink in surprise. "What?"

"I made some pretty rude insinuations." She looks down at her feet. "I have a hard time coming to terms with Sophie spending the bulk of her time with someone who isn't me."

I can almost see past her tough exterior then, genuine emotion peeking through as her brow furrows and her mouth turns down. "Oh, well . . ." I shift my weight from one foot to the other. "I imagine it's got to be hard." I go back and forth on whether or not I should involve myself more in this strained situation, finally deciding that I won't be able to live with myself if I don't. "You know, I would never want to get in the way of you spending time with her," I stress. "Maybe we could work together here. Sophie needs you," I say. "Like I said the other day . . . she needs everyone she can get."

Iris looks genuinely surprised, her mouth parting slightly as she processes what I've said. She nods finally, a slow concession, taking a deep breath only to expel it. "You're right. She does need that." She looks down at her feet again. I get the sense that apologies don't come easy to her. "Aiden hinted that you might be responsible for my invitation to her trip the other day."

"Oh, no," I argue. "Sophie wanted you there! I just told Aiden it might make things easier if he—" Iris is looking at me strangely, and I clamp my mouth shut. "Anyway. I just want Sophie to be happy."

"I'm starting to understand that," Iris answers sincerely.

Little victories. I celebrate internally.

"You guys!" Sophie calls from the floor above. "Are you coming?"

Iris shares a small smile with me, and this feels like a victory too. "I think we're being summoned."

"I've learned patience isn't her virtue," I chuckle.

Iris follows me up the stairs, where Sophie is sitting in the middle of the living room beside a now-empty sack and a pile of tissue paper, holding three new games for her Nintendo Switch.

"Cassie!" Sophie holds out one game in particular. "Aunt Iris got me *Animal Crossing!*"

"Oh boy," I gush, falling to my knees beside her. "That's exactly what you wanted."

"You can build your own island in this one!"

"Well, that sounds like a dream," I tell her.

Sophie is already reading the back covers of each of her new games, and I turn to Iris, who is standing nearby with her arms crossed to give her a thumbs-up. I'm rewarded with another small smile; today is full of all sorts of victories, I think.

Sophie holds up another case. "She got me *Sonic*, too!"

"Oh, that's the movie you've been bugging me to go see, right?"

Sophie rolls her eyes. "That's *Sonic Two*," she corrects me. "It looks so funny!"

"I know, I know, but I have labs this weekend. Maybe we can go one day after school next week, or maybe—"

I have an idea then, striking me out of nowhere. I can feel my mouth hanging as I turn to Iris, thinking that maybe I can gain more points here with the terse aunt who is just starting to warm up to the idea of liking me.

"Hey," I call, pointing at Iris while my idea still pings around in my head. "Do you have to work today?"

Iris frowns. "Later? I have to take over for my clerk at two. She has an appointment."

"Why don't you and Sophie go to a movie? You could get breakfast, or lunch after—whatever you want. I mean, if you want to?"

It's the second time I've surprised Iris this morning, if her expression is any indication. "Do you think Aiden would be okay with that?"

"I'll text him," I assure her. "I'll tell him it was all my idea, promise. But I think he will be fine. We can just swap numbers in case something comes up, and I need to come get her. What do you think?"

"That sounds . . ." Iris's arms slowly uncross as she looks between Sophie and me, still a little stunned. "That sounds great, actually. If you're sure it's okay."

Technically, I'm not one hundred percent, but I am pretty confident, at least.

"Sophie." I turn to address her. "Do you want to go with Aunt Iris?"

Sophie nods enthusiastically. "Yes!"

"Why don't you go upstairs and change while I text your dad? I'm sure he'll be fine with it. You two can have a proper girls' day for your birthday."

Sophie hops up, snatching up her games but leaving her mess, practically sprinting past us toward the stairs as she heads up her room. I pull my phone out of my pocket to shoot a text to Aiden, fairly positive he will be okay with this idea but wanting to make absolutely sure before I send them out the door. I'm prepared to convince him that it is, if need be.

"Thank you," Iris says behind me. I turn to find her features have softened considerably, gratitude shining in her eyes. "Seriously."

"Don't worry about it," I tell her. "Sophie's happiness is the most important thing here, right?"

Iris nods. "Right."

"Well, you're a part of that."

"I really appreciate that," Iris says, almost like she's relieved to hear it.

Maybe she'd begun to doubt it.

"You two go and have fun," I urge. "I've got some homework I can catch up on. You're practically doing me a favor here."

Iris's mouth quirks. "Right."

I grin back at her, doing a mental fist pump. It seems like I may be finding the cracks in this woman's armor after all. Even if only a little.

Good thing I'm incredibly patient.

After an hour of hanging out in my room staring at my laptop, I finally relax enough to stop checking my phone. I have had to remind myself numerous times that Aiden approved Iris and Sophie's outing, and that someone will definitely let me know if I'm needed.

It's funny, I'm worrying about Sophie like she's actually my kid or something.

I'm lounging on my bed with the door to my room slightly ajar, and I hear it when Aiden's keys jingle in the door, when it opens and closes to signal his arrival.

"Cassie?"

"In here," I call, closing my laptop.

He appears in my doorframe to lean against it, and it is . . . a sight. A sweat-drenched Aiden Reid. On all the days he's come back from the gym, I've had to avert my eyes, to make sure that I didn't stare for too long. Which, now that I'm able to look my fill, I'm realizing was an actual tragedy.

He crosses his arms, his biceps pressing against his T-shirt sleeves. "Are they still gone?"

"Yeah, I imagine they will be for a little while. They were going to get breakfast, I think." I check the time on my phone. "The movie didn't start till eleven, so . . . I doubt we'll see them until at least one."

"It was nice of you to offer," Aiden says.

I shrug. "I'm determined to be the first nanny who Iris *doesn't* hate." I hold up my phone and shake it back and forth. "I even got her number. Bet none of the other nannies can say that."

Aiden grins. "No, they can't."

"It looks like you at least got a good workout while you were hiding at the gym," I tease, eyeing the darker patch of cotton at his chest where the sweat is still drying.

"I wasn't *hiding*," he huffs.

I roll my eyes. "*Sure* you weren't. I think someone might be a little afraid of big, scary Iris."

"Am I," he murmurs, eyeing me.

I feel a flicker of desire lick low in my belly with the way his eyes move over my body, watching them travel up my legging-clad thighs and across my chest. A girl could get all sorts of ideas with a man like Aiden looking at her like he is.

"You said it will be a few more hours," he repeats, still eyeing me, "until they get back."

I nod slowly. "I did."

"I need a shower," he says deliberately. "Would you be interested in joining me?"

My mouth is curling just as all the reasons why that's a bad idea hits me—realizing that a shower means being completely exposed and out of control. Thus far I've been able to hide the scar on my back that will surely give everything away, but naked and wet will one hundred percent ensure that Aiden sees it, subsequently discovering just how *well* he knows me, even outside of our newfound intimacy.

I try to mask the building anxiety in my chest, keeping my expression even as I push my laptop to the side. "What if I like you like this?"

"Like this?" He looks down at his damp clothes. "I'm a sweaty mess."

"I can think of a lot better reasons for you to be a sweaty mess," I tell him coyly.

His expression changes. "Can you."

"Mm-hmm."

I pat the bed beside me, and he immediately pushes away from the doorframe to press a knee to the edge of bed before crawling up toward me. His hands brace on either side of my hips to cage me in, and I have to admit that the smell of his sweat mixed with his deodorant and something that is just inherently *Aiden* isn't at all unpleasant.

"And how do you propose we fill the time, Cassie?"

I reach to let my fingertips tuck under his shirt, grazing his abdomen and feeling it tense under my touch. "I can think of a few things."

"Hmm." He ducks his head to press his lips to my throat, and I close my eyes, curving my fingers around either side of his hips. "Are you asking me to fuck you, Cassie?"

My stomach clenches. It's still a little difficult to reconcile the shy-smiling Aiden with the dirty-mouthed *A* that I now know are one and the same, and I can't help but wonder just how much Aiden has been holding back with me.

"I might be," I gasp, feeling his knee wedge between my legs, applying pressure between them. "If you're not too tired. I know at your age all that activity might—"

I yelp when his teeth nip at the base of my throat, his hand covering my breast through my shirt to squeeze as his thumb teases my nipple through my thin sports bra. His hands are already tugging at my leggings—the cool air of the air-conditioning hitting my skin as he rolls them down, with my underwear following close behind.

"You're already soaked," he murmurs. "I think you want me to fuck you very badly."

I turn my face to kiss his jaw, tucking my fingers into the waistband of his athletic shorts. It takes only one motion to pull him free, and he makes a pained sound when my hand wraps around his already-hard cock to give him a teasing stroke. "You're no better off, Mr. Reid."

"I'm learning that I *always* want to fuck you, Cassie. It's becoming a problem."

"I'd hardly call it a problem," I breathe, pressing my thumb against his slit to smear the bit of precome there. "Especially since I feel the same way."

He's starting to ease my T-shirt up my belly, and that same

panic bleeds through my heavy arousal as warning bells set off in my head. I push at his hips to urge him to turn, guiding his body until he falls to his side and then rolls on his back. He situates himself so that he's resting against the headboard and my pillows, and I crawl into his lap immediately, sliding my wet center against his hard cock in a slow back-and-forth while his hands settle at my hips to grip there.

"Let me," I say. "Wouldn't want you to tire out."

He tries to smile, but it's short-lived when I rock against him again. I brace my hand on his shoulders as I reach between us to grab his cock, holding him steady as I slowly lower down onto him. I can see the raised tissue of his scar near my fingers where they've rucked up his shirt, and there is a flash of guilt that surges through me, but it fades away quickly when he starts to fill me.

I like the way his mouth parts and his eyes grow heavy as he watches himself disappear inside me, his teeth settling against his lower lip as my hips meet his, completely full of him. "Do whatever feels good," he murmurs, his voice like a thick honey that I can almost feel dripping down my skin. "I want to watch you use me." His hand slides over my hips to palm my ass, looking at me with eyes that seem to be burning. "Because after that . . . I'm *going* to fuck you, Cassie."

I can *feel* the way liquid heat courses through me, the way I practically *drip* with his words—clamping down around nothing as the air in my lungs seems to catch fire. His eyes are fixed on the place where we're joined now, waiting for me to move at my own pace. He feels so much larger like this, so much deeper—and I whimper as I involuntarily constrict around him—a fruitless effort because there is no room left, no give. Nothing but *Aiden*.

I try to lift up slowly, feeling every inch of him sliding against me inside as I pull off. The sensation of lowering back down feels like I might burst with the thickness of him, but the slight burn is delicious, the friction heavenly.

"Good," he grinds out, the sound harsh in my ears. "Good girl."

I shiver, making a pitiful sound as my insides give another vain squeeze. Aiden rubs soothing circles at my thigh.

"You like that?" I feel his hand slipping between us, his thumb pressing against my clit to tease me. "Like hearing how well you take me?"

I think I nod; it's a barely there movement that feels like too much—and Aiden hums in approval as he rolls his thumb against the most sensitive part of me.

"Fucking dream inside you," he murmurs. "Keep moving like that, Cassie. I want to watch you fuck yourself on my cock."

I try to lift my body, but it takes effort; I'm so fucking *full* that it's a stretch just to lift off him. I can hear the way he hisses through his teeth when I lift my hips to slide up the length of him, hear his heavy exhale when I slowly sink back down.

"*Good,*" he grates. "Do it again."

I do it again—a slow lift and a tight slide, my nails digging into his shirt as I roll my hips at the end of the movement this time. It brings him deeper—and I can't help the long, loud moan that slips past my lips as my head lolls to rest against his shoulder.

"Aiden," I gasp as I push up on my knees to lift off his cock, dropping back down as the girth of him nearly steals my breath. I'm just so *full.* "Aiden, I need—"

"Do you want me to fuck you now, Cassie?" His hand finds my cheek to urge my face away from his shoulder, cupping my jaw and pushing his fingers into my hair as I look back at him through hooded eyes. "Do you need a little more?"

I bite my lip, rocking my hips forward as I nod. I feel his hands grip my hips then, holding me steady. "Hold on to me."

I wrap my arms around his neck as his lips tease at my jaw, the softness of his mouth a stark contrast to the hardness of his cock, which is still deep inside me.

"Cassie." I pull back to find him watching me with eyes that seem darker than usual. He leans in slowly until his mouth hovers only inches from mine, curving it against my lips to linger briefly before he breathes, "You're better than anything I ever fucking thought about."

There's a rush of sensation in my chest that flutters down into my stomach, the softness of his voice filling me with something that borders giddiness—but I hardly have any time to dwell on it. Not with the way he begins to *move*.

"*Oh.*"

He lifts me like it's nothing, his hands tight at my hips as he pulls me up off his cock only to slam me back down again, thrusting up to meet me with a grunt. I feel him deeper like this, deep enough so that it's *almost* uncomfortable—but there's that slide of him against my inner walls, that wet friction as every ridge rubs me in just the right way. I hold on tight to steady myself as he thrusts into me with what feels almost like desperation, like he needs each one just a little more than the last.

"You feel"—each word sounds like an inhale, and then an exhale—"*so goddamned good.*"

He pulls my hips back and forth just to accentuate how full I am, to feel me. There's a broken stream of muttering where I pick up things like *can't believe* and *so fucking tight* and *such a perfect little pussy*—each one making my heart beat a little faster, making me squeeze around him again and again.

He finds a rhythm, a heavy lift and a sharp drop that has me bouncing on his cock. His head falls back against the headboard as his mouth parts in a throaty moan—alternating between eyes rolling back and homing in on where he disappears inside me again and again.

"Gonna come," he warns through gritted teeth. "But not without you." He takes to rocking my hips back and forth again—not actually thrusting but giving me minute amounts of friction anyway, just enough to keep me on the precipice. "Can you touch yourself? Want you to come on my cock."

He leans in to kiss my neck while I find my clit with shaking fingers—swiping at the swollen little bud that is already so sensitive, so *close*. I tilt my head back to give his mouth better access while I work myself quickly, his sudden stillness making the throbbing of his cock inside obvious, making the fullness—the *heat*— that much more heady.

He's lifting me again, bouncing me on his cock at that same rhythm that makes it hard to breathe, but it feels so *good* that I can't even be bothered. My whimpers turns to moans that I can hardly contain—and his breath hisses between his teeth as he keeps trying to fuck me even as his thrusts grow erratic, resulting in a messy pace that *still feels fantastic.*

My fingers slip against my clit with how wet I am, but I just keep going, moving as fast as he is, chasing after the end with a bit of that same desperation.

"Aiden. *Fuck, Aiden.*"

"*Come,*" he bites out. "Fucking *come*, Cassie."

I'm not even sure where it comes from now—be it my fingers on my clit or his cock that hits deep, touching me in all the right ways—but it doesn't matter. It's a slow, tumultuous pressure that swells and *swells* until it *bursts*—like fireworks exploding in my blood and my vision and deep, deep inside where his cock still moves—the sparks of it floating down to tingle at my skin as I shudder through it.

There are more filthy mutterings and heavy breaths that are hardly audible with the way my blood pounds in my ears, but I *feel* it—when he falls over the edge. His hips get tight to hold against mine, his cock pulsing against my walls like a steady throb. He pulls me close with thick arms wrapped around me, lips moving hungrily over my throat and my jaw and eventually my mouth as he empties deep inside.

"So good," he breathes. "Fucking perfect."

I shiver from both the praise and the sparks of my orgasm that are still zinging inside, falling against him in a boneless heap as his hands move across my back in heavy presses, like he can't help but keep touching me. Even after, he keeps kissing me lazily, his lips a pleasant pressure against my skin.

"I can't seem to touch you without losing control," he murmurs eventually.

"Mm." I snuggle closer. "I don't mind."

"It's becoming a problem," he says with a snort. "I'm finding that I *always* want to touch you."

I pull back to give him a lazy grin, shrugging. "I don't mind that either."

"How are you so . . ." His words trail off as he shakes his head, deciding against whatever thought he had and pulling me in to crush his mouth against mine instead.

I melt into his kiss, letting the weight and heat of his body seep into my muscles like a relaxing balm, hardly even noticing that he is still rooted deep inside me.

"*Now* you're a sweaty mess," I tease as I break away.

I feel his lips curl against mine. "It feels a lot more worth it now."

"I'm glad," I answer, kissing him again.

"Although, I still need that shower."

That familiar flash of guilt, and I hastily shove it back down as I remain calm.

"As tempting as that is . . . you *did* interrupt my homework."

He chuffs out a laugh. "Oh, did I?"

"Also worth it."

"I guess I wouldn't want to get in the way of your education."

"Any more than you already have, you mean," I tease.

He smiles as he gives me another quick kiss, wincing as he pulls out of me and rolling me to my back to loom over me again. "I guess I'll just have to find you later then."

"Twice in one day? Scandalous."

His smile is slow, inching across his face as he lowers to let his mouth hover against mine. "It still wouldn't be enough."

My pulse quickens as he kisses me again, and I close my eyes and enjoy the plushness of his mouth as I will the traitorous muscle to calm down. It's almost disappointing when he finally pulls away, tucking himself back into his shorts, and part of me is tempted to say to hell with it and follow him right into that shower.

But then I remember all the reasons why I can't, and again I feel that heavy weight of guilt settle at still not telling him of our past. Still too afraid to risk losing this to bring it up. I want to believe that it wouldn't matter, that Aiden likes me enough to look past it—but the uncertainty makes me keep quiet, feeling like shit for doing so.

"Well, if you change your mind," Aiden says as he slides off my bed. "You know where to find me."

He winks at me from the door before he disappears through it, and I fall back against the covers in a huff, closing my eyes as my boneless, spent body settles into the mattress. In a second I will get dressed again and go back to what I was doing; I *won't* follow Aiden, as tempting as it might be to do so, because I know deep down that I'm not ready yet. I'm not ready to face the truth and all the risks that come with it.

Even if, deep down . . . I know I'm just making it harder by waiting.

CHAPTER 14

Cassie

I never did cave to the urge of jumping in the shower with Aiden, but that doesn't mean I wasn't *incredibly* tempted. I spent the rest of my Friday morning being a good girl and finishing up my homework, knowing that Saturday's Cassie would be all the more grateful for it when she wasn't having to rush through slides before heading to labs. That proved to be true, since Aiden let me sleep in a bit this morning while he and Sophie snuck off to the New Children's Museum at Sophie's behest. I have to say this for the kid, she is all about milking her birthday week. It makes me laugh just thinking of Aiden's huge form trying to crawl around on some of the more interactive exhibits with her. It also makes me a little wistful that I couldn't go with them.

Currently, I'm sipping my morning coffee at the kitchen counter, living in a dazed sort of state as thoughts full of vibrant flashes from the day before, hell, the last *several* days (and nights, for that matter) flit through my head. My brain is saturated with thoughts of a deep voice and a hard body that can't seem to get enough of *me*, of all people. If I close my eyes, I can still feel the heat of Aiden's palms at my thighs, hear his low murmur of dirty words that might be becoming my own personal addiction. And sure, the guilt is still there, and I know without a doubt that I should be making plans to find a way to tell Aiden the truth—but it's hard to focus on any of those things when I'm getting dicked down within an inch of my life every night.

I should really get finished up here and start getting ready to leave for St. Augustine's. I need to leave within the hour, and I still haven't dried my hair from my shower, and I have every intention of doing that, really.

If I can manage to stop being distracted by Aiden's texts.

My phone buzzes at the counter as if summoned, and I'm biting back a grin as I swipe it over to read what he's sent.

There's a picture attached of Aiden looking disgruntled as he attempts to step out of a giant inflatable rainbow tube—his big body obviously too much for the children's attraction. I can't help but wonder how he manages to still look so good when he's frowning.

CASSIE

> I'm assuming Sophie took this? You look like you're really struggling.

AIDEN

> I told her I was too big for it.

CASSIE

> We wouldn't want to stifle her inquisitive mind though.

AIDEN

> Hilarious. Have you left for
> school? You're not texting and
> driving are you?

I can't help but roll my eyes at this. It's such a dad thing to ask. Still, I won't pretend there isn't a little flutter in my stomach that he's concerned about me.

CASSIE

> No, Dad. I'm still at home. I'm
> leaving soon though.

AIDEN

> I don't know how I feel about
> you calling me dad.

CASSIE

> Would you prefer Daddy?

AIDEN

> You realize they will take
> me to prison if I get hard
> in a museum full of children
> right?

CASSIE

> Lol good thing for you I
> don't have a daddy kink, or
> I would totally have some
> fun with this.

AIDEN

You're evil.

CASSIE

You'll just have to pay me back later. ;)

AIDEN

Completely evil.

CASSIE

Is Sophie having fun?

AIDEN

A blast. She's kind of shy though. I can tell she'd like to join in with some of the other kids, but I can't get her to take the first step.

CASSIE

She's at a weird age. It can be hard making friends.

AIDEN

I know. I just hate seeing her struggle with it.

CASSIE

You can't force it. It will happen. She's too amazing for it not to.

AIDEN

> You're right.
> Now hurry and get going so you
> don't have to speed.

CASSIE

> Okay, okay. Will do, Daddio.

AIDEN

> Evil.

I laugh as I stow my phone in the pocket of my pajama pants, finishing the rest of my coffee and rinsing the mug before putting it in the dishwasher.

It's funny, really. School used to be a greater source of anxiety; how I would pay for the next semester, if my loans would process, if I'd have to defer for another year—but with the salary I've been getting here, I've hardly needed to think about it at all, this last month. If it continues, this will be the first year of school I can pay for out of pocket without even thinking about student loans.

I don't think I will ever fully get over what this job pays.

And that's another part of this whole thing that makes me feel guilty; that's on *top* of the knowledge that I still haven't figured out how to tell him that this isn't the first time we've been intimate, even if it's the first time he's touched me. There have been moments this week where I've wondered if it should bother me, the fact that I'm receiving wages from the man I'm sleeping with—but I tell myself that the two things are wholly separate. The fact that we're making sure to keep our . . . antics away from Sophie's eyes means it's not *completely* sordid. It's only a slight differentiation, one that probably doesn't offer nearly as much justification as I would lead myself to believe—but it's something, at least.

Still, it's a little wild to think about only having one more year left of school—what should have been two years of grad school turning into four thanks to the wonderful experience of having to work my way through it. It's a complete relief to see it coming to an end, to finally be close to the opportunity to get out there and do some real good, but I won't pretend that it's not a little unnerving, thinking of what I'll do with my life after this. There's a certain pressure that comes with graduation, with getting out into the world and *doing* something that has me reflecting on all the other aspects of my life, wondering where I might be in five years.

Thoughts that are only made more confusing by the distracting man with a dizzying smile thrown into the mix. I know that it's entirely too early to even be *daydreaming* about anything with Aiden Reid, but can I really help it if some part of me is constantly thinking about the possibility of losing all of this? And not just Aiden but Sophie too. And that's the driving factor that keeps me from telling him everything. For the first time in a long time, I feel almost like I belong here, that I'm doing good here, and given that it's the first real family to welcome me . . . is it my fault that I would want to do anything I could to hold on to it a little longer?

This entire line of thought leaves my head a complete mess.

I am not naive to the fact I don't have a lot to offer Aiden and Sophie outside of myself, that there are years and vast differences between us that I can't change—but I can't help but think about his quiet "I shouldn't be thinking about you as much as I do" and its sequel, "I feel like I'm going crazy," and that means something, right?

It's silly of me to pin such notions to something so new, something that neither of us really knows what it even is—but I can't help it, really. It's just that Aiden Reid makes me feel a little crazy too. It's enough to make anyone wonder.

It's enough to make anyone worry about what waits for us at the end of this.

Our labs this time focus on assistive-pediatric-seating equipment, and focusing on the functions and parts of the different types of chairs they've brought in for us to study is a great distraction. I've been testing out the different tilting functions of the Rifton I've been assigned for the last twenty minutes or so, and I think I'm nearly ready to move on to the next model.

"Help me install this harness, would you?" Camila holds up the optional butterfly harness that can be added to this model. "I can't figure out where it clips in."

"Here," I say, holding out my hand. "I think it clips in here."

Camila watches as I find the attachment points for the harness, clipping all four into position until it's properly installed.

"I totally missed that," Camila huffs. "Some of these chairs are a doozy."

"They're amazing though," I say. "There's so much they can do now."

"For real." Camila examines the back of the chair, finding the tilt function and bringing the chair back into its first position. "I think we've got it now, don't you think? Should we move on to the Leckey?"

"No tilt function with that one, at least," I note.

"Right. Looks like that group is almost done with it. We can go grab it next."

We take a seat near the other group who is still studying the different functions of the Leckey, Camila sprawling out next to me in the plastic chair and blowing out a breath. "Just this last year, and we're done."

"It's crazy."

"Do you think the boards are going to be brutal?"

"Probably," I laugh. "But we'll be fine."

"Says you," she snorts. "You're top of the class."

"You're doing just fine."

"How's the nanny gig going? You were acting so weird last time I saw you."

"Oh . . ." I blush, hoping she doesn't catch it. I can't exactly tell her that I've complicated matters further by *sleeping* with the person from my past who *still* doesn't remember me. "Things are great. I really love Sophie, the little girl I nanny. She's . . . a character."

"I told you," Camila laughs. "They can be something at that age."

"You said you had a niece that age, right?"

"Lucia," Camila tells me. "She's a gremlin. Cute little thing though."

I nod absently, watching the other group test the different modes of the chair as my thoughts wander. I can't say why the idea pops into my head; maybe it's just because I'm remembering Aiden's texts earlier about how he wished Sophie had an easier time putting herself out there—but an idea sparks nonetheless.

"Hey, Camila . . ."

She turns to regard me. "Yeah?"

"Do you think your niece would enjoy a trip to the zoo?"

"I sense I'm walking into a trap."

"It's just . . . Sophie, she—she's new at her school this year, and she's had a hard time making friends. I just thought . . . if she could play with someone her own age without all the pressure of being in a swarm of kids at school . . . Is this a terrible idea?"

"For me maybe," Camila snorts. "Didn't I tell you Lucia was a gremlin?"

"Oh, come on. She's *your* niece. She's got to be a *little* cool."

Camila narrows her eyes. "Are you trying to butter me up?"

"Is it working?"

She rolls her eyes. "Unfortunately. *Fine*. You're buying lunch that day, by the way."

"Of course. Anything. This is going to be so great."

Camila is still grumbling even as I'm quietly celebrating my own genius.

The zoo?"

I refuse to be distracted by Aiden in his element, his arms crossed over his chef coat and his apron stained with bits of something or another as the rest of his staff works diligently behind him.

"She'll love it," I urge. "And my lab partner is going to bring her niece, so it will be a great chance for Sophie to get to know someone her own age."

"Don't let her hear you scheming like that," he warns, leaning to peek into his office, where Sophie is still playing on her Switch at his desk. "I mean, I'm fine with it, but are you sure you want to? That's going to make for a long day."

"Of course! It's going to be so fun. Especially for Sophie. Has she ever been?"

"Maybe once when she was smaller . . ." He rubs the back of his neck. "We haven't gotten a chance since . . . well."

"I get it." I reach unconsciously for him, my fingers tripping over the edge of his apron at his waist before I remember where we are. I draw my hand back, clearing my throat. "You could always come with us. Play hooky?"

Aiden laughs, looking back at the flurry of activity behind him. "I think they might stick me in the oven if I tried it."

"Just a thought."

There's a hint of a smile at his mouth when he turns back to me, and his eyes are warmer, making my stomach flutter. "Trust me, that's where I'd rather be."

"Well, I'll send lots of pictures, at least."

"Perfect. Text me a reminder in a bit, and when I have a break, I'll order the tickets."

"Oh, no, I can—"

"I'm getting them," he says bluntly, leaving no room for argument.

My lips twitch. "Well, yes, sir."

"We should probably add that to the list of phrases you can't say to me in public."

I raise an eyebrow, lowering my voice. "You're becoming a regular pervert, aren't you?"

"I think you just bring it out of me," he chuckles.

The fluttering in my stomach is worse now, because I'm not just thinking of this last week together—I'm thinking of all the times he's been even filthier than this in the dark of my room, where I couldn't see his face. I have to suppress a shiver, trying to stow those thoughts away and focusing on Sophie instead.

"I'll go tell her the news," I say.

Aiden laughs again. "Just make sure you don't let her know that it's a playdate. She's liable to kick you in the shins."

"She would never," I protest. "She loves me."

"Don't say I didn't warn you."

I roll my eyes as I stride past the kitchen toward the office on the other side, giving the doorframe a knock as I peek my head around it. "Hey, Soph. Got any plans tomorrow?"

"It's Sunday," she says with a frown. "And I'm ten."

"What do you say to us having a little adventure?"

She tries her best not to look *too* excited, her Switch lowering to her lap as she gives her best impression of nonchalant.

"What kind of adventure?"

"I still can't believe you watched that
last video at work," I laugh.

It's becoming a weird habit of ours—talking for a while after
we Skype. He still watches me come, and honestly, I enjoy it
just a little more when it's him, and isn't that silly?

"It was worth it," he murmurs. "Although,
my coworkers might disagree. They probably
think I have stomach issues now."

I can't help but laugh again. I adjust the mask on my face,
my fingers lingering there as my teeth worry at my lower lip.

"I'm trying to imagine it," I answer quietly. "It's so
weird that I don't know what you look like."

"It is." I hear him clear his throat. "But then again, I don't
know exactly what you look like either."

"Kind of weird," I chuckle nervously,
my heart rate quickening.

"Yeah," he chuckles softly. "Weird."

He doesn't ask me to take off the mask, which is a good thing.

Because right now I can't say that I wouldn't do it for him.

CHAPTER 15

Cassie

This is a really lame adventure," Sophie comments from the passenger seat of my car.

I huff out a sigh. "Just give me a minute."

I try to crank the ignition again, hearing that fatal rumbling whine as the engine of my old car tries its best to turn over for a few seconds before it sputters and gives out again.

"Come on," I groan. "Don't do this to me."

"Does it need gas?"

"It has plenty of gas."

"What about oil?"

"What are you, a mechanic?"

Sophie shrugs. "Just trying to help."

"I know, I know. I don't know what's wrong with it. It probably just hates me."

"How are we going to get to the zoo?"

I drop my head on the steering wheel, sighing as I think. "We could call an Uber."

"It's a peak time," she says casually. "They'll take forever."

I cock an eyebrow in her direction as I lift my head. "How do you know about peak times?"

"Mom didn't have a car," she says. "We always Ubered if it was far."

"Okay. What about the bus?"

Sophie makes a face. "The bus?"

"You've never taken the bus?"

"It's hot."

"Well, I'm not seeing many other options. My friend Camila lives on the other side of the zoo. By the time she could get out here, we'd waste half our zoo time."

"We could call Dad."

And let Aiden hear about how shitty my car is? No, thank you. Knowing him, he'd probably try to leave his car here from now on and take the bus himself. It would be just like him to do something like that.

"We don't want to bother him."

"But I want to *go*," Sophie whines.

"I know that, but if we can't Uber, and you won't take the bus, I don't see how we'll be able to—"

I pause, an idea striking me. It might be a bad one, since I've only just begun to win brownie points with the person I have in mind, but I think to myself that this could be a chance to earn more, if I play my cards right.

"Hey, Soph," I say, turning to flash her a grin. "What time does your aunt's shop open?"

Thanks for coming to get us," I say again as we climb into Iris's car. "You're really saving us here."

"It's fine," Iris says. "I don't want Sophie on the bus."

What do these people have against the bus?

I decide it's not the time to try to gain the answer to that question.

"And you're sure you won't come with us?"

"I would," Iris says, and I think she actually means it, based on her tone. "But I don't have anyone to cover for me until this afternoon. I only have two other employees right now."

"Wow, that sounds tough. Is it crazy busy?"

Iris nods. "We're getting into the fall wedding season, so we've had a lot of orders. I'm doing my best to keep up with the staff I have. I can't really afford to hire anyone else at the moment."

"I'm sorry," I say lamely, not knowing what else to say.

"It's fine." Iris shrugs. "Just part of it." She eyes me from the side as she pulls out onto the main highway. "Was this your idea?"

"Oh . . . yeah. I have a friend from school who has a niece Sophie's age. I thought . . ." I stop myself, glancing back at Sophie, who is listening curiously. "I mean, my friend asked me if I knew anyone around the same age as her niece that might want to have a zoo day with them."

Iris gives me a knowing look, and then surprises me by actually *smiling*, like she knows exactly what I'm not saying. "That sounds fun."

"Have you ever been?"

"Oh, yeah," Iris says. "Rebecca and I took Sophie when she was, what . . . six?"

Sophie shrugs. "Maybe. I was little. I remember petting a giraffe!"

"We did the wildlife safari," Iris clarifies. "Rebecca was obsessed with the giraffes."

There's a wistfulness to her tone, her expression far away, and I see the minute she catches it, quickly masking her features to that of her usual indifferent look.

"That sounds like a great time," I note.

Iris nods. "It was. I think I have a picture of the three of us somewhere with a giraffe."

"I'd love to see it sometime."

Iris eyes me again. "I'll try to find it next time."

Next time.

Iris and Sophie start chatting about some book Iris left, and I turn my face toward the window to hide my smile. I hadn't planned to see Iris today; I hadn't even thought to invite her to the zoo, which I'm feeling bad about now, but I'm sort of glad that my car was dead this morning. It feels like every time I see Iris, I understand her just a little better. Little by little, I know I'm slowly chipping away at her armor.

It's become my own personal mission at this point.

The rest of the drive goes smoothly, and Iris even promises to text me that photo when she finds it before she drops us off. I take it as another victory. The entrance to the zoo is bustling even on a Sunday, and it takes us a good ten minutes to track down Camila and Lucia outside of it even while texting each other constantly.

"Finally," Camila says when she finds us. "Thought we'd lost you."

I glance around. "It's busy today."

"Yeah, Lucia was acting like she was going to die if we had to wait anymore."

The little girl who has the same midnight hair and dark brown eyes as her aunt makes a face at Camila. "I didn't say that."

"Uh-huh," Camila scoffs. "Oh. Yeah. You're Sophie, right?" Camila bends to offer her hand to Sophie, who takes it to shake gently. "This is my niece, Lucia. I promise she isn't as mean as she looks."

Lucia rolls her eyes. "I'm not mean."

"Hi," Sophie says, looking shy.

Thankfully, Lucia doesn't seem to have a shy bone in her body, pointing to the drawstring bag Sophie has slung on her back. "Is that an *Encanto* backpack?"

"Yeah." Sophie nods. "I got it at Disneyland."

"Lucky! Me and my mom are gonna go next year. Did you see Mirabel?"

Sophie's eyes light up. "Uh-huh! And Bruno!"

"Oh my God. Did they—"

The pair of them huddle closer as they continue to gush, and we follow them toward the ticket booth as Camila flashes me a wry smile. "I don't think we're going to have to worry about those two."

"Praise to the family Madrigal," I laugh.

"Hardly. If I have to hear that damned song one more time, I'll—"

"So, you don't talk about Bruno?"

Camila narrows her eyes as we get in line to show our tickets, shaking her head. "Now it's lunch *and* a snow cone."

Lucia and Sophie are practically best friends by the time we make it to the Lost Forest, our plan of attack being to try to make one big circle so that we can catch everything before we get back to the exit.

Sophie presses her nose to the glass to get a better look at the hippos, *ooh*ing appreciatively. Lucia is busy reading the information panel.

"It says that hippos kill up to five hundred people a year," Lucia reads, not like she's shocked, but like she finds this fascinating.

Sophie looks back at her with disbelief. "Hippos?"

"What," Lucia snorts. "Do they sit on them?"

"No," Camila sighs. "Look at those tusks! They'd make a shish kebab out of you."

"Yuck," Sophie says. She looks down the way. "Are we close to the kangaroos? I want to see the kangaroos."

Camila checks the map. "They're on the way back in the Outback. We have a little ways to go before we get there."

"Did you guys know," I cut in, "that male kangaroos are called boomers?"

"What?" Sophie's nose wrinkles. "No way."

"No, no," Camila sighs, shaking her head. "I'm sure it's true. She probably read it off a peach tea lid."

"Oh, and koalas." I snap my fingers. "They sleep like twenty-two hours a day."

Camila rolls her eyes. "Can you please start drinking Dasani like a normal person?"

"Nope," I laugh. "I'm addicted." I notice Lucia and Sophie are both huddled near the glass now, and I pull out my phone. "Hey, kids. Turn this way. Let me get a picture."

Lucia throws her arm around Sophie, who looks mildly surprised for a moment before returning the gesture and smiling big, and my chest squeezes with a happy sensation as I snap a few photos. I immediately busy myself with sending one to Aiden, knowing he'll get a kick out of Sophie and Lucia hitting it off so well.

With the picture I add:

CASSIE

> They're practically besties and we aren't even halfway through the zoo.

"Are you sending that to Dad?"

I notice Sophie eyeing me, and I nod. "He wanted lots of pictures."

"Tell him he has to come next time," Sophie says. "I want to tell him about how the hippos murder people."

I grimace. "Maybe we leave that part of the trip out."

I feel my phone buzz, looking down to see what Aiden's response is.

AIDEN

> That's amazing. It looks like everyone's having a great time.

And then only a second later:

AIDEN

> I really wish I could be there with you guys.

My stomach clenches as my face splits into a grin involuntarily. I have no idea how one text can make me so happy. Then I remember who it's from. I tap out a reply without thinking.

CASSIE

> **It was a bitch getting here, but it's worth it. Sophie is having a blast.**

His reply is instant.

AIDEN

> What do you mean? Did
> something happen?

Oh. Shit. I still haven't told Aiden about my car.

CASSIE

> Oh. Well . . . my car was acting
> up this morning.

I decide telling him Iris brought us here is probably a conversation better had in person.

CASSIE

> We can just Uber back . . . or
> take the bus.

AIDEN

> No. I'll come get you. Just tell
> me what time.

CASSIE

> You don't have to. I know how
> busy you guys are.

AIDEN

> I said I'm coming. Just tell me
> what time.

CASSIE

> Okay, okay. Bossy.

AIDEN

> See you then.

It's silly to still be grinning over this, but I can't help it. I wonder if I should tell him that I kind of like him bossy.

Camila is looking at me strangely when I look up, and I quickly mask my smile into a more casual expression. "You guys ready to move on? I think we're close to a few cafés. We can grab some food."

"I'm *starving*," Lucia whines.

"Yeah, yeah," I chuckle. "Let's get you gremlins fed."

I pointedly ignore the way Camila is still eyeing me.

Camila blessedly waits until after lunch to comment, when the kids are both distracted by the pandas.

"So . . . what's Sophie's dad like?"

"Hm?" I try for a blank face. "Oh, Aiden? He's . . . great. Really nice."

He also has a filthy mouth and a dick that defies science, but that's probably not a good thing to mention right now.

"Uh-huh."

"What?"

"You said he's single, right?"

I roll my eyes. "What does that matter?"

"Oh, I don't know . . ." Her grin is mischievous. "Most people don't giggle at texts from their boss. Made me curious."

"I did not *giggle*," I protest.

"Sure you didn't."

She walks ahead of me to trail after the girls on the Panda Trek, and I fidget nervously as I follow. Is it really that obvious? I have to do a better job of keeping things under control. I sidle up beside Camila, not looking at her.

"It's not what you think," I say.

I mean, it is, but I doubt that's something I should be openly sharing with people.

Camila gives me an innocent look. "I wasn't thinking anything."

"Oh yes, you were," I huff.

"Is he hot?"

"*Shh.*" I glance up a few feet to where Lucia and Sophie are still chatting excitedly. "What does that matter?"

"So, he is," Camila laughs. "Whew. And you're living with him? Please tell me you're hitting that."

"*Oh my God,*" I hiss. "Can you be any louder?"

"I haven't had a date in months," she says. "You know what our schedule is like. Honestly, good on you for finding dick with our workload."

"It's not *like* that," I say again, but it sounds feebler this time.

"Hey, no judgments here," Camila assures me. "Sophie's a cool kid. Her dad has to be pretty cool too."

I chew at the inside of my lip, turning my head to watch Sophie's smile, grinning when she catches me watching and gives me a little wave that I return.

"She is a really cool kid," I agree.

"Much less of a gremlin than Lucia."

I elbow Camila. "Lucia is great."

"Yeah, yeah, she's all right."

I hesitate a moment, wrestling with the desire to tell someone *something* and knowing I should keep my mouth shut. I let several more steps pass in silence as it weighs on me, and then I let out a slow breath.

"Her dad *is* really great," I say quietly.

Camila's grin is slow, but she leans into me conspiratorially, stealing my move as she elbows me in the side. "Yeah, I bet he is."

B y the end of the day, the entire group is exhausted. We've had more than a normal human's fill of lions and tigers and bears (oh my), and by seven o'clock, we're all just ready to go home.

"Are you sure you don't want me to take you guys home?"

I shake my head at Camila. "It's so far out of your way. Aiden said he'd come get us."

"He's late," Sophie grumbles beside me.

"Seriously," Camila tries again. "It's not a big deal. Just text him and tell him that—"

"Oh, there he is," I say, spotting his car approaching the drop-off point.

"*Finally*," Sophie huffs.

Aiden's car comes to a stop at the curb, and he puts it in park before stepping out of the driver's side to lean on the hood. "Sorry I'm late," he offers. "Traffic."

He's still in his chef coat, so I know he came straight here from work and that he'll probably even most likely have to go back—and why does it make me warm all over again that he would put everything on hold for us?

Lucia and Sophie are hugging goodbye, and I can hear them talking about exchanging friend codes on the Switch, but it falls to the wayside when Camila leans in to murmur in my ear, "Jesus Christ, Cassie. If you aren't hitting that, then you should be arrested."

I bark out a laugh. "That doesn't even make sense."

"It's a crime against humanity. Think of the rest of us. Swamped. Overworked. Dickless."

"Okay, we are leaving now."

"I'm just saying—"

I throw my arms around her neck for a hug. "Thanks for today. It was great."

"Apparently the kids are ride or die now, so we'll have to do it again."

"Right."

Camila lowers her voice again. "And I *sincerely* hope that you have locked down that dad di—"

"Okay, girls!" I pull away from Camila. "Time for Sophie and me to go. But we'll hang out again soon, okay?"

They both nod and hug goodbye again, Sophie waving back at Lucia as I help her in the car.

"I really am sorry I was late," Aiden says again as we all buckle up. "I should have left a little earlier."

"It's fine," I assure him. "We weren't waiting long."

"I'll have to head back for a while after I drop you guys off."

"I figured," I say.

Aiden looks in the rearview mirror as he pulls away from the curb. "Did you have fun today?"

"*So* much fun," Sophie gushes. "Did you know that hippos murder people?"

I groan, and Aiden gives me a strange look from the side.

"Don't ask," I say. "Don't ask."

help Sophie out of the car when we pull up outside of the house, making sure she has her bag of souvenirs before she starts up the walkway. She turns back to look at me halfway. "Are you coming?"

"Just a sec," I call after her. "I need to tell your dad something."

"Okay, but you promised to do the kangaroo puzzle with me."

"Yeah, yeah, we're going to do the puzzle."

I wait until she disappears through the front door before I crawl back into the passenger's side of the front seat, pushing over the middle console and cupping my hands to Aiden's face to pull him in for a kiss. There is a moment of surprise on his part that dissolves quickly, and then I feel his fingers in my hair and his tongue at my lower lip before it dips inside to touch mine.

I kiss him *hard*, much harder than feels appropriate for the inside of a car in the middle of the street—but I decide I don't care. I had a phenomenal day with a phenomenal kid, and now I'm being carted home by a phenomenal man who lets me attack him with kisses out of nowhere.

Things could be a lot worse.

He looks a little dazed when I break away. "What was that for?"

"Because you're great."

He blinks. "I am?"

"Very."

"Are you trying to entice me to bail on work? Because it's working."

My lips curve against his, and I press another soft kiss there. "Later," I promise. I crawl backward out of the car, and I notice he's frowning when my feet touch the sidewalk, my hand on the door. "What?"

"You really might be evil," he grumbles.

I give him a sly grin. "Good thing you know where I live, Mr. Reid."

I think I can still hear him grumbling even after I shut the door.

You sent @lovecici
 a $50 tip

I sent you a new toy. I want to watch you use your mouth and imagine it's my cock.

CHAPTER 16

Aiden

Returning to work is a lot harder with the sensation of Cassie's lips still against mine, but I manage somehow. The restaurant is still as busy as I left it when I slip in through the service entrance, and Marco looks like he's at the end of his rope, running to meet me with a frazzled look.

"We're out of shallots."

I rear back. "How the hell are we out of shallots?"

"Inventory error? I don't fucking know. But we just used the last of them in a poulet au vinaigre, and I have two more orders for it waiting."

"Why does it feel like I'm going to be yelling at Alex tonight," I sigh.

"He's out sick," Marco says. "So unless you want to yell at him over the phone . . ."

Fuck.

Maybe I really *should* have played hooky for the rest of the night. I could be putting together a puzzle at home with the girls right now.

The girls.

It takes me by surprise, the way my brain instantly lumped them together that way. I don't know when I started to think of them as a package deal, waiting for me at home, but I *do*, I realize. And it's getting increasingly more aggravating that I have to spend so much time here away from them.

"Um, hello," Marco says, waving his hand in front of my face. "Why are you smiling like that? You're creeping me out."

"Nothing," I say, collecting myself. "Do we have yellow onions?"

"Probably." He turns to yell at one of the line cooks to go check before turning back to me. "Think we can use them as a replacement?"

"It's likely they won't even be able to tell. Just add a little bit more garlic. That's the best we can do."

"Shit. I didn't even think of that," Marco tuts. "That's great. God. I'm glad you're back. I was about to have a breakdown."

I clap him on the shoulder, chuckling, "It's going to be fine."

"Fine," Marco echoes dumbfoundedly. "Who are you and what have you done with Aiden Reid?"

There's still a ghost of a smile at my mouth as I reach to grab for a clean apron, tying it around my waist as I ready myself for the rest of a busy night. Strangely, it feels less daunting than it did when I walked in.

And I know it's one hundred percent because of *the girls* waiting on me at home.

———

We don't get the doors to the restaurant closed until after ten, and Marco assures me that he and the others can handle breakdown since I had to come in earlier today. Normally I would fight him on this, but with the possibility of catching Cassie still awake back at the house . . . it doesn't take much convincing to get me to duck out.

I think it's because she and Sophie have weighed so heavily on my mind tonight—their day together, the fact that I couldn't be there—maybe that's why I decide to call the owner, Joseph, on my way home. It doesn't take long for him to pick up, his voice ringing through the car speakers after only twenty seconds or so. Normally I would worry about calling someone at this hour, but Joseph is a notorious night owl.

"Aiden? Everything okay?"

"Oh, yeah. Everything's fine."

"Easy night, I hope?"

"Mild shallot disaster, but nothing we couldn't handle."

"Yellow onions?"

I laugh. "Yeah, yellow onions."

"Always does the trick."

"Actually . . . I was calling about something else."

"Oh?" I can hear him rustling around, no doubt settling deeper into his favorite leather chair that he likes to smoke in. "Everything going all right?"

"Yes, everything is going great, it's just . . ."

"Well, spit it out, boy," he laughs. "I've never known you to be tongue-tied."

"I was considering the possibility of handing off some of my duties to Marco. Lessening my workload a bit."

"You're not thinking of quitting are you?"

"*No*," I stress. "Of course not. I love it there, and I love working for you. It's just that . . . ever since Sophie came to live with me full time, I've really started to realize just how much I've missed out on her life. It's more obvious when I'm seeing her every day, when I'm reminded every day of how much I'm *not* seeing. Does that make sense?"

"Of course it does," Joseph says, and I sigh in relief. "You know I will work with you however I can."

"I would of course understand if you wanted me to step down as executive chef, or if you needed to cut my wages to make up for the lesser responsibilities—"

"Oh, nonsense," Joseph scoffs. "No one wants that. We can find a way to make sure you have more time at home without taking you down from the position." He laughs then. "Marco would shit his pants if we suggested it, anyway. Everyone there knows that the kitchen can't run without you."

"I just want to be fair to you."

"Son, you've been fair to me for years now. You've worked yourself to the bone. I always hoped you'd find a reason to start taking some time for yourself. There's no better reason than family."

I nod heavily, my voice feeling thick. "I really appreciate that."

"Now you just need to get yourself a girl, and I can really stop worrying about you."

I'm very grateful that Joseph can't see my face right now. "About that . . ."

"Oh?"

"I was just wondering if I could bring a plus-one to your birthday party in a few weeks."

"Well, lo and behold, I have seen it all. You're coming to the party? *And* you're bringing a date?"

"Well . . . I haven't brought it up yet . . . but I'm hoping that she might like to come with me."

"Trust me when I say, I cannot wait to meet whatever woman has gotten you to take a step back and start enjoying your own life outside of work. She must be something."

My mouth twitches involuntarily. "She is."

"Well, you get on home, and I'm going to get on with the rest of this nice brandy I've just poured myself."

I chuff out a laugh. "Sounds like a fine night."

"We'll talk more tomorrow about your plus-one. Hurry up and ask her."

"Yeah, yeah, I will."

"Night, Aiden."

"Night, Boss."

I feel lighter after I hang up; I had no idea how that conversation might go, but I think it's safe to say I couldn't have imagined it going any better than that. And it really is time, I think. To start stepping back and being more present at home. When Sophie first came . . . everything in my life was such a mess. I didn't know how to be her father and run the kitchen at the same time. And maybe that's still a little true, but . . . I know that if Cassie hadn't shown up, I would still have my head in the sand, too ignorant to even see how much I was making Sophie suffer. Without her . . . I might never have learned how to properly talk to my daughter.

Realizing this only makes me want to get home to her faster.

There's very little that could ruin the good mood I'm in now, but when another call signals on my Bluetooth, and Iris's name pops up on my console display, I find that it's the one thing that comes dangerously close to doing so. I just never know how the conversation will go with her, and that's why it always makes me so nervous.

"Hello?"

Iris sounds tired. "Hey. Sorry to call so late. I figured you'd be breaking things down."

"I actually left early. Decided to head home."

"That's unlike you," she points out.

"Yeah, well, it's just been a long day."

"Did Cassie tell you I drove them to the zoo today?"

This throws me. "You did?"

"Her car was acting up and she gave me a call. Even invited me to go with them."

"Why didn't you?"

"Couldn't get anyone to cover for me at the store." She's quiet for a moment. "She's tenacious, for a nanny."

I can't help but laugh softly. "That's true."

"Listen, it's not something I wanted to discuss around Sophie, but I did feel the need to say . . . that I know Cassie is very pretty and likable. Hell, *I'm* starting to like her."

I feel myself prickle, not knowing where she's going with this. "And?"

"I'm just saying . . . I don't know how any single man could live with her without something happening."

"Iris, I don't know what you're implying, but I don't think this is any of your—"

"I'm not *attacking* you, Aiden," she sighs. "Honestly."

"Then what are you trying to say?"

"I just want to make sure that, regardless of whatever relationship may form between you and Cassie—and I do not want to know what that is—I don't want Sophie to fall to the wayside. Just make sure she's your number one priority, okay?"

I can't help but get a little irritated. "I know that without you telling me."

"Don't get pissy. I just worry for my niece, okay? I just want to make sure she's being taken care of in the best humanly way possible."

"Again, I don't need you to tell me this."

Iris sighs again. "Okay. I'm sorry I even called. It's just been weighing on me. I know from watching them that Sophie *loves* Cassie, it's clear to anyone that's around them for more than a minute, and I just hope that you consider the consequences of Sophie suddenly losing Cassie's presence in her life if you two were to start something up and it goes sour."

This makes me pause. Admittedly, it's something I haven't had time to consider. Mostly because I don't want to imagine a possibility of a future where things between Cassie and me go sour.

"I appreciate your concern," I say tightly, trying to remain civil, "but I can promise you that Sophie has been and will always be my number one priority."

"All right," Iris says. "That's all I wanted to say."

"Okay, well then, if you're done—"

"For what it's worth," she cuts in, and I feel myself tense in waiting. "I really do think she loves Sophie very much. I think she's good for her."

I keep quiet for several seconds, considering that.

"So do I," I answer finally.

Iris hangs up to leave me in the silence of the car, left with all the things she's said and the new possibilities that I hadn't considered. I absolutely *haven't* thought about what it might mean for Sophie if Cassie and I were to suddenly fall apart, knowing deep down that it would devastate Sophie if that were to happen, just as much as I'm realizing it would me.

I grip the steering wheel tighter.

All the more reason to make sure that doesn't happen.

The house is quiet when I step through the door; Cassie's room is dark and it's well past Sophie's bedtime, so my first assumption is that I'm the only one up. I'm still a little rattled by Iris's call, and that might be why I bypass Cassie's room and clod up the stairs wearily in search of the fridge. Maybe a beer will help calm my thoughts.

So it's a surprise when I step onto the landing to be met with the soft light glowing over the oven—Cassie leaning over the sink with a spoon in hand as she eats directly out of an ice cream carton. I've caught her in midbite, the spoon perched at the tip of her tongue as she licks the last of the sweet treat away, and it's like a Pavlovian response, the way my cock twitches at the sight of it.

She smiles around her spoon. "We have gotta stop meeting like this."

"It is becoming a habit," I murmur back, distracted by her mouth.

"How was the rest of your night?"

"Long." I move toward the counter, closing the distance between us. "Exhausting."

"Poor baby," she teases.

If you two were to start something up and it goes sour.

I hate that I'm still thinking about it. This thing between Cassie and me has barely had enough space to breathe, and I'm already worrying about how it might end. Who does that?

"Everything okay?" Cassie sets her spoon in the sink, stowing the carton back into the freezer while I circle the counter to go to her. "You look tense."

I pull her against me, breathing in the scent of her shampoo and letting it calm my errant thoughts. "Just a really long night."

"Oh?" She pushes away, smiling up at me coyly as her fingers tease a path down my sternum. "Anything I can do to help with that?"

I reach to cup her face in my hands, my thumbs brushing against her cheeks. How have I only known her for such a short time? Why does it feel like it would be something unsurvivable if she were to suddenly walk away?

I try to push this ridiculous train of thought far away. "What did you have in mind?"

"Well, I happen to know for a fact that you have a preferred method of being comforted."

I grin against her mouth when she pushes up on her toes to meet me, and the thought of making her scream on my tongue *does* immediately ease some of the tension in my shoulders. "I'd be happy to indulge if you want to hop up on the counter," I murmur against her mouth.

"Oh no," she says sweetly, kissing me again gently. "I was thinking I could return the favor."

"What do you—"

I suck in a breath as she sinks slowly to her knees, tugging at my hips until I'm pressed against the counter, and I brace myself with my hands behind my back.

"Cassie, you don't—"

She's already unbuckling my belt. "You don't think this will make you feel better, Mr. Reid?"

"Fuck," I hiss, tensing when her hand slips between the fabric to palm me through my boxer briefs. "Jesus, Cassie." My head turns back towards the empty living room behind the kitchen island I'm currently leaning against, eyeing the dark landing of the stairs. "Sophie . . ."

"Out like a light," Cassie assures me. "We'll be quiet." She peeks up at me with a flicker of hesitation in her eyes. "Unless you don't want to . . . ?"

My good sense wars with the overriding sensation of Cassie's hands on me, noticing that from the bottom of the stairs, the only thing someone might see if they came along would be my back, given that Cassie is kneeling on the opposite side of the island that hides my legs. It's a bad idea, probably, but then again, I am still finding it incredibly difficult to think with my brain right now.

"Quiet," I murmur back, focusing on Cassie's triumphant grin. "Quick." I swallow. "You're sure?"

"Very," Cassie practically purrs, making my cock twitch under her palm. "Just be still."

She continues to touch me gently, tracing my shape with her forefinger and thumb before she hooks into the waistband. She grabs at the elastic, inching it down until my cock bobs free, already hard just from her light touch. Her fist immediately wrap around me to give me a heavy stroke from base to tip that has my breath hissing past my teeth, her slim fingers gripping my cock and making my blood heat. The way she strokes me slowly is enough to make me unhinged.

"You have to be quiet, Aiden," she says with that same coy smile. She teases the tip with her tongue, just enough to make me gasp. "Can you be quiet for me?"

"Careful," I whisper in warning.

She slides her fist to rest just under the head of my cock, swirling her tongue around it as I shiver, her voice just as soft as mine. "What should I be careful of?"

"You should be careful that I don't actually fuck that pretty mouth."

"You can," she teases, wrapping her lips around me to suck before she lets me go with a wet *pop*. "If you want."

God. What is it about Cassie that makes me lose control? I want to be gentle with her, I want to be as sweet to her as she deserves—but every time she touches me, I seem to devolve into some crude state that can't focus on anything other than fucking her as hard and as deep as I'm able to.

"Then open wider," I urge through gritted teeth. "Give me your tongue."

She keeps her eyes trained upward to keep looking at me when she extends her tongue and flattens it just under the broad head, closing her lips around the tip to swirl around it. My mouth parts as my lashes flutter with the heat of her mouth, and I raise my hand almost instinctively to slide my fingers through her hair, pushing it away from her face just as she lets the head of my cock bulge against her cheek.

I could come from the visual alone, if I really wanted to.

She pushes up on her knees a bit as she grabs my hip with one hand, letting the other fist at the base of my cock as she slowly, *slowly* begins to push her lips down the hard length. Her eyes drift closed as she takes me as deep as she's able—lips meeting her fist as she swallows around the fat head that nestles in the soft warmth of her throat.

"*Fuck*, Cassie," I grind out under my breath. "Just like that. Jesus *fuck*."

My head falls back as my hips jerk, trying to keep still as she draws back up to caress the underside of my shaft. My stomach clenches when her tongue teases the flared lip just beneath the head before giving the tip a light swirl, and I nearly choke when she starts to flick her tongue against the little slit there.

She lets the entire head slip past her lips after, holding it in her mouth, giving me a heavy stroke up and down before releasing me altogether. She offers up some of her saliva to let it drip down on my cockhead, immediately slicking her fist down the length in steady strokes before she pulls me back inside her mouth, beginning to bob her head in time with her still-stroking fist.

"You're gonna make me come in your fucking throat," I say breathlessly, trying and failing to maintain any semblance of control. "That what you want?"

She hums around my cock as her head gives a jerky little nod that only shoves me deeper inside, her nostrils flaring as she breathes in deep through her nose.

I grind my teeth together so hard I fear they might chip. "You want my come in that hot little mouth of yours?"

She moans softly as she pushes down to meet her fist that works the base, and I can see the way her other hand disappears between her legs, the way her wrist moves in a way that can mean nothing else but that she's touching herself.

"Are you gonna come with my cock in your mouth, Cassie?" My words come out harsh and grating as I try to keep my voice low, trying my best to be as quiet as I'd asked her to be that first time. "Your mouth is a fucking dream," I pant, my fingers winding through her hair until I'm half gripping it. "Knew it would be. *Fuck.*"

I fist her hair just above her head, not tight enough to hurt her but tight enough to hold her there—and her hand slips from my cock to reach for my hip, squeezing me in encouragement as she looks up at me through heavy-lidded eyes.

I nod down at her, and then a slow, curious thrust into her mouth—and Cassie just closes her eyes with another soft hum around me. I slide over her tongue slowly but purposefully, pushing deep into her mouth, as deep as I can until I hear the little sounds she makes in resistance, immediately drawing back out as I gauge how much she can take. I repeat the entire process to get a feel for her, my teeth grinding together and my cock painfully hard with the need to come, but I hold on as I do it all again, and *again*—each thrust coming just a little faster than the last.

"There is no goddamned part of you"—I close my eyes as I give her hair a soft tug and tilt her head back as I start to rock in and out of her mouth faster—"I don't want to fuck."

She whimpers when I drive a little deeper—eyes bleary and

wet—but she doesn't shy away. She pushes herself up straighter on her knees, wrist still working furiously as she teases her clit—opening a little wider as my cock nudges at the back of her *throat*.

"*Fuck,*" I rasp. "Gonna come. Are you close?"

She only closes her lips around me in answer, forcing me to feel every wet inch of her mouth as I delve inside again and again and *again*. There's a soft mewling in her throat that is sharp and staccato as it builds and builds, morphing into a quiet moan as her body begins to tremble, one that reverberates around every inch of my cock and pulls me right over the edge.

My breath leaves me in a rush as I grunt through it, holding my cock in her mouth with a heavy press against the back of her head as I spill into her throat. I can feel her swallowing around me, taking everything I give her—stars blooming in my vision from the sheer pleasure of it all.

My ragged breath is the only sound that remains in the quiet kitchen after—my fingers unwinding from her hair one by one as I pull away to let my softening cock fall from her mouth. I help her up on shaky legs as I pull her against my chest, not caring in the slightest that my come is probably still on her tongue as my hand wraps forcefully around the back of her neck to pull her in for a kiss.

Her hands flatten against my chest as I cage her in, kissing her deeply as my heart slowly begins to cease its erratic pounding.

She scratches her nails playfully against my shirt. "Feel better?"

"I don't think they have a word for how I feel," I say with a huff of a laugh. I let my lips slant against hers again briefly before muttering, "How are you so perfect?"

She doesn't answer, but that shy grin at her mouth speaks volumes—at least for me. How am I supposed to get a handle on all the things she makes me feel when she looks at me like that?

"You know . . . if you set an early enough alarm, you could probably get away with sleeping in my bed."

"Is that so." My eyes dip to her mouth. "I can't promise you I'll let you sleep."

Her smile hitches up a fraction as she gives my hand a tug, leading me out of the kitchen toward the stairs. I go easily, because how can I not—thinking about the trouble that I'm in. Because I still have no idea how to make sense of the things I'm feeling, the things I *want*—nor do I have any way to combat the strange worry they bring, the anxieties that come with getting myself deeper and deeper in this thing we've started until we get to a point where I might not survive the end of it. But at this point . . . I'm not sure if there's anything I can do about it—no way to turn any of it *off*.

I know deep down . . . it's too late for that now.

It's also kind of weird just calling you "A."

 I know. I'm not very creative.

I wonder about that too. What your real name is.

 Sometimes I wish you knew.

 I want to hear you screaming it when you come.

CHAPTER 17

Cassie

W hy didn't you bring my girl with you?"

I cock an eyebrow at Wanda. "Oh, so Sophie is your girl now? Have I been replaced by a younger woman?"

"The heart wants what the heart wants," Wanda says with a shrug.

"Right," I laugh. "Sophie doesn't get out of school for a couple more hours."

"Well, boo." Wanda shuffles out of the kitchen to settle down in her chair. "Seems like she had a lot of fun on her birthday. It's all she talked about that day you brought the cake over."

"She had a blast. She'd have worn that princess dress to school if we'd let her."

"I forgot to give her the present I bought her the other day," Wanda says. "Make sure you take it to her, yeah?"

"Just keep it," I tell her. "I'll bring her by again after school tomorrow. Aiden has inventory anyway, so he'll probably be late."

"How are things on that front?"

I keep my face neutral, appearing interested in a piece of fuzz on my shirt. "Oh, you know. They're okay."

"Just okay, huh?"

"Yeah." I manage to pick the bit of lint away, rolling it between my fingers to look busy. "I think it's all going to work out fine. Aiden still doesn't know who I am, so as long as I keep being careful, I think that everything will be—"

"What have I told you about lying to me?"

I look up at her with surprise. "What?"

"I told you, only liars use 'fine.'"

"Oh, that's a bunch of bullshit, and you know it."

"Now, don't think you're so spry that I can't whoop your ass."

I roll my eyes. "Seriously, everything is okay."

"Cassie."

I worry at my lower lip, averting my eyes to the old shag carpet beneath my feet. I think I'm afraid if I say it out loud that it will somehow jinx everything. It's only been a week since we got back from our trip, and every time Aiden touches me (which seems to be any stolen moment he can find the chance to do so), I think that this will be the time he finds out. I've been careful to keep my scar hidden from him, and if he thinks it's weird that I keep avoiding taking off my shirt or that I'm always pulling him into a position that hides my back—he hasn't said anything yet.

"He hasn't figured it out," I say again. "Who I am."

"But something is different," Wanda accuses. "You look more nervous than a prize turkey in November."

"Did you know only male turkeys gobble?"

"Little girl, if you don't tell me what happened right this second . . ."

"I—" I make a frustrated sound, falling back against her couch cushions and grabbing for one of the throw pillows to press to my face to whine her name. "*Wanda.*"

"Oh boy. What did you do?"

I keep the pillow against my face, mumbling into the fabric. "I slept with him."

"What? Can't hear you."

"I *slept* with him," I say louder, peeking over the pillow.

Wanda blinks back at me with an unreadable expression, dumbstruck for a few seconds before she blows out a breath through her lips with a shake of her head. "Well, shit."

"I know."

"Was it good?"

"*That's* your follow-up?"

She raises her hands innocently. "What? If you're going to hell anyway, you might as well enjoy it."

"Aren't you supposed to tell me what a bad idea this is?"

"Oh, it's a terrible idea, but it's also been, what? Like eighteen months since you got any?"

"I told you that in confidence," I grumble.

"If anyone deserves a good trip to Pound Town, it's you."

"Please don't ever say Pound Town to me again."

"You still haven't answered the question. I'm old, Cassie. I need some excitement in my life."

"You get more play than anyone I know."

"I was trying to spare your feelings."

I throw an arm over my face. "It was great, okay? It *is* great. We haven't stopped since we got back from Anaheim."

"Oh boy."

"I know. Am I a horrible person?"

"For which part: sleeping with your boss, or not telling him he used to watch you diddle your skittle on camera?"

"Oh my *God.*"

"What? What do the kids call it?"

"I want to die."

"No, you don't," Wanda laughs. "You know I'm just pulling your leg."

"But you're right. I'm terrible, right? I should tell him the truth."

"I mean, yeah. You probably should. The longer you wait, the worse it'll be, you know?"

"I know that. I do, but . . ."

"But what?"

"I'm scared, okay? I *like* him. He's not just some voice on my laptop anymore, he's *Aiden.* And he's perfect, and I'm afraid of fucking it up and him disappearing again."

That's an understatement. I'm *terrified.* Everything about the last week has seemed like something out of a dream, and deep down, something tells me that if Aiden were to find out what I'm keeping from him, it would all be over. It already happened once, so it stands to reason that it will happen again.

"First of all," Wanda starts. "Nobody is perfect. So knock that off. Second, I don't care if Aiden has two dicks and a seven-inch tongue—he'd be a damned fool to toss you aside."

"Again," I point out. "Happened once already."

"He didn't know who you were," Wanda insists. "And you didn't know him. Not really. You can't plan your whole future just because of one bad day from the past."

"I guess."

"But that doesn't mean you need to be keeping secrets."

I frown. "I knew you were going to say that."

"Because you know I'm right, Cassandra."

"Ouch. Full name. Pulling out the big guns, huh."

"You always think the worst of people," Wanda sighs. "You can't just assume something will go wrong before you give it a chance."

"Well, in my experience, that's exactly how it's been."

"Oh, horseshit. Only when it comes to those garbage parents of yours. And you don't even talk to them anymore. You can't let the bad taste they left in your mouth ruin your whole dinner."

"Well, that's a fun analogy."

"I'm just assuming Aiden is tasty."

"Oh, gross."

Wanda chuckles, shrugging at me. "But am I wrong?"

"You are just entirely too old to be this horny."

"Don't be ageist."

"Yeah, yeah."

"So, are you ever going to tell him? You know I'm right. The longer you wait, the uglier it could get."

"I know that. I know. I'm going to tell him. I am. I just . . . I'm not ready yet."

"You might never be," she tells me. "Doesn't mean you shouldn't do it."

I groan. "Why do you always have to be so right?"

"It's because I'm—"

"Old," I finish. "Yeah, I know."

"Just give him a chance. People can surprise you, if you let them."

"Maybe," I sigh. "I don't know."

"Well, I do," she says forcefully, grumbling as she pushes up from her rocker. "You know why?"

"Yeah, yeah," I huff, waving her off.

"You want a drink?"

"It's two o'clock in the afternoon."

"You think time matters when you pass seventy?"

"I have to pick up Sophie in a bit."

"More for me then," she says.

I watch her shuffle into her kitchen, pulling at her terry robe and belting it tighter around her waist. I'm left staring at the popcorn ceiling of her apartment as she begins to rummage through her fridge. I know that she's absolutely right, that continuing to keep things from Aiden will only make it that much harder when he inevitably learns the truth; it's not like I can keep the scar on my back a secret forever, after all. And given its size and its meaning and that he's one of maybe four people who know it exists—I don't think I can explain it away easily.

You can't plan your whole future just because of one bad day from the past.

I hate that she's always right.

don't tell him that night, or several nights after, and a week later, I'm still vacillating between whether or not I should tell him at all. I could argue that there is hardly time for a discussion like that since all our alone time is filled with secret kisses and touches that make me lose my head, but I'm well aware it's a threadbare excuse at best. How in the hell do I even start a conversation like that?

Oh, by the way, you actually used to watch me touch myself. I thought you liked me, but then you ghosted me. Isn't it funny how we found each other again?

Even in my head it sounds ludicrous.

I'm frowning at the coffee maker on this particular morning, watching coffee drip into the pot while my thoughts are far away, and it's probably for that reason that I don't hear him coming down the stairs. I don't realize he's there until I feel Aiden's arms sliding around my waist to pull me against a solid body, and I can't help the silly grin that forms when I feel his lips at my throat.

"Good morning."

"Sophie . . . ?"

"Still passed out," he tells me. "I just checked."

"Someone's getting bold," I tease.

"Mm. Addicted, maybe."

"I call that job security."

He pulls away from me laughing. "Hysterical."

"What do you want for breakfast?"

"Whatever it is, we better start now before Sophie wakes up, or we'll be having pancakes again."

"I think you're just sore that she doesn't like *your* pancakes."

"I've cooked for senators, and I can't satisfy a ten-year-old. How would you feel?"

"Maybe try something else. Even *you* can't mess up eggs and bacon."

I catch Aiden rolling his eyes beside me, and I wink at him before I return my attention back to the now beeping coffee machine. "Go on. I'll make the coffee. You can be the breakfast hero."

"She'll probably hate that too," he grumbles.

"Don't worry. I'll show you how to make them right," I say seriously. I turn on my best Norman Osborn impression. "You know, I'm something of a chef myself."

"Should a Spider-Man reference turn me on?"

"Probably not," I deadpan. "Something is probably seriously wrong with you."

I yelp when he suddenly lands a smack against my ass, grinning back at him while he starts to rifle through the cabinets for a pan. It's moments like this that make it so hard to entertain the thought of telling him the truth, this easy routine between us making it even more difficult to try to find some sort of opening to reveal our history. Things have been so perfect, and don't I deserve a little perfect in my life? It's been ages since I've had any. There has to be some universally accepted perfect-to-shit ratio for everyone.

I *do* hear Sophie when she comes down the stairs, turning to catch her stretching her arms over her head when she reaches the last step, looking just like her dad when he first wakes up. I feel like I shouldn't feel so happy to have noticed it.

You've got it bad, Cassie Evans.

Sophie lurches sleepily into the kitchen to join us like a newly turned zombie, mumbling, "What's for breakfast?"

"Your dad is cooking," I tell her.

She makes a face. "Not pancakes, right?"

"Hey," Aiden counters, sounding offended. "What if I'd been practicing?"

"Have to be a *lot* of practice," Sophie snorts.

Aiden looks at me incredulously with a spatula in one hand and a skillet in the other. "Do you see what I deal with?"

"Oh, poor baby," I coo, pouring a cup of coffee for him. "So mistreated."

He shakes his head, returning his attention to the stove. "Everyone is against me."

Sophie grins at me from the counter, where she's found a seat, and I return it conspiratorially as I grab my own mug. I watch quietly as Sophie and Aiden continue chatting back and forth while he busies himself with breakfast, and again there is that creeping sense of guilt that settles in my chest like a sticky weight. It's something I've never experienced, this warm sense of *family time.* When I was a kid, I was usually making my own breakfast, and more often than not, I did it in an empty house. Is that why I'm so hesitant to screw things up here?

Thinking about it makes my head hurt.

"Cassie?"

I turn too quickly, realizing Aiden is talking to me. "Hmm?"

"I said, how do you like your eggs?"

"Oh. Just however you guys have them is fine. I'm not picky."

"Over easy it is," he decides.

Sophie blows a raspberry. "I like scrambled!"

"Scrambled it is," Aiden corrects.

Sophie leans on her elbows over the counter. "Can we go back to the park after breakfast?"

"You have school today," Aiden reminds her.

"She's off today," I tell him. "Parent-teacher conferences."

Aiden frowns. "I didn't know that. Am I supposed to go?"

"Nope," Sophie says smugly. "I exceed expectations."

Her grin makes me laugh. "She got a note in her backpack that said she didn't need a sit-down. She's making straight As." I cast an apologetic look in Aiden's direction. "Sorry, I meant to tell you."

"No, no, it's fine. Thanks for staying on top of it."

"So can we go?" Sophie looks expectant. "To the park? Please?"

"I don't know," Aiden says with a cluck of his tongue. "I don't know if I can manage the walk while I'm still so devastated about my terrible pancakes."

"You're good at other things," Sophie tries. "Like . . . you always know where the batteries are!"

"Wow," Aiden says dryly. "Suddenly my life has meaning again."

I'm trying to hide my smile behind my coffee cup when he looks at me, feeling my stomach flutter when he flashes me a lazy grin that shows just a bit of teeth. Even after everything we've done, it still takes me by surprise, how effortlessly gorgeous he is; just looking at his mouth is enough to make me flustered. Not for any particular reason, of course. I'm absolutely not thinking about the way his mouth was between my legs last night, that's for sure.

"You know," I tell Sophie, trying to push those thoughts away before I start blushing. "I found a Frisbee in one of my boxes I've been putting off unpacking the other day. I bet we could totally kick your dad's ass."

"Yeah, let's kick his ass."

Aiden frowns. "*Sophie.*"

"Oops." I shoot him an apologetic look. "Sorry."

He doesn't look angry, in fact, I think he's trying not to smile. "Also, you should both probably know that I was on an Ultimate Frisbee team in college."

"Oh, wow," I say amusedly. "I can't tell if that's impressive or sad."

Aiden raises an eyebrow but says nothing.

"Go ahead and go shower," he tells Sophie. "I'll be done with breakfast by the time you finish." He turns to point his spatula at us both. "And then I'm going to kick *both* of your asses at Frisbee."

Sophie giggles as she hops off the barstool, bounding back upstairs to leave us both alone. Aiden flips the bacon in the pan again before he lets the spatula rest at the edge of the skillet, sneaking a glance toward the stairs before he crowds me against the counter.

"What was that about kicking my ass?"

I peek up at him through my lashes, smiling slyly. "Are you worried, Mr. Reid?"

"Not at all," he says with confidence. "With full respect to you and my sweet little girl who I love dearly—I'm going to destroy you both."

That probably shouldn't make me so excited.

"Maybe I'm a secret Frisbee champion? Maybe I played at nationals in high school."

"I don't think that's a thing."

"See, the fact that you don't know about nationals doesn't instill confidence about your skill."

Aiden grins, leaning in to let his nose run along my jaw, distracting me. "Would you be willing to make a bet?"

"Mm." I close my eyes when I feel his lips at my throat. "A bet?"

"Just to make it interesting."

"And what happens when I win?"

"*If* you win," he corrects.

"Keep telling yourself that."

"If you win," he says, his lips tilting against my skin, "I'm going to fuck you on this counter tomorrow after I take Sophie to school."

"Oh?" My laugh is shaky now, his hand curling at my hip and making it difficult for me to keep my mug steady. "Is that a prize for me or for you? What happens if you win?"

He pulls away, smiling lazily as he looks down at me before closing the distance between his mouth and mine. "If I win," he murmurs against my lips, "I'm going to fuck you on this counter tomorrow after I take Sophie to school."

"Wow. Those are some serious prizes. It sounds like I win either way."

"I promise, I'm the winner here."

His lips brush against mine, and my lashes flutter closed as he applies more pressure, my head doing that thing where it goes all fuzzy just like it always does when he kisses me. I feel the warmth of his tongue as it teases the seam of my mouth, opening to let him in as he kisses me in a slow, dizzying way.

"Your bacon is burning," I mumble distractedly.

Aiden sniffs as he breaks away from me. "Fuck."

"Are you sure you're a chef?"

Aiden scoffs as he attempts to save the bacon. "Everyone's a critic."

I'm still smiling as I take another sip from my mug, my thoughts less focused on my guilt after his touch but not gone entirely. It's this that I don't want to fuck up, I think. This easy morning that could become a norm if I let it. I don't want to lose Aiden's touch or Sophie's smile or their cute bickering about pancakes. I don't want to lose any of it.

Maybe it wouldn't matter, my brain hopes. *That we knew each other. Things are different now, right?*

I take another slow sip, trying to push this line of thought down.

I'll tell him, I assure myself.

Although, at this point, I'm trying to convince myself more than anyone.

I should have asked her to do this a long time ago. Seeing her bent over her bed as she fucks herself with the vibrator I bought her—I can see everything like this.

I'm imagining how soft she'd feel if I slipped my fingers inside her, how wet she'd be if I gave her my cock. It's all I think about anymore, and seeing her like this . . . her ass in the air and her pretty pussy fully on display for me?

I might actually be going insane.

CHAPTER 18

Cassie

I'm going to tell him today, I've decided.

I know it's not a good look that I waited yet another day, but it's just that we had such a good time at the park yesterday (I lost at Frisbee, but with the bet we made, did I really?), and then Aiden worked late, and it's just not something I could bring myself to talk about over text. Even face-to-face, there is a good chance he'll get irreversibly angry and tell me to get out of his house, which is something I've been trying to brace myself for, but deep down I know it isn't something I could ever be prepared for.

I've been pacing around the living room while Aiden takes Sophie to school, running through every possible outcome in my head. In some versions, Aiden is confused but understanding. In others, he is so angry that he can't even look at me. And in the more delusional possibilities—he's even *glad* to have found me again.

But that seems unlikely.

I have to tell him though. Today. Before he can get back here and distract me with his kiss and his touch and all that comes with it. I know if I let him touch me, I'll lose my resolve, even if something in the back of my brain begs that I keep it quiet just a little longer, because what if today is the last time he ever does? It's something I don't even want to consider, but I know that I have to.

And I can live with that, if it happens. Or at least, that's what I'm telling myself. I did it once, right? Sure, it was shitty, but I got over it. Mostly.

You know it's different now, my brain whispers.

And that's the crux of it all. Aiden is no longer that faceless person who turned me on and whispered to me in the dark. Now, he's this person who seems like so much more than I deserve, with his nice smile and his pretty eyes and his addictive laugh. Now, Aiden is dad jokes and forehead kisses (Sophie) and secret kisses (me) and sweet, filthy words whispered in the dark that are murmured directly in my ear rather than through my computer speakers. He's *real* now, and that means it will be a thousand times harder to get over him.

I've been going over my speech in my head, trying to hammer out exactly what I'm going to say so that I have a fighting chance of convincing Aiden that I had no idea about our history before coming here, and that I've only kept it from him since learning about it for fear of how he might react. Surely he can't fault me for that, right? It's reasonable for me to react the way I did. It feels like it is in my own head, at least.

Fuck.

This is going to be a disaster.

My phone buzzes on the counter a foot away from where I'm pacing, and I'm so on edge that it actually makes me jump before

I snatch it up. There's a text from Aiden waiting for me on my lock screen, and I slide it open to check it as my stomach twists more into knots.

AIDEN

On my way back.

Even as nervous as I am, there is still a bit of fluttering underneath all the anxiety, because despite my determination to sabotage his plans, I'm still thinking about the alternative course of action where I just keep my mouth shut and let Aiden make good on his promise to fuck me on the countertop.

You have to tell him.

I really, really, hate doing the right thing.

After a round of wearing a Cassie-sized path into the living room carpet, I step over to the kitchen sink to run some cold water so that I can press it to the flushed skin at my cheeks and neck, trying to calm my nerves even as my heart starts to pound in my chest with building anxiety. I had thought about calling Wanda for courage, but I'm afraid that if I talk to anyone else before I go through with this, I might break down from the stress of it all. I reach for the towel hanging on the handle to the oven door to dry my face, closing my eyes and taking deep breaths to try to calm my racing heart.

I have no idea which part of this mild panic attack I'm experiencing causes me to miss the door opening downstairs sometime later—but it means that I actually *jump* when I feel Aiden's arms sliding around me, pulling me back until my ass is flush with his hips and kissing my neck.

"*Jesus*," I gasp. "You scared the shit out of me."

He laughs against my throat. "Wasn't trying to sneak up on you."

His hands are already sliding up and over my waist, my lashes fluttering when he cants his hips, revealing that he's already hard.

"Wow, someone is impatient."

"I've been thinking about fucking you on this counter since the other night," he murmurs, still kissing my neck.

I close my eyes. "I guess that's what inspired the stakes you laid down for the Frisbee game you cheated at."

"Catching the Frisbee isn't cheating."

"It is when you're gigantic."

"I'm sorry." I feel his hand slipping under my shirt to palm my stomach, teasing the waistband of my shorts. "Can I make it up to you?"

My mouth tilts up slowly, getting lost in his touch. "Mmm. Maybe."

Wait. No. This is what we wanted to avoid.

I turn suddenly, trying to put some space between us so I can focus but finding myself caged in by his arms now as he braces them against the counter behind me. "Aiden, actually, I—"

"Is someone trying to back out of our bet?"

Christ, he still thinks I'm playing around. Playful Aiden might be my kryptonite.

"No." I press my palms to his hips, going for a gentle push but distracted by the brush of his cock against my thumb through his sweatpants. *Be strong.* "That's not it—"

His head lowers, his lips feathering against mine. "Because I won fair and square, Cassie," he utters sensually.

"I know," I manage.

He only has to lean in a *little* so that the shape of him, hard and wanting, slots between my thighs, and a shiver passes through me.

"And I'm *going* to fuck you on that counter."

I am not strong. I am so not strong.

I can sense it happening, can feel the way I'm forgetting all about what I resolved myself to do—losing my sense of focus when his mouth slants against mine. My eyes drift closed as his tongue slips inside, teasing me with its softness that is a stark contrast to the hardness between my legs. I slip into it so easily that I hardly even notice his hands finding my ass, hoisting me up against him in one fell swoop before spinning to set me on the kitchen island behind us.

And he never stops kissing me, not for a second.

Fuck it, I think distantly. *I'll tell him after.*

I try not to think about the fact that that decision might make this the last time he touches me like this.

He takes me by surprise all over again when he spins me, maneuvering my body until I'm lying over the counter on my stomach, my toes pressing against the tile. His hands grip my waist to hold me steady, leaning his body over mine, his breath washing against the back of my neck.

"Hold on," he says roughly, a satisfied growl tearing out of him when I reach to grip the edges of the countertop.

His hands slide over my hips, dragging my shorts down my thighs slowly—humming softly when he's got me in only my pale pink cotton underwear that is covered in cartoon cats.

"More print," he laughs quietly.

He grips me through the fabric, squeezing my ass roughly as I wriggle in his hold. His fingers slide between my legs, and I know he must immediately be able to feel how wet I am already. The cotton is practically soaked through even though he's barely touched me, and he rubs his fingers there slowly as a soft moan slips out of me.

My legs are trembling when he finally drags my panties down my thighs as well, leaving me bare and waiting and *so open* for him. He pushes a finger inside, and then another, holding me by the hip to keep me steady, giving me just enough to work me up but not enough to completely satisfy.

"Aiden," I hear myself whine. "Can you—"

"In a minute," he mutters huskily. "I want to look at you."

I'm completely exposed like this, maybe more than I've ever been with Aiden given that it's the middle of the day in the middle of the kitchen at the fucking counter where we eat *breakfast*. But I still can't seem to rustle up any embarrassment for my compromising position. Not with the slow slide of his fingers in and out of me, careful, like he's memorizing the way I feel around then.

"You're so pretty here," he whispers reverently, pushing his fingers deep to make me gasp. "So soft."

I turn my face against the granite to peer back at him, and his expression is heady, eyes transfixed between my legs as he continues to tease me. I catch it when he finally draws his hand away, slipping his fingers into his mouth, his eyes meeting mine to hold my gaze as he licks any remnants of me away.

I don't think anyone would judge the way I've started to squirm needily, not with the way Aiden is looking at me.

I'm still watching as he pulls himself out, grabbing my hips to hold me still and sliding his cockhead between my folds. I'm struck again with the idea of how on display I am like this when he starts to push inside, warmth flooding deep into my stomach because I know that he can see *everything* like this. And he is watching . . . *intently*.

I can feel every inch of him pressing slowly inside, and through hooded lids I continue to watch as Aiden's lashes flutter, his teeth pressing against his lower lip as he fills and *fills* until my ass is wriggling against his pelvis, my toes skirting along the floor as he holds me suspended.

I'm so *full* of him. It makes it hard to think.

He pulls out carefully, drawing it out, making sure I feel every inch as he goes. It's a little faster when he pushes back inside, Aiden hissing between his teeth as he bottoms out just to repeat the process all over again, each thrust coming harder than the last. The way he has me bent at the waist means I feel each one even more so than usual, that each one hits just a bit deeper. It's as frustrating as it is delicious.

"I can't—" I feel breathless now, my eyes screwed shut and my mouth slack as I focus on the sensation. "I can't touch myself like this."

"Are you asking me to?"

"*Aiden*," I pant.

He dips into me a little harder. "I want you to ask me," he grunts. "Ask me to make you come, Cassie."

"Aiden I swear if you don't"—I cry out when he fucks me more roughly, my body jolting against the counter—"fucking *touch* me."

"I will." He chokes out a laugh, pushing up my shirt just a bit and sliding his hands over the smooth expanse of my lower back before leaning to kiss my spine. "I just want to hear you ask me for it."

His fingers tease over the top of my thigh, tracing a line down the inside and lingering as he draws it back up inches away from where I need him. But my focus is suddenly zeroed in on the hand that strokes my back. My heart begins to pound for reasons that have nothing to do with his cock inside me, knowing that if he pushes up my shirt just a little more—he'll see everything.

His fingertips skirt just below my bra strap, his other hand still teasing between my thighs even as he continues to stroke into me at a steady pace. "Ask me, Cassie."

"Fucking *touch* me," I grind out, my pulse pounding in my ears in both pleasure and fear. "*Please.*"

He hums against my skin, obliging instantly and dipping his fingers between my legs to find the little bud of my clit. I moan when he rubs it, my body practically sighing in relief when the palm at my back slides back down to the safer zone near the base of my spine.

Thank fuck.

He finally pulls it away altogether to wrap it around one of my hips, gripping me there as he works me steadily, as he fucks me *unsteadily.* He's thrusting deep now, his body curling until his breath pants against my spine and his skin is slapping against mine. I can tell by the way his hips begin to stutter that he's close, can hear it in the soft groans that escape him.

"It feels so good when you come," he huffs. "*So good.*" He slides deep, rolling his fingers against my swollen clit. "It's better than anything I've ever felt."

His words wash over me, making me burn hotter, and I can feel that sweet pressure building between my legs, anticipating the moment when it bursts into an allover pleasure.

"Right there," I breathe. "Don't stop."

His fingers are slipping against my clit with the way I'm soaked, but he keeps rubbing me in that same spot that makes me whimper for more. "Never."

My fingers clench and unclench at the edges of the counter, and my back attempts to arch even though I have no room against the hard surface, and the *sounds* that leave my mouth are breathy, deep, *needy*—and then I feel it.

It starts with a trembling inside, a spasming of my inner walls that is only made more intense by his cock, which still continues to rock into me. He lets out a loud, guttural sound as he pushes deep one last time, and he doesn't withdraw, doesn't *move*—just sheathes himself and allows my quivering body to pull him over the edge.

His cock twitches heavily, filling me—filling me with his come, his warmth, *him*—and he's too heavy to be covering me like he is, but I don't mind it. He feels so good pressed against me, his big body molded against mine as his mouth wanders. My nape, my throat, my jaw—any bit of bare skin he can reach.

"Good thing you're so bad at Frisbee," he huffs against my hair.

I puff out a breath. "With stakes like yours, it didn't matter either way."

"True." I catch his soft chuckle, and he shudders against me as his forehead rests against my spine. "I don't want to pull out of you."

"Sir, that's how people get UTIs."

He barks out a laugh. "Sexy."

"Proper vaginal health is *very* sexy," I stress. "Besides, if you don't, I'll be dripping all over the—"

We both freeze as the doorbell sounds, struck for a moment like maybe we imagined it. But then it rings again—and it's like a switch has been flipped, Aiden pulling out of me with a hiss and wince as we both make a comically mad dash to make it look like we *didn't* just fuck at the kitchen counter.

Aiden gives me a frazzled look as he pulls up his sweatpants. "Are you expecting someone?"

"No," I scoff, situating my panties. "Are *you?*"

"I have no idea who that could be."

"Maybe it's the mailman."

"Well, let me—" He tugs his shirt from the waistband of his sweats where it's tucked inside. "Then I'll—"

"Fuck." I make a face. "I'm leaking."

Aiden pauses what he's doing. "I shouldn't be turned on by that, right?"

"Not right *now* you shouldn't," I snort, waving him off. "Go get the door while I use the bathroom."

"Give me a second, and I'll come help you clean up," he says with a sly grin.

"*Go,*" I laugh.

He turns to hurry down the stairs as the doorbell goes off again, and I make for the opposite direction to duck into the half bath just off the kitchen. I shut the door behind me and breathe out a heavy sigh, a laugh chasing after it as adrenaline rushes through me. I know that there's an entire floor and a front door between where we were and whoever is waiting on the front porch, but the way my heart jumped into my throat when the doorbell rang felt like actually being *caught*, and my entire body is still thrumming with energy from the surprise of it.

I clean myself up quickly before Aiden can come in after me and make good on his promise to "help"—I've been exposed quite enough for one day, thank you—still laughing under my breath as I wash and dry my hands before going back out into the hall. I make it about five feet before I hear her voice, my laughter dying on my tongue as that same rush creeps back inside but darker, trying to brush it away as I remind myself there is *no way* that she could have any idea what we were just doing.

I see the face that matches the voice when I step back into the kitchen, Iris sitting on one side of the couch in the adjoining living room as Aiden sits tensely in the chair opposite it. She looks up when she sees me, smiling in a small but noticeable way, and that's a good sign, right?

"Hey," I greet, keeping my tone casual. "When did you get here?"

"Just now," she answers.

"Oh, sorry." I try for a smile. "I was in the laundry room. Didn't even hear the doorbell ring."

I don't miss the way Iris's eyes move between Aiden and me, but I do my best to ignore it.

There's no way she could know.

Her eyes cut to Aiden. "I was surprised you were both here. Don't you work out in the mornings?"

"Oh." Aiden shrugs nonchalantly. "Not every day."

God. We are not good at subtle.

I pad over the kitchen tiles to the fridge, opening it up to grab a water bottle. "Did you want anything, Iris?"

"No, thank you," she calls. "Actually . . . I just came to see you."

I pause by the fridge. "Me?"

"Yeah." She almost looks embarrassed. "I just remembered us talking the other day in the car . . . about those photos?"

"Oh!" I shut the door to the fridge hastily. "Right! The ones of you and Sophie and her mom?"

"Right . . ." She reaches into her purse, rifling around for a moment before pulling out a thick photo envelope. "I went ahead and ordered some prints of a bunch of random photos on my phone." She holds it awkwardly for a moment as I make my way to the living room before finally turning slightly to offer it to Aiden. "And you, too, I guess. I don't know. You might not have wanted this many."

"No, this was so sweet," I gush, reaching to snatch the envelope from Aiden, who still looks a little stunned. I open the flap and am met with a much smaller, much toothier Sophie, her cheeks round as a beautiful woman hugs her from behind. "Oh my God. Look at baby Sophie. She was such a little doll." I pause, noticing Iris watching me. "Rebecca was beautiful."

"She was," Iris agrees.

"Oh, shit, sorry." I hand the envelope back to Aiden, remembering myself.

He takes it gingerly, still looking a little out of sorts. "This was . . . really nice of you, Iris."

"I can be nice," she says tersely. Her lips press together before she adds, "Sometimes."

Aiden actually laughs, shaking his head. "Yeah, I guess so."

"Seriously, thank you for bringing them," I say.

Iris shrugs. "I had time, and I was in the neighborhood. It's no big deal."

"Right," I say with a smile. "Well, I'm sure Sophie is going to love going through these."

Iris's eyes soften, her lips turning up ever so slightly. "I hope so."

"You know, you could—"

I'm interrupted by the trilling of a cell phone, and it takes Aiden several seconds to recognize that it's his. "Oh. Sorry." He pushes up from the chair, moving into the kitchen to grab it from the counter, where he must have tossed it earlier. He frowns at the screen before casting us an apologetic look. "It's work. I'll take this in the other room."

I nod back at him before he disappears down the hall, presumably toward the laundry room, almost forgetting my train of thought before my eyes fall on the envelope of photos Aiden left in his chair. I move across the living room to settle into it, picking up the envelope and looking back inside to thumb through the pictures.

"Anyway," I try again. "I was going to say that you could come back after school. When Sophie is home." I peek up to gauge her expression. "If you wanted."

I wonder if there will ever be a time that Iris isn't taken by surprise by me trying to include her. "Really?"

"Aiden will be at work, so we usually eat something simple for dinner, but you're welcome to join us. We could go through the pictures? I'm sure Sophie would love having you there to tell her about the ones she was too young to remember."

"That would be . . ." She trails off, her eyes searching my face in a daze before she swallows. "That would be great, actually."

"Good." I flash her a smile. "Sophie and I usually get back around four . . . and dinner is usually between five and six . . . so, just whenever you want to stop by."

"That sounds great," she says again, still looking like she's processing.

I nod. "Terrific."

There's a moment where we both just sit in silence—me holding the envelope and Iris looking at me like she's trying to figure something out, but after a minute, maybe, she shakes her head as if clearing it, making a move to stand. "I'd better get to work," she says hastily. Her voice is thicker than it was a moment ago. "I can probably be here around six, though, if that's okay."

"That's perfect," I tell her. "Sophie will be so excited."

Iris looks up at me after gathering up her bag, a small, cautious smile at her mouth. "I am too."

"Perfect." I realize I'm just grinning like an idiot, and I shoot up from the chair. "Oh, let me walk you out."

"No, it's fine." Iris waves me off. "I know where the door is." She shuffles her weight from one foot to the other. "But I'll . . . see you guys later."

My tiny victories feel like they're piling one on top of the other to make for one *large* one, but I tell myself it's too soon to be getting excited. Iris is like a doe. You have to be careful with her.

She gives me a hasty goodbye before rushing down the stairs, and I don't settle back into the armchair to start flipping through the pictures until I hear the door shut behind her. I don't even realize for a bit that I'm still grinning.

"Did Iris leave?"

I turn to see Aiden coming back into the room, and I nod. "Just now." I jut my chin out smugly. "*But* she's coming back for dinner to hang out."

"Seriously?" Aiden scoffs as he shakes his head. "How in the hell did you make best friends with Iris in like a month when we've been butting heads for a year?"

"I'm told I'm very charming."

His lips twitch. "Are you?"

"How else would I ensnare a professional cook?"

He breaks into a full grin, rolling his eyes. "Hopefully this isn't some sort of long con. I might wake up without a kidney and find out Cassie isn't even your real name."

It's a joke, and I know that, but apparently that's all it takes for everything to come crashing back. In all the excitement, I'd completely let myself push aside all my worries from this morning, let myself get wrapped up in Aiden's touch yet *again* without coming clean.

And now we're alone again, and I'm out of excuses.

If he notices the shift in my mood, he doesn't immediately say, pulling his phone from his pocket and checking the time as my smile falters.

"By the way, Aiden, I wanted to—"

"Shit," he mutters. "I'd better hurry."

I blink. "What?"

"That was work that called," he sighs. "Some sort of oven-related disaster happened during prep. I have to go see what the damage is."

"Oh . . . boo."

Try to sound more disappointed. Don't make it so obvious that you're relieved.

"I know." He shuffles over to lean down, brushing my hair away from my face before pressing his lips to my forehead. "I'm starting to regret my career path."

"But you love being a cook," I say seriously.

This only makes him smile wider. "One of these days, I'm going to make you regret all the teasing."

"Say less," I laugh.

It's still there, that worry in my stomach that comes with knowing that I should be spilling my guts right now, but I assuage my guilt with the reasoning that it would be a bad idea to broach this conversation when he's got one foot out the door. Something like this will take more time to hammer out, I tell myself. It's better to wait.

Although if this is for his benefit or mine, I can't be sure.

"Oh. What were you going to say?"

"Nothing," I say after a beat, trying not to sound like I'm not sinking back down into an infinity pool of anxiety. "I was just wondering when you might be home tonight."

"Hopefully not too late." He ducks lower, his lips hovering near mine just before he kisses me. "Knowing you're waiting up for me will make the night more bearable."

It wouldn't, I think. *Not if you knew the bomb I'm going to drop on you.*

"I'll be here," I murmur back.

Another quick peck at my mouth, like he can't help himself. "I'm going to change."

"Okay."

I don't exhale until I hear his footsteps fading up the stairs, left with a melting pot of emotions that are equal parts our present and our past and everything in between. I'm realizing now that the more time I wait to tell Aiden everything only means more time wrestling with the anxiety that comes with it, knowing I have hours ahead of feeling this way before I find out whether or not Aiden will hear me out or kick me out of the house once he learns what I have to say. And now I've added an extended visit with the aunt who is only *just* starting to warm up to me, realizing I will have to bottle all of this up until she's gone.

I sink down into the chair with a sigh.

It's not even ten in the morning, and I could already use a drink.

Well, if you want to hear something REALLY crazy . . . sometimes I get jealous of everyone else watching you.

Do you think that's weirder than me getting excited every time it's just you and me?

I may be biased, but I don't think that's weird at all.

Did you know you're the only person I've ever shown my scar to? Does that make you feel any better?

It's a start. Being the only one to ever see you naked would be another.

CHAPTER 19

Cassie

Pretending that I was A-OK with Sophie and Iris this evening had been a real struggle. Sophie thankfully had a bonding experience today with a girl who was interested in Sophie's Disney birthday trip, so going over every facet of that conversation had been Sophie's main focus for most of the evening. I was genuinely happy to hear about her potentially making a friend, and if I hadn't been so nervous about what I had to do when her dad gets home, I might have even suggested taking her out to celebrate. Then there were the pictures, and since Iris had been the one recounting all the memories that were attached to each photo, I was able to mostly just sit nearby and listen to Iris remember it all.

It had been a good night, outside of my inner turmoil. It's one that I could see myself making more of a thing, having Iris over.

Well, if I even get to after this. It could be my last night here, for all I know.

Don't think like that. There's still a chance this will work out.

I've been doing assignments to keep myself preoccupied ever since Sophie went to bed, realizing after I logged into the portal that I've let myself get a lot more behind than I meant to this last week. And as if I haven't experienced enough stress today, I even missed a deadline entirely, meaning that I now have my first failing grade. I know that one failed assignment isn't going to get me kicked out of the program or anything, but it sure doesn't help my current mood.

I did get that drink; I had to wait for Sophie to completely pass out to get it, but the very large glass of wine from the bottle that I can't pronounce, which tastes like it is worth more than I get paid in a week, helps take the edge off. I pilfered it from Aiden's wine fridge, so if this night goes south, it might be another nail in my coffin. Doesn't stop me from drinking it though.

For the last hour, I've been watching the front door from the settee by the stairs, where I'm lounging with my laptop, every car passing by outside making me perk up as I wonder when Aiden will get home.

I'm wearing the same pink shirt that has gotten us into trouble a few times; it's probably cheating to try to arouse memories of, well, *arousal* at a time like this—but I figure working whatever angle I can in my favor can't hurt. Like Aiden will somehow be so distracted by my tits that he will forget that I've been lying to him for weeks.

Not lying, my brain corrects. *It's just an omission.*

Because that's a huge difference.

I take another slow sip of wine, letting it swish in my mouth for a second before I swallow it. It's dry and a little bitter, but the taste of it helps keep me awake. The screen of my laptop is starting to blur as my eyes burn with fatigue, and I reach to rub them with my fingers as I stifle a yawn. You'd think with all the anxiety

I'd be wide awake, but it seems to be having the opposite effect. I've been so up and down with worry today that my body seems to be revolting. I would guess that all the late nights I've spent with Aiden recently haven't exactly helped the situation, either, but I can't find it in me to complain about that.

I shut my laptop and put it beside me before I reach to set my glass on the little side table nearby. I stretch my arms above my head afterward, my neck cracking as I turn it this way and that. My phone puts the time at just after eleven, and I know that Aiden could walk through the door at any moment.

God, maybe I *should* have called Wanda.

She would have probably known the perfect thing to say. That, or she would have just told me to take off my shirt as more of a distraction. It could have gone either way. She'd probably be proud of me for wearing the thinnest bra I own tonight. Me on the other hand . . . Yeah. Still feels like cheating.

I sigh as I reach for my wineglass again, holding it near my mouth as I stare at the railing that lines the stairs, getting lost in my own thoughts and contemplating the worst possible outcome. I've always been of the mind that if you *expect* disappointment you can never be disappointed, so maybe that's why I'm playing out in my head what the worst ending looks like.

Worse comes to worst, Aiden tells me he doesn't feel comfortable keeping me on as the nanny, let alone as his . . . whatever I am to him. (How pathetic is it that I'm just now realizing we haven't even defined what the hell we are.) Worse comes to worst—Aiden will tell me that I will need to pack up my things tomorrow, he'll cut me a nice severance check (he seems the type), and then he will escort me out of his house and out of his life. For the *second* time.

Don't be dramatic. He didn't even know your name then.

I shake my head as I bring the glass to my lips again, closing my eyes as I tip it back to try to down the last little bit of red liquid.

Now, I'm not actually drunk; I'm hardly even *tipsy*—so I can't say why I would choose this moment to be clumsy. Maybe it's the nerves, or maybe it's just the soul-crushing stress I've been under these last couple of days . . . I don't know. Regardless, my glass chooses this moment to miss my mouth, the last of the wine dribbling over my bottom lip and spilling all down the front of my shirt.

"Shit."

The damage is done; apparently there was a lot more wine left in the glass than I realized. (Why did I have to choose the largest one in the cabinet?) My shirt is soaked through from tits to navel, and when I stand up quickly to avoid getting any on the settee, I realize that I'm dripping all over the tile.

"Great," I mutter, turning to set my glass back on the side table. "Perfect."

I have my shirt over my head before I can second-guess it, and it isn't until I'm down on my knees mopping up the bit of wine that's dripped on the floor that the full hilarity of this situation hits me. Wasn't this exactly how I'd found Aiden that night I'd waited up for him? He'd called it stupid then. What a damned pair we make.

I'm swirling the sodden cloth on the tile even as my breasts and belly are still damp with lingering drops of wine, cursing my luck as I clean up my mess so I can hurry and change before Aiden gets home.

But my luck with meeting Aiden in any capacity has proven to be mostly shitty in the past, and this is no exception. Hearing the keys in the door at that moment leaves me too stunned to move, left frozen on my hands and knees with an open mouth and a wine-stained shirt in my grip. He steps through just like he always does, hanging his keys on the hook and slipping off his shoes at the door, and it takes him a second to notice me there, gawking back at him.

"Cassie?"

I suddenly forget how to speak, still staring at him. The cold air on my back feels like a scary thing now.

He takes a step closer. "What happened?"

"I spilled my wine," I manage, pushing up so that I'm resting on my knees to keep my back hidden from him. "Soaked my shirt."

"Wow," he laughs. "And your first instinct was to tear it off? I think you've been spending too much time with me."

The closer he gets the more panicked I feel, and I scramble to a standing position as fast as I can as he closes the distance between us. He's still smiling at me as he runs a finger over the damp skin of my breasts, and my voice is lodged in my throat as I think about nothing but escaping.

This isn't how I wanted to tell him.

"I should go get another shirt," I try, sidestepping away from him.

Aiden's arms encircle me, pulling me against him. "Just so I can take it off of you again?"

"Oh, I—"

My heart is rattling around in my ribs, so loud I find myself wondering if he can hear it. It's the first time I've ever been shirt-less with him that I wasn't on my back or on top of him—in total control. Something I don't feel like I am right now. In control. His fingers are sliding up my spine to climb higher, and with every inch I find it harder to breathe.

"Aiden, I need to talk to you."

He hums softly, bending to let his lips skirt along my jaw. "About?"

"There's just"—he makes it hard to think when he kisses my neck like that—"something I've been meaning to tell you."

His hands are so close now, and I know any second he's going to feel it, and then I won't have a chance to ease him into this like I'd planned. I bring my hands between us to press against his chest gently, warring between wanting to bring him closer and knowing I should push him away.

"Aiden, I—"

Fuck.

I can feel it, when he goes still. It's curious at first, his touch—his fingertips tracing the edge of my scar like he hasn't quite figured out what it is. I feel his hand flatten against the entire shape of it, no doubt feeling the difference in texture between my scar and the rest of my skin.

"Cassie, what's—?"

I do push away from him then, looking down at my feet since I'm having a hard time looking at him. I know this could be it, that after this he might never smile at me again, and why does that feel so devastating all of a sudden? We've only known each other for a short while, only given in to these urges for only a few *weeks*—so why does it feel like this could be the end of something important?

"I should have told you as soon as I realized," I mutter quietly at the floor. "I didn't—at first I didn't know how, and I was afraid to lose my job, and I *know* that I should have said something after we had sex, but I just . . . It's awful, I know, but I was just so afraid you'd disappear again, and it just felt so shitty the first time, and I realize this all sounds pathetic, but—"

"Hey."

I finally look at him then, feeling his hands at my shoulders as he brings his face level with mine.

"Cassie, what are you talking about?"

There's genuine confusion in his eyes that blends with actual concern, like he has no idea what I'm talking about. And why would he? I'm barely making any sense. I can feel my eyes growing wet as I feel genuine fear for whatever is about to happen, but I take a deep breath, knowing it's still the right thing to do.

I turn slowly, trying to keep my back straight so I don't look as pitiful as I feel, staring at the wall of the alcove by the stairs as I wait for him to say something. It takes seconds, or maybe hours, I can't be sure, but then I feel his hands at my skin, tracing again. Maybe he's trying to place it. Maybe he doesn't even *remember* it, and right now that almost feels like it might be worse. Being such a blip on his radar that he doesn't even *remember.*

His voice is impossibly soft when he finally says something. "You were making dinner."

He remembers. I shouldn't be excited that he remembers.

"Because I was home alone," I whisper back.

"And you accidentally pulled the pot of boiling water onto yourself."

I can barely hear myself when I answer, "I couldn't get out of the way in time. I caught it with my back."

"I . . ."

I'm shivering, but I don't think it's the air-conditioning.

"Cassie, are you—?"

I can only nod.

He's quiet again after that, impossibly quiet. I want to look at him, but I'm too afraid to. I'm too scared to find out what look he'll be wearing when I do. Disappointment? Anger? I don't know which would be worse.

"How long have you known?"

I swallow. "Since I saw your scar."

"So, the entire time that we've been . . ."

I nod again.

"*Jesus,* Cassie. How could you not tell me?"

I shut my eyes tight. He definitely sounds angry. "I was afraid."

"Afraid of what?"

"It's just . . . you disappeared so suddenly back then, and I thought—God. I guess I was naive. I thought you actually liked me, and that you actually wanted to meet up. So when you were just . . . *gone*, I just—" I blow out a shaky breath. "I didn't want to have to go through that again. Especially now that I . . . know you. It would be so much shittier now."

"Were you ever going to tell me?"

My eyes fly open, and I can't help it then, turning to face him so that he can hopefully see the sincerity in my face. "Yes! I was going to tell you tonight. I was going to tell you *today*, actually, but then you . . . um, distracted me, and there was all of that shit with Iris, and you had to go to work, and I just thought we needed to have an actual conversation about it, and—"

I go quiet, finally noticing his expression. It's angry, to be sure, and confused, sure, but I notice that there is none of the emotion I had been most afraid to see.

Disappointment.

Aiden doesn't look disgusted, or put out; sure, he looks like he's mad that I let him in my bed so many times without telling him the truth, but somehow it doesn't feel as dire as I thought it would be.

"I'm sorry," I say quietly. "I should have told you sooner."

His eyes are still hard. "Yes. You should have. I still can't believe you didn't."

"I know." I look down at my feet again. I'm still half-naked and covered in fucking wine. This couldn't get any worse. "I know. I'm sorry."

I'm still staring at my toes while I wait for him to say something, feeling my pulse pounding in my ears as I wait and see whether Aiden will choose to try to talk this out with me, or if he'll ask me to leave. I'm not ashamed of my past, and I won't let someone make me feel like I need to be, not even Aiden—but damn if it won't hurt if he turns out not to be who I thought he was by trying to make me feel that way. Then again, I did keep things from him, so maybe he would be justified? I don't know. It's making my head hurt, and at this point, I wish he'd just get it over with.

Whatever "it" is.

CHAPTER 20

Aiden

I'm too stunned to say anything. Of all the things I could have imagined coming home to, this wasn't even in the immediate vicinity of possibilities.

I know that she's waiting for me to open my mouth and say something—staring down at the floor with resigned defeat as if she's already made up her mind that I'm going to push her away over this. I can't pretend that I am not angry that she kept it from me, but probably not for the reasons she might think. I just hate the idea of her putting herself through hell with worry when she could have been honest with me. I even understand, I think, all the reasons why she didn't. After wondering where she went for so long, even now, would I have also been hesitant to chance her disappearing again?

I thought you actually liked me, and that you actually wanted to meet up.

That's the part that's sticking out to me. All this time I assumed that it was *me* who had misunderstood things. Has she spent all this time thinking the same thing?

I didn't want to have to go through that again. Especially now that I . . . know you.

Had she felt as disappointed when I pulled away as I had been when I thought she'd done the same?

"Cassie, I . . ." I feel a bit calmer now but no less dumbfounded. "I did like you. I *did* want to meet up."

She finally looks at me, and I hate that her eyes are wet because of me. "What?"

"I didn't mean to disappear," I explain. "When it happened . . . I had just found out that Rebecca died. That month was insane. I was worrying for Sophie, and making arrangements, and trying to figure out how to restructure my entire life. By the time I was able to pull my head out of the water and breathe again, weeks had passed by without me realizing it. And when I came back to apologize . . ."

"I'd deleted my account," she whispers.

I nod solemnly. "I thought that I was the one who misunderstood."

I watch her mouth part with surprise, all the pieces clicking together, and I realize none of this had occurred to her before this moment. That she's actually spent the better part of a year thinking that after everything we said, it had all been transactional after all. That I never cared about her like I made her believe. She'd been so afraid, that even now, even after I can't seem to go a day without touching her or without being close to her—I'd toss her aside.

I can't help it; it's the question that's been on my mind ever since I logged back in to find her account scrubbed. "Where did you go?"

"I . . ."

I watch her teeth worry at her lip as her cheeks redden. Her eyes dart away like she's embarrassed.

"I couldn't do it anymore. After you disappeared. I know it's probably silly, but . . . I missed you, and I thought that you had dropped off the face of the earth, and I just . . ." She sucks in a breath, her eyes still wet. "I couldn't do it anymore."

It all feels surreal. Like any moment I'll wake up in my bed and none of this will have happened. How is it even possible that out of all the people in this city who could have answered my ad it was her? That the one person that Sophie needed most, could also be the one person that *I* needed most, without even having realized it?

"I understand if you need me to leave," Cassie says stoically, her lip trembling. "But I didn't mean to keep it from you like this. I just . . . didn't know how to tell you."

Maybe asking her to leave *is* the sensible course of action. Maybe a more rational man would scold me for not even considering the thought. But regardless of our strange past and our stranger present and everything in between, the thought that bothers me most is Cassie walking out my door and never coming back. It probably doesn't make sense for me to feel that way; we know *nothing* about each other that could warrant me feeling so possessive of her, like I can't let her go, but . . .

It doesn't stop me from feeling that way.

"I don't," I tell her finally, my voice thick. "Want you to leave."

Her eyes are wide when they find mine again. "You're not mad?"

"No, I am," I assert, and when she starts to look crestfallen again, I add, "but not because you kept this a secret."

"What?"

"I'm angry that you dealt with this alone. I'm angry that you spent all this time worrying that I would push you away without giving me the chance to tell you that there is absolutely *no* way I'm letting you get away again."

Her breath catches, and she looks so sweet in this moment; her hair is falling down from her messy bun in pieces around her face, her mouth is parted in a soft, quiet way that begs for me to kiss her, and her eyes—her eyes hold so much relief that it makes something in my chest hurt.

I'm careful when I reach for her, approaching her like a frightened animal that might run, and for all intents and purposes, she could still do that. I notice she's still trembling slightly when my hands cup her jaw, her lashes fluttering closed as her fingers wrap around my wrist. Maybe it's imprudent of me to be as elated as I am to know that it's *her*—that the person I find myself losing all my senses for today is the same person who drove me crazy back then. Her eyes are closed when I lean in, and I can feel that slight wetness at her lashes against my cheek when my lips touch hers.

She tastes sweet. Like wine and something that is inherently Cassie, and I find myself pulling her closer to try to taste more, something that is becoming a habit whenever I touch her. Like no matter how much I have of her, it's somehow never enough.

I feel her fingers sneaking under my shirt, finding the raised skin near my navel as she teases at my scar. It makes me shiver, her touch paired with the knowledge of everything attached to these marks on our bodies—the realization of all I've said to her and all I've seen of her crashing down on me like a wave. How many times did I wish I could touch her like this? How many times did I wish I could find out if her lips were as soft as they looked?

How is it possible that after all this time, I would find the answer to all those questions in such an unexpected way?

I should take her to her room, I know that, but I can't seem to stop touching her long enough to do that. Almost as if I give her an inch she might slip right through my fingers. I push her deeper into the alcove behind the stairs, my hands at her waist and her hips and everywhere else I can reach as her tongue touches mine sending me into a bit of a frenzy.

I dip my head to rest my lips against her shoulder as I urge her to turn, and there is only a hint of hesitation as she obliges, giving me her back as her hands brace against the wall. I let my mouth wander, teasing the raised skin between her shoulder blades in a way that I haven't had a chance to do yet. I feel her shiver as my tongue traces the shape of her scar, her spine curving to bend into the insistent press of my mouth even as my fingers find the snaps of her bra to pop them open. Her back being bare only makes it easier to explore, and if I didn't feel so restless right now, it might even be something I could spend all night doing. I tell myself I'll have time later.

She looks breathless when I turn her to face me again, helping me when I urge her bra off to let it drop to the floor. Her breath is heavy, and for a second I am mesmerized by the rise and fall of her breasts as if begging me to touch them. I hold her gaze when I bend down to slide my lips against the swell, closing my eyes and focusing on the thumping of her pulse against my mouth.

"Your heart is beating so fast."

She bites her lip, pushing her fingers through my hair to sweep it away from my forehead. "Did you know that on average, women's hearts beat faster than men's?"

"Oh?" My lips curve against her breast as I leave another kiss there, messier this time so I can taste her. "Snapple just hasn't ever heard mine when I'm touching you."

She gasps when I wrap my mouth around her nipple, and I'm entranced by the way her lips roll together—the way she looks at me through hooded eyes. I'm wondering if there had been signs I should have picked up on; how many times did I watch her come from the safety of my monitor? It feels like I saw her in every way possible, all those nights, but something about the time we've spent together feels different than it did back then, and I can't help but wonder if it's because it's *me* touching her, rather than herself. I'd like to delude myself into thinking so.

Her skin tastes sweet, too, the lingering flavor of the wine she spilled coating my tongue as I let it swirl around one taut peak. I tweak the other between my fingers as I let one hand slide down her belly, dipping past her shorts to tuck inside her underwear so I can see how wet she is.

Fuck, she's already soaked.

"Is it weird?"

I release her with a wet *pop*, tilting my head up to see her more clearly. "What?"

"I don't know . . . with everything that happened . . ." She lets out a nervous laugh. "I mean, there's . . . a lot of stuff you asked me to do."

My lips tilt as I press my fingers deeper between her legs, curling them to let them slip inside her as her mouth forms a quiet *O*. "I remember everything I ever asked you to do, Cassie."

"Mm." Her hips cant toward my hand as her eyes shut. "I liked it."

"You liked it when I told you what to do?"

She nods lazily. "Mm-hmm."

"I can do that," I rumble. "Why don't you start with taking these off?"

I let my fingers slip out of her to grip the front of her shorts, giving them a tug. When I pull my hand out entirely, rising to my full height to see if she'll obey, I feel a familiar thrill coursing through me. It had been one thing to watch from the other side of a screen as she did whatever I asked her to, but this is different.

This isn't some faceless woman that I'm harboring some ill-advised crush on, this is *Cassie*—warm, soft, *real*. A woman that invades my thoughts more and more with every passing day.

I watch as she reaches to roll her shorts down her thighs, her underwear going right along with them until she kicks them off to let them land on the tile. It's darker here in this little corner, the light over the front door not enough to illuminate her entirely, but I can make out every soft swell and gentle curve, from the fullness of her breasts to the slight slope of her belly and the roundness of her hips that make my palms twitch with a need to touch. The rosy color of her lips match the tight points of her nipples, and I know from experience that both complement the pretty pink between her legs.

Everything about Cassie seems to be designed to drive me crazy.

"I can't believe that I spent all that time wondering"—my knuckles brush over the tops of her thighs as she shudders, and I slide my fingers between them, curving my hand and dragging it higher—"what it would be like to touch you." Her lips part in a quiet gasp when my fingers slide back and forth between her wet folds, and I can feel my cock pressing insistently against my zipper. "I had no idea how much *better* the real thing would be."

"Aiden," she sighs, her slim fingers teasing the front of my jeans. "Take these off."

"Here?" I push deeper, feeling her clench around my fingers. "You want me to fuck you out here?"

Her finger tuck into my waistband, tugging insistently. "*Aiden.*"

It feels like we're in a different moment in time, one where she's waiting on me to give her a cue, like the only thing that matters is whatever I'm about to ask of her. It makes me feel heady and a little out of my mind.

She squeezes me through the denim, and I hiss through my teeth. "*Fuck.*"

"I like it when you swear," she says with a breathy laugh.

"You do?"

She nods.

"Really." I keep pumping my fingers in and out of her, bracing my other hand by her head as I watch her touch me. "Do you want my cock, Cassie?"

There's a noticeable shiver that passes through her, and she barely manages her shaky nod.

I tilt my hips further into her hand. "Well."

She bites her lip as she unzips me, reaching with both hands to ruck down my pants before she teases the shape of me through my boxer briefs. I have to close my eyes when she pulls me out, her hands warm and soft as she drags her fist from base to tip. She pushes up on her toes to let her lips brush against mine, stroking me in a slow back-and-forth that's driving me wild.

"Tell me what you want me to do," she murmurs into my mouth. "You know I'll do whatever you want."

She's slipping into the past with me now, whispering things I haven't heard since she'd said them in a dark room with her face hidden. Just hearing them is nearly enough to make me come all over her hand, but that's not what I want.

"Put your arms around my neck," I urge. I regret the loss of her hand on my cock when she immediately obeys, but I know that inside her will feel that much better. "Hold on to me."

She does what I ask, and I slip my hand from between her thighs to grab her hips, hoisting her up against me and pressing her to the wall as she wraps her legs around my waist. We're close enough that my cock slots between her legs, coating me in her slick heat as I tilt my hips just enough to feel her. I pin her there against the wall and whisper that she hold on tight, reaching toward my back to pull my T-shirt up and off before I drop it to the floor. Her arms are immediately back to hold on to my neck, and it takes hardly anything at all to angle myself enough to slip inside her.

She makes a sound, something between a whimper and a moan, and I lean closer to let my lips whisper at her ear, "*Shh.*" I adjust her so that I can push deeper. "You have to be quiet, remember? Be good."

"Yes—*oh.*" Her heels dig into my ass, her fingers pushing into my hair. "I promise." She's whispering now as if to prove her point. "Keep going."

It only takes a slight bit of movement to root all the way inside her, her hips flush with mine as she trembles with it. I have to take a moment to collect myself so that I don't immediately come inside her—it's always a danger, as good as she feels—letting my forehead drop to her shoulder as I steady her with my hands on her hips.

"You wouldn't believe how much I thought about this," I huff. "I wanted to touch you so bad, Cassie. Then . . . now . . . fucking always."

She kisses at my throat, her tongue licking there afterward. "You can touch me whenever you want."

"Yeah?" I angle my head back to look at her. My hands slide to cup her ass, sliding out of her a fraction only to push back in. "Whenever I want?"

"*Yes,*" she hisses.

I lift her to pull her off of me, enough so that I'm only a little bit inside her before I let her fall back down. "Just like this?"

"*Ah.*" Her head falls back against the wall. "Whatever you want."

"I just"—I grunt as I pull her up and back down on my cock harder—"want you."

"Like that," Cassie pants. "Mmm."

"Can you come like this? Tell me what you need."

"I think—if you—"

She arches to bend back against the wall, so much that I have to hold her hips tighter to keep her upright. It means that every time I thrust into her, I bump against that place that makes her gasp, her body jolting with every slap of my hips, and her legs tightening around my waist impossibly further.

"Right there," she moans, struggling to keep her voice down now. *"Oh*—don't stop."

As if that was actually an option right now.

I can feel her nails digging into my shoulders, deep enough to leave a mark, but the sting barely registers with the way she's started to tense up. I can hear the pops in her toes and feel the trembling of her body, evidence of her tipping over the edge. It's difficult to duck my head so I can suck at the soft swell of her breasts, but I need my mouth on her, wherever I can reach. I feel that pressure building deep while I push into her again and again and *again*—my legs weak and my pulse throbbing under every inch of my skin.

"Cassie, I'm—*fuck.*"

I hold her close as we shudder through it, her breath hot against my ear as I bury my face in her throat. My teeth sink into the supple skin at the bend in her neck to stifle my groan, and she presses fevered kisses against my jaw as I try to come down from the high of it. I hold her close through all of it, unable to let go of her. It only occurs to me that I'm still gripping her tight, buried inside her, when I feel her fingers pushing through my hair while she strokes my shoulder in soothing circles.

When I finally pull away to look at her, the feeling it gives me to see her debauched and mussed and satisfied, smiling at me like I've given her a fucking present—it's indescribable.

"Please consider leaving a tip," she whispers.

I huff out a laugh, dazed at the idea that this is happening and that she is here and that so many things came together to put us in each other's lives again. It still feels like it might be a dream, and maybe I would actually worry that it was, if she wasn't so very warm and so very *real* in my arms. It has me wondering how many days we need to spend together for it to be socially acceptable to entertain the idea that I might be gone for this woman. Surely more than we have, I would think.

And what's even more unbelievable is that even now, even just having had her . . . I already want her again.

"How much sleep do you need?"

She cocks an eyebrow at me. "Really? Again?"

"You did ask for a tip," I say seriously.

Her mouth drops open as she smacks my shoulder, but her eyes say she's more than happy to sacrifice her eight hours. I know reasonably at some point I *do* have to let her sleep; I'm aware of that.

But that isn't going to be anytime soon.

@alacarte

Ⓢ **sent you a $100 tip** Ⓢ

♥

I wish I was spending this to take you out instead. How's that for cheesy?

CHAPTER 21

Cassie

When I notice the sunlight on my face in the early morning, my first reaction is panic. I shoot up in my bed, feeling Aiden stir beside me as I clamor for my cell phone on the bedside table.

Just after seven. Whew.

Sophie doesn't normally crawl out of bed until eight thirty, at least. Especially on weekends. Still, I have labs today, and since Aiden's and my late-night activities prevented me from remembering to set my alarm, I'm a good twenty minutes behind. I yawn as I replace my phone where I found it, rolling my shoulders and stretching as I try to wake myself up. I'd wager we only got four or five hours of sleep last night, and I have sore muscles I didn't even know existed until today, but still. Seeing Aiden sprawled out in my bed, his hair falling into his eyes and his mouth parted softly in sleep—I'd say it's worth it.

Last night had been one of immense surprise and relief; I had been so convinced that Aiden would ask me to leave that his understanding had knocked me on my ass. And what's even more remarkable is his apparent *happiness* to know who I am, who *we* are. It's like a huge weight has been lifted off my shoulders, knowing that there are no more secrets between us. It feels now like maybe we can actually give this thing a real chance. If that's what Aiden wants, that is. I'm well aware that in our frenzied arousal that followed his discovery last night, Aiden and I haven't gotten a chance to talk. That is something I think we'll need to do at some point. I'd feel a lot better hearing that I'm not the only one who is invested in this thing between us beyond just the physical aspect.

I know I'm still behind, and that I should be jumping in the shower, but I feel greedy with him next to me like he is. His body seems too big for my queen-sized mattress, one of his thick arms draped above his head and the other resting over his stomach above the sheets, which are tangled around his hips. There are things more easily noticed in the bright light of the morning that I haven't been able to appreciate during our usual late encounters— things like the soft smattering of hair on his chest that is lighter than that on his head. I let my fingers brush through it carefully as he stirs, not enough to wake but enough to shift his body so the sheet slips further from his waist, leaving him mostly nude.

And I am definitely not complaining about that.

I check the time on my phone again, weighing my options before telling myself that dry shampoo is a thing for a reason. Sure, they probably didn't invent it for the sole purpose of early-morning sexcapades with your long-lost camgirl knight in shining armor, but whatever. I'm careful as I scoot next to him, lightly tracing the bottom half of his scar, which spills out from under his draped arm. I lean in to press my lips there afterward, feeling his skin twitch under my mouth, but his soft snores don't stop.

I smile as I press another kiss lower, right along the relaxed V near his hip, flicking my tongue there as Aiden makes some soft sound in his sleep.

His cock lies heavy against his thigh, and I steal a glance at his face as I run a finger down the length of him, feeling him jump slightly at my touch. His thighs are already parted, one of his knees angled out to one side, so it's not that difficult to wedge myself between them, bringing me up close and personal with the most intimate part of him. He's heavy in my hand when I slide my palm underneath, and even with this I can feel him twitch.

It makes me wonder how much I can get away with before he wakes up.

I'm careful with my tongue, running it along the entire length of him with a barely there touch, and under my other hand that is braced over the top of his thigh, I can feel him tense. I swirl my tongue around the head before I try to take more inside, and I can feel how he's starting to get harder in my mouth. I close my eyes as I push deeper, not able to fit all of him but making up for the leftover inches with my fist as I grip the base.

I don't notice he's awake until I'm pulling back up, my eyes popping open when I feel the weight of his palm on the back of my head. Now, it's hard to smile with a dick in your mouth, so I'm sure I look ridiculous, but I try to make up for it by bringing the flat of my tongue under the head to cover more of him.

"That's—" His voice is gravelly with sleep, his eyes glazed and half-lidded as he watches me. "That's some wake-up call." He's fully hard now, making it easy to kiss along his shaft as he groans low in his chest. "What time is it?"

"Early," I tell him. "She'll be asleep for a while."

His lashes flutter when I slide my tongue back up his entire length. "Okay."

"But I have labs today," I tell him, pumping him lazily with my fist. "So I have to be quick."

One side of his mouth tilts up. "If you keep touching me like that, I don't think time is going to be an issue."

I like the way he watches me when I take him inside my mouth, looking at me like I'm some sort of mythical creature he can't believe he's seeing. It's enough to make any girl feel confident. I bob my head to take as much as I can, still using my fist to work what my mouth can't reach.

He's gentler this time—none of the frenzied roughness like the last time I had him in my mouth, but I'm enjoying this side of him just as much as that one. Idly I wonder if there are *any* sides of Aiden I won't like. The pressure of his hand on my hair is slight, hardly even there, but that, too, is making me feel heady. I kind of like being the one in charge for once.

His head falls back against the pillow, his mouth parting as his breath comes more roughly to spur me on. I can feel every twitch against my tongue, every little press of his fingers against my hair—all of it only making me want to push him over the edge that much more. I can tell he wasn't kidding when he said this wouldn't take long; I've barely had him in my mouth for more than a minute or so, and his breathing has been reduced to a series of ragged pants, and his hips tilt up almost reflexively every time I take him as deep as I can manage.

"Cassie," he rasps. "You should—I'm gonna—"

I know exactly what he's saying, and maybe it's hubris on my part, but I like this. I like it because it feels like he can't help it. I like it because *he* likes it. I could do this as many times as it takes to blow his fucking mind so that he won't even be able to *look* at his cock without imagining my mouth on him.

Although with the way he's panting, I don't think it will take all that much.

His body is impossibly tense now, and his fingers have actually tangled a bit in my hair, but I'm so concerned with the way he swells against my tongue that I barely feel any of it. I work my fist in tandem with my mouth, hearing his stuttered groan before I feel the warm splash against the back of my throat. I try to focus on the sounds he's making, the way his body shakes beneath me, closing my eyes as I swallow everything he gives me. The way he goes boneless afterward is intensely satisfying, and it makes my watery eyes and my lack of breath when I pull away from him all worth it. He looks dazed as he stares up at the ceiling, hardly even moving when I crawl up his body to drape myself across his chest.

"Good morning," I tease.

Aiden blows out a breath. "Alarm clocks are going to seem incredibly lackluster now."

"Job security," I laugh, enjoying my little running joke. I lean in to kiss him, and Aiden doesn't seem put out at all that I just had him in my mouth, pulling me in to deepen the kiss. I give him a softer peck after. "I do have to get out of here though. You cost me my shower."

"I'd like to say that I feel bad, but . . ."

I grin. "Yeah, I'd hate to make a liar out of you."

"I'll return the favor later."

"Oh, absolutely. I have a mental orgasm tally. Don't worry."

"Wow, no pressure or anything."

My smile hitches up another notch, and I give him one last kiss. "I'm supposed to get my car from the shop after class, so I'll pick Sophie up from the restaurant later, okay?"

"They fixed it?"

"Apparently the check engine light is *not* something you just ignore and hope it goes away."

"I really could take you to class, you know," he insists.

It's a conversation we've had a few times since my old clunker gave out on me, and I roll my eyes now just like I have every other time.

"I might be the only person in this house that doesn't hold a grudge against public transportation."

He pinches my ass, and I yelp. "I'm glad it's fixed, at least."

"My slightly less-broken hunk of junk and I will be perfectly fine to come get Sophie after class."

"She'll be anxiously waiting for you to save her, I'm sure," he snorts.

I roll away from him, feeling his eyes on me but not hating the attention, and I cast another look back at him before I head into the bathroom to do a rush job of getting ready. "Maybe today she'll give your pancakes another chance?"

I laugh as I close the bathroom door behind me, hearing him grumbling the whole way.

The rest of my day doesn't go as well as my morning.

The wake-up call I'd given Aiden hadn't officially made me late leaving the house, but since I left later than usual, the traffic jam my bus got stuck in following an accident *definitely* made me late. Between the missed assignment this week and being almost thirty minutes late to my first lab, my instructor had a few choice words to say about getting my head in the game. It colored my entire day, throwing me off in a way that had me dropping things I shouldn't and charting things incorrectly—making all sorts of errors I wouldn't normally make had I not been so rattled.

I'm exhausted by the time I leave campus, my ride back to San Diego seeming much longer than usual. Picking up the car helps—but the hefty bill certainly doesn't. Hell, before becoming Sophie's nanny, this same bill would have meant eating microwave ramen for a week or two.

I'm trying to pull myself out of my gloomy mood by blasting Taylor Swift's entire discography on the drive to the restaurant, but even my Spotify seems to be against me today, playing entirely too much *evermore* and not nearly enough *Red*. It's like the universe *wants* me to cry today.

Fickle bitch, I'm telling you.

I've been to Aiden's restaurant to pick up Sophie a few times now since our first interview, and while the hostess doesn't side-eye me as much about my body spray anymore, she seems to have an opinion on my shoes, if the way she looks at my worn Chucks every single time I step through the doors is any indication. I don't even acknowledge her tonight, giving her a dismissive wave as I head straight for the kitchen. I have to pass through the bar area to get there, but I've developed a good routine of moving around the bartenders while staying out of their way as I push through the double doors that lead into the kitchen area.

Now, I'm fully aware that I'm not in the best of moods right now, but I can't pretend that seeing Aiden in full *executive chef* mode—barking orders to the other chefs and peeking over their shoulders with a discerning look all while wearing that jacket that I shouldn't probably be so attracted to—helps a little. He doesn't notice me at first, too busy criticizing the braising of some meat sitting in a pan that's out of my view.

Sophie is perched on her usual stool in a safe corner near the sinks, waving when she catches sight of me and setting her Switch on the counter before hopping down from her seat. "Can we go home?" She casts a wary glance toward her dad. "Dad is in a bad mood."

It's like we're linked or something.

"What happened?"

Sophie shrugs. "I don't know. Some customer was mad about something."

"Yikes."

I peek back at Aiden, still chiding who I assume is one of his sous-chefs, wondering if it might be better to sneak out and send him a text. I'd hate to make his night any worse. Before I can land on a decision, Aiden finally notices me standing on the other side of the kitchen, and his expression immediately changes as he offers one last word to his sous-chef before coming over.

"Hey," he says, smiling with tired eyes. "How was your day?"

I roll my eyes. "About as good as yours, it sounds like. What happened?"

"Bullshit," Aiden grumbles. "I didn't catch a steak going out overcooked, and it got sent back with a nice note about whether or not we deserve our stars."

"Ouch." I make a face. "They sound like they're a lot of fun at parties."

"What happened with your day?"

I know if I tell him I was late today he'll blame himself, and since it was entirely my choice to hang back and enjoy him this morning, I don't want to make his night any worse with needless bitching.

I shrug noncommittally. "Just a lame day. Nothing in particular."

"I'm sorry," he offers.

I wave him off. "Eh. It's fine."

"Sophie," Aiden addresses his daughter. "Why don't you go get your stuff from the office?"

"Okay!"

When we're alone, Aiden peers at me from the side. "I really want to kiss you right now."

"How gossipy are your chefs?"

"Oh, the entire world would know before you got to your car."

This makes me laugh. "You'd better not risk it then."

Aiden nods like he agrees, but there's a set to his mouth that says differently. His jaw clenches as he hesitates to continue, looking like he's wrestling with something.

"You know," he starts. "My boss is throwing a party next weekend."

I perk up. "A party?"

"For his birthday. He does it every year."

I guess he's telling me that me and Sophie will have a night alone soon.

"Oh." I bob my head aimlessly. "Sounds fun."

"I thought maybe we could go together."

This catches me off guard. "What?"

Shy is a strange look for such a large man but not an unappealing one. "Like a date?"

My mouth parts in surprise. "But . . . what would we tell Sophie?"

"Well." Aiden's hand reaches just enough so that his pinkie brushes against mine, and it can hardly even be called a touch, but it makes me shiver all the same. "I guess we would tell her the truth."

I can feel my heart start to beat faster, a heavy fluttering sensation setting off in my belly at the seriousness of Aiden's expression. "And you're . . . okay with that?"

"She's going to find out eventually," he tells me. "It's not like you're going anywhere anytime soon." There's a flash of uncertainty in his features then, like he's not entirely sure himself but looking for some comfort in this regard. "Right?"

My mouth opens and closes like I'm doing a goldfish impression; I thought that we'd have to talk soon about what we are and where we saw ourselves going, but I never expected Aiden to dive into it headfirst without any hesitation. I've barely had time to wrap my head around the idea, and Aiden is ready to lay all his cards out on the table. It feels a little reckless, and a lot endearing, but ultimately, it's an easy answer.

"No," I tell him. "I'm not."

His smile is brilliant, so much so that it nearly takes my breath away, and I'm experiencing an intense need to kiss *him* now. "So? Do you want to go?"

"Is it fancy? I doubt I have a dress that works."

"Let me worry about that," he urges. "Say you'll come."

I bite my lip as I consider, still concerned about how Sophie will take this news but too elated by the idea of Aiden *wanting* to tell her to even entertain the idea of saying no. Because who am I kidding? There's no way I'm going to do that. Reckless or not, I know that I'm as ready to dive in headfirst as he is. How could I not be?

"Yeah," I tell him. "I want to go."

Another distracting smile for my trouble. "It's a date then."

It's a date.

I've had plenty of first dates before, but I don't think I've ever been on one with a guy I'm already sleeping with. And still I feel a thousand times more excited for this one than any other I've been on. I practically feel like I just got asked to prom.

Sophie comes back before I have time to say anything else, but I think the goofy grin on my face I can't seem to wipe away probably says more than enough. At least Aiden's looks mildly similar, so I don't feel completely ridiculous.

"Can we watch *Encanto* after dinner?"

Normally I might groan—it's a good movie, but we've seen it a dozen times now—but strangely I don't even feel put out. I pat her head with that same smile plastered on my face. "Sure. We can watch it."

"Yes!" She turns to wrap her arms around Aiden. "Bye, Dad. Love you."

"Bye," he answers back, squeezing her into a hug. "Love you too."

Sophie flounces past me, and I give Aiden one last look before following her. "See you later?"

"Yeah." The look he gives me is heavy, the green and brown of his eyes seeming warmer than usual. "You will."

It takes me at least an hour to stop smiling.

*My heart is beating so fast. This could be a terrible mistake.
He could be someone entirely different than he seems to be.*

But that doesn't seem to be deterring me in the slightest.

And he's still waiting on my answer.

"I want to see you too," I breathe. "Really see you."

*I can hear his exhale, rushed, like he'd
been holding his breath.*

*I reach for the mask, but he stops me,
making a sound of protest.*

"But you said—"

*"I want to be able to touch you, when I first see you," he
says. Heat pools in my belly. "Because when I see you . . .
I have a feeling I won't be able to stop."*

CHAPTER 22

Cassie

We don't tell Sophie until the day of the party. It's probably not the smartest thing either of us has ever done, dragging our feet like this, but I think Aiden has been as nervous about her reaction as I've been. She's sitting in the armchair opposite the couch, her fingers steepled under her chin like a mob boss as she regards us thoughtfully.

"So . . . you're like, boyfriend and girlfriend?"

Aiden and I share a look, and I shake my head. That one's all him. "Yes," he answers, clearing his throat. "We're dating."

Sophie looks from me to her dad to me again. "Why did you keep it a secret?"

"We weren't trying to keep it a *secret*," I urge. "We just—"

"Didn't want to confuse you," Aiden finishes.

Her little face is still as blank as an empty canvas. The way she is looking at us is almost enough to make me squirm; it feels like

I'm telling my dad about my first boyfriend, which is hilarious since I know he wouldn't have given a shit. Clearly, telling Sophie is a much more nerve-racking experience.

"I *know* what dating is," Sophie says. "It's like kissing and stuff."

I notice Aiden looks like he'd rather be anywhere else. "And going out together," he says, ignoring that comment. "Like tonight. I want to take Cassie to a party."

"On a date," Sophie clarifies.

"Yes," he says. "On a date."

Her eyes narrow, like she's thinking. She looks like the damned Godfather. Like a four-foot-five crime lord. Or maybe I'm projecting.

"But Cassie is still my nanny. Right?"

"Of course I am," I assure her. "None of that will change."

Her nose wrinkles. "Do you have to kiss?"

"We can try to keep the kissing to a minimum," Aiden counteroffers, even though I'm pretty sure he intends to keep doing it as much as possible out of Sophie's line of sight. "If that makes you more comfortable."

"It's gross," she says, making a *blech* sound.

This makes me laugh. "You won't think that one day."

"Yes, I will," she argues.

Aiden snorts. "Forever, I hope." He regards his daughter carefully then. "Are you . . . okay? With this? It's very important to me that you're okay with all of this, Soph."

"Oh. It's fine." She shrugs. "But if you break up, I get to keep Cassie as my nanny."

"I'm glad to know where I lie in the pyramid of your priorities," Aiden mumbles.

I pat his shoulder, grinning. "Don't you forget it."

"Can I go play my Switch now? I almost beat the boss last time."

"Yes, you can go," Aiden tells her. "If you're sure you're okay."

She moves to leave but turns back with a puzzled expression. "Wait. Where am I going tonight?"

"Oh," I pipe up. "So. If you're okay with it, Wanda asked if you wanted to hang out with her tonight."

Her eyes light up. "Can I spend the night?"

"Sophie," Aiden interjects. "I'm sure Wanda didn't mean for you to—"

"I'll ask her," I cut in, knowing Wanda won't care. I turn to Aiden. "She'd probably love it, honestly. As long as you're okay with it."

He frowns. "If you're sure it wouldn't put her out."

"Wanda will be the first to let me know if so," I laugh.

I shoo Sophie upstairs, waiting until she's gone to lean my head on Aiden's shoulder, grinning up at him. "That was relatively painless."

"Am I the only one who felt like I was in an interview?"

"Oh, no, she definitely had a Don Corleone–vibe going on."

He's still frowning at the stairs where she disappeared. "It's good that we told her, right? I hate lying to her, anyway."

"I think it'll be fine," I assure him. "Sophie's a smart kid. She'd have caught on eventually."

"You're probably right."

I reach to trace a finger down his jaw. "Especially since I don't see the whole 'kisses to a minimum' thing working out very well."

He scoffs. "Are you implying that I can't keep my hands to myself?"

I don't answer, instead looking down and tapping the back of his hand that rests on my knee where his fingers have been unconsciously tracing a circle for the last ten minutes.

Aiden rolls his eyes. "Okay, fine."

"So, I hope you made sure my corsage matches my dress. I expect fanfare tonight."

"Fanfare," he echoes, shaking his head as he laughs. "Well, I didn't get you a corsage, but I did get you a dress."

I push away to raise an eyebrow at him. "How did you know my size?"

"I . . . might have looked in your closet," he says sheepishly.

I clap my hand over my mouth in a dramatic faux gasp. "Oh my God, next thing you know you'll be rifling through my underwear drawer."

"I prefer your underwear on the floor more than I do in your drawer."

I bite back a smile, turning my face down at my lap so he can't see my blush. I trace a circle of my own on the back of his hand that still rests on my knee. "So . . . I'm curious about this dress. What kind of dress would Aiden Reid buy me?"

"Something with a questionable neckline."

I shake my head admonishingly. "Pervert."

"Maybe," he chuckles.

He leans in then as if to kiss me, but I reach between us to cover his mouth with my hand. "Hey, now. Kisses to a minimum."

I squeal when he licks my palm, snatching it away as his hand darts out to grab my wrist so he can tug me closer. He keeps ahold of me while he covers my mouth with his, my teasing protests no match for the softness of his lips. He hums contentedly as he lingers for a moment, only pulling away when I've completely melted into it.

"That'll have to do until later," he murmurs.

It only hits me at this exact moment that *later* means an entire house to ourselves after our first official date, for the first time since I've been here, and seeing the way Aiden is looking at me—I have to assume he's thinking about that fact as well. It takes all I have to keep my voice even when I speak again.

"So," I say in a totally normal way that doesn't betray the fact that I'm thinking about future uninhibited sex. "Let's see this dress."

S top fidgeting," I laugh as we stand outside Wanda's door.
Aiden adjusts his tie (I could probably write an entire essay on why Aiden should wear a tie every day, because holy shit), making that same nervous face that makes me want to giggle every time I look at him. "Why does it feel like I'm meeting your parents?"

"Well, Wanda is closer to that than my actual parents, so. It's not too far off."

"Right. Shit. I'm sorry."

"Bad word, Dad," Sophie chides from beside us.

"I know," he apologizes. "Sorry."

Sophie leans to look at her dad from my side. "Is Dad scared of Wanda?"

"I am not scared of Wanda," he argues.

I nudge Sophie with my elbow. "He's totally scared of Wanda."

"I am *not* scared of—"

Aiden falls silent when the door finally opens, Wanda pulling open the door in her house shoes and her robe and her pink flannel pajamas. Basically the polar opposite of intimidating. Doesn't keep Aiden from standing as stiff as a statue next to me. She smiles brightly at Sophie, who immediately rushes her in a hug, and Wanda leans into it as she pats the little girl's head. Seeing the way Wanda lights up with Sophie makes me feel all fuzzy inside.

Wanda gives Sophie a serious look. "You ready to get whooped in gin rummy tonight?"

"No! I'm going to win this time. I've been practicing."

Wanda looks unconvinced, shooting her a look. "She's got a long way to go before I start dragging her to the casino with me."

Aiden is still completely mute beside me during all of this, and Wanda doesn't acknowledge him at first. Not until she directs Sophie into the house to go find her deck of cards. Sophie gives us a rushed goodbye, but I can tell she has higher priorities than us now.

Wanda's face loses its kindly warmth when she finally turns back to Aiden, her hands moving to her hips as she looks him up and down. "You Aiden?"

He nods stiffly. "Yes, ma'am."

"None of that ma'am stuff. Wanda's fine."

"Right. Wanda. Sorry."

Wanda purses her lips as she taps her foot. "You got a hell of a kid in there," she tells him.

"Thank you," Aiden answers. "She speaks highly of you. We appreciate you watching her tonight."

"Well, since you snatched this one"—she hitches a thumb in my direction—"I could use the company."

Aiden looks like he wants to melt into the floor, and I have to force myself not to laugh. "Sorry about that," he offers. "I, ah, didn't mean to snatch her away."

Wanda looks my way then, whistling. "Look at you," she praises. "That dress makes your ass look like a million bucks."

I tuck my chin, batting my eyelashes at her as I turn to give her my side profile. "Doesn't it? Aiden picked it out."

"Oh?" She peeks over at Aiden, looking amused. "Did he?"

I smooth my hands over the silky black material that hugs me like a glove, patting the roundness of my hips as I nod. "He did good."

"I'm sure he wasn't thinking about your ass at all when he bought it," she teases.

I turn again to peek back at the ass in question. "Pretty sure this doesn't happen by accident."

When I sneak a glance in Aiden's direction, I notice the tips of his ears are red, and I decide to cut the teasing short. He might never take me out again if he thinks this is what he has to look forward to. I try to tell Wanda with my eyes to cut it out, but it doesn't work in the slightest.

"So, Aiden." She leans in to lower her voice. "You aren't still looking at those booby cams, are you?"

"*Wanda*," I admonish. "Oh my God."

Aiden looks about three seconds from short-circuiting, and I can feel my neck getting hot with mortification. He is absolutely never going to ask me out again. Wanda finally smiles as I start silently begging for death, squawking out a laugh as she pats Aiden on the chest.

"I'm pulling your leg, boy," she cackles. "You be good to my girl, all right?"

Aiden nods mechanically. "Yes. Of course."

"She tell you I got a fake hip? If you break her heart, I'll—"

"Okay," I cut in. "We'd better get going. You have our numbers, so, if you need anything at all . . ."

Wanda is still laughing, and I shoot her a look that says I will be tearing her a new hide later. "You kids go have fun," she says, shooing us off. "I got the little terror handled."

"Seriously," Aiden urges. "Call us if you need anything at all."

"Don't worry," Wanda says with a smile. "I got this, Dad."

She gives us a wave as she closes the door, hollering something about shuffling the cards before the door closes behind her. Aiden doesn't immediately move to leave, still looking dazed when his eyes find mine. "I can't tell if she hates me or not."

"Oh," I laugh. "She loves you."

He bobs his head. "Well, okay then."

"Come on," I tell him, reaching for the red silk of his tie and letting it slide through my fingers. "Let's go get your money's worth on this dress."

A iden's workplace looks different when it isn't full of chattering customers and packed tables. The owner has closed most of the restaurant down save for the main dining area, where they've set up groups of tables for the staff. I notice the hostess who is always giving me looks (Aiden has informed me that her name is Laura and that it's just her face) at a nearby table with one of the bartenders, and she gives me a nod when our eyes meet. Maybe even a smile. I can't tell.

Maybe it really is just her face.

The lighting is the usual muted glow that feels romantic, and when Aiden guides me across the space and helps me into one of the fancy chairs that I haven't sat in since our weird first meeting—it fully hits me that this is a *date*. It makes my heart beat faster while I settle into my chair, Aiden taking the one opposite me and giving me a warm smile when he catches me staring.

"What?"

"It's funny," I tell him.

"What is?"

"The last time we were here like this, I almost spit on you."

"It was very cute," he tells me.

"Really?"

"How creepy does it make me seem if I tell you it made me think about your mouth for the rest of the night?"

"Incredibly creepy," I deadpan. "Straight to jail."

His smile widens. "I'll be sure not to tell you any of the other creepy thoughts I've had about you since you moved in then."

"Oh, no way," I protest. "I want to know everything. I already know you're a pervert, anyway."

"But how creepy does it sound if I say I only want to be a pervert with you?"

I blow out a breath, reaching for the little purse I've brought as if going for my phone. "Wow. Yeah. I'm calling the police." Aiden laughs, and I drop the act as I grin back at him. "It's fine. I spent most of that first night thinking about your hands, so we're even."

"My hands?" He looks down at his fingers with a furrowed brow. "What about them?"

"They're very big."

"So?"

"You know what they say about guys with big hands."

He raises an eyebrow. "Wow. Now who's the pervert?"

"I guess we're made for each other," I say with a cluck of my tongue.

His expression softens. "Yeah."

I notice someone approaching our table then, a middle-aged man who can't be any older than fifty, judging by his thinning gray hair. He waves when he catches Aiden's eye as he nears. He's dressed in a black suit and matching tie, more snazzy looking than the other partygoers, and I have to assume this is Aiden's boss. "Aiden! So glad you came. I was sure that you were going to give me the old 'parties aren't my thing' line again this year."

"Ah, well." I notice Aiden flushing. "I thought it would be nice to come out for once."

The man turns his smile on me then, his teeth just visible beneath his thick, graying mustache. "And your lovely date would have nothing to do with that at all, I'm sure." He extends his hand. "Joseph Cohen, dear. I own this old place."

"It's beautiful," I tell him. "I'm Cassie."

"Cassie," he echoes. "How did such an ugly guy land a looker like you?"

I can tell he's joking, noticing the way Aiden rolls his eyes from behind Joseph, and I shrug as I throw up my hands in mock disbelief. "He wore me down. I'm talking poems-outside-my-window level of wooing."

"I have no doubt," Joseph laughs. He points a finger at Aiden. "I like this one." Then to both of us: "You both have fun tonight, yeah? Have some wine. Dance a little. It's my birthday, so I insist."

"I would hate to offend you by not taking free wine," I say seriously.

Joseph chuffs out another laugh. "Exactly." He pats the edge of our table. "I have to make the rounds. Everyone loves a visit from their boss on their off night, right?"

I wait till he's out of earshot before I lean across the table. "Okay. Is that an act, or is your boss cool?"

"No," Aiden chuckles. "He's great. He went out on a limb for me when he gave me this job. I had been a sous-chef at a three star for a couple of years after I got out of school, and I wasn't getting any bites on any of the other places I was applying. Joe walked in one day on a whim, and he liked the food so much that he asked to meet whoever made it. He insisted I come by for an interview, and well, the rest is history."

"He sounds great," I tell him. "Definitely better to like your boss than work for an asshole."

Aiden's mouth twitches. "And you know this from personal experience?"

"Oh, absolutely. My boss is a real hard-ass. Very demanding."

Aiden laces his fingers as he leans in closer. "I'd be happy to be more demanding, if you want."

Warmth pools in my belly, and I have to remind myself we

still have drinks, dinner, and dancing to get through before he can take this dress off me. Not that Aiden seems to have any intention of making the wait easy. I try to look unaffected even though I'm pressing my thighs together now, nodding my head toward the open bar.

"I think you'd better buy me a drink first."

The rest of the night seems to pass by in a blur; dinner is some amazing beef dish that I can't pronounce but melts in my mouth, and after the main course, they bring out a blackberry sorbet that makes me want to live inside their freezer. If we weren't in a five-star restaurant, I'd have probably licked the bowl clean. Joseph comes and sits with us for a while between courses, telling stories about Aiden and the restaurant and all sorts of fun anecdotes in between. At some point a woman starts crooning softly from the overhead speakers, some French song I can't understand, and I watch as people start moving from their tables to find the open floor in the middle of the room.

Now, I'm a twenty-five-year-old woman who has dated and dined and danced on more than one occasion before this, but when Aiden rises from his chair to offer me his hand and quietly asks me to dance—I feel downright giddy. Almost like it's the first time.

He guides me out onto the floor and pulls me close, and his wide palms settling at my hips are a warm, pleasant weight through the silk of my dress. I wind my arms around his neck and grin up at him shyly as he starts to move me to the music; there's nothing inherently complicated about the way he does it, just a shuffling of our feet in a slow back-and-forth, but I feel fluttery all the same.

"As far as first dates go," I tell him, "this one has set the bar pretty high."

I feel his thumb slide against my hip. "That's good to know. It's been a long time since I had a first date."

"Me too," I admit. And then a little quieter: "Over a year."

His smile is faint and barely there, but I can just make it out. "Me too."

"Sometimes none of this feels real," I admit. "I keep expecting to wake up on Wanda's couch."

"How do you think I feel? I have to convince myself every day that someone like you would want to hang around."

"Um. Pump the brakes there, Mr. Reid. Let's not pretend that you aren't a six-foot-something temptation station with sex eyes."

"Sex eyes?"

"Oh, come on. They're so pretty it isn't even fair."

I feel his hand slide minutely up my side to press at my waist only to drift back down as if only to feel the shape of me. It makes my stomach flip. "I think yours are nicer."

"You, my friend, are crazy."

His laugh is so low I might almost miss it over the music, but then he leans in so that I can feel the warmth of his breath at my ear, making me shiver. "You make me feel crazy, Cassie."

I close my eyes when I feel the soft press of his lips at my jaw, my knees giving a ridiculous wobble that I thought was only a thing in movies.

We've been at this party for more than an hour, closer to two, really, and suddenly all I'm thinking about is getting out of this classy place and going back to Aiden's to do far less classy things. The things I'm wanting to do might even be called downright rude, to some.

I have to press up on my toes to get close to his ear, dropping my voice to a whisper. "How much longer do you have to stay?"

I feel him tense when my fingernail teases the collar of his shirt on the back of his neck.

"As long as you want," he murmurs back, pulling me closer against him.

"I think I'm ready to leave, Mr. Reid."

He makes a sound low in his throat that puts my knees in danger again, squeezing my hip for good measure. "Then let's get you home."

Home.

Weirdly, the word makes me shiver.

I'm incredibly grateful that we don't have to wait for the check.

have no idea how we make it in the house, let alone up two flights of stairs to Aiden's bedroom. I don't have time to let it marinate that this is the first time I've been in Aiden's room, since we've never been brave enough to sneak up here with Sophie normally down the hall. Somewhere in the back of my mind I'm aware of the general color scheme of Aiden's room; it's the same black and gray throughout every other facet of the house, but it's a *very* distant thought. I don't exactly have time to tease him about it right now. Not with the way he's holding my face, tongue laving against mine while I fumble with the buttons of his shirt.

He's already torn down the clip holding up my hair, fingers tangling in the thick mass as his palm slides up my thigh to ruck up my dress. He groans when I get his shirt open, my hands running over his chest and shoulders to tug at his head, trying to somehow deepen the kiss. Everything about tonight feels somehow *more* than any other time we've been together; some heady combination of the date and coming clean to Sophie making all of this feel more *real* somehow.

I don't come back down from my kiss-related high until I feel him undoing the zipper at the back of my dress; I've already managed to work his shirt and tie off and undone the fly of his pants when I come to my senses.

"Wait, wait."

Aiden's eyes are wild when he pulls away from me. "Wait?"

"The dress," I huff. "I need to hang it up."

"Fuck the dress," he growls, trying to kiss me again.

"It's the nicest dress I own now! It'll get all wrinkled on the floor."

"I will buy you another dress," he argues.

This makes me laugh, the neediness in his voice doing all sorts of things for my ego.

"Get on the bed, Mr. Reid. I'll be right back."

"Oh, no. You're not going all the way back downstairs," he snorts. He nods his head toward a door nearby. "Hang it in my closet."

I leave a quick peck at his mouth, his frustrated expression like that of a toddler having a tantrum—the tented front of his pants saying otherwise. I cross to the closet hastily, pulling open the doors and flipping on the light in search of a hanger.

"Jesus," I mutter.

Aiden's closet is as big as my bathroom downstairs. I notice empty hangers near the back beyond a sea of black shirts and gray sweats and dark denim, stepping further inside to grab for one as I start to shimmy out of my dress. I'm unclasping my bra for good measure to save Aiden the trouble when I spot something interesting, pausing for a good second as an idea pops up in my head. I bite my lip as I consider.

Would it be silly or sexy? I wonder.

"If you don't get out here," Aiden calls impatiently. "I'm going to come fuck you in the closet."

Ah, what the hell.

I grab the garment that caught my attention from a hanger

before I can change my mind, putting my arms through the sleeves. His chef coat is entirely too big for me, the hem hitting midthigh and the sleeves nearly covering both my hands, but when I turn to the floor-length mirror on the back wall of his closet, I have to admit that the overall effect—gapped fabric that hints at my breasts and leaves the black lace of my underwear (I bought non-printed for tonight, thank you very much) on complete display—isn't half bad.

I try for my best Jessica Rabbit impression when I step out of the closet, backlit by the light inside as I slide one arm up the side of the door to lean against it. Aiden sits up in bed when he sees me; he's shucked off everything except his underwear, and his eyes go wide as they rake down the entire length of me.

"On today's edition of Who Wore It Best . . ." I say with a nervous laugh.

Aiden isn't laughing. In fact, he looks downright tense. "No contest," he says tightly. And then with a crook of his finger: "Come here."

I manage to cross the room without tripping or doing anything else that might break the sexy vibe I'm going for, crawling up the bed to meet him at the headboard where he's resting against (of course) black pillows. He pulls me over his lap so that my core rests directly against the length of him that strains against his underwear; the heat making everything between my legs tingle. Aiden's eyes follow the movement of his hand when he lets his palm rest flat over my belly, watching as he slides it higher between my breasts to push open the front of his coat so that my chest is left bare.

"How are you so fucking perfect?"

I arch my body so that my nipples graze his chest, both of us shuddering as I turn my face to press a line of soft kisses at his jaw. "How are you not touching me yet?"

"I'm trying to decide how I want to touch you first." His hand slides over my hip to dip inside my underwear so he can palm my ass. "With my hands?" He ducks his head so that his tongue can circle my nipple, drawing a quiet gasp from me. "My mouth?" His hand at my ass pulls me closer against him, close enough so that he can roll his hips to let his cock rub between my legs. "Something else?"

Words are hard right now, but I manage a breathy, "Is there an all-three option?"

"There is always an all-three option," he chuckles dryly.

His fingers find a nipple to tease it, rolling it languidly as his mouth meets mine. His kiss is quiet, even lazy—a sharp contrast to the needy urgency from earlier. Almost like he's taking his time. Drawing it out, maybe. I'm torn between urging him to hurry up and relishing the sensation.

He nibbles softly at my lower lip, kissing the corner of my mouth after. "I watched you for so long." Another slow, lingering kiss. "I was obsessed, Cassie."

"I stopped doing private shows at the end," I confess. "It was only yours."

His cock twitches between my legs. He likes that. "You were so fucking stunning. Doing everything I told you to do."

"I liked it," I whisper.

He pulls away to look at me with dark eyes. "Would you like it right now?"

"What?"

"I always imagined what you looked like—what you *really* looked like—when you came. Doing what I told you. Can you show me?"

My stomach flutters with nerves and excitement, and I bite my lip as I consider. The eagerness in his expression makes the idea that much more appealing, and it only takes me a second to come to a decision, leaning to kiss him deeply.

"And what kind of show would you like tonight, A?"

His breath is ragged when it puffs against my mouth. "I've thought about that for a few days, actually."

"Mm. Have you."

His hand fumbles with the nightstand by the bed, popping open the drawer and digging inside until he brings out a long, silk pouch. "I got you a present."

"A present?"

He hands me the pouch, watching eagerly as I loosen the drawstring to reach inside. My fingers meet soft, velvety silicone that is all too familiar, and heat drips down into my belly and deeper as I pull out a bright pink vibrator that looks . . . very realistic.

"You shouldn't have," I murmur.

I scoot back until I'm straddling his legs, putting enough room between us so that he can see everything. It's been a long time since I've done this, but with Aiden watching, it feels easier to slip back into it.

I press the tip of the vibrator between my breasts, letting it trail down my belly. "I'm glad you're back," I say sweetly. "I missed you."

The effect it has on Aiden is immediate. His breath comes harder, and his nostrils flare as his entire body tenses. "You make it hard to stay away."

"Oh?" I circle the tip of the vibe around my navel, making sure to keep eye contact. "Is that all I make hard?"

"I like your outfit," he rasps.

I smile down at one shoulder of his jacket, reaching with my free hand to push it slightly off-kilter. "This? It's my boyfriend's."

"Is it."

"He'd be mad if he knew I was wearing it for you."

I notice Aiden's fists clenching at his sides as I start to tease the vibe closer to the waistband of my underwear, and I wonder how long he can actually keep up with the game. "We'd better not tell him then."

"You haven't told me what you want, A," I simper. "You know I'll do whatever you want."

"Really?" His chest rises and falls roughly. "What if I want you to tease that pretty little pussy with that toy there?"

"Oh, this?" I slide it higher, making a lazy path up and over my sternum until I can bring it to my mouth to lick the tip. "I don't know. Do you think I can take it?"

"You'd better," he grinds out. "You'll need to get nice and soft if you're going to take me later."

My breath hitches. "Am I going to do that? Are you going to give me your cock later, A?"

"Would you like that, Cici? Would you like me to split you open on my cock?"

"Mm." I don't stop as I trail the toy lower this time, letting it slip past my underwear to slide the thicker head through my folds, getting it wet. "That sounds so much better than this silly toy."

"Later," he promises, and I cannot describe how elated it makes me to know that this time, there *will* be a later. "Take off those panties so I can see how wet you are."

It takes maneuvering to get my underwear off in this position, but I manage to work them down my legs enough to drop them on the other side of the bed before I return to a straddle. I know he can see everything now, especially with the light from the closet still casting a glow inside the room, and it's made more obvious by the way his eyes home in on the toy that I'm still teasing through the wet mess between my legs.

I cock my head. "Like this?"

"Just like that," he says roughly. "A little slower, maybe."

I make slow, exaggerated movements, keeping my legs spread as wide as I can manage so that he doesn't miss anything. The motion of my hand is causing his jacket to slip from one shoulder, practically falling off me now.

"Touch your nipples for me," Aiden murmurs. "Tease them."

I close my eyes as I do what he asks, feeling strangely powerful from the raw *need* in his voice. Like it's taking every bit of restraint he possesses not to reach out and touch me. How had I never recognized it before?

"Can you put it inside? Let me see how you fuck yourself."

I suck in a breath as I nudge the head of the toy against my entrance; it slips in easily with how wet I am—not to mention how much smaller it is than Aiden. I don't even know how I could ever go back to this after him. I start to thrust it in and out of me slowly, slick, wet sounds ringing out in the air as I continue to use my other hand to pinch my nipple.

"I bet your cock would be so much nicer than this toy," I muse coyly. "I wonder if I could even take all of you?"

"You could take everything," he rasps. "I'd keep you on my cock for *days* if I could, Cici."

"That sounds nice," I answer airily. I push the toy deeper. "But for now . . . I can pretend this toy is you, if you want."

"Then you're going to need to fuck yourself harder than that, Cici. Because that's what I'd be doing. I'd be fucking you until you were screaming for it."

It's getting increasingly hard to keep up with the game, especially since I know how much *better* it will be when he *actually* touches me.

"Can I turn the vibration on, A? I need a little more," I pout.

"I don't know," he says carefully. "Do you think you've been good enough for that?"

"I've been so good," I breathe. "Please, A?"

"Turn it on," he grates. "Get that pretty pussy good and ready for me."

I flip on the vibe, ticking it up a few settings until there is a steady, humming vibration deep inside me that makes me gasp. "*Oh.*"

"Does it feel good, Cici?"

I nod, my eyes drifting closed as I focus on the way the toy moves in and out of me. "Mm-hmm."

"You think it feels better than I would?"

I shake my head. "You would feel so much better."

"Because you'd prefer it, wouldn't you. Being stuffed full of me."

"*Yes,*" I sigh.

"Tell me how badly you want my cock, Cici."

"I w—*ah*." I hit that place inside that makes me shudder, and my wrist starts to ache slightly as I try to keep up my pace. "I wish it was you. I wish I was full of you instead of this toy. I *need* it, A."

"Yeah? Can you beg me for it? Beg me for my cock, Cassie."

My eyes peek open, noticing how utterly *wrecked* Aiden looks. His chest is flushed red, and there are slight veins bulging in his arms from the way he's clenching his fists so hard. His mouth is slack and his eyes are heavy, and I decide to forgive his slipup, trying to focus again on the play.

"Please, A," I whisper, thrusting the toy inside just a little harder. "Please give me your cock."

"I don't believe you. Are you sure you want it?"

My mouth falls open as I hit that place again, trembling all over as an orgasm begins to build. "I think about it all the time. How nice you'd fill me up." My head lolls back as my thighs shake, so close I can almost taste it. "I bet you'd—" My breath catches, my hands shaking. "I bet you could—"

I tense up when it hits me, not as all consuming as the one I know Aiden can give me but enough to leave a thin sheen of sweat across my body, to leave me a gasping mess. When I can finally open my eyes again, I can see that Aiden is looking at me like I'm some sort of mythical thing, his expression full of wonder and awe and a little of something else that makes my chest hurt.

"*Fuck*, Cassie. How are you so—"

"Cassie?" I smile at him even as I'm struggling to catch my breath. "Who's that? You know my name is Cici."

"Cici," he says tightly.

"Do you wish you could touch me, A?" I slip the toy out from inside, turning off the vibration but bringing the head to my belly to smear some of my fluids there. "I wish you could touch me."

His jaw tenses. "I don't know if I can do this."

"Oh? What's the matter? I thought you liked to watch me?"

He surprises me by pushing away from the pillows, crawling over to meet me until he can urge me to my back. He braces his hands on either side of my head while I'm sprawled beneath him.

"Aiden?"

"I changed my mind," he tells me seriously, his eyes on mine. "I want Cassie." He plucks the sleeve from my arm to slide it further down. "Just Cassie." My heart starts to beat a heavy cadence in my chest as he urges me out of his jacket, tossing it away. "And I don't want to watch anymore."

I can hardly breathe when he lowers against me, easing me into a kiss that makes my toes curl. His tongue slips inside my mouth to lick against mine, and I close my eyes as my skin tingles and my stomach flutters. I feel his hand move to my hip to squeeze there, wandering after—up my ribs and under my breasts and back down again over my belly until he can dip between my legs.

"You're so wet," he marvels.

I let my fingers graze against his hips, pulling him closer. "Because of you."

"Fuck."

That urgency is back when he kisses me, but the rest of his body goes slow. He holds my hip to keep me pinned beneath him, rocking against me so that I can feel the heat of his cock against my center. The thin fabric of his boxer briefs feels like entirely too much, and I start to tug at them impatiently, needing to feel all of him. He manages to get his underwear off with less difficulty than I did, and in only a matter of seconds he's completely bare against me.

I sigh into his mouth when I can feel him against my core, continuing that slow rutting that has the head of his cock bumping against the most sensitive part of me with every stroke.

"Aiden," I whisper between kisses. "Aiden, can you—"

And like he can read my mind, I feel the nudge of him against my entrance, notching against me before slowly pushing inside. He never stops kissing me while he gives me inch after inch, filling me in a lazy, torturous way so that it feels like forever until I'm full. It's so much different from the toy, so much *better*, and again I wonder how I could ever be fully satisfied with anything other than this now that I've had it. I hope I never have to find out.

His body against mine is a warm, satisfying weight, and his lips, which have begun to wander again, elicit little sparks against my skin wherever they touch. He doesn't move inside me while his mouth presses against my cheek, my jaw, down to my neck— and after a moment of this torment, I start to squirm with impatience.

"Be still," he says, not a demand but a plea. "Let me feel you."

I go still as he lets out a ragged breath against my throat, kissing there gently after as his hand slides down my thigh. His hand curves around the back of my knee to urge it upward, pushing it high to open me up more as he pulls up his head to look at me. His throat bobs with a swallow as he looks at me through hooded eyes, holding my knee against my chest and smiling dreamily before he kisses me again.

And then he starts to move.

He draws back his hips to push back inside at that same slow pace, his lips and tongue keeping me too distracted to even complain about the slow rhythm. Not that I want to. Every slide inside brings a delicious friction, every inch of him touching every part of me. I'm still sensitive from the orgasm I just gave myself, and it means that every sense is heightened, every touch feels like so much *more*.

I feel his arm snake under my back, pulling me against him and pinning my knee against his chest. He falls to his elbow on my other side, his mouth never leaving mine. We're so close that I can feel the base of his cock rubbing against me with every thrust, a tingling pressure building between my legs as he rolls his hips against mine again and again.

My thigh starts to burn with the way he has it pushed up toward my stomach, but the angle means he hits impossibly deep with every thrust, the pleasure of it overriding any discomfort. His kisses are stuttered, like he's having trouble keeping his focus, his head finally burying against my throat, groaning. I hold on to his shoulders as he picks up the pace, his breath washing hot against my neck.

"*Aiden*," I gasp, feeling that tingling heat inside swell to the point of bursting. "Oh. *Oh.* I'm—"

"Are you gonna come?"

I try to nod. "Don't stop."

"Never." His thrusts are erratic now. "Fuck. I *never* wanna stop."

"Just—just keep—*right there.* I'm—"

It's like a shower of fireworks bursting behind my eyes and all over my skin, lights and colors flashing in my vision as my entire body tenses with my orgasm. Aiden is still moving, his pants growing louder and rougher against my ear, and I slide my fingers over his shoulders, leaving dazed kisses wherever I can reach.

He also goes stiff when he tumbles over the edge, his big body shaking against mine and his cock twitching deep, deep inside before he goes slack against me. He's heavy and entirely too large for this, but I like the weight of him. I keep pressing kisses against his jaw as he tries to catch his breath, shivering with every pass of my fingers against his skin.

He keeps me close until his breath is less shallow, inhaling deeply just to blow it out before he pulls out of me with a wince. He doesn't go far, rolling slightly to the side so he can keep me close against him without crushing me with his weight, and watching as I bring my hands up to let them rest under my head. He looks spent like this; his head rests on one bicep, and the other is draped lazily over my hip, but his eyes are expressive and bright as they study my face.

I bring the tips of my fingers to his mouth, tracing its shape lightly. "Did you know that the most sensitive parts of your body are your fingertips and your lips?"

"Yeah?" He kisses my fingertips. "Seems pretty suggestive for a Snapple lid."

His hand drifts up my side until he can wrap his fingers around my hand, turning it to press a kiss against my palm. There's a ghost of a smile at his mouth when he looks up at me, like he's keeping a secret he can't share, and it feels infectious with the way it has me grinning shyly back at him.

"Do you ever wonder what would have happened if we'd met up back then?"

His mouth is still grazing my palm. "If we'd met up?"

"Mm-hmm. Like, what do you think would have happened?"

His laugh is nothing more than a quick rush of air through his nostrils, and he turns my hand again to brush his lips against my knuckles. "I think we'd be right here."

Butterflies swarm in my stomach and up into my chest, and for a moment it feels like I might float away if Aiden's hand wasn't tethering me to his bed. It's an entirely new feeling, but not one I dislike.

"This still feels like a dream," I whisper. "I keep thinking I'll wake up."

Aiden smiles, and I don't even have time to be fully twitter-pated by it before he rolls, bringing himself half on top of me again. "That's fine," he says, eyes flicking to my mouth for a moment before he lowers to kiss me. It's slow, and sweet, and everything he is, and I can feel my lashes fluttering dazedly when he pulls away. "I don't plan on letting you sleep tonight, anyway."

"Pervert," I tease.

I can feel him growing stiff against my thigh when he kisses me again. "Don't worry," he murmurs against my mouth. "You're going to wake up right here in my bed."

The weight of that sentiment feels heavier than his body, and I let it wrap around me like a blanket as I melt back into him, letting him dizzy me with his kiss and his touch and everything else.

Maybe I could hold a rose. Like they do in The Bachelor. So you'd know it was me.

You watch The Bachelor?

I can neither confirm nor deny that statement.

CHAPTER 23

Cassie

I dream about my parents that night, which comes completely out of left field, considering that I haven't spoken to them since I left home at eighteen. I dream about the day I left, about my dad's disappointed expression and my mom's irate ranting—a fight I can barely even remember anymore. Mom's face is a fuzzy static that matches Dad's, and even if I squint, I can't make them out. Have I forgotten what they look like?

There's an ache that comes with the dream, one I haven't let myself feel for a very long time—some crushing anxiety about being alone. A stifling worry that comes from being such a disappointment to the two people whose love should have come easy.

I feel my feet sinking into the grass outside my house as my mother's voice starts to fade, and panic claws at my chest as I struggle to climb back out. I throw out my arms as I open my mouth to scream, but no words come, and I realize that the ground is literally going to swallow me up without me being able to do a thing about it.

But then I hear my name, like a soft sigh on the wind, and strong hands grasp mine to pull me back up. There's a flash of warm brown and green looking back at me, a blinding smile that comes with it. He whispers my name again and again, and the panic in my chest ebbs to some blooming heat that makes me tingly all over.

Cassie.

Cassie.

Cassie.

"Cassie."

I wake to soft sheets beneath me and softer lips at my shoulder, groaning as I stretch my arms to shove them beneath the pillows as I come to. Aiden's hand is rubbing gently against my spine as his lips continue to leave barely there kisses at my back.

What a weird dream, I think.

Not that I have time to dwell on it, humming like a content housecat when I feel his mouth at my scar, tracing one side.

"Good morning," he mumbles against my skin.

I yawn, turning my face so I can peek back at him from over my shoulder. "What time is it?"

"Early, I think," he answers. "My phone's still in my pants."

"Mine's downstairs." Moving sounds like the last thing I want to do right now. "How are you so chipper this early?"

He grins before he leans to kiss my shoulder again. "I had a great night."

"But aren't you exhausted?"

"I'm used to running on low sleep," he says. "You're just giving me better incentive."

It takes incredible effort to roll to my side, my eyes still heavy with sleep as I prop my cheek against my fist. I know that like this my breasts are almost fully on display, and I won't pretend it isn't intensely satisfying to see Aiden eyeing them hungrily.

"Don't even think about it," I warn him. "I am out of commission. My poor vagina is on strike. I actually think I have temporary paralysis down there."

"I highly doubt that," he chuckles. "I don't remember hearing any of these complaints last night."

"I will not be held accountable for things I did or said mid-orgasm."

He laughs again, closing the distance between us to kiss me instead. "Is this allowed?"

"As long as you behave," I murmur, leaning into it.

Aiden sighs against my mouth before his forehead comes to rest against mine. "We need to get up. I'm sure Wanda is ready to put Sophie out on the street by now."

"Doubt it," I tell him. "When I called her on the way home last night, she said Sophie was still hustling her at cards. Wanda probably won't even let her leave until she gets back on a winning streak."

"Maybe Wanda will make pancakes for breakfast so Sophie can add one more person to the list of people making them that she prefers over me."

"Wow, someone's bitter."

Aiden scoffs. "I'm not bitter."

"Sure you aren't." I fall to my back, stretching my arms over my head again. "You might have to carry me downstairs."

"Only if I can do it while you're naked."

"*Fine*. I'm getting up. I need some water, anyway."

I swing my legs over the side of the bed, feeling a burning in my thighs and an aching in my back—but all of it brings back memories of how I got so sore to begin with, making me not mind so much. Aiden is stretching in bed behind me when I pick up the discarded white T-shirt he'd been wearing under his button-down last night, pulling it over my head. It dwarfs me, but I figure it'll do for a trip downstairs for some water.

I can hear him rolling out of bed as I leave the room, turning my neck back and forth to loosen it up as I head toward the stairs. The house is much quieter without the sound of Sophie milling about; usually I can hear the sounds of her Switch or maybe even *Encanto* playing for the dozenth time, and I realize that as amazing as my night with Aiden was, I miss the little gremlin.

I grab a bottle of water from the fridge as I check the time on the oven. It's only eight in the morning, which is normally around the time Sophie wakes up, so by the time we get dressed and on the road, I imagine Sophie will be bouncing off the walls of Wanda's kitchen. I laugh at the thought; I can already hear Wanda pretending to be put out by Sophie's energy.

I've just filled my glass and brought it to my mouth for a drink when I hear thudding footsteps coming down the stairs—heavy and urgent almost as if Aiden's running. And then I hear him talking.

"No, of course," he says in a tight tone. "I'll be there immediately. And Sophie, is she—? Right. Yes. Yes, I know. Her aunt? Is she there? That's—" Aiden stops at the bottom of the stairs, gripping his phone tightly in his hand and closing his eyes as his other hand makes a fist at his side. "Okay. I'm glad Sophie isn't alone. Yes. I'll be there in fifteen minutes."

I set my glass on the counter when he hangs up, watching as he stares at the floor for a moment, looking lost. I move quickly to his side to try to get his attention, bringing my palm to his jaw to force him to look at me. "Hey, what's wrong?"

Aiden blinks at me like he's only just now seeing me; his mouth parting and his eyes searching my face as if he's trying to find what he should say. "Cassie, it's—"

"Did something happen?" I can feel worry creeping into my limbs like a chill. "Is Sophie okay?"

"She's fine," Aiden assures me, reaching to wrap his hands around my wrists. "She's okay. It's . . ." His lips press together, his expression pained. "It's Wanda."

Every part of me goes cold. "What?"

"Wanda, she . . ." He swallows, and it looks like he'd rather say anything else than what he's about to say to me. "Wanda had a heart attack."

I don't say a word as I run to my room to change.

learn more details about what happened on our drive to the hospital; sometime early this morning, Wanda started having chest pains and woke Sophie up. Sophie called 911 at Wanda's instruction before she inevitably passed out, which left a terrified Sophie alone, trying to get a hold of us.

And our phones were forgotten on the floor somewhere.

The guilt I feel is palpable, and I can only imagine that Aiden feels the same, if not worse. His knuckles remained stark white against the steering wheel the entire drive to the hospital, and he doesn't utter a word the whole way there. I know that we were told that Wanda is stable, and that the worst is behind her, but still. I feel that looming sense of dread at the idea of the first person to really love me lying in the hospital.

When we finally arrive, I have to sprint to keep up with Aiden as we rush down the corridor of the floor Wanda is on, and when we finally round the corner near Wanda's room to spot a tired-looking Sophie clinging to her aunt Iris, I feel equal parts relieved and terrified. Sophie doesn't notice us at first, sitting next to Iris on a bench in the hall as Iris looks straight ahead with an angry expression. I know this isn't going to go well.

Iris notices us first, turning her head at the sound of our footsteps and glaring at the pair of us as she tightens her arm around Sophie's shoulders. "Nice of you to finally join us."

Aiden ignores her, going straight to Sophie to crouch in front of her. He reaches out to cup her face, forcing her eyes to meet his. "Are you okay?"

"Yeah," Sophie mumbles, her little lip trembling. "Wanda's sick. I tried to help, but she—she fell asleep, and I couldn't wake her up."

"Shh," Aiden soothes, loosening Iris's grip on his daughter and pulling Sophie into his arms. "You did amazing. It's not your fault. I'm sorry we didn't answer the phone."

Iris looks livid, her expression darker than I've ever seen it as she glances between the pair of us with what can only be described as contempt. "How could you leave her with an elderly woman and then just ignore your phone all night?"

"I didn't hear it go off," Aiden answers tightly. I can tell he's doing his best to remain civil, but I can also sense how stressed he is right now. "It was a mistake."

"A mistake," Iris snorts, moving to stand as she gestures between us. "I wonder why that is? Do you think that maybe it's because you decided to go off"—she gives me a deliberate look that is anything but pleasant—"and have fun on your own?"

I feel my stomach twist with more guilt, hating that I'm the reason he's being berated right now. Iris is looking at me like I'm something she is trying to scrape off her shoe, and Aiden's weary expression makes me feel pretty equivalent to that. I can see every bit of ground I've gained with Iris blowing away like dust in the wind, every victory circling down the drain. It's all over her face that she blames me for this just as much if not more than Aiden.

"Iris, it wasn't his fault, it was—"

"Just don't," Iris practically spits. "You know, you really had me fooled. I thought you *cared* about her. But you were just trying to get something else. Weren't you."

I rear back as if she's slapped me, and I hear Aiden take a deep breath. He smiles at Sophie, reaching into his wallet to pull out a few bills and handing them over to her. "Why don't you go get yourself something from the vending machine? It's right down the hall." He points to the large machine at the end of the hallway we're standing in. "I'm sure you're hungry."

Sophie nods solemnly, taking the bills and looking warily between the three very tense adults surrounding her before she shuffles off.

Iris is looking at me again like I'm garbage, and it makes my face hot with embarrassment. It feels like I've deluded myself into thinking that we were making progress, because with one mistake it's all crumbling away.

Aiden's voice is cautious when he speaks again. "Hey, I'm glad you were here for Sophie, but—"

"Of course I'm here for Sophie," Iris hisses. "I'm *always* here for Sophie. Which is exactly why she should be with me." She pokes a finger at Aiden's chest. "You left Sophie with an elderly woman you barely know so you could run off and fuck your nanny. What the hell were you thinking?"

I can feel the air rushing from my lungs like I've just had the wind knocked out of me. The way she says it makes it sound like some dirty, cheap thing—like I'm someone Aiden picked up for a quick lay. It makes me *feel* dirty, hearing it said like that.

Aiden looks livid, a tic in his jaw as if it's taking all of his restraint not to completely tear Iris a new asshole. "You don't know what you're talk—"

"Actually, I think I do," Iris laughs derisively. "I've turned a blind eye to it, because I thought she cared about Sophie, but it's clear that she cares more about *you*. Apparently, Sophie is just an afterthought to the both of you."

"Iris," Aiden says tightly. "Don't you dare—"

"Don't *tell* me what to do, Aiden Reid," she seethes, clearly keyed up to the point of no return. "I sit back and watch you bumble your way through trying to be a father, and I have done everything I can to try and help you, to find a solution that's actually *in* Sophie's best interest. But you've been so wrapped up in your own ego, you've never even tried to consider what might be best for her. Which is clearly not living with you."

"My *ego* has nothing to do with it," he snaps back. "Sophie is *my* child, not yours, and you're not going to sit here and tell me that—"

"I don't have to sit here and tell you anything," she says with a humorless laugh. "I can tell it to a judge, instead. I think one might find this entire situation extremely interesting."

That panic is back, scratching at my chest from the inside like it might burst right out of me at any second. "Wait," I interject. "Iris. I'm so sorry. This is my fault. I would never do anything to hurt Sophie. I'm the one who suggested—"

"I don't care," Iris interrupts, her eyes wild and wet with unshed tears. "The only thing I care about is my niece calling me completely terrified this morning from the back of an ambulance because her *father* wouldn't pick up the phone. All because he was getting his dick wet."

"That's *enough*." Aiden's face is red, a hardness to his eyes I've never seen before. "Get the fuck out of here, Iris. Right now."

"You can't tell me what to—"

"If you don't leave at this very second," he says darkly, "I'm going to go straight to the courthouse tomorrow and file a restraining order. Do you want to spend the money it will take to fight that?"

She narrows her eyes. "And you think that will stick?"

"Do you want to find out?"

A second passes between them as I stand by the wayside, silent and stunned.

"Fine," Iris says finally. "But this isn't over, Aiden. I've known from the beginning you were going to fuck up. I just had to bide my time and wait for it to happen." She pauses midstep beside me to regard me directly, her expression a mixture of disappointment and hurt and rage all rolled into one. "I hope you were worth it."

Aiden stares at some spot on the wall behind her as Iris stomps off, and I turn my head to catch her telling Sophie goodbye at the end of the hall. I reach for Aiden, to do what, I don't know—comfort him, maybe—but I draw my hand back, battling with some strange feeling.

I hope you were worth it.

Suddenly every good feeling I've had in the last twenty-four hours drains away, leaving nothing but worry and guilt and shame in its wake. I hadn't considered before this moment what it might mean for Aiden in the long run, the two of us being together—hadn't even entertained the thought of what people might say about him, for lack of a better expression, fucking his nanny.

Aiden finally looks down at me, a multitude of different emotions playing out in his features. Fear, anger, regret—it's all there. But what's worse than that, I think, is that flicker of disappointment in his eyes. I don't know who it's for, him or me or just this situation, but it rouses all sorts of old emotions from days when I'd been all too familiar with this look. It's practically the only one my parents ever gave me.

I'd been a burden to them too.

"I'm sorry," I whisper, still feeling that icky sense of guilt.

Aiden shakes his head. "This isn't your fault, Cassie."

Yes, it is. How can it not be?

I want to cry, but I force myself to hold it together.

"I made a mistake," he says flatly, looking down at the floor. "And I'll deal with it."

A mistake? Does he mean me? I can't bring myself to ask. I swallow around a growing lump in my throat, trying to find words but coming up short.

"You should check on Wanda," he tells me, his expression one of defeat and fatigue. "I'll take Sophie home."

He's pushing you away.

Part of me thinks he wouldn't, but that part is being shushed by a very loud, pathetic voice right now.

"Okay," I say quietly. "Yeah. You're right."

"I'll see you at home," he says, trying for a smile but not quite managing it.

I nod as he pats my shoulder, the gesture holding none of the warmth that I feel he would have given me before this. It only makes me feel worse. I watch him go and join Sophie, who has taken residence on a bench further down the hall, and she casts a glance back toward me when she starts to leave with Aiden, waving feebly.

I return it with a smile, but like Aiden's, it doesn't meet my eyes.

Seeing Wanda hooked up to machines only worsens my darkening mood. The nurse said that the meds they gave her would make her sleepy, and she's been out for a good hour, but I'm determined to wait until she wakes up. My phone's been dead since we left earlier, a by-product of leaving it off the charger all night. Another mistake I've made in the last twenty-four hours.

I lean my head back against the wall of Wanda's room, rubbing at my arms to fight the chill of the hospital. I've had nothing to do for the last hour except replay the confrontation with Iris over and over—reliving her angry words and Sophie's worried face and Aiden's defeated exhaustion again and again.

I made a mistake.

Maybe he didn't mean me, I keep telling myself. Maybe he was referring to this situation. I'm not even sure that it matters. Regardless of how we ended up here this morning, I know deep down that I have now completely become something Iris has tucked away in her arsenal to use in her unyielding fight to take Sophie. I'm now the *biggest* piece of ammo she has, it seems. And how in the hell do I live with that?

I hope you were worth it.

I press the heels of my hands against my eyes, breathing in and out as tears threaten to gather there. It feels like I'm against a wall, stuck between what I want and what's best for this little family I care about so much. Will I always be a stumbling block for them? Just something to be used against Aiden? What happens when Iris takes him to court and he decides I'm not worth the trouble? It's not like he would choose me over Sophie, and I wouldn't want him if he would. Half the reason I love him is because of how devoted he is to Sophie.

I pull my hands from my eyes, blinking up at the ceiling in a daze.

Do I . . . love him?

The realization hits me like a bag of bricks, but instead of elation, I only feel more dread. If I love Aiden, and we keep going as we are—he'll get so deep in this thing with me that he will stubbornly hang on long after I've proven to be bad for him and Sophie. Or what's worse, he'll toss me aside. Both options make my chest hurt, and I know that going through either would break me to pieces.

I can't escape the sick suspicion that the longer I stay, the more of a burden I'll become for them.

"You look like shit."

I sit straight up, seeing Wanda squinting at me from her bed.

"Oh my God, you're awake," I say with relief, pushing out of my chair to go to her bedside. "How are you feeling?"

"Eh. They didn't have to open me up, at least. I'm sure they'll be on my ass about changing my diet after this."

"Which you *will* be doing."

"My mama has been dead for years, girl. Quit talking like you're her."

Despite everything, this makes me laugh. "You scared the shit out of me, Wanda. I need you to live for at least another twenty years."

"Lord, I hope not," she grumbles. "How'd you sneak in here anyway?"

"Told them I was your granddaughter."

"Slick. Real slick."

I frown. "Seriously, are you okay?"

She gives me a tired smile. "I told you that you were gonna give me a heart attack one of these days." Her smile dissipates at my crumpled expression. "Oh, stop it." She struggles to sit up in bed, and I put a hand behind her back to help her up. "I'm not dead yet." She looks worried then. "Where's Sophie?"

"Aiden took her home." Just the mention of both of them makes my chest throb. "How much do you remember?"

Wanda shrugs. "I told her to call 911 when I started having chest pains. She did real good. There's bits and pieces from the ambulance but nothing much after that."

"She couldn't get in touch with us," I say guiltily. "We both forgot to keep track of our phones last night."

Wanda chuckles. "Imagine you were too busy shaking the sheets."

"It isn't funny! We both feel like shit. Sophie had to call her aunt Iris."

"Damn. That harpy that keeps bothering your fellow? That sounds like a fun time."

"It was awful, Wanda. The way she tore into Aiden . . ." I can feel my eyes welling, and I have to take a moment to stave it off. "She threatened to take it to a judge."

"Oh, let her. She's just being bitter."

"She threatened Aiden because of *me*, Wanda. If he hadn't been with me last night . . ."

"Then I might be dead for all we know," Wanda says assertively. "That girl saved my damned life. That's how fate works, girl."

"I know that, but if I hadn't—"

"Shut that shit up," she says, clucking her tongue. "Quit trying to put this on you. It isn't your fault I got a shitty ticker."

"I don't know what to do," I admit quietly, those tears I'd been willing away are pooling at the corners of my eyes and threatening to spill. "If I stay with them, she's going to use it against Aiden."

"The hell do you mean 'if I stay'? You aren't thinking of leaving, are you?"

"I—" I swallow thickly, feeling a single trickle over my cheek. "I can't be the thing that ruins things for them. I don't—" I suck in a breath, trying to choke back a sob. "I don't want to be someone's burden. Not again."

Wanda is quiet, watching as I hang my head and wipe my eyes. So many emotions are hitting me all at once, and I feel even shittier sitting here whining about my problems when Wanda just lived through a damned heart attack. She waits for me to calm down, waits for the sniffling to stop as I stare at my knees.

"You done?"

I shrug noncommittally, wiping my nose. "I guess."

"How many times have I told you that not everyone is like your parents? I'm pretty sure those two were actually assembled in some kinda angry dick factory. It was never *your* fault."

"Wasn't it? They never wanted me. All I ever did was cause problems for them. They haven't called me *once*, Wanda. Not once in seven years. They were ecstatic to see me go. How can that not be my fault?"

"Because they're shitty, selfish people. Your parents shouldn't have been parents. Especially to someone as special as you. They were bitter people with bitter lives who turned up their noses at a beautiful gift instead of appreciating it."

"I don't know . . ."

"You think running away is going to solve things? It won't stop that lady from hounding that family. Stubborn doesn't quit at a roadblock, Cassie. It finds another damned road."

"I'm sorry," I say pitifully. "I can't believe I'm sitting here complaining after the night you had."

"My only other option would be some grainy-ass soap opera," she says, waving me off.

"Still."

"Don't shoot yourself in the foot, honey. You can have good things, but you have to *let* yourself have them."

What she's saying sounds reasonable, or rather, it would, to a more reasonable person. I don't feel very reasonable right now. I feel angry and sad and mostly just . . . beat. Like I'm trapped in a corner with only one way out, but the way out is paved with rusty railroad spikes.

I wipe my eyes again for good measure as I hear the door to her room opening, some chipper nurse stepping inside to greet us both as she gushes over Wanda being awake. The nurse mentions something about vitals and tests, and even though Wanda doesn't say it, I can hear the dismissal in her voice.

"I'll come back later," I tell Wanda. "Don't be mean to the nurses."

Wanda rolls her eyes. "Haven't bit one yet, at least."

If I didn't feel like shit, I would laugh at the look the nurse gives her.

"You remember what I said," Wanda reminds me. "Don't do anything stupid."

I nod, but even as I do it, I know it's a lie. I walk out of Wanda's room with a heavy weight on my shoulders, begging my eyes to keep the tears in until I can find a quiet spot outside to host a pity party before I try to flag down a cab. Because I *can't* be the thing that stands between Aiden and Sophie. I won't allow that to happen. No matter how much I . . . care about them. Both of them.

They'll be better off if I do it now, before we get too deep. Before we reach some point that we can't turn back from. Before Aiden realizes that I was never worth it in the first place. I can't say whether or not the decision I've come to is stupid, but . . . I know it's going to hurt like hell.

I've never been so nervous in my entire life. I've been waiting for this day for weeks, ever since we decided to meet in person. It's ridiculous that I would be so terrified of a date at my age, and yet I've checked my hair three times, I've changed my outfit at least five.

My hands itch to touch her, and I'm desperate to hear her voice, hear her for real.

And today I finally can.

I check my appearance one more time in the hall mirror, jolting when my phone ringing from the kitchen counter distracts me. I frown when I notice who's calling—there's absolutely no reason for Rebecca's sister to be calling me.

Dread settles into my stomach. Could something be wrong with Sophie?

I answer the call, bringing it to my ear with bated breath. "Iris?"

CHAPTER 24

Aiden

Sophie doesn't say a word the entire ride home. I've told her three times since we left how sorry I am that I didn't answer her call; I can't even describe how much of a failure as a father I feel knowing that she spent hours on her own without anyone to comfort her. It's left me with a pit in my stomach since the moment I saw her sitting in that hallway looking more desolate than I've ever seen her.

She's quiet when we get home, too, trudging up two flights of stairs toward her room while claiming to be tired, and I war with myself on whether or not I should give her space or beg her to talk to me. At this point I have no idea which course of action will make things better, if they will at all, but in the end I decide she's spent enough time on her own today.

I follow her into her bedroom and help her take off her shoes as she sits at the edge of her bed, staring down at me with unseeing eyes. I sit beside her after I help her settle under the covers, noticing her dark circles.

"Sophie, I'm so sorry," I tell her again, wishing I had some way to make this right. "I should have been there. I feel horrible that you had to go through that alone."

Sophie shrugs. "It's okay."

"It's not, Soph," I stress, leaning to press my hand to her hair. "I'm supposed to protect you. It's my job to make sure you don't ever feel like this, and I didn't do a good job. I'm going to do everything I can to make sure I never mess up like this again."

"I'm not mad at you," she tells me quietly.

I shake my head. "I would be mad at me, if I were you."

"I'm not," she assures me. "Promise."

"But you're not okay," I urge. "Talk to me. Let me help."

She nuzzles into her pillow, shutting her eyes and squeezing them tight as tears collect there. "Wanda was hurt," she says pitifully. "I didn't know what to do. I thought she was gonna die."

"Oh, honey." I carefully crawl over her, settling behind her in her bed and pulling her back against my chest to hold her tight. She turns to bury her face there, and I rest my cheek against her hair. "You did amazing, Soph. Today was scary. Way scarier than anything you should ever have to go through. But you did great. *So* great. You saved Wanda's life. Do you understand?"

I can't see her face now, but I feel her nodding against my chest. "Is she okay?"

"They told us she's going to be fine after some rest," I tell her. "Cassie is with her right now."

"Do you think Cassie is mad at me?"

"What?" I turn my face down to look at her. "Of course she isn't. Cassie could never be mad at you. She loves you."

Sophie's voice is softer now. "I don't want Cassie to get mad and leave."

"Sophie." I feel a squeezing sensation in my chest. "Is that what's got you so worried? That's not going to happen."

"You promise?"

"I'm going to do my very best to make sure that never happens."

"I love Cassie too," she whispers into my shirt.

I close my eyes as I rub her back, leaving soothing circles there to keep her calm and comfortable. It takes a while for her breathing to even out, but I can tell when she drifts off to sleep, her body going limp in my arms as the tension of the morning finally gets the best of her. I keep my arms around her even after she falls asleep, taking advantage of this quiet moment as I think about our exchange.

I can't imagine what Sophie felt when she was alone with Wanda—unable to reach me or Cassie and not having any idea what to do. The panic she must have felt leaves me a mess inside, racked with guilt and outright shame for not having been there for her. Especially with how amazing last night was, how happy I was up until the moment I saw all of the missed calls. Things felt fucking perfect up until that part. Now I just feel like shit.

There's an additional guilt on top of everything else for having left Cassie at the hospital, but I hadn't known what else to do. I'm sure that Cassie understands how much Sophie needed me, how distracted I was by everything going on—but it doesn't ease the guilt.

And Iris. Fucking *Iris*.

She's never liked me, not when Rebecca got pregnant, not when we tried to make things work, not when we decided we were better apart—especially not when my life got so hectic after I got my current job. Everything had only gotten a thousand times worse after Rebecca passed and Sophie came to me. Now it's like Iris's entire life's mission is to prove me an unfit parent. And here

I am, having hand delivered the knife she's been looking for to stab in my back.

What a fucking mess.

I keep thinking about Cassie's face at the hospital—her crestfallen look telling me that she was blaming herself for Iris going off the rails. I should have done more to assure her, I know that, but with Sophie looking nearly catatonic, all I could think about was getting her home and safe and herself again. I plan to thoroughly apologize to Cassie whenever she makes it back. Not that I have any idea when that will be, since her phone is dead.

I love Cassie too.

It's the only part of this whole mess giving me any level of happiness. Sophie's quiet admission. The way Cassie loves my daughter, the way Sophie loves her back—it makes me feel things I've never felt before. Makes me imagine all sorts of things I have no business imagining with Cassie after our short time together, even *with* our strange shared history. Still. I imagine them all the same.

I pull Sophie tighter, shutting out the buzzing in my head. There's time to figure all of this out later, preferably on a day when we all haven't been put through the ringer. I close my eyes, yawning as I silently assure myself.

We have plenty of time.

don't know when I dozed off, but Sophie is still sleeping soundly beside me in her bed when I wake, so I roll away gently to let her keep resting. I yawn as I scratch the back of my neck, grabbing my phone from her bedside table where I'd stashed it to check the time. It's after lunch, but there is still nothing from Cassie. I wonder if that means she's still at the hospital.

I frown as I tuck it inside the pocket of my jeans, not liking the fact that I haven't heard from her. I know her phone was dead when we left, but I was hoping she might call from the room at least to give an update. I imagine she's busy with Wanda, telling myself she'll check in when she has a spare moment. I decide to distract myself with lunch while I wait, figuring I can let Sophie sleep until I've whipped something up, at least.

I close her bedroom door quietly behind me when I leave her room, stepping carefully down the hall so as not to make any noise. I'm halfway down the stairs before I notice anything amiss, pausing only three steps from the landing when I'm surprised by the sight of Cassie on my couch, her head in her hands.

"Cassie?"

She looks up at me immediately, her eyes red and her face haggard, like she's been crying. Seeing her so out of sorts makes me uneasy, and I hurry down the last few steps to cross the living room.

"Hey," I say soothingly, sitting beside her on the couch. "When did you get back? How is Wanda?"

She's looking at me strangely, her eyes lingering over the lines of my face even as her lip quivers. She sniffles once as she nods, everything about it stiff.

"She's fine," she tells me. "They're going to keep her for a few days for observation."

I sigh in relief. "That's good news, right? You knew she was too tough to let something like this get the best of her."

"Yeah," she answers quietly. "She'll outlive us both."

Something about her flat tone is unsettling, and it's obvious that something is still weighing on her. "Is something else bothering you? What's wrong?"

"We—" She swallows, clearing her throat like she's having trouble. "We need to talk about what happened at the hospital. With Iris."

Shit.

I squeeze my eyes shut as I huff out a frustrated breath. "Fuck, Cassie. I'm sorry. She shouldn't have ever spoken to you like that. I should have done more, but everything was so—"

"It's not your fault," she says urgently. She reaches her hand to lay it over mine against my knee. "*None* of this is your fault."

"I know I couldn't have predicted how this morning would play out, but it doesn't mean I don't feel terrible about the things she said to you. I hate that you got dragged into my bullshit." I try to smile then, mostly because I'm desperate to see some expression on her face other than the melancholy nothing she's giving me now. "Strange ending to a great night."

She doesn't smile; in fact, her eyes water as if she might cry again.

"Cassie." I lean in to cup her face with my palm. "Please talk to me. Tell me why you're crying."

"I just . . . I don't think I realized how hard this was going to be."

My brow furrows. "Do you mean Wanda? She's going to be fine. In a few days she'll be back home and everything will be okay. You'll see."

"I'm going to stay at her place," she tells me.

This catches me off guard, and it isn't until this exact moment that I notice the duffel bag sitting on the other side of her, next to the couch.

"Okay . . . sure." I nod encouragingly, pushing my own feelings aside, wanting to put hers first right now. "Of course. I'm sure Wanda is going to need some help when she comes home. You should take all the time you need with her."

A lone tear slips over her lashes to trail down her cheek, and I notice it then, what I haven't seen until this very second. I haven't noticed the way she's looking at me like she's never going to see me again.

I feel something stinging and sharp in my chest.

"How long do you think you'll be gone, Cassie?"

Her lower lip trembles, and that pain in my chest becomes an ache, like I need to breathe but am not able to get any air.

"Cassie," I try, my voice coming out wrong. "Please don't—"

"I can't do it, Aiden," she says desolately. "I can't be something used to hurt you. Or Sophie, for that matter. I just can't."

"Cassie, what Iris said—it's going to be okay. She's just angry right now. She'll calm down. I'm not going to let anything happen."

"It already has," she chokes out. "And it's going to get worse. They're always going to point to how this all started. They're going to use me like a trump card. I can't be that. You won't *want* me to be that. I'll end up as a burden to both of you."

I can't comprehend what she's saying. How can she actually think that her leaving could be a good thing? Just the thought of her walking out my door right now makes me feel like I'm swallowing water far beneath the surface, struggling to swim upward but suspended far below. It feels like *drowning*.

"Cassie. Let's talk about this. It's been a stressful morning, and you're upset. You don't have to make any decisions right now. If we—"

"I'm not going to change my mind, Aiden."

I'm months shy of being thirty-two, and I have never in my adult life felt as helpless as I do right now. I can feel her slipping through my fingers, and it feels unfair, *unreal*—I've barely even had her at all, and now I'm going to lose her.

"You're really leaving. Aren't you?"

She nods, and I feel something breaking inside.

"I've got some of my stuff in that bag"—she nods toward the duffel that I'd like to toss out the window—"and I'll send someone after the rest."

She's going to disappear. Again.

"Sophie," I say dazedly. "She's asleep. I should go—"

"No." She shakes her head. "I think it would be easier on her if I didn't say goodbye."

I feel something hot at my neck then, pushing up from the couch as my sadness and my frustration collide with anger. "Easier for who, Cassie? You? Or her?"

"Both," she whispers, fresh tears springing up in her eyes. She rises from the couch then, hardly even looking at me. "It'll be easier on her if she hates me."

"Do you actually believe that? She *loves* you. She's the happiest I have seen her since her mom died, and it's because of you. If you disappear, it's going to absolutely wreck her."

Not just her, I want to scream. *It's not just her.*

"I know," she whispers dejectedly.

"You said you weren't going anywhere," I remind her. "Why did you let me tell her about us if you were going to leave?"

"I'm sorry," is all she says, reaching for her duffel. "I wish there was some other way."

"There *is.*" I reach for her shoulders, turning her towards me before I hold her face in my hands. "Stay. Figure it out with me. I just found you. Don't throw it all away before we even have a chance. *Please*, Cassie."

Her eyes dip to my mouth as her lips tremble, and I feel my restraint crumbling away. She doesn't stop me as I lean in, and I hear her soft intake of air seconds before my mouth touches hers. The kiss is wet from her tears, only making me feel more desperate, and I try to pull her closer, try to bridge the gap between us that feels like it's widening by the second.

There's a moment when she leans in, when I think maybe she'll fall into my arms and forget this entire conversation—but it's fleeting, slipping through my fingers just like she is. She pulls away, keeping her eyes shut tight as her fingers wrap around my wrists to gently pry them from her face. She steps away from me, and it's only a foot of space between us, but it feels like miles.

"I'm sorry."

Two words, but they're enough to rip me to shreds. But I'm not ignorant to the look in her eyes. I can see how much this is killing her. How much she doesn't want to go. How can I let her go, when she's looking at me like she is? Like she wants me to hold her?

"You don't want to go," I say desperately. "You know you don't. I'm not going to let you walk away for some bullshit reason. I *need* you."

She sucks in a breath, eyes widening as her resolve seems to waver. Her mouth closes just to open again, like she's trying to form words but can't remember how. Her next breath is shaky, her lips pressing together and her eyes turning to the floor, and for one second I think I've gotten through to her. That she won't leave.

"Aiden, I . . . it's not just the Iris thing."

"Then what is? Whatever it is, we can work it out together. You just have to give me the chance to—"

"This is all too much for me," she says flatly.

It feels like someone knocked the wind out of me. I feel all my surety and confidence trickling down the drain, having no way to be prepared for the possibility that she might not just be leaving for me but for *her* as well.

"What?"

"I . . ." She rubs at her arm nervously. Is it because of guilt? "I've been too distracted by all of this. I've been messing up at school, and I just . . . I don't have time for everything that comes with this. With us. I love Sophie, I do, but I'm not ready to be anyone's mother. It's way more than I signed up for. It's not the right time in my life for me to try and be what you need."

Every emotion that has raged inside me from the moment I realized her intention fizzles out and dies. In their wake is a cold, empty void that I find is somehow more terrifying than the idea of her leaving only moments ago. It feels like the end of something. Or maybe it feels like something that never really was.

"Oh."

I don't know what else to say. How can I possibly respond to that? I'd deluded myself into thinking that Cassie felt as strongly for me as I've come to feel for her. How naive of me.

A dry, hollow laugh escapes me. "Right. I didn't—" My voice is thick now. "I didn't realize that's how you felt."

"I'm sorry," she says again.

I'm sorry.

What a ridiculous phrase. Meaningless. How is it that in millions of years we haven't managed to come up with a better string of words to offer someone whose heart's being stomped on? *I'm sorry* feels like offering a Band-Aid for a shark bite.

Utterly. Useless.

"Don't be," I tell her. Now I'm the one who can't look her in the eye. I don't know if I'm embarrassed or just numb. "It was my mistake." I move past her to drop down on the couch to take the pressure of my now-unsteady legs. "I shouldn't have assumed that we felt the same."

I hear her choke back a sob, but I still can't bring myself to look at her. I'm afraid if I do, I'll lose it.

"Aiden, I—"

"I'll say goodbye to Sophie for you," I say hollowly. "Eventually, she'll understand."

In my line of vision I can make out her legs moving toward her bag, and I can see her hands reaching for the strap. They're trembling. I think she's crying again. I still want to hold her, but knowing that she doesn't want me to keeps me on the couch, my hands fisted at my sides and my eyes trained on the floor.

"Goodbye, Aiden," she tells me softly, hardly even a whisper. "I'm so sorry."

I don't tell her goodbye. I don't think I'm physically able to make my mouth form the word. Almost like it's wired shut in rebellion. As if not saying it will somehow make all of this go away.

But I can see her walking away from me, and the crushing realization that she won't be coming back is a heavy, tangible thing settling on my shoulders. I don't breathe until I hear the front door close behind her; I think I was hoping during her entire walk downstairs that she would change her mind. I have no idea what I'm going to tell Sophie, just like I have no idea how I'm going to pick myself up off the couch and figure out how to deal with losing Cassie only moments after I found her.

I don't cry. I think I'd like to, but everything is so numb. Instead, I put my head in my hands, my shoulders shaking as I close my eyes and try to forget the way Cassie kissed me like she didn't want to go. Even if I already know it's going to haunt me. I have a terrifying feeling that all of her will.

Part of me thinks I should have told her I love her.

Part of me knows it wouldn't have made her stay.

I can't believe you stood me up.

Did something happen?

Please tell me something happened. Otherwise I am going to feel really stupid.

Hello?

CHAPTER 25

Cassie

"You know, eventually you're going to have to stop mop-
ing."

I raise my head from the aged velvet of Wanda's couch, glaring
at her from the living room. "Shouldn't you be more sympathetic?"

"Why?" she scoffs at me as she stirs her soup. "I'm not the one
who told you to go and act like a dummy."

I groan as I press my face back against the couch, the place
where I've been sleeping for the past two weeks. It's been more
than two months since I last wallowed here, and after everything
that's happened, it feels like some awful irony that this is where I
find myself. Sometimes I catch myself wondering if it might be
better if I could somehow go back and stop myself from ever taking that job to begin with.

At least then I wouldn't be so miserable.

Lying to Aiden and making him think that I didn't have time

in my life for him and Sophie will go down in history as the hardest thing I've ever done. I know that ultimately it was necessary, that they will both be better off without me in their lives—but it doesn't make it hurt any less. I don't think I will ever get his heartbroken expression out of my head. And I have definitely tried.

I can't even let myself wonder how Sophie might have reacted when she'd learned I was gone—dwelling on that for too long makes me feel like complete garbage instead of *mostly* garbage. There's no way a ten-year-old can understand complicated nonsense like sacrificing for the greater good. Hell, after weeks of obsessing over the decision, even I think it's bullshit. Nothing for the greater good should make you feel so shitty.

"You haven't talked to him since then?"

I shake my head against the couch cushions. "I'm sure that they both would be happy to never see me again."

"Oh, horseshit. There isn't anything you could have said that can't be fixed with a good romp in the hay."

"There are so many things wrong with what you just said."

"Everything I say is brilliant."

I roll my eyes. "I'm not even sure where you would find hay in San Diego."

"You know what I mean."

"He hates me, Wanda," I whine, burying my face. "And he should. I was a real asshole."

"You were doing what you thought you had to," she offers. "Even if it was stupid as hell."

"Gee. Thanks."

"I did try to talk you out of it."

"I know." I close my eyes to keep from crying for the hundredth time since I left Aiden's house. "But it's better this way."

Wanda makes a noise that suggests she has a lot to say about that but blessedly says nothing. Not that she hasn't said plenty since I brought her home from the hospital. I've been trying to throw myself into school and the useless endeavor of looking for more work; I would like to say that I've been making myself useful to Wanda while she recovers, but it only took about twenty-four hours after she came home for her to decide she had no desire to be "coddled." Stubborn as a mule, that one. With all the sulking I've been doing, it's more like she's been taking care of me.

"Why don't you get out of the house?"

I shake my head. "Don't want to."

"You're haunting this damned place like a ghost. If you don't go outside soon, you're gonna start collecting cobwebs."

"I'm fine, Wanda."

"Tell that to your hair," she snorts. "When's the last time you brushed it?"

"Really great to have you in my corner," I deadpan. "I feel very nurtured."

"You want nurturing, get out of my house and go tell that big pretty man that you love him. I bet he'll give you all the nurturing you want."

I push up from the couch, rolling my body to the side and getting to my feet. "Okay. I'm going out."

"To Aiden's?"

"To the *store.*"

"Stubborn ass," she grumbles.

"Yeah, I love you too."

I shuffle into my shoes by the door, not bothering to brush my hair like she suggested. As I grab my keys, I catch sight of myself in the little mirror hanging by the front door and notice that I really do look like shit. My auburn hair is sticking up every which way, my normally nice-looking skin sallow—made worse by the bags under my eyes from the lack of sleep. Plus, there's the overall look of general misery I can't seem to wipe from my features. I make a mental note to force myself to take a long, hot shower when I get back from the store as I use a hair tie from my wrist to throw my hair up.

"Get some bread," Wanda calls after me.

"Yeah, yeah," I toss over my shoulder as I shut the door behind me.

haven't been outside other than to my lab last weekend, and even then, I had done my very best to avoid conversation with actual people as much as possible, especially Camila. The trip to the store is a short one—just a few blocks from Wanda's house—but it's the furthest noneducational journey I've taken in weeks, so I'm going to chalk it up to a win.

I don't actually need anything from the store. Truth be told, I just wanted to show Wanda that I *am* capable of doing things without crying—but I throw a candy bar (two, actually) onto the conveyor belt at the last second along with a hastily snatched peach tea before the cashier rings up Wanda's bread. Maybe the snacks will help me remember what endorphins feel like.

I sound like a less cool Wednesday Addams lately.

It's still light out when I leave, not quite enough time for Wanda to have finished dinner, and as I start to walk back, I consider finding a bench to squat on for another twenty minutes or so to give the illusion of me getting out and about. Maybe that will get Wanda off my back. Although I doubt it. I open my drink as I walk, turning the lid over out of habit to read whatever is written on the other side.

Cherophobia is the fear of happiness.

I pause on the street, frowning with disdain at the offensive little circle. I really can't make this shit up. If Aiden were here, he'd probably accuse me of lying. Thinking about him only makes my heart hurt more. I put the lid back on aggressively, tossing the bottle in my plastic sack as I continue on toward Wanda's, planning to toss the drink in the first available trash can.

There's a café I like on the way back to the apartment, the familiar smell of freshly baked pastries assaulting my nostrils when I pass and giving me the first real hit of endorphins I've had since I left Aiden's. I linger outside the door as I weigh my options. A cheese Danish sounds a hell of a lot better than a random bench, now that I think about it.

I have to push the fact that I look like I've been living in a cave for the last few weeks far out of my mind to find the courage to go inside, telling myself that these people have surely seen weirder things than a hot-mess grad student who looks like she might burst into tears at any minute. That's probably par for the course for us, anyway. It's not very busy inside, at least, and I say a quiet thanks for small blessings.

I pull my phone out of my pocket as I fall in line to order, staring at the empty notifications with an increasingly familiar feeling of melancholy. Aiden hasn't reached out since I left, and why would he? I practically told him I didn't want him. Something that is so far from the truth it might as well be in the *National Enquirer*. Right next to the bit about some pop singer keeping an alien in her basement.

I don't even know how many times I've wondered whether or not I'll ever stop loving him at this point.

The line moves, and I shuffle along, peeking around the café to see how many people I'm subjecting to my rough appearance. Most of the tables are bare save for a few along the back wall; there's an older man sipping something from a mug while he reads a paper, a young couple chatting across the table from each other animatedly, and in the very back corner, typing furiously at a laptop and looking less than enthused about her lot in life is—

I can't help but stare.

I know exactly how large this city is, and therefore I am fairly aware of the odds of seeing someone at random you don't want to see. I can't rattle off a percentage or anything since I don't care about population study and I don't work for the Census, but I can still conjecture that it is a *very* small number.

But there sits Iris, tucked in the corner of a café I've visited a hundred times like a regular.

She doesn't notice me as she glares down at her laptop screen, and I catch myself wondering what she's focusing on so intently. Despite my desperate attempts to mentally detach myself from Aiden and Sophie, seeing Iris is a harsh reminder that I have made absolutely no progress. Seeing her irritates the hole they left behind, making it feel as raw and as fresh as the day I carved it into my own chest when I walked out on them.

It's not a conscious decision, going to her; I don't think I even realize I'm walking over to her until I'm nearly at her table, my feet moving on their own as they carry me one after the other to where she's sitting. She doesn't even notice me until I plop down into the seat opposite her in the little booth, dropping the sack with Wanda's bread beside me as Iris's eyes widen with surprise, like she's trying to process the fact that I'm here.

"Hi," I say.

She still looks out of sorts to see me. "Cassie? What are you doing here?"

I don't know how to answer that. I'm not entirely sure myself.

"I . . . I saw you sitting here, and I just . . ." I notice for the first time the dark circles under her eyes, looking hardly any different from mine. I notice how much she looks like Sophie—same cheekbones, same nose—and I realize I barely know anything about this woman, and now she's uprooted my entire life. I realize at this very moment how much I need to know why it had to come to this. "Do you hate Aiden? Do you really want to take Sophie away?"

She rears back, looking incensed. "Excuse me?"

"I need to know," I urge. "I need to know that I didn't have any other choice."

"You're not making any sense," she snorts, slamming her laptop closed. "And I don't owe you or Aiden a damned thing. So you can tell him—"

"I can't tell him anything," I inform her softly, feeling that familiar sting in my eyes. I silently beg them to stay dry. "I left. The day we saw you at the hospital."

Iris snorts. "What, did it stop being fun when you realized how inappropriate it was?"

"No." I shake my head. "I left because Aiden is a good dad."

"Because that's a real reason."

"It is," I say matter-of-factly. "He's a great dad, and he loves his daughter, and I wasn't going to be the reason someone takes her away from him."

"Your leaving doesn't change the fact that he left her with an elderly stranger and then went radio silent when she needed him because he was with *you.*"

"And I can't change that," I tell her. "I know that. It was a mistake. I can't take it back. But I can make sure I don't cause them any more pain. Even if it means hurting them to do it."

Iris looks at me for a long time, her blond brow knitted and her mouth pursed while she studies me.

"Why exactly are you telling me this?"

"Because you need to hear it," I insist. "I know that Aiden's schedule is crazy, but he's been working so hard to find a balance for Sophie. He *adores* that little girl. All he wants is what's best for her. I don't understand why you would try so hard to take her away when she *wants* to be with him."

"She doesn't know what she wants," Iris says a little quieter, averting her eyes.

"I think she does," I argue. "I saw it every day for weeks. How much she wanted to be with her dad. You have to know that it would hurt her if you separated them, so why the hell are you trying so hard?"

"Because I *have* to," she huffs, running her fingers through her hair. "You don't get it."

"Then explain it to me."

"And why should I?"

"Because I'm offering to listen, and I'm starting to think there isn't anyone else in your life who has."

"You don't know anything about my life," she scoffs. "You can't possibly know what it's like to lose your only family."

I smile at her, but it's hollow. "You might be surprised."

"Oh? You know what it's like to wake up one day and your sister is just . . . gone? Your other half, the most important person in your life"—she snaps her fingers—"gone. Just like that." Iris looks up at the ceiling, her eyes shining. "She was all I had. Our parents are dead. Did you know? Since we were teens. I basically *raised* her, and I didn't even get to say goodbye. You can't *possibly* know what that's like."

"You're right," I tell her truthfully. Unfortunately, I was subjected to my parents for a very long time before I was able to get away. "I don't know what that's like."

"And then my niece, the only part of Rebecca I have left—suddenly she's ripped away from me too. *Days* after we buried Rebecca." Iris runs her fingers through her hair, looking lost. "My sister was suddenly gone, and then some guy who only saw her once or twice a month comes and takes her? Just because he shares her DNA? How is that fair? I watched Sophie come into this world. I held Rebecca's hand while she pushed. I cut Sophie's cord. *Me*. Not Aiden. *Me*. And now she's . . ."

Her eyes are red, a wetness there that threatens to spill, and for the first time since I met Iris, I don't see the guarded woman that she's been every time we've met. I see a scared, grieving sister, a lonely aunt—someone who doesn't know where she's going or what to do next. For the first time since I met her, she seems . . . sad. Not any different than I am right now, really.

"I can't lose Sophie too," Iris whispers, a quiet sob in her throat. She wipes her eyes. "I'm sure you're enjoying this."

I shake my head. "I'm not. I'm just thinking that we all could have avoided a lot of heartbreak if you and Aiden could have a real conversation."

"You don't think I've tried?"

"But *have* you?" I give her a pointed look. "Listen, I know Aiden. He's a good man. He's definitely not an unreasonable one. He wouldn't keep Sophie from you out of spite. Look at how these last few months have been. Haven't we been finding ways for both of you to be in her life?"

Her mouth snaps shut, a guilty look in her eyes as she stares down at the table. "That wasn't Aiden. That was you."

"I'm glad to hear that at least some part of you still believes I cared about Sophie."

"Listen, I'm sure you do, but you have to understand—"

"*You* have to understand that Aiden is going to make mistakes. With or without me in his life. I don't think the measure of a parent is the mistakes they make. I think it's how hard they work to fix them."

Iris stares at me with a bewildered expression, turning her head slightly like she's trying to figure me out. "I don't get why you want to help so badly. You said you left."

"Yeah." I laugh bitterly. "And it was the hardest thing I've ever done. Now I wonder if it was even the right thing."

"So why are you trying to help me?"

"I'm not," I correct. "I'm trying to help *them*. I want Aiden and Sophie to have every bit of happiness that they deserve. If that means spelling out to you how to have an actual conversation like a normal human being . . . well. It's worth the awkward conversation."

Iris blinks. Then the wrinkle in her brow softens, her eyes following suit as she looks at me as if seeing me for the first time. "You love him. Don't you."

"I—" I swallow, just the thought of it rustling up a fresh wave of pain that I suspect won't ebb for a long time to come. "Yes." I nod slowly, looking down in my lap. "I do. Both of them."

Iris doesn't say anything, and really, I don't think there's anything left for either of us to say. I nod awkwardly at the table before I lay my fingers on the top to drum them absently.

"I'm going to leave you alone now," I tell her. "Just . . . think about it. There's no reason for any of you to keep hurting like this."

Iris nods dazedly, still looking at me like I have a second head growing out of the side of my neck. I guess I can't blame her, since this is the strangest encounter I've ever had in my life. I can't even say if it will do any good, but at least I can say I tried.

"Cassie," Iris calls as I move to slide out of the booth.

I pause at the edge. "Yeah?"

"I'm sorry," she says. "For the things I said. I was hurting."

Another dry, hollow laugh escapes me. "Yeah, well. There's plenty of that to go around."

I don't say goodbye as I leave Iris sitting at the table, and I don't look back. I step out of the café with Wanda's sack of bread still in my hand and my Danish forgotten. I have no way of knowing if anything will come from what I've done, but the hole in my chest feels smaller, less raw. Maybe it will never close. Maybe this will be the best I can hope for—that Aiden and Sophie will find happiness.

Even if it's without me.

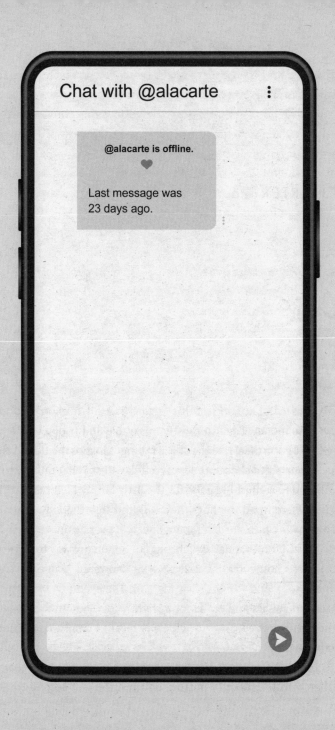

CHAPTER 26

Cassie

Days after talking to Iris, I find myself feeling strangely less mopey. I'm still mostly miserable and a lot angry at myself, but I don't feel like the sky is falling. Most of the time. I think it's because I've chosen to let myself daydream that talking to Iris will lead to something good for the little family I left behind. That somewhere in all the hurt they will find their happily ever after. That I won't be a burden for anyone. Not ever again.

I'm still on Wanda's couch, but I'm not on my way to achieving complete homeostasis, at least. I've showered (multiple times, thank you), and I've brushed my hair. I've even put away my depression sweats and opted for a slightly less sad outfit of leggings and an oversized T-shirt, which is clean, I might add. That's a definite plus.

I've spent most of the day working on assignments that I've fallen into the habit of putting off until the last second to allow for more crying time, and by the time that I've gotten fully caught up with my lessons—the first time in weeks that I've done so earlier than the night before my labs—I'm feeling almost like myself again. Almost.

I can hear Wanda stepping down the hall from her bedroom as I close my laptop, pulling her robe closed as she peers at me over her glasses. "Look at you," she says, sounding impressed. "There was an actual woman living under all that funk."

I roll my eyes. "Again, so happy to have you in my corner."

"I'm just pulling your leg. I'm happy you look more like yourself. I was starting to consider calling an exorcist or something."

"Yes, we are all very amused by your haunting jokes."

"Dialed that old Ghostbusters line at one point," she deadpans. "Got some poor schmuck in Kentucky."

"Isn't it time for you to get ready for bingo?"

"I've got time." She moves over to her chair to plop down into it, studying me over the tops of her glasses. "You do look much better. You think that mean broad heard anything you said?"

I shrug. "I don't know. I want to think she did though. It makes me feel better to think that."

"You'd probably feel even better if you go check yourself."

"I'm not having this discussion again."

"We haven't actually had it to begin with. You're always skulking off to the bathroom or burying yourself in my couch like a real squatter."

"Wow. A couple months ago you were begging me to stay here."

"Yeah, well. That was before you had a whole-ass family out there wishing you'd come back."

There's a squeezing sensation in my chest. "They don't. Trust me."

"You think they'd write you off after a few weeks?"

"I told him I didn't have time for them. I told him I didn't sign up for any of that."

"Yeah, well. We all do dumb things sometime when we love people."

"Yeah," I laugh. "We do."

"I don't want you to end up with any regrets."

"Maybe I'll be like you," I chuckle. "New boyfriend every week. Sounds like a dream to me."

"It's not," Wanda says flatly. "You think that sounds like a dream to you?"

I rear back. "What?"

"You think I like living in this tiny apartment all by myself?"

"I . . ." I feel at a loss for words. "I don't understand."

"Cassie," Wanda laughs. "You are too smart to be this dumb. Of course I'm not living the dream." She clucks her tongue. "The dream is coming home to someone who loves you every day."

"But, if that's how you feel, then why do you—"

"Because I had my chance at that once, and I ruined it. Just like you're trying to do."

I have no idea what to say. In all the years I've known Wanda, she's never given me any indication that she had any qualms about her life. Sure, it's a little out of the box that she could get to this age without having ever settled down, but I assumed that was the life she chose. It had never occurred to me that she might want anything different.

"Why is this the first time I'm hearing about this?"

Wanda shrugs. "You've never needed to hear it until now." She crosses one leg over the other as she sighs deeply, looking down at her foot that's tapping the air as she considers. "I wasn't much older than you were, when I met Henry."

"Henry?"

Wanda smiles, remembering. "Your typical surfer beach bum

living in La Jolla in the seventies. Blond hair, blue eyes . . . way too pretty for his own good. And of course, since I was such a looker, he obviously couldn't stop thinking about me after we met."

"Naturally," I say with a grin.

"I thought I was hot shit in those days. I'm telling you, Cassie, if booby cams were a thing back then, I'd have made a killing."

"I have no doubt."

"So there I was, this stacked little brunette who thought her shit didn't stink, and along comes Henry. I tell you, Cassie. He knocked me right on my ass. He bought me an ice cream on the boardwalk that first day, and I can't even remember what we talked about, but I was just"—she claps her hands in a shooting-off motion—"gone. Right from the start."

"What happened?"

"We were together every day that summer. We would lie on the beach, we would make out in his car, we'd do . . . other things." I make a face, and Wanda snorts at me. "Oh, shut up. You and I both know neither of us are strangers to a penis."

Words I would never like to hear again, thank you very much.

"Anyway," Wanda goes on. "Of course I loved Henry, and of course he was obsessed with me—"

"Obviously," I tease.

"Damn right," she huffs. "But . . ." She sighs, shaking her head. "I was foolish. Twenty-seven years old, and I still didn't know anything about anything. I was always looking for the next party, the next big thing, and Henry, surprisingly enough, well . . . he wanted more."

I notice the slight furrow in her brow now, the sad quality of her eyes that tells me this isn't a wound that's ever healed for her, whatever it may be.

"He asked me to marry him," she says in a faraway voice. "At the end of that summer. Got down on one knee and everything.

He had . . ." Wanda smiles, but again, there's a sadness to it. "He even had this ring. It was tiny and pitiful, but I know he had to have saved all summer to buy it." She closes her eyes, and I can tell she's remembering this moment like it was yesterday. Like she's never stopped thinking about it. "He'd gotten this job with a construction company in San Francisco, and he wanted me to come with him. Wanted to start our lives together all the way across the state."

I know what happened, of course I do, since Wanda is here and Henry isn't, but the way she goes quiet then tells me that she has trouble talking about it even now after all this time, and I find myself stating the obvious, anyway.

"You said no," I say quietly.

She nods. "I said no."

"Why?"

"Why," Wanda laughs dryly, turning her eyes up at the ceiling and shaking her head. "I thought I needed the party. That I wasn't ready to settle down and play the housewife. I thought that somehow this life Henry was offering would hold me back." Wanda breathes in deep just to blow it out, that same sad smile at her mouth. "So he left. Packed his bags and took that job. He left me behind just like I forced him to."

"Wanda, I—"

"Don't." She waves me off. "It was damn near half a century ago. I made my bed."

"But I had no idea."

"Because you didn't need to then, but you do now. Do you know why?"

I shake my head. "Why?"

"Because," she says. "Eight months after Henry left, I found myself miserable. I missed him so terribly that I could barely get out of bed in the morning. It took me *eight* whole months to realize that I had made the worst mistake of my life, and that I didn't want to keep chasing the parties. I wanted Henry."

"So what happened?"

"Tracked him down." She nods. "Yes, I did. I flew all the way to San Francisco with this grand plan to win him back. I was determined to do whatever it took. Grovel, beg . . . anything."

"But?"

The pain in Wanda's expression is palpable, and it's astounding that it could still be so fresh for her, even after all this time.

"But he'd moved on," she tells me softly. "He'd married this pretty little thing who was a receptionist at the place he worked. I saw them on one of the job sites I'd run off to trying to find him. She was handing him a sack lunch in a white dress, and they looked . . . they looked so *happy*. I couldn't even bring myself to confront him. I turned around and went right home." She looks me in the eyes then, pointedly, like this is the most important part that she wants me to grasp. "And I *never* felt anything close to what I felt for Henry. Not for the rest of my life."

"Wanda, I'm—I'm so sorry. I always thought you loved your life."

She blows out a breath. "I make do. I have fun, I do. And I have you now, and that's been enough for me. But I see you sitting there, making the same mistakes, and I can't sit by and watch my life play out all over again with you. Trust me, Cassie. You don't want to see Aiden someday with his pretty blonde in a white dress. You don't forget pain like that. You don't ever forget loving someone that could have been yours if you hadn't pushed them away."

I look down in my lap, trying to think of a response. I feel horrible for having spent so much time with Wanda without having any idea about this part of her past; why hadn't she ever told me about this before now? Maybe if I'd known this story, maybe I'd have been less likely to . . .

No.

I can't sit here and try to blame someone else for my choices. *I'm* the one who said those things to Aiden, and I'm the one who made the decision for us both that he was better off without me. I could have talked to him, and we could have tried to find a solution together, but I robbed him of that option when I lied to him and told him I didn't want him. I have no one to blame but myself for the hell I've been through these last few weeks. Is this what the rest of my life will look like? Will I always regret what could have been between us?

I already know the answer to that. I know it because even before I ever knew Aiden's name, before I knew what he looked like or where he came from or about his smiles and his kisses and everything else—I missed him. I missed him for a year when I knew nothing. I know that I will miss him *forever* now that I know so much.

"God," I mutter, hanging my head. "I fucked up."

"Mm-hmm," Wanda agrees. "But you still have time to fix it. You can go and apologize. Tell that man you love him and that you're a complete idiot."

"Just like that, huh," I chuckle, peeking up at her.

Wanda bobs her head. "Easy peasy." She looks at the wall clock, checking the time before she rises from her chair. "Now, if you'll excuse me, I have to go get ready."

"Bingo?"

"Nope," she tells me. "I'm going on a date."

My mouth falls open. "What?"

"That's right," she says with her head held high. "A bona fide date."

"With who?"

"Fred Wythers."

"*What?* I thought you dumped him."

"Yeah, well. That's because he wanted to see me more. I wasn't looking for anything like that then."

I still feel flabbergasted by this new revelation. "And you are now?"

"A heart attack really puts things into perspective, girl. I could be dead tomorrow." She shrugs. "Maybe I decided I might not want to kick the bucket all alone."

"That's . . ." I'm still trying to wrap my head around everything I've learned in the last twenty minutes. "That's great, Wanda."

"We'll see," she humphs. "I'll get a free meal out of it, at least."

I can't help it, I grin at this very classic Wanda outlook. "Right."

"Now, I want you to sit there on that couch—"

"No problems there," I snort.

"—and you think about what I've said. Maybe you'll figure out that you don't want to be like me, after all." She winks at me then. "Even if I am cool as hell."

I laugh as she heads back down the hall to get ready for her date—that's going to take me some time to get used to—leaving me right where she found me but with a hell of a lot more to think about.

Wanda left an hour ago, and while it was strange to see her in one of her nicer pantsuits and being picked up at her front door like she was running off to prom, I like how cute she was, trying not to seem excited. Fred had given me a friendly hello before they left, waving with one hand and holding a bouquet in the other, and I hadn't missed the blush on Wanda's cheeks when he'd handed over the flowers. It's definitely new, but it looks good on her, I think.

Although, the "don't wait up" she'd tossed over her shoulder made me feel like a loser. Seventy-two, and she still has more game than me.

I haven't done much since Wanda left, not that anyone's surprised, but I have been doing a lot of thinking. About Wanda's story, about my own predicament . . . but mostly about Aiden and Sophie. I've gone over every possible scenario that I can think of in regard to how I might apologize, or if I even should, and every spiral only brings me right back to the same guilt and the crushing fear that nothing I could ever say to them will make any difference. How could either of them forgive me after the way I left? Like they didn't even matter.

I know at some point I will need to drag myself off this couch and make myself something to eat if I am going to keep up the facade that I am slowly getting better, but my brain is mush after all the thinking I've been doing, and I won't pretend that turning off the lights and going to bed early at—I glance at the clock and groan—seven o'clock sounds like a much more appealing option.

I'm still going back and forth between my riveting options when there's a knock at the door, and I frown at the other side of it as I wonder who might be here. There's no way that Wanda would be back this early, and as far as I know I'm her only real friend, so who else could it be? With my luck, it'll be the old man from 2B again with my package he "accidentally opened after they delivered it to him by mistake." Right. He was just disappointed there wasn't anything good in there. I huff as I'm forced to leave the sad velvet throne I've made a home on, trudging over to Wanda's front door and looking through the peephole, but the hall looks empty. I frown as I look again, confirming that no, there isn't anyone out there. Are we still ding-dong ditching in 2023?

I unlock the chain before fumbling with the lock in annoyance, finally managing to get everything undone so I can wrench open the door in the hopes that I can catch the little bastard who dares to give me shit while I'm still half wallowing. I find immediately that I hadn't been wrong, exactly, since I couldn't see anyone out of the peephole, but I hadn't been right either.

Because there is someone on the other side of the door, someone who is too short to spot from the peephole and who has no business being here, especially by themselves. I gape at chestnut hair and freckles and a tiny face that makes my heart hurt, stunned for a moment as I try to make sense of her being here. I turn my head down the hall to confirm that yes, she actually is alone, squashing the slight disappointment and focusing on the little girl at the door who makes me feel both elated and incredibly guilty.

"Sophie?"

I think I feel more foolish than anything else.

I'm not a stupid girl. I don't do things like this.

But half falling for someone whose name I don't know and whose face I've never seen . . . well. It doesn't do anything to help my case.

I stare at the settings page in the same way I've done so a dozen times in the last few weeks, wondering if I am a stupid girl. Would I be so hurt over a relative stranger that I was considering deleting my entire account otherwise?

But I miss him.

And it feels like I can't do this anymore, not without thinking of him every time I log on.

I take a deep breath as I hit the delete button.

Are you sure you want to delete your account?

I lied.

I definitely feel more hurt than foolish.

CHAPTER 27

Cassie

W hat are you doing here?"

Sophie is still standing on the faded carpet of the apartment hallway. I think I'm actually too stunned to even think to invite her in at first, stuck in the doorway as she rubs her arm guiltily.

"Sophie," I press, gently grabbing her arm and pulling her inside the apartment before shutting the door. "How did you even get here?"

"An Uber," she tells me matter-of-factly.

"An Uber," I echo dumbly. "You took an Uber?"

"Yes."

"All by yourself?"

She holds up a cell phone that I recognize. "I used my dad's phone."

"You used your dad's . . ." I blink, trying to wrap my head around what she's saying. "Where is your dad?"

"Working," she tells me. "I snuck out of the office."

"Sophie, that was *extremely* dangerous. Do you understand me? You are way too young to be hopping into Ubers and going across town. How did you even get the address?"

"Dad had it on his phone."

Everything she is saying sounds perfectly reasonable and logical, but nothing about it makes any sense. I know Sophie is an incredibly smart little girl, but this feels impossible, even for her.

"What are you doing here, Sophie?"

She looks down at the floor. "I needed to see you."

"You needed to see me."

"Yes. Dad wouldn't let me call you."

My stomach twists. She wanted to call me? The guilt I feel for not having said goodbye to her flares up like it's brand new. "Sophie . . . your dad is probably freaking out."

"No, he isn't," she mumbles. "He's going to give me away."

"What?"

She looks at me with a helpless expression. "He's going to give me away! To Aunt Iris!"

"Come here." I tug her hand, leading her to the couch, and pat the space beside me so that she can sit. "What are you talking about?"

"I heard him talking to her," Sophie tells me. "On the phone. He was talking about me going to her house. He doesn't want to keep me anymore because I ran you off."

"Oh, Sophie." My heart breaks a little more. "You didn't run me off."

"But I always run off the nanny. I . . ." Her eyes well with tears. "I couldn't help Wanda. Is that why you left? Dad wouldn't tell me, but that has to be why you left, right?"

"Oh, honey." I pull her against me, crushing her in my arms as the familiar scent of her watermelon shampoo hits my nostrils. I breathe it in, my emotions lodging in my throat. I thought I'd never smell it again. "That's not why I left. You did nothing wrong. *Nothing.*"

She turns her face to press deeper against my chest, her arms winding around my waist. "Then why did you leave?"

"It's . . . complicated."

"Were you mad at my dad?"

"No. *No.* I wasn't. I wasn't mad at anyone."

"Dad misses you," she mumbles into my shirt. "He never talks about you, but he seems so sad all the time."

I have to shut my eyes so that I can keep from crying again. "I miss him too," I admit quietly. "I miss you both."

"Then come back! Maybe if you come back, Dad won't give me away!"

"Soph . . ." I urge her backward, looking her in the eyes. "Your dad isn't going to give you away. There's no way he would ever do that. He loves you."

"Then why was he talking to Aunt Iris about me going to her house?"

My conversation with Iris drifts through my thoughts, and I can't be sure that whatever is going on between Iris and Aiden means progress, but I have to hope that's the case. I know that Aiden would never give Sophie up. Not under any circumstances.

"I'm sure it's not what you think," I tell her. "Maybe they're trying to stop fighting so much. I'm sure they both want to make you happy."

"I don't want to leave Dad's house," she says pitifully. "I want to stay with him."

"Of course you do," I soothe. "And I know that he wants you to stay there too. He loves you so much, Sophie, which is why I'm sure he is out of his mind with worry right now."

"Maybe," she mumbles.

"I'm sure of it," I insist, "which is why we have to take you back."

"But even if I stay with my dad," Sophie goes on, "you won't come back."

Everything in my chest feels like it's being squeezed too tightly, my eyes stinging as her piercing gaze holds mine. Her green eyes are so similar to the green of Aiden's right eye, and her expression now feels like looking at a smaller version of him. It makes me miss him all the more.

"I don't think your dad would want me to come back, Sophie. I said . . . a lot of terrible things when I left."

"Why?"

"Because . . . I thought that I had to. I thought that I needed to leave to protect you guys."

Sophie's nose wrinkles. "That's silly. You can't protect us. You're too small. My dad's *way* bigger than you. You should let him protect us."

I can't help but laugh; her ten-year-old logic is so simple and yet completely spot-on in a roundabout way. I reach to run my fingers through her hair, brushing it from her face before cupping her cheek.

"I don't know if it's that simple," I tell her. "I'm sure I'm the last person your dad wants to see."

"But don't you love him?"

This takes me completely off guard. "What?"

"You went on dates," she insists. "And you were"—she makes a face—"kissing and stuff. That means you love him, right?"

"I . . . wow. You really know how to put someone on the spot."

"What does that mean?"

I pinch the bridge of my nose, sighing. "Never mind. I don't think it matters if I love him."

"Yes, it does. My mom always said that you can fix anything with love."

My lips press together, something tugging at my heart. "She did?"

"Yes." Sophie nods enthusiastically. "So if you love him, we can fix it! You can come back, and then he won't send me away, and everything will be okay again!"

"Sophie, it's not that simple."

"But if you—"

"Just trust me," I huff, cutting her off. "I wish things were different, but they aren't."

Sophie hangs her head, and I feel that hole in my chest—the one I'd been so sure was starting to heal—throb with fresh pain as if it had been opened moments ago. I would give anything for things to be as simple as she thinks they are; I would love to take her back and apologize and throw myself in Aiden's arms or even at his feet, but I know that's not how the world works. She didn't see the look on his face when I told him that they were more than I signed up for. I took every warm moment we had together during my time there and threw it right back in his face. I don't think there's anything I can say to come back from that.

"But I do have to take you back to him," I say resignedly. "So I'm going to need you to call the restaurant and see if he's still there or if he's gone home."

I can't even imagine the level of panic Aiden is at right now; he's probably got the entire San Diego police force out on the streets right now. Sophie looks dejected, and I know none of this is what she wanted to hear, and I wish that I had better answers for her. I wish I could make everything okay for her—but I don't think it's in the cards. Not for me, and not for us.

I help Sophie dial the number to the restaurant and hand over the phone, because I'm way too much of a coward to call myself. I hold my breath while she dials, realizing in a very short time I am going to be forced to see Aiden again. I can't imagine what kind of speech Aiden will have for Sophie when she gets back to him, and I can see that she's thinking the same thing, judging by the nervous look on her face, but I think I have more to be scared of.

Because I doubt Aiden will even talk to me at all.

Aiden had already left the restaurant—his coworkers said he left immediately after discovering that Sophie had snuck out, and he headed back to his house to try to look for her there. I had been right about his level of panic; it's evident by the flashing lights we are met with outside the town house when we pull up alongside the street. Sophie looks at me with fear in her eyes as I park in front of the gate, obviously regretting her decision entirely as she is no doubt anxious about how her dad will receive her when she gets inside.

"Will you come in with me?"

I frown, looking from her in my passenger seat to the front door that is awash with red-and-blue lights. "I don't know if that's a good idea . . ."

"But he wants to see you," she urges. "And maybe if you come with me, he won't be so mad."

"Oh, I think he's still going to be mad," I warn her. "You did a silly thing, Soph."

She hangs her head. "I know."

The idea of seeing Aiden again is something I am torn between wanting terribly and wanting terribly to avoid, but the helpless look on Sophie's face tugs at my heartstrings, and I know that despite my discomfort, I owe her this much. Probably more.

"Okay," I concede. "I'll go with you. Just to take you inside, okay? Then I have to go."

She nods eagerly, looking a tad relieved. "Okay."

I feel like *I'm* the ten-year-old in massive trouble when I walk behind her through the gate, my hand gently between her shoulder blades as I urge her up the path. The front door is ajar, and all the lights are on in the house, but the first floor is empty when we step inside. I can hear voices upstairs, a cacophony of different people talking over each other, but above them all, I can hear one that I recognize. One that makes my stomach flutter, even now.

Sophie reaches for my hand at the bottom of the stairs, giving me another worried look as I wrap my hand around hers. I don't let go of it as we ascend, and at first, when we reach the top, no one notices us. They're too busy taking notes and making calls, and there, in the middle of all of it, is a frantic-looking Aiden Reid. He's still in his chef coat, his arms crossed tightly across his chest as he speaks heatedly with an officer, and I can see that his hair is messy like he's been running his fingers through it repeatedly. He looks out of his mind with worry.

I can tell when he finally sees us; he stops midsentence and turns his face with wide eyes and open mouth, like he's completely forgotten what he was about to say. I watch as he looks from Sophie to me and back again, trying to make sense of her being back, especially with me.

"Sophie," he breathes, stomping across the carpet and falling to his knees to pull her against him. "Where were you? Do you have any idea how worried I was about you? You can't disappear like that." He pushes her back, looking over her body. "Are you hurt? Are you okay?"

She nods feebly. "I'm okay."

"Where did you go?"

"To Wanda's," I offer quietly.

Aiden looks up at me then, and even like this—frazzled and confused and slightly dazed—it breaks my heart to look at him. I can feel every kiss and every touch all at once, all of it rushing back with one look. He swallows thickly as he rises to stand, staring at me like I'm a ghost.

"Wanda's?"

I nod. "She took an Uber."

"An Uber," he repeats flatly. He looks down at her with a knitted brow. "You took an Uber?"

She pulls his phone out of her pocket, handing it back to him sheepishly. "I found the address in your phone."

"You found the . . . Jesus Christ, Sophie. That's all the way across town. Do you have any idea how dangerous this was?"

She looks down at her feet, shifting her weight from one to the other. "I'm sorry."

"Why did you do this?"

"Because . . . I thought you were going to give me away."

This visibly takes him by surprise. "What? Why on earth would you think that?"

"I heard you talking to Aunt Iris this morning," she mumbles. "You said you were going to bring me to her house."

Aiden sighs, running his hands down his face. "To *visit*, Soph. Not to stay. Your aunt and I . . . we're trying to find some common ground with you. We're trying not to fight so much." He ducks to cup her chin gently. "I would *never* give you away. Do you understand? Never."

"That's what Cassie said," Sophie answers, her voice trembling. "But I was scared."

"I'm sorry," Aiden says wearily. "I was going to talk to you about this tomorrow. I had no idea you even heard the conversation. But you have to understand that there is nothing you could do or say that will make me send you away. Okay?"

I can tell it's difficult for him to acknowledge me. I can see it in the way he stares over Sophie's head for a moment or two before finally turning my way stiffly. "Thank you," he says. "For bringing her back."

"Of course," I say awkwardly. "I wanted to make sure she got home safely."

"Right." His jaw works subtly. "Of course."

I rub my arm, still feeling awkward. "Okay. Well. I guess I'd better leave you guys to it then."

I start to turn back toward the stairs, finding it incredibly difficult to keep looking at him. I hope that with time, my brain can at least smudge the memory of his face, because if I have to recall his perfect face every other day, I might go insane.

Aiden surprises me when his hand darts out to snatch my wrist, pulling me back. "Is that really all you want to say?"

"What?" I glance down at his hand holding me before meeting his eyes. "What do you mean?"

His eyes seem to burn as they hold mine, the brown a dark, warm honey and the green a rich, bright seafoam. I don't think my brain could forget those if they tried, unfortunately.

"Iris and I did have a long talk this morning," he says. "She had a lot of interesting things to say."

"O-oh." My pulse quickens. "Really?"

"Yes. Really. Apparently someone plopped down across from her at a café and convinced her to call me and work things out."

"Oh, well . . . I figured it was the least I could do."

"But what I don't get is . . . Why?"

"What do you mean, why?"

"I mean, if you wanted to toss us aside, if we were more than you signed up for—why would you care about what happened between Iris and us? Why would you insist that she try to work things out with me?"

"I—"

"And why would you tell her all about how wonderful I was with Sophie, and how much we deserved happiness?"

"Oh, well, I—"

"Why would someone who wanted to push us aside care about any of that?"

"Aiden, it's just—"

"Because she *loves* you," Sophie pipes up.

Both of us look down at her with surprise, her expression nonchalant and, frankly, annoyed. Like she's over this argument.

Aiden looks back up at me with a hopeful expression, and even this tiny flicker of need in his eyes is enough to make my stomach swoop with anticipation. Neither of us says anything, and I think maybe he is waiting for me to confirm or deny this, but I can't seem to find my voice. I open my mouth to let it gape as I try to form words, but Sophie, once again, decides to help us out.

"Don't worry," she says in that same bored tone. "Dad loves you too."

I imagine my expression appears as astounded as his when our eyes meet again, and I notice the way his eyes search mine for any sign of a lie. "Is that true?"

"I—" I swallow, my mouth feeling dry. "Yes."

"You love me?"

I try to look surer than I feel. "Yes, I do."

He catches me by surprise when he pulls me against him, my shock dissipating in only a moment when his mouth covers mine. There's desperation in his kiss that melds with relief, and my arms wind around his neck as if by instinct, trying to bring myself as close to him as I can possibly be. My fingers shove through his hair as his hands curve against my spine to pull me tighter, and it isn't until we hear the clearing of a throat behind us that either of us seems to remember the situation we're in.

I feel my cheeks warm with a blush when I notice the police officer lingering awkwardly nearby, trying to look anywhere but at us as he gets our attention. "I guess we can call this matter closed then, yeah?"

"Oh." Aiden looks dazedly between me and his daughter before laughter bubbles out of him. "I guess we can. Sorry, Officer."

"Well, uh. We'll get out of your hair." The policeman throws his finger in a circle, rounding up his fellow officers before he gives Sophie a pointed look. "Next time, maybe tell someone where you're going, little lady."

Sophie pales. "Yes, sir."

"Right." The officer's mouth tilts with a smile as we move out of the way of the stairs, and he gives us both a nod. "You folks have a good night."

I don't think any of us move until we hear the front door close downstairs, Aiden still looking at me like I might disappear any moment before he gives his attention to his daughter. "You and I have a lot to talk about, Sophie."

"Yeah." She hangs her head. "I know."

He releases me then, bending to press his lips to Sophie's hair. "But I'm glad you're okay."

"I'm sorry," she says again.

"Why don't you head up to your room," he tells her. "I'll be there in a minute."

Sophie grimaces. "Are you guys going to kiss again?"

"Yes," Aiden says. "We are." He smiles when she sticks out her tongue. "But I think you owe us this one."

"*Fine,*" she groans.

She trudges off toward the stairs that lead up to her room, and

Aiden waits until he hears her bedroom door close before he regards me again.

"You know you shouldn't have lied to me," he scolds. "It's been a shitty few weeks."

"I know." I turn my face down. "Me too."

He reaches to tilt up my chin, his knuckle lingering below it as he forces me to look at him. "I missed you," he admits. "So fucking much, Cassie." He scoffs as he shakes his head. "Even your damned Snapple facts."

One side of my mouth tilts up. "Did you know that no two lip imprints are the same?"

"That feels like one I'd want to test."

I press up on my toes, closing my eyes as I brush my mouth against his. "I missed you too."

"If you want to make it up to me," he says as he pulls me closer, "move back in."

I can't even pretend that my heart doesn't skip a beat as my lips curl in a grin. "Are you offering me another job?"

"No." He shakes his head, leaning in so that his lips hover inches from mine. "I'm offering you my whole damned life, if you want it."

Everything inside me lights up like a sparkler bomb going up in a flare, my skin tingling and my heart pounding and all of my senses going into overdrive in what I can only describe as pure happiness. I know there is more to talk about, more to say, but I think there will be time for that later. I think right now I can revel in the fact that we're here, and that he still wants me—even after everything. Right now, that's more than enough.

I pretend to consider this. "Will you be making pancakes?"

"I will not be making pancakes."

"Hmm. Well, in that case . . ."

He smiles as he pulls me in for another kiss, and I melt into it, my heart doing a happy little dance as I feel that hole in my chest quietly close, like it was never even there. I realize then that it wasn't so much of a hole, but a piece that was missing—and it was right here, with them, just waiting for me to pick it back up.

"Oh," he murmurs, still half kissing me. "In case it wasn't clear . . ." His lips press against the corner of my mouth, and I can feel his smile there, like it's imprinted on my skin. "I love you too."

I'm sinking into his kiss again, mentally calculating how long we can get away with making out downstairs before Sophie comes to scold us, and at that thought, I feel a mild flicker of panic. I push Aiden away, looking at him seriously. "We can never, *ever* tell Sophie how we met."

Aiden laughs, already pulling me in again. "Whatever you say, Cici."

I'm sure that later we will have to figure out this whole kissing thing; I know that Sophie will insist on keeping it to a minimum, as is her way, but I think tonight we get a free pass. It's not every day that you find love because of a booby cam. I think that warrants a few celebratory kisses. I can already hear the jokes Wanda will be making. There's no way she will *ever* stop talking about this.

Strangely . . . I find I absolutely don't mind.

I've refreshed the page a thousand times.

It sounds exaggerative, but it has to be true.

But my brain can't seem to comprehend the idea of her just being . . . gone. Without a trace.

I mentally calculate the number of days between this one and when I last spoke to her—and it makes my chest hurt, realizing how many there've been. They've all blended together this last month, and with everything that's happened . . .

I should have said something.

I could have said anything, anything to let her know I didn't mean to stand her up.

But I didn't, and now she's gone.

I don't even know her real name.

EPILOGUE

Aiden

ONE YEAR LATER

S top refreshing," I laugh. "It's not going to change in five seconds."

Cassie shoots me a look from the kitchen counter, an adorable pout at her mouth as she glances at the laptop screen again. "They said the results would be posted today."

"Right, but we have no idea what time. You're going to drive yourself crazy checking obsessively." She brings her thumb to her mouth to bite at her nail anxiously, and I pat the couch beside me. "Come over here and sit with me."

She's been running herself ragged over the pending results of her boards; the final hurdle she has to clear in her long-grad-school journey. I completely get her anxiety, given that this test will tell whether all her hard work has paid off and if she will be a fully licensed occupational therapist, but I hate seeing her stress like she has. She drags her feet as she comes from the kitchen, and I grab her wrist before she can pass by me, tugging her into my lap.

"It's going to be fine," I assure her, pulling her face to my chest. "You're going to pass."

She makes a frustrated sound. "What if I don't?"

"Then you try again. It won't be the end of the world. But . . . it doesn't matter, since you *will* definitely pass."

"I'm scared of failing it," she admits quietly. "I've already taken so much help from you, and if I can't start contributing soon, then—"

"You don't have to contribute," I chuckle. "I don't care what you do. As long as you do it here with me."

"Why does that sound perverted?"

"I think you're projecting."

She scoffs. "Sure I am."

"Stop worrying or I'll call Wanda."

She groans. "Don't do that. She'll come over."

"So?"

"She'll bring Fred with her."

I laugh. "Well, they are married now."

"Right. But they are way too touchy-feely. It's been three months since the wedding. They have to stop kissing all the time at some point, right?"

"You sound like Sophie," I tease.

She makes a face. "This must be what she feels like when she catches us kissing."

"Wanda would tell you to stop being silly."

"Yeah, well. Wanda didn't have to sit through a timed exam questioning everything she learned."

"You're *fine*, Cassie." I kiss her hair. "Everything is going to be fine."

"You might not be saying that after your girlfriend tanks her future."

I cup her chin to turn up her face, smiling at her disgruntled expression. I rub my thumb along her lower lip. It's amazing that after a year of having her here, I could still be so struck by her. Her bright blue eyes are like a clear sky that I could get lost in, and I do, frequently—and for what must be the thousandth time, I'm just grateful that she's here.

I lean in to kiss her, enjoying the way some of the tension leaves her body. "Do whatever you want with your future. As long as I'm part of it."

"Gosh." She smiles against my mouth. "You've gotten cheesy."

"You like cheesy."

"Maybe a little."

"Stop worrying," I urge.

"But what if—"

I kiss her again. "Stop."

"But I could—"

I kiss her harder. "*Stop.*"

"*Aiden,* but what—"

"Hey," a voice calls from the kitchen. "You passed."

Both of us jolt apart, noticing a very annoyed eleven-year-old judging us. She shakes her head as she points to the computer. "You passed," Sophie says again.

"What?" Cassie looks from Sophie to me to Sophie again. "I passed?"

Sophie checks the screen again. "That's what it says."

"Oh my God." Cassie's face lights up as she throws her arms around my neck. "I passed!"

She pulls me in for a kiss that has me closing my eyes and wishing very much that we were alone, and I keep my arms tight around her body to keep her against me.

"*Ugh*," Sophie groans. "You promised to stop kissing so much."

I smile against Cassie's mouth. "We're celebrating."

"Well, do something less gross to celebrate," Sophie huffs.

"Actually that's a great idea," I say, leaning back to shoot her a grin. "Which is why I made reservations tonight."

Sophie perks up. "We're going out?"

"Mm-hmm." I rub a slow circle against Cassie's back. "I invited Iris and her new girlfriend. Wanda and Fred too."

Cassie still looks surprised. "You made reservations?"

"Yep."

"But what if I didn't pass?"

I brush my fingers against her temple, sweeping one loose strand of her hair away to tuck it behind her ear. My palm lingers against her cheek, and in that clear blue sky of her eyes, I can see my whole life looking back at me.

"I knew we'd have something to celebrate," I tell her quietly.

Her smile is slow, her lips tilting on one side and then the other until she's beaming, and when she leans in to kiss me again, I can hardly even hear Sophie's half-hearted groaning. I think she'll let us have this one, most likely. I let my hand drift to my pocket where the little velvet box sits, grinning against Cassie's mouth, because we *do* have plenty to celebrate.

And we're just getting started.

It's probably a stupid idea.

*When Marco had suggested I check it out,
I think he'd meant it as a joke. Just another way of ribbing
me for not dating.*

*So why am I sitting here, staring at my computer
with a freshly made account for OnlyFans?*

*I do a quick scroll, and honestly, I can't tell the difference
between this and any other porn site. That brings me back to
the question: Why am I here?*

*I'm about to log out and forget this ever happened,
because Marco can never know . . . but then
I see her account as a suggestion.*

*I don't know what it is about her; her face is covered, her
hair is a bright lavender that has to be some sort of wig—
but something about her picture draws me in.*

*I click her profile, scrolling through the free
content just out of curiosity.*

Cici.

Maybe I won't log out after all . . .

ACKNOWLEDGMENTS

Please allow me to get this off my chest first and foremost: *holy fool of a Took, I published a book.*

And by "I published a book," I mean a fantastic team of people—that I do not deserve and will never fully be able to express my gratitude toward—did a million things that I am not smart enough to comprehend to put my words out in the world all while petting my hair and assuring me that "they've got this." Let's acknowledge the true heroes, eh?

In no particular order:

Cindy Hwang, my wonderful editor, who practically plucked me out of the gutter and pushed a metaphorical pen in my hand and said: *go forth and be dirty.* Meeting her changed my life for the very best, and how she continues to put up with my shenanigans and barrage of constant needy emails is beyond me, but I am forever grateful for it; Jessica Watterson, an actual angel in agent form, who is kind enough to withstand more anxious texts and emails than one person should ever have to endure, all while (as one does while dealing with me) petting my hair and telling me everything is going to be great; The Real Ones™: a group of ladies that are also kind enough to endure several lengthy rants that mostly consists of: *omg I can't do this is this terrible should I hide in my closet* all while (you guessed it) petting my hair and telling me everything is going to be great; my tall girlfriend for always, always, *always* being there to yell at me about how great I am even when I don't believe it (rarely ever), and for being a constant bright spot in a sometimes dreary space; my meemaw (she's not much older than me, but her spirit is that of a meemaw, and we love her for it) who read this book at least four dozen times in various bits and pieces all while (*Is this joke old yet?*) petting my hair and telling me I was an idiot for doubting myself; my common-law wife, who got so good at recognizing an impending meltdown that she can now just look at my face and say: *Do we need to go to the office and talk*? Not much of a hair petter, that one, but her voice of reason kept me sane on more days than I'd like to admit; my emotional support girlfriend, who has stuck by me through the worst of times even when I wasn't sure I deserved it, always knows exactly what I need to hear and who has yet to forsake me for my terrible puns like the saint she is, and they are *pun-ishingly bad;* my *actual* grandmother (non-meemaw type), who put a Johanna Lindsey book in my hand one summer and was cool enough not to tell my mom there was (gasp) *sex* in it—I would not be here without it; to the rest of my family for proudly shouting about this sexy book to all who would listen because that's *their* daughter/sister/cousin/niece that's writing that smut, thank you very much; Jessica Mangicaro and Kristin Cipolla for their superior taste in dad jokes and Taylor Swift (respectively) and for making me think people might actually want to read this book (and for being awesome at convincing *others* that they want to read this book); Angela Kim for enduring a barrage of emails from a certain author who will remain nameless during the stressful catastrophe that is copyedits (and always being incredibly helpful and generally lovely, despite her questionable taste in Batman portrayals); my therapist (yes, I am thanking my therapist) for stitching me up and putting me back together during the last couple of years. Can confirm I am only here because of her kindness, her wisdom, and her ability to sit through hours of me rambling all while petting my hair and telling me—(*okay, you get it*); Monica Roe for the amazing cover, as well as everyone at Penguin Creative (special shout-out to an amazing Art Director, Rita Frangie, for showing me that blue was the obvious choice for the cover color, we stan a visionary genius); Alaina Christensen, Alissa Theodor, and Kristin del Rosario for doing such an amazing job on design and graphics and making those message exchanges really *pop* (they made the book *chef's kiss*); everyone at Berkley who did all those million things that made this book possible; to every single person who has popped into my DMs and guided me through the strange land that is social media, adopting me into their little communities, shouting about the concept of this book, the excerpts—but mostly for putting up with my ramblings and my inability to have casual conversations; and to *you*, dear reader, for picking up this book, for sifting through my babbling gratitude (if you've made it this far), for making this *real*.

When I look back at my fifteen-year-old self—sitting in her room with a bulky, Gateway desktop—pecking away at Microsoft Word and trying to write some strange (and truly awful) romance novel because she couldn't get enough of the books she'd been swiping from her grandmother's shelf . . . I can honestly say that that girl had no idea she would someday have her *own book* sitting on shelves (even her grandmother's, because she is quite frankly, the coolest, and has, at the time of writing this, preordered a copy). Every step of this journey has been surreal, and fun, and terrifying, and *incredible*. No matter what happens going forwards, I am happy to look back at that gangly, starry-eyed teenager and know that she did it, even when she never dreamt she could.

Oh, and to that person I steal the covers from . . . thank you for keeping me starry eyed, after all this time.

Mackenzie

'm seeing someone."

In retrospect, the lie comes much easier than I thought it would. It feels icky lying to the woman who has raised me since I was twelve, but in the face of my seventh bad date (or has it been eight, now? I've honestly lost count) in three months—it also feels necessary.

My grandmother Moira has a reaction that is as immediate as it is expected. "*What*? Who? Someone from work? Is it someone I know?"

I know if I don't shut down this line of questioning quickly, it will spiral into a full-blown interrogation.

"No," I say quickly into the phone. "You don't know him."

I think that this part at least isn't as much of a lie, since I don't know him either. Since, ah . . . he doesn't exist.

My grandmother means well, she does, but her taste in men—

be they human *or* shifter—is downright terrible. I have been to movies with shifter model-train experts that wanted to scent me on the first date. I have gotten coffee with human data analysts who asked if I could somehow keep my tail in human form (I don't even want to explore the thought process there); every bad date has only solidified the idea that I am better off focusing on my work rather than my grandmother's wishful thinking that I will find a nice man to settle down with and give her a litter of grand-children. As if I don't have enough to deal with. Sometimes I think Gran is no better than the dates she sends me off with when it comes to my omega status.

It's rare, what I am, but it doesn't make me all *that* different from any other shifter. Maybe in the past it did, back when shift-ers were still living in secret underground hierarchy systems un-beknownst to everyone else, but now it just means that I have an annoying stigma following me around that I'm somehow better in bed than other shifters. That I'm better off barefoot and pregnant than participating in the working class. I swear, anyone I've ever told has expected me to spontaneously go into heat at whim.

That is why I mostly keep it to myself nowadays.

"How long have you been seeing him? How old is he? Is he a shifter? I know how busy you are, dear, but I'm not getting any younger, and it would be so nice to hear the pitter-patter of—"

"Gran, it is *way* too soon to be thinking that far ahead." I shud-der at the thought of crying babies. "It hasn't been that long. It's still new. Like, very new. Practically still has the plastic wrap on it."

"Oh, Mackenzie, why didn't you tell me? Are you trying to break my heart?"

"You know work has been insane. We've had four bar fights in the last month—not to mention the pileups from all the black ice we've been getting . . . It's been an utter nightmare in the ER. I think I'm getting carpal tunnel from all the stitches I've administered lately."

"You work too hard dear, couldn't they transfer you somewhere not so . . . fast-paced?"

It's a question she asks often, but she knows my answer already. I love working in the ER. Even after the most harrowing of days, I go to bed at night knowing that I'm saving lives.

"Gran . . ."

"Right, right. So tell me about your mystery man. At least give me a species, dear."

Human would be safer—since it's harder for interspecies couples to procreate, but I know the most obvious choice to keep her appeased.

"He's a shifter," I say, still feeling icky for lying. "You'd love him." I make a quick decision based solely on knowing that Gran will see right through me if I try to say I met my mystery man anywhere else, since I don't really *go* anywhere else. "I met him at work."

I can practically hear her clicking her heels together. She's probably doing a little dance in her kitchen as we speak, thinking that her granddaughter is finally going to settle down with a nice wolf who will give her and my grandpa grandchildren. It makes me feel that much more guilty. Thinking about the model trains strengthens my resolve though.

"I have to meet him. When can I meet him? You could bring him to dinner . . . You haven't been to visit in too long, honey. It would be so nice to see you and your new friend."

"No, no," I say quickly. "I told you, it's new. We're taking things slow. I don't want to jinx it, you know? It could . . . make things awkward at work, you know?"

"At least give me a name, will you?"

I panic, unable to think of a single name. There are dozens of eligible fake boyfriends working on my floor at this exact moment, and I can't recall a single name. Is this punishment for lying to Gran? Is the universe cursing me for being a bad granddaughter? I can feel my hippocampus practically melting into a puddle of goo in my head, blanking on even one syllable that might wrap up my poorly-planned lie in a neat little bow.

"Oh, well . . ." I can feel my mouth going dry as I scramble for something, *anything*. "His name? His name is—"

Now, I can count on one hand the number of hospital staff at Denver Memorial that I don't vibe with. One of the benefits of being one of the youngest ER doctors (at twenty-nine) is that everyone on staff treats you like the baby, and while it *can* get annoying sometimes, it means that I have made very few enemies while working here over the last year. In fact, I would even go so far as to say that most people I've met while working here *like* me. But that doesn't mean there aren't exceptions. I mean, I'm likable, I think. As long as the other party in question isn't trying to sniff my neck.

However, that isn't to say that every one of my work relationships are all sunshine and roses. And of course, it's with this thought that the break room door opens from across the room, revealing thick, midnight hair that nearly grazes the top of the doorframe attached to the massive form of one of the few physicians that fall into the "don't vibe with" category. His permanent frown set in a wide pink mouth turns my way, settled below piercing blue eyes that regard me in the same way they always have in the time I've known him—a stern look that says he's unhappy to have another living, breathing person in the same room he's entered. And of course, because the universe seems to be punishing me for my white lies before I can even finish getting them out—

it is *his* name, unfortunately, that is the first one that my brain seems to be able to formulate.

"Noah," I tell Gran in a hushed tone, so that he can't hear me. "His name is Noah Taylor."

Gran is gushing, her voice fading as I watch the surliest shifter I've ever met give me his back in order to crowd the coffee pot, gears turning in my head. It's not the *worst* idea I've ever had, I think. I mean, it's certainly not the best, but there are more terrible options. Probably. And besides, it's not like he would actually have to meet her or anything. Maybe he snaps a picture with me and cracks a smile for the first time in his entire life. That could give me at least a few weeks reprieve, right? What could be the harm in an innocent little picture? Surely even Noah Taylor takes selfies.

Actually, I wouldn't put money on that, now that I think about it.

"Gran, I need to get back to work," I say, cutting off her incessant line of questioning that I can't hear anymore anyway. "I'll call you tomorrow, okay?"

"All right, but I want more details when you do. Don't think this is the last of this conversation."

"Right," I tell her, absolutely knowing it isn't. "Sure thing."

I'm still staring at Noah's back as he pours coffee into his mug, watching his wide shoulders rise and fall with a sigh after what must have been a long night. Noah is an interventional cardiologist on staff at the hospital, not to mention the head of his department, and he comes in pretty high demand. Anyone that walks through our doors with a bad ticker gets an instant referral, and from what I can tell, the guy might actually sleep here. I'm not convinced he hasn't made a den (no pun intended, especially since our kind haven't slept in dens in like, a century) of some sort in the basement. He's been working here far longer than I have, years even—but it took me only one meeting to recognize how much of an ass he is. Especially since in our first meeting he said that I "barely looked old enough to tie a suture." Let's just say he's not one to rub elbows with his fellow shifters for camaraderie's sake alone.

He catches me staring when he finally turns to take a sip from his cup, one perfect brow raising in question as he notices me. "Can I help you?"

"Maybe," I say honestly. "What sort of night have you had?"

He looks uncertain as to why I would ask the question, or why I would even care in the first place, pausing for a moment before he huffs out a breath.

"Horrible, if you must know," he tells me. "Two heart attacks. Back to back. I've placed seven stents in the last five hours. And if that isn't enough, now I have to deal with the damn board and their ignorant—" He narrows his eyes, seeming to realize he's actually holding a conversation with a fellow employee that doesn't involve glowering. "Why do you ask?"

"Oh, because . . . professional courtesy? You looked . . . tired. Sounds like you had one hell of a night."

Noah appears unimpressed by my attempt at friendly conversation. I think idly it's probably the first time anyone has ever attempted it with him. "Exactly. So forgive me if I'm not up to chat."

I roll my eyes. "As if that's anything new."

"Right," he says flatly, holding up his mug. "I think I'll take this in my office."

"No, wait!"

Noah turns, that perplexed expression still etched into his features as he's probably realizing that this is the longest conversation he and I have had in at least the last six months; I can't actually remember the last time he returned my polite *hello* when I pass him in the corridor, now that I think about it. I think the last time we spoke, he told me my shoe was untied without even slowing his pace. I'm not sure that even counts as conversation.

He's looking at me with annoyance now, like I'm burning his precious time. "Yes?"

I can't believe I'm considering asking the Abominable Ass of Colorado to help me. It might be the worst idea I've ever had, but I'm in it now.

"I was wondering"—I know I'm going to regret this—"if you would take a picture with me."

Noah looks utterly confused. "Pardon?"

"A picture. Maybe you could smile in it too? I'm willing to pay. In better coffee, or snacks—" He looks like he doesn't know the definition of the word, and honestly, that tracks. "Okay, so no snacks. Whatever you want. I just need a picture."

"Explain to me a situation where taking a picture with me helps you somehow."

"Well, you see, that's complicated." Noah blinks at me for about three seconds before he turns to leave, seemingly done with the conversation, and I call after him again. "Okay, okay," I sigh. "Look. I know this is going to sound ridiculous, but I need to use you."

His eyebrows nearly shoot into his hair. "Excuse me?"

"It's not a big deal, it's just, I needed someone from work, and I sort of blanked when she asked, and your name sort of spilled out since you were *right there*, and all I need is a picture, really. I think that would buy me some time at least to—"

"What on Earth are you *talking* about?"

I take a deep breath, regretting this already. "I need you to be my fake boyfriend."

He lingers in the doorway for a good number of seconds, ones where I can feel my stomach churn in embarrassment. I *know* that I should have given Gran a random name. I *know* that I could have told her I was fucking a random male nurse on the side and properly silenced her with a blush, but I didn't do any of those things, and if I can't buy myself some time, I'm looking at fun-filled Friday night with some egghead explaining cryptocurrency to me. (Did I mention that I have been on some *really* bad dates?)

Noah takes a sip from his mug, swallows it, then closes the break room door. He crosses the space to pass the other little wooden tables that fill the room, his frame that seems ridiculously too big when settling into one of the padded chairs on the opposite side of the one I'm occupying. For a moment he says nothing, studying me with a mercurial look as the old wall clock ticks the seconds away to my right, but then he takes another sip from his mug, swallowing it with a bob of his Adam's apple before he sets it down on the table.

"Explain."

S o." Noah's cup is almost empty, his expression hardly any different than it had been ten minutes ago when I began to explain my horrible dating history and my aversion to experiencing even one more bad date—all leading up to my lie. "You want me to pretend to be your boyfriend . . . so that you don't have to get a boyfriend?"

"You don't even have to do anything."

"I fail to see the need for me at all then."

I'm pretty sure I've never been this close to Noah. At least not for this long a time. I can sense a sharp tinge of suppressants rolling off him, which I find odd; most male shifters choose to forego them, too hung up on their male ego to miss out on clouding a room with their scent in the hopes that a female shifter will come running. Maybe it's a professional decision? His scent might not be pleasant. Although, I think I can discredit that theory, given that despite his attempts to hide it, I can faintly make it out even under the chemical tang of his suppressants, making me think he needs a stronger dose. Not that I'm complaining, since I think it might be a nice scent. It's woodsy. Like pine needles and crisp air. It reminds me of running in the snow on all fours.

But this isn't what I should be focusing on.

"Well, a picture, maybe. So I can prove you're real. That will hold her off for a few weeks, at least, with my schedule. Surely you know how to smile, right? You can think of something you enjoy, like glaring at small children or criticizing baristas at Starbucks."

"I don't do either of those things," he snorts. "Thank you very much."

I shrug. "It was a guess. Come on, it will cost you nothing, and you'd be helping me out."

"Helping you out." Noah looks pensive as he stares down into his mug, raising it to his mouth to drink the last of his coffee. "And tell me again why I would do that?"

I scowl. It's honestly so annoying that he might be one of the most good-looking men I've ever come into contact with—shifter or otherwise. His features are angular, and his blue eyes are sharp as if he sees more than you want him to, and I won't pretend that his aquiline nose doesn't rustle up ideas about having it somewhere I shouldn't even be considering . . . if only his personality wasn't so sour.

"Intraspecies camaraderie?" Noah looks unmoved, and I groan. "Seriously, would it kill you to do something nice for once? This is based on the assumption that you recognize what doing something nice looks like and know how to properly execute the task."

Noah is studying me again, eyes moving over my sandy blonde hair and my amber eyes and even my mouth that is currently pressed into a pout, almost like he's considering. *What*, I can't be sure. I can't tell if he's thinking about helping me out, or if he's trying to find the most satisfying way to tell me I'm screwed.

"I have never been much for intraspecies camaraderie," he says finally, and I feel my stomach sink, knowing this was the worst idea I've ever had. "But . . ."

I perk up. "But?"

"I think we can reach an agreement that is more mutually beneficial."

Now it's my turn to look confused. I can't think of a single thing that Noah Taylor would need from me, or anyone else for that matter, given that I've never seen him speak to anyone for even a fraction of the time he's been speaking to me without barking orders at some point.

"And what could I possibly do for you?"

Honestly, I'm preparing for the worst. He's probably going to ask me to pass the buck on his consults to one of the other cardiologists, which would be a total pain in the ass, given that he knows he's the most highly requested one. Maybe he'll ask me to clean his office for the pure enjoyment of watching me do it. That feels like the sadistic torture Noah might be into. I can't even imagine what his office looks like. I bet it doesn't even need cleaning. He probably has plastic covers on all the chairs and surfaces. I could offer to put in admission orders for him for some agreed on span of time. That would be annoying but doable, at least. Definitely worth staving off a few more horrible dates since I am apparently too spineless to simply say "no" to my Gran's puppy dog eyes.

Oh God. What if he asks me for sex? I've pegged him as some celibate sourpuss who gets by with angry masturbation on the weekends, but what if Noah is like every other horndog I've come across? That is absolutely the one thing that is completely off the table, and I will kick him in his stupidly large shins if he is dumb enough to suggest it. It's not like he knows I'm an omega; there's no way he could, so surely it isn't going to be anything kinky he's after.

I tense when Noah leans forward in his chair, his fingers lacing together as his hands rest on the table, and his piercing eyes meet mine with that blazing intensity that they never seem to lose when I am unlucky enough to cross paths with him. They don't look like the eyes of someone who is about to ask me for sex, at least. Or maybe they do, given the context. I don't know. It's hard to think with him staring at me like he is. But as it turns out, Noah has no intention of asking me for any kind of sordid favors. What Noah proposes is much worse, and the craziest part is the way his expression absolutely doesn't change, not even a *tiny* bit when he says:

"I need a mate."

Now it's my turn to blink at him. Stupidly, if I had to guess. "You need . . . a mate?"

Noah nods, like it's a perfectly reasonable thing he's said. Like he didn't just propose the shifter equivalent of marriage—and the *last* thing I'm interested in—to a veritable stranger that I don't think he even likes (I'm not taking it personally or anything; he doesn't seem to like anyone) over bad hospital lounge coffee.

"And fast," he adds.

I really, really *should have told Gran I was sleeping with a nurse.*